# HIS
# EVERY
# NEED

## TERRI L. AUSTIN

sourcebooks
casablanca

Published by Sourcebooks Casablanca, an imprint of Sourcebooks, Inc.
P.O. Box 4410, Naperville, Illinois 60567-4410
(630) 961-3900
Fax: (630) 961-2168
www.sourcebooks.com

Library of Congress Cataloging-in-Publication Data

Austin, Terri L.
  His every need / Terri L. Austin.
     pages cm
  (trade paper : alk. paper)  1.  Young women—Fiction.  2.  Domestic fiction.
I. Title.
  PS3601.U86365H57 2014
  813'.6–dc23

                        2013045381


       Printed and bound in the United States of America.
            VP 10 9 8 7 6 5 4 3 2 1

*To Jeff.*
*Thanks for always believing.*

# Chapter 1

Allie Campbell frowned at the black SUV parked in her driveway. One of Monica's friends? Damn it, if her sister ditched school again, Allie was going to handcuff herself to that kid and haul her delinquent butt into class. And even though Monica was an adult—*technically*—and could make her own decisions—*really stupid ones*—she was going to graduate high school this year if it killed them both.

Allie parked on the curb and shoved open the driver-side door. It groaned, sounding as tired as it looked. And for a Ford Festiva that had seen seventy-five thousand miles too many, it looked exhausted.

Before she could grab groceries from the backseat, a man strolled around the side of the house, clipboard in hand. Middle-aged and slightly paunchy, he waved at her with a tape measure.

"Great, you're home. Would you mind letting me in so I can get some measurements, ma'am?"

Allie shut the car door with a bump of her hip and adjusted her purse strap. *Ma'am?* Twenty-five wasn't ma'am territory. She walked across the narrow strip of yard, stopping directly in front of the stranger who wore a polo shirt with the name *Dave* embroidered on his chest.

She had been on her feet for the past nine hours soothing unhappy hotel guests. The Festiva's air conditioner was on the fritz. Again. And her polyester uniform—hot and itchy on a good day—stuck to her in all the wrong places. Add the *ma'am* comment, and she didn't have any niceties to spare. "Who are you and what are you doing in my yard?"

He pointed at the truck. "Dave Buchanan, home appraiser. I'm taking measurements for the owner."

Allie glanced at the white magnetic sign affixed to the truck's door. Sure enough—Dave Buchanan, Home Appraiser. "My dad is the owner, and he didn't mention this to me."

Dave examined the clipboard. "Says here Trevor Blake ordered an inspection." He shrugged. "Maybe he forgot to tell you?"

Who the hell was Trevor Blake? "No, you've got the wrong house. Would you mind moving, so I can pull into my driveway?" She turned and walked toward her car. Crisis averted. No need to have another pointless argument with Monica. At least not about this.

"Nope," Dave called after her. "This is the place. I need to get inside. I have a couple more houses to see this afternoon."

A small tingle shot up Allie's spine. She spun around to face Dave, if that was even his real name. Was this some kind of scam to get into her house? If so, he'd picked the wrong place. They didn't have anything worth stealing.

Pulling her phone from her pocket, she glared at the man. "If you don't leave immediately, I'm calling the police."

He shrugged. "Whatever, lady. It might speed things up."

Well, that wasn't the response she was expecting.

He squinted down at the form. "The signature says Trevor Blake. There's a second one here too—a Brian Campbell?"

Alarm bells started clanging in her ears. This had to be a mistake. She speed-dialed her dad's cell number, her eyes tracking the stranger as he pointedly looked at his watch.

"Yeah, Al," he answered, "I already know. School called this morning. Monica never showed up. I don't know what to do with her. I'm out of ideas." He sounded weary.

Allie pinched the bridge of her nose. "It's okay. I'll deal with it. Listen, a guy's here at the house, says he's an appraiser?"

There was long pause on the other end. "Damn, he's there already?"

She blinked. Something was wrong. Seriously wrong. Her dad didn't make a sandwich without asking her opinion. "You're not thinking about refinancing, are you? You never even mentioned it."

"I, uh." He cleared his throat. "I don't know how to tell you this, honey."

His answer scared her. The afternoon sun seemed brighter, hotter, making her skin feel prickly. A bead of sweat slid down her back. "Just say it." For some reason, her voice didn't sound like her own.

"We…" He trailed off. "No, not we. Me." He stopped. "This is my fault. I did this. I lost the house, Al."

Despite the dry Vegas heat, Allie went cold all over. "What are you talking about?"

Dave tugged on his earlobe and wouldn't make eye contact.

"I'll explain it all tonight." Another drawn-out pause. "I didn't know how to tell you."

She shook her head, gripping the phone like it was a lifeline. "Tell me now. And who is Trevor Blake?"

"He's an investor. English guy." His breath sounded ragged, his voice shaky. "I borrowed money for the business. But when your mom…" He didn't finish. He didn't need to.

Allie staggered backward a few feet until her ass hit the Festiva's taillight, her stomach in free fall. She felt a little woozy. "No," she whispered. "It's all we have left." *Lose the house?* They'd already lost so much. "The business will pick up. We just need more time to pay off this loan. I could get a second jo—"

"No. The business is busted. It's over. You don't know how sorry I am." She heard his pain, as clear and sharp as her own. "Trevor Blake's the new owner."

A thousand thoughts flooded Allie's brain. How were they going to survive? Where would they live? How much time did they have before the new owner kicked them out?

No, she couldn't think about any of that. She needed to fix this. Now.

She gathered herself together and pushed off the car. "Dad, I've got to go. We'll talk about this tonight." Without waiting for his reply, she hit the end button and tossed her hair over her shoulder as she strode back to Dave, shoving her phone into the pocket of her slacks.

Another day, another freaking crisis. She needed to get rid of this guy before her youngest sister got home. If Brynn thought they were losing the house—well, Allie had to make sure that didn't happen.

"Mr. Buchanan?"

A red-faced Dave looked at her with pity. "Sorry. These things are tough," he said. "The economy's bad for everyone right now."

God, Allie was so tired of pity. So tired of empty platitudes. She squared her shoulders and clung to her purse strap with both hands. "This isn't a bank thing. We're not in foreclosure." Realizing how defensive she sounded, she swallowed and tried for a softer tone. "Can I see that?" Allie nodded at the clipboard.

"Sure, of course." Dave handed it over and stared at the Garcia's house next door. With its freshly painted exterior and decorative yucca plants, it was the complete opposite of Allie's raggedy place with peeling brown paint and a crumbling driveway.

She read through the form, making a few mental notes. "Mr. Buchanan? I need you to put off this appraisal until tomorrow." She held out the clipboard.

"Not possible. Look, I'm sorry for your troubles, but I've got a job to do."

*All right, Dave, time to pull out the big guns.* Allie widened her eyes, glanced up at him through her lashes, and took a deep breath. "Please? Just twenty-four hours, that's all I'm asking." She placed a hand on his forearm and squeezed. "Please, Dave?" she whispered.

He gulped and licked his lips, his eyes darting back and forth. Finally, he let out a gusty breath. "Okay, what the hell? But I'm coming back tomorrow. And I'm getting in the house, one way or another."

Allie smiled. "Thank you." *Ma'am my ass.*

He sniffed and hitched up his jeans before climbing into his truck.

She had bought herself some time, but how was she supposed to get their house back in twenty-four hours? And what if she couldn't?

She closed her eyes for a second. Focus. One thing at a time. Groceries first.

Allie made three trips, hauling bags into the house. As she shoved a box of cereal in the cupboard, she heard the front door slam. "Brynn, is that you?"

She stuck the milk in the fridge and glanced at the kitchen doorway to find her fifteen-year-old sister propped against the jamb. With a bulging backpack, she looked like a turtle ready to topple over. Brynnie was pale. And too thin.

"How was your day?" Allie asked.

Brynn studied her thumbnail and shrugged.

"You hungry? I could make you—"

"No, thanks."

Allie grabbed four potatoes out of the bag and dropped them in the sink. "What about your geometry test? Did you kick ass and take names?"

Brynn scuffed her toe over the worn, beige linoleum, causing a high-pitched squeak. "It was easy. Boring."

"Your art teacher emailed me this morning." Allie glanced over her shoulder. "She said you didn't want to enter your drawing in the art show this year."

"So?"

"That's the drawing of Mom, right? The one of her in the hospital." Their mother had been beautiful, even if she had lost all her hair and forty pounds. Her frame was thin, her face gaunt, but her smile was radiant. Brynn had captured that. "Mom was proud of that picture, Brynn. And your teacher said you could win an award." Allie scrubbed at the potatoes and blotted them with a paper towel.

Brynn rolled her eyes. "Who cares about awards? I'm not showing it. Ever. And why're you making so many potatoes? Dad will be late and Monica won't be home." Digging a hand in her pocket, she whipped out her phone, her thumbs flying over the keyboard.

"Have you heard from her?" Allie asked.

"Right. Like she talks to me."

"She skipped school again today."

Brynn ignored her.

"Did Monica even get on the bus?"

"No." Brynn paused and glanced up. "One of her stupid friends picked her up at the bus stop. As usual."

Fantastic. Banking her anger and frustration, Allie dried her hands on a dish towel. "We're having pork chops for dinner tonight." Pork chops were Brynn's favorite. That's why Allie'd bought them, even though they weren't on sale. She knew the chances of Brynn coming out of her room for dinner were almost nonexistent, but she kept trying.

"I'm not hungry. Sometimes…I just wish we could all be together again." She said it so quietly, Allie barely caught the words.

"We can be. I'll text Monica and tempt her with chocolate cake. A family dinner would be nice." The cheerful note Allie forced into the words grated on her nerves. She knew what Brynn meant. But if she thought about it right now, she'd completely fall apart. And she couldn't do that in front of her little sister.

"Monica would never pull this crap if Mom were here. I miss her so much." Brynn pressed a hand to her abdomen. "I remember how it was before she got sick."

Allie remembered too. The house had been filled with chatter and laughter and the smell of her mother's sweet perfume. But the chatter had been replaced by Monica's bitching and Allie's nagging. Deep lines of stress and worry etched their way across her dad's face, and he seemed older than his fifty years. Losing Mom changed everything. For all of them. And Brynn was right. Monica wouldn't dare act like this if Mom were alive. Allie was doing her best, but she made a poor substitute parent. And Monica resented the hell out of her for it.

Allie glanced away from the pain in her sister's eyes. "Dinner will be ready soon. Do you have homework? When is that English essay due?"

"I know what I need to do," Brynn said. "You don't have to keep reminding me. I'm not a six-year-old."

Allie stepped forward, her hand outstretched to pat Brynn's shoulder, but her sister turned and walked out of the kitchen. As Allie's arm fell, so did the fake smile that left her cheeks sore.

She wanted to follow Brynn, hold her close, tell her everything would be all right—even though it was a lie. *Everything will be fine. It gets better. We'll be okay.* Lies. She said them over and over and felt like a fraud every time.

A hug wouldn't make Brynn feel better. Wouldn't bring her mom back. Wouldn't heal her family.

Allie glanced at the wooden doorjamb Brynn had been leaning against and the growth marks her mother had charted. Each sister had a different color. She traced a finger over her own red marks. This was her family's history.

Crossing her arms, Allie cast her eyes over the dated kitchen, took in the red-and-white-checkered curtains and the rooster wall clock. Her mom loved that stupid rooster.

Allie made a promise. *Take care of the family.* She was supposed to hold everything together, but she was failing. Big time.

Losing the house would be like losing her mom all over again.

She had to talk to this Trevor Blake, make him understand, beg if she had to. Allie was prepared to do anything to keep the promise she made. She would take care of everyone—starting with the house. She was going to get it back.

And she wouldn't take no for an answer.

—~~~—

Trevor Blake sat behind his polished desk and stared at the girl—woman, really—who'd come to plead her father's case. Her lips were full and pink. Her cheeks were bright with color. She was flustered, nervous, hand trembling as she repeatedly tucked her pale hair behind one ear.

Lovely. Although that uniform should be burned. The bright green waistcoat hid a spectacular pair of breasts.

"So, that's why we have to keep the house." She looked at him and waited.

Chin propped on his palm, he stared at her. Truly lovely. He roused himself and straightened in his seat. "I don't care, Miss Campbell."

With wide blue eyes, she stared back. "Excuse me? I don't understand."

Trevor placed his elbows on the desk and steepled his fingers. "I said I don't care. Not about your problems, not about your house. I don't care about any of it."

She blinked a few times. "But my mother died six months ago. We're still trying to recover."

"I'm terribly sorry for your loss. Now, if you'll excuse me, I have work to do." He gestured toward the door.

She shook her head and a few blond strands slid over those amazing tits. "No, I won't excuse you. Didn't you hear what I said? I don't know what my father owes, but we can pay you back. We just need time."

"I was only half listening, really." He leaned forward, his gaze resting on her face. "You're rather beautiful. I find it distracting."

With a clenched jaw, she clutched the armrests of her chair until her knuckles were white. As she took a deep breath, the green buttons on the waistcoat strained and looked ready to pop right off the bloody thing. Very distracting indeed.

"Please, I'm trying to keep my family together, Mr. Blake. Since my mom died, that house is all we have left. Surely you understand that?"

"I don't have family, Miss Campbell. Relatives are considerably more trouble than they're worth." A pain in the bloody ass was more like it. He flatly refused to acknowledge his own.

"Please?" Her voice was a breathy whisper and she tugged on that full bottom lip with her teeth. "Can you give us an extension? Just a month or two. I promise we'll pay every cent."

He bit back a smile. Oh, she was good at this. Very practiced. Most men probably tripped over their own cocks to give her what she wanted. But he wasn't most men. And her sad eyes left him as unmoved as her tragic little family drama. "Do you know what I do, Miss Campbell? Who I am?"

She met his gaze. "Who are you, Mr. Blake?"

"I am, for lack of a better phrase, an investment angel. When I loaned your father money to expand his business, he put your house up as collateral." He lifted his shoulder. "But he's hemorrhaging money, an astounding feat given that he has a commercial refrigeration repair business and we're in the middle of a desert. He even sold off the tools and equipment, which were also mine." He raised a brow in annoyance. Brian Campbell had gone behind his back. Did he think Trevor wouldn't find out? And even though the loss was trivial, Trevor hated losing money, no matter how small the amount. "How your father's managed to keep his head above water this long is something of a mystery."

"What? No, you're wrong. He wouldn't do that without telling me." She scooted to the edge of her seat and placed her hands on top of his desk. Her nails were ruthlessly short, the skin around them red and rough. "You can't do this. My sisters will be out of a home. I'm begging you."

"I am sorry for your plight, but it changes nothing. Now, I trust you can find your way out." Dismissing her, he turned his attention to one of the computer screens and checked the commodities prices. Wheat held steady, oil down, gold up.

Hmm, he'd made a nice little sum today. Not a fortune, but tidy.

When he glanced back, she still hadn't moved. The heat drained from her cheeks, leaving her pale. That lush bottom lip trembled.

Trevor sighed. *Oh God, not tears.* He narrowed his eyes and gave her a nasty, calculated smile. "You know, Miss Campbell, with assets like yours, you could make money in this town. I'm sure you could work a pole as well as the next girl. Or there are the brothels. Prostitution is legal in parts of Nevada, after all." Just as he'd planned, the tears that clung to her lashes didn't fall. Color flushed her cheeks. He'd lit the fuse, and now he waited for the explosion. *Anger—so much better than tears.*

She leaped to her feet and slammed her palm on his desk. "Fuck you. Take your loan and your investment angel bull crap. Just…" Her gaze darted from his face to the multiple computer screens and her mouth flattened into a straight line. Angry eyes met his. "Fuck. You."

He took in her pink cheeks, the determined tilt of her chin, then his gaze slid downward, landing on her breasts, which were rapidly rising in agitation. "If you'd like, I'll be happy to oblige."

"My God, do you think this is funny? My mother is dead, my father is now unemployed, my sisters are about to get kicked out of their home, thanks to you, and you're joking about sex?"

He splayed his hand over his chest. "I never joke about sex, Miss Campbell. I take my fucking very seriously."

She froze for a moment, her lips forming a perfect O before she turned and stalked across the room to the fireplace. Clasping the edge of the marble mantel, she remained silent.

Even in those hideous black trousers, her ass looked nice and firm. She was rather magnificent.

He was a bastard for saying those things to her, for taking her family home. But it was business. It wasn't personal. Why didn't people understand that?

She swung toward him. "All right. If that's the only way, then I'll do it."

"What?" Her ass had him in a bit of a daze. What had they been talking about?

"I accept."

He replayed the last couple of minutes over in his mind. Then it finally hit him, like a cricket bat to the head. She was offering to fuck him in exchange for her house. Dear God.

She licked her lips and glanced at the door.

*Already regretting her hasty offer?* Good, she should be. And of course, the idea was ridiculous. She was hardly the type to offer up her body in exchange for anything as mundane as a small house in a rather shabby part of the city.

He stood and stepped from the behind the desk, strolling toward her slowly, purposefully. His gaze lowered to her mouth. She audibly swallowed but stood her ground. He liked her spirit. She was tall, but he towered over her, forcing her to crane her neck to glare up at him.

He placed his hands on the mantel and caged her between his arms. With his head angled, he leaned forward. Their lips were only inches apart. Her pupils dilated, her breathing became shallow. If he leaned just a little closer, those breasts would graze his chest. *So tempting.*

She smelled good enough to eat—a light, fresh fragrance that wasn't too delicate, wasn't overpowering. It made his cock stand up and pay attention. "All right then, I'll forgive the debt if you agree to cater to my needs. At my beck and call, fulfilling my every whim, for as long as I want you. How does that sound?" Dropping his hands, he pulled back and smiled. Positive she would throw his offer and probably her fist in his face, he waited. Baiting her was rather delicious. But he needed to get back to work. He couldn't spend the rest of the afternoon taunting Allie Campbell, as delightful as that sounded.

She stared at him with those impossibly blue eyes. "All right," she said after several seconds, "for one month, but I want it in writing."

His jaw dropped for an instant, gobsmacked. "Sorry?" He'd just been teasing her. He couldn't have a mistress. Didn't want one. Especially one that came with so much baggage. A party girl who knew her way around? Possibly. A woman who had sisters to take care of, a widowed father? He resisted the urge to shudder.

"I said yes." She tilted her chin and studied him. "You expected me to say no, didn't you? Are you trying to welsh out of it?"

Was she challenging him? Questioning his word? He crossed his arms over his chest and regarded her coolly. "I've never *welshed* on anything in my life."

She mimicked him, also crossing her arms, and nodded. "Good."

"Three months, not one, and there's a catch, Miss Campbell." He smiled at the panicked look in her eyes.

"What's that?"

Ah, now he had her. "You have to comply with whatever I tell you to do, when I tell you to do it, no matter how…depraved"—his voice deepened on the word, drew it out—"or the deal is off."

Her arms fell and she shook her head. "No. Forget it."

Excellent. "Well then, good day." Turning, he walked back to his desk.

"Wait," she said, a thread of desperation in her voice. "Two months. And I won't do anything that could hurt me."

He wasn't sure what possessed him to turn around, but when

he did, he saw a flicker of fear in her eyes. And it made him feel…
He rubbed his chest. He didn't know what the feeling was, but he
didn't like it. He quickly dropped his hand. "But a little pain can
be very pleasurable."

Instead of running for cover, like a sensible girl, she met his cool
gaze with her own.

"Then we'd need a safe word or something. And no other partners."

Truly, he'd never been into pain, either delivering it or receiv-
ing it. Doling out the occasional light spanking—well, quite. But
that wasn't painful. That was foreplay. As for other partners, he
didn't like to share. Not that he was planning on actually having
Allie Campbell.

*So. Tempting.*

He told his cock to shut up. He'd never let it do the thinking
before and he wasn't about to start now.

But what was he to do? Knowing there was no way out of his
offer, not without *welshing*, he stalked toward her and held out his
hand. "You're mine for two months. Deal."

She hesitated for the briefest moment. "Deal."

When she placed her hand in his, he felt a rush of anticipation.

"And you'll forgive my father's debt, let us keep the house, and
pay off the existing mortgage," she said in a rush.

He sighed. "Fine."

Her face relaxed a bit. "Fine."

Bloody hell. He wasn't sure when things had gotten so out of
hand, but somehow Trevor had acquired himself a mistress.

# Chapter 2

ALLIE LEFT THE MANSION, blinking against the bright sunlight as if she had emerged from a strange dream. She just agreed to become a mistress. To a man she didn't know. A man who, in fifteen minutes, made her angrier than Monica ever had.

Yes, she had vowed to do anything to keep the house, to keep her promise. And when she'd seen the way Trevor looked at her, like he wanted to gobble her up and lick his fingers afterward, it popped out of her mouth. She'd figured she could screw him once, get the house, and bury the memory so deep, she'd never think about it again. But this... She'd signed up to become the man's sex slave. This wasn't a onetime thing, this was two months of sex servitude.

Under other circumstances, she'd probably be flattered by his interest. It's not like he was hard on the eyes. Okay, so Trevor Blake was beautiful, with that wavy, black hair and the broad shoulders. Even beneath his expensive suit jacket, she could tell he had a nicely muscled chest. Still, he was an asshole. An English asshole, with that superior, upper-class, snobbish accent and taunting gray eyes. Despite the heat, she shivered.

But what other option did she have? She barely scraped out a living wage at the Lucky Shamrock Hotel and Casino. Even if she worked double shifts, it wouldn't be enough to pay rent on an apartment big enough for four people.

Maybe there was some way she could hold Trevor Blake off—at least until she came up with a better plan.

Walking on the circular brick drive toward her car, she rubbed her head. Sharp pain started throbbing behind one eye. Perfect.

Allie climbed into the Festiva and propped her arm on the open window. How was she going to explain this to her father? Or manage to do her job around mistress duty?

With a growl of frustration, she beat her fists on the steering wheel. Goddamn it, when had her life fallen apart?

Dumb question. When her mom got cancer, Allie's world came to a screeching halt. She closed her eyes and shut down the thought, feeling guilty that it even crossed her mind.

Allie was ready to get away from this house. Away from him. But when she tried to start the car, it refused to cooperate. She twisted the key again and pumped the gas pedal. "No, please no. Start, you worthless piece of crap. I swear, I'll give you premium next time." The engine wouldn't catch.

She glanced back at the house and tried to start the car once more with the same result. Resting her head against the back of the seat, she thought about what to do next.

Trevor's solitary property sat on the edges of Henderson, forty minutes away from home. She could call a cab, but somehow, the fifty dollars that had been in her wallet last night was mysteriously missing this morning. Of course she couldn't prove Monica had taken it, but…

There were no bus stops for miles, but it was only about ninety degrees and she could hoof it. She could walk past the guard at the gate and leave her shit heap of a car in Trevor Blake's pristine drive. Ten or twelve miles tops—that was doable, right?

No, that would be stupid, and unfortunately, she'd reached her stupid quota for the day. Pulling her keys from the ignition, she took a deep breath and swallowed her pride.

When she rang the bell, the butler, another Brit, answered the door. With sparse, dark hair and of average height—although his stiff demeanor made him seem taller—he peered at her with a calm expression.

"Back so soon, miss?"

She didn't know if he was being sarcastic or not. "I'm sorry to bother you again."

"It's no bother at all."

"Um, okay. My car won't start." She wagged her thumb over her shoulder.

He looked past her to the junker in the drive. "How very shocking. Do come in."

When she stepped inside, cool air touched her hot skin. Allie glanced around the huge foyer. She hadn't really paid much attention her first time through because she'd been too nervous about meeting Trevor Blake. But this time she took in the expensive round table with a dragonhead pedestal, the large Chinese vase filled with bright orange roses, and a suit of armor in one corner. The wooden banister was polished to a bright sheen, and the gray marble floor gleamed in the late afternoon sunlight.

"Please follow me." With his back as stiff as his starched shirt, he moved swiftly through the house.

Allie tried to keep up but got distracted by oil paintings and large, ornate pieces of furniture. There were glass cases filled with collectibles—knives, antique guns, coins. Swords and spears decorated the walls.

The fastidious butler stopped more than once to adjust a frame or straighten a knickknack before picking right back up and zipping through the house at a quick pace. He led her to a conservatory filled with colorful, exotic flowers. A stone fountain trickled softly in the middle of the room. A wrought-iron table stood to one side, and he held out a chair for her.

"I'll bring tea, shall I?" With a bow, he left before she could decline.

Allie's gaze traveled around the room, and she spied a potted orange tree in the far corner. She took in the tranquil setting, breathed in the heady, perfumed air. It was like something out of a movie, and Trevor Blake actually lived like this. His electric bill alone must be in the hundreds. Maybe thousands. She couldn't wrap her head around it.

Oh God, she'd agreed to become his mistress. How was she supposed to follow through with something like that? She'd only had a couple of boyfriends and the sex had been okay. Nothing earth shattering. But a man like Trevor would expect hot, crazy sex. Tricks and weird positions. As for weird positions, she'd tried the pretzel— once—and it had been very uncomfortable. Allie didn't do hot and crazy. In fact, she hadn't done sex at all in the last four years. At least not with a partner.

Images of a naked Trevor Blake ran through her mind. She may have hit the replay button on her imagination a couple times before she snapped out of it. She was certain she wouldn't be able to satisfy him. He was sophisticated. European. Rich. She was just Allie Campbell, a college dropout from North Las Vegas. Not bad to look at, but gorgeous women were plentiful here. She was nothing special.

Allie glanced at her watch. All she wanted was the number for a tow truck. Fixing the Festiva was going to cost more than it was worth, but it would be cheaper than buying a new car. Probably.

As she continued to wait, Allie listened to the calming splash of the fountain in the background, her eyes resting on a bright purple trumpet flower. The sweet fragrance soothed her. Exhausted, she let her eyes drift shut and, for the first time in long time, felt her shoulder muscles, usually stiff from anxiety, begin to relax.

Then something tickled her ear.

"Couldn't bear to leave me?"

His breath teased a strand of her hair. She twisted in the chair and found his face inches away. He was so close the woodsy scent of him filled her senses. So close she could see the thin black outline surrounding his light gray irises.

She leaned forward, trying to get as far away from him as possible, since he was violating her personal space. Again. "My car wouldn't start."

Straightening, he strolled to the opposite side of the table and sat down, his tall, muscular body at odds with the dainty chair. "Yes, it was an eyesore. I took the liberty of having it towed to the scrap yard." When she opened her mouth to speak, he held up a hand. "No, no, Miss Campbell. No need to thank me."

She stared at him for beat. "You took my car?" Gripping the sides of the table, she leaned forward. "You took my car? Where is it?"

Trevor flicked an imaginary fleck off the sleeve of his dark suit. "It's gone for good, I'm afraid."

When she jumped to her feet, the chair crashed backward. "How dare you?" Her voice bounced around the glass walls and slate tile floor. "I need that car. You can't get rid of it."

"And yet, I did." He glanced toward the door. "Oh look, Arnold's brought tea."

Clenching her hands into fists, she fought the urge to reach across the table and pop him. The arrogance of this man was unbelievable—telling her to work a pole, junking her junker, sitting there like he was God. And she couldn't just walk out of here or speed off in her car—*her* car—and never see him again. Oh no, she'd made a bargain, and for her family's sake had to stick around and see it through.

The butler approached the table with a large silver tray bearing a teapot, cups, little sandwiches, and cookies. Frowning, he stared from his employer to Allie as he set the tray on the table. "Is everything all right, miss?"

"Everything's fine, isn't that right, Miss Campbell?" Trevor smiled pleasantly and waited.

Realizing her muscles were rigid with tension, she took a deep breath and forced herself to relax. "Yes, I'm fine, thank you."

The butler, Arnold, bent down and picked up her chair, holding it out until she sat. Then he handed her a napkin and poured a cup of tea. "Would you like sugar, cream?"

"Um, sugar please." Her hands were shaking, so she thrust them in her lap. Allie rarely lost her cool, not even with the rudest hotel guest. Sometimes Monica brought out Allie's claws, but this man and his high-handed ways made her so angry, she reacted before she could stop and think.

After doctoring the tea and setting it before her, Arnold placed three small sandwiches on a plate. "Here you are." Then he served Trevor and, with a bow, left the conservatory.

"I need my car back." She tamped down the panic rising in her chest. "Please," she forced out, her jaw clamped tight.

"Your vehicle was ugly and didn't work properly." He took a sip of tea. "By the way, I've decided you're moving in."

---

He watched the blood drain from her face. Oh, he was going to hell, tormenting Allie Campbell this way. As soon as she left his office, he wanted to call her back and tell her he'd changed his mind. But when Arnold told him she was still here, her car disabled, he thought about how delightful it had been playing with her. And if he pushed her a bit, he might force her to give up on this insane idea. She didn't want to be his mistress. And he didn't want her. Well, that wasn't quite true. Actually, he did want her. In several positions. But she was entirely too much work. It was best to nip this in the bud, now.

She shook her head. "I can't move in with you. I have to look out for my sisters. I have a job."

He peered at her over his teacup. "But you'll still have a job,

Miss Campbell, servicing my needs." He tried not to smile at the blush that flamed her cheeks. Really, this was too easy.

He surveyed the tray of treats before him. "Mmm, Jammie Dodgers, my favorite. Arnold never puts on a spread like this for just me." He plucked a biscuit from the tray and popped it into his mouth. "These are delicious. Here." He picked up another and held it out to her. "Try it."

"No."

"Every whim, remember? You're not backing out of the deal already, are you? What a pity."

With a mutinous expression, she opened her mouth and allowed him to place the biscuit on her tongue. Snapping her mouth shut, she almost bit his finger, but he pulled away so that she only grazed him with her teeth. "What a temper you have, Miss Campbell."

"I still have to work," she said once she'd finished chewing. "I told you, we have medical bills and my sisters need to eat."

"Another sandwich?" He gestured to the tray.

Slamming her hands down on the table, the crockery rattled and her untouched cup spilled its contents onto the saucer. "No, I want you to listen to me."

She was a lovely woman, ripe, lush. But when she was angry, she was stunning. Those eyes flashed blue fire, her whole body practically vibrated. He had no doubt that she would be a passionate lover. He didn't plan on finding out, of course. Still, he wondered if she was a moaner. Would she rake her nails down his back? Was she a screamer? If not, he could turn her into one, he was sure of it.

Despite wanting to talk her out of this crazy scheme, Trevor was reluctant to let her slip away so quickly. If she stayed the two months, or until he grew tired of her—and really, how long would that take—she could save her family's home and wipe out the debt that must be crippling them. She'd even thank him in the end.

He kept his expression neutral. "I am listening, my sweet. You have medical bills, two teenage sisters who won't make it through another day without your guidance, and an unemployed father who depends on you. Do I have that right?"

She shifted in her chair, obviously uncomfortable with the situation, uncomfortable with him. "They need me. I can't just leave them. You don't understand."

"I'll pay the medical bills. Without having to pay me or the hospital, your father will find some way to support your family. See? All better."

She sighed, looking him in the eye. "It's more than that. I have to go home. I'll come back every morning, every evening. Mr. Blake… Trevor. Please."

He stared back, mesmerized. This "please" had been sincere, not angry, not manipulative. But he wasn't ready to let her go. Not yet. "I'll have my driver take you home to get your things." He rose from the table. "When you come back, Arnold can show you to your room. I'll see you at dinner."

He stood, tossed a last biscuit into his mouth, and sauntered out, leaving behind a seething Allie Campbell.

For some reason, he didn't feel triumphant at getting what he wanted. Instead, he felt almost the slightest twinge of guilt.

―⁓―

Allie sat in the back of the limousine, seething. She hated him, hated that her father had borrowed his money, and most of all hated that she wasn't in a position to rip that perfectly pleasant smile right off his face.

Bad enough she'd agreed to have sex with him, but now he was forcing her to abandon her sisters. Brynn had always been shy, but lately, she'd become withdrawn, sullen. She hardly ever smiled anymore. With Allie gone, Brynn might never come out of her room. Monica, on the other hand, had become uncontrollable after their mom died—staying out late, skipping so much school that graduation was up in the air. If Allie wasn't home to keep a handle on things, there was no telling what Mon would do.

When the car pulled in front of the house, both of her sisters stepped onto the porch, watching as the driver opened the door and offered Allie a hand. Monica, in dark skinny jeans and a sparkly tank top, ran toward her and peered inside the car. Brynn held back, watching from the porch.

"Whose car is this, Al? Oh my God, can I go for a ride?" Monica hopped inside and began fiddling with the buttons. "I want to go to Amber's house. She'll piss herself." She turned on the radio, switched stations until she found a song with a thumping bass. Then she hit the moonroof, popping her head out as she raised her hands and swayed to the music. "This kicks ass, Al."

Allie reached in and turned off the radio. "Get out."

Monica looked down at Allie from her perch atop the seat and scowled. "Why are you so against having a good time? You're like, anti-fun." She climbed down and scooted out of the car. "Whose car did you say this was?"

Allie had decided to go with the truth—or as much of it as she could, without telling her sisters she'd sold herself to a stranger. "My new boss, it's his car. Come on. Let's go inside. We need to talk."

"Shit, I hate it when you say that. Lecture time." Her voice became a parody of Allie's. "Monica, you're ruining your life. Boys are bad. Just say no. Blahdy blah blah."

"You are ruining your life, but that's not what this is about. Not this time." Allie mustered up a smile for the driver. "Thank you. I'll be half an hour, maybe forty-five minutes."

He nodded. "I'll be waiting."

Well, the chauffeur was American, a Southerner by the sound of his accent.

Monica smiled at the cute man and gave him a finger wave. "Does he come with the job?"

Allie ignored her and strode toward the house. Brynn waited until Allie walked up the cracked concrete steps before she began her interrogation. "What are you doing in a limo, Al? What's going on?"

Placing a hand on Brynn's shoulder, Allie gently pushed her into the house. Monica shoved her way past them and stepped inside. "Allie needs to talk."

"Sit down a second, okay?" She waited until her sisters parked themselves on the shabby blue sofa. Monica looked just like their mom—the same long, honey-blond hair and light blue eyes, down to the little dent in her chin. Brynn, on the other hand, looked more like their father, with dark hair and deep blue, almost navy eyes. And right now they were wide and frightened.

Brynn sat huddled, arms wrapped around her stomach. "Tell us what's going on, Al."

"You know with Mom's hospital bills and the cost of the funeral, things have been pretty tight lately."

"Yeah, no shit. Like I *need* a car. And those shoes are from last year." Monica pointed at the green canvas shoes in the middle of the room, their long strings trailing across the floor.

*God, not again.* "Monica, we've been over this. You want a car? Get a job and buy one."

Rolling her eyes toward the ceiling, she sighed. "How am I supposed to get a job if I don't have a car? And I thought you said this wasn't going to be another lecture."

Brynn pulled her knees up to her chest. "Would you two shut it? All you do is fight and I'm sick of it."

When Allie thought she could open her mouth without blasting Monica, she said, "Dad's business has taken a hit and even with my paycheck we can't make ends meet. So, I took a new job today. I'm an assistant to a man named Trevor Blake. He's an investor and he needs me to start immediately. But I have to move into his house because he keeps such crazy hours."

Monica smiled. "Score. Can I come over and use the pool? He's got a pool, right?"

Allie ignored Monica and sank down on the sofa, brushing her shoulder against Brynn's. "It's going to be all right. I'll call every day and I'll come home to check on you all the time."

Brynn narrowed her eyes. "No, you won't. You're going to leave and not come back. And I don't care. I'm not a kid. I can take care of myself." She jumped up and ran out of the room.

Guilt lodged in the middle of Allie's chest. What was she supposed to do? If she didn't keep this bargain, the medical bills alone would probably bankrupt them. And Trevor Blake would evict them.

The house itself was a relic. Old, scarred furniture. Ancient brown carpeting. A secondhand refrigerator that made an annoying, high-pitched whine. The place was in desperate need of a paint job and more than a few repairs. But at least it was a home.

Slouching against the back of the sofa, Monica sighed. "God, she's such a drama queen. It's not like you're dying too."

A lance of pain shot through Allie. But she let it pass. Monica only wanted a reaction. "It wouldn't hurt you to be nice to her. She's having a tough time right now." She sat for a moment, debated whether she should tackle the next subject. But she was already having the shittiest day ever, why not go for the gold. "Want to tell me why you skipped school? Where were you? Who were you with?"

Monica shook her head. "Here we go again. My life is none of your business. You're not Mom, all right? I don't have to answer to you. Stop telling us what to do and just leave already. The only reason Brynn cares if you're here is because you do all the shit jobs."

"Believe me, I'm aware of that. And I could use some help."

Monica batted her eyes. "But then you couldn't be Allie the Perfect. Your life wouldn't be complete."

These same old arguments exhausted her. "Do you ever get tired of being so bitchy, Mon?" Allie glanced at her sister. "Because the rest of us are sick of it."

"Maybe I'm sick of you," Monica yelled. "You're the bitch, not me."

This was how it always ended—angry words, hurt feelings, and childish disagreements. Allie ignored Monica's parting shot as she walked to her room.

She closed her door with a quiet click. Monica and Brynn shared a room, while Allie had the smallest bedroom to herself. She guessed one of the girls could move in here now.

Well, maybe not. She wasn't exactly mistress material, so maybe Trevor would get bored sooner rather than later. Unless he felt cheated by her lack of experience and tried to renege on their agreement.

No, it was in her family's best interest to keep him happy. Every damn whim.

# Chapter 3

"WILL THESE ACCOMMODATIONS WORK, miss?" Arnold asked.

A charcoal duvet covered the king-sized bed. A lovely antique dressing table took up one corner of the room. Above it all was a tray ceiling. The other side of the room, beyond an archway, contained a small sitting room decorated in dove gray and pale pink.

"Yes, Arnold—may I call you Arnold?" she asked.

"I'd be pleased if you would."

"Thank you. The accommodations are beautiful."

"Very good. The en suite is through there." He pointed toward a door next to the bed. "And Mr. Blake requested that you wear the dress hanging in the closet."

Well, that couldn't be good. She didn't trust Trevor Blake to pick out something nice and normal for her to wear. He probably wanted her to wear some sheer, slutty dress that showed off her boobs. Mistress wear. She blinked and noticed Arnold waiting for her response. "Sure, thanks."

"If you require anything, simply dial nine on the phone next to your bed."

"Thank you," she repeated.

Once he was gone, Allie made her way to the closet and opened the doors. A lone black dress hung inside the walk-in. Floor length, with a modest V-neckline and a side slit, it was simple and beautiful. The back, however, was nonexistent. Two narrow crossing straps held it together. There was no way she could wear a bra with it. Black satin sling-back shoes, with wispy feathers across the toe, sat on the floor. She wondered if any of it would fit.

Trevor Blake had bought himself a real live Barbie doll. *Freak.*

She spent the time before dinner unpacking her bags and took a quick shower in the black marble bathroom. An hour later, Allie stood at the top of the staircase, her back straight, head high, feeling exposed and awkward in the backless dress. As she stepped forward, the silky material flowed over her legs.

Trevor waited for her at the bottom of the steps. She hoped to God she wouldn't fall on her ass in front of him. She wasn't used to wearing such high heels.

"You look lovely, Miss Campbell." He wore an evening suit with a black tie and a crisp, white shirt.

Putting on one of her customer service smiles, she willed herself not to show signs of discomfort as the slit parted with every step, revealing her bare leg almost to her hip.

His eyes strayed there as he watched her descend. "I'm so glad it fits."

Opening her mouth to say something clever and cutting, she forgot to kick her foot out ahead of the dress so she wouldn't trip on the hem. She stumbled on the last step and stretched her arms toward him to keep from falling. He reached out at the same time and caught her.

By the boob.

---

Trevor cupped her large breast in one hand. Definitely real. His cock twitched in response.

He wanted to do more than simply cup it. Oh, the very dirty things he longed to do to Allie Campbell. It was good she couldn't read his mind. Her poor little head might explode.

"I'm quite used to women falling for me, Miss Campbell, but you needn't be so literal."

She jerked herself up and stared at his hand. "You're still touching me."

Smiling cheerfully, he left his hand where it was. "So I am."

She tried to smack it away, but he remained unmoved. He watched her pull herself together and attempt to throw an apathetic look on her face. He wasn't fooled. A hot flush stole over her cheeks and those flashing eyes revealed everything she was feeling. And right now, she wanted to punch him.

"When you're through feeling me up, may we eat? I'm starving."

He gave her points for the cool note in her voice. He assumed a serious expression. "Yes, of course, Miss Campbell." He gave her breast one last, gentle squeeze and winked before letting go. Then he offered his arm to escort her to dinner.

The dining room was large, with a table that could easily seat twenty. Not that he ever had guests. His home was a tranquil sanctuary in a chaotic world. Yellow and white flowers from the garden made up a floral arrangement in the middle of the table, and lighted tapers shimmered throughout the room.

Trevor led Allie to a seat next to the head of the table. When she sat, he saw the back of the dress for the first time. He was willing to bet she hated being on display. That made him smile.

Arnold served a salad and discreetly disappeared. Pouring them each a glass of wine, Trevor watched her from the corner of his eye.

Allie appeared stiff and uncomfortable as she placed the napkin on her lap. He liked it better when she was hissing at him.

"How is your room?"

"It's fine, thank you." She proceeded to eat a small bite of lettuce, keeping her eyes on her plate.

"And what about your family, Miss Campbell? How did they take the news?"

"They were upset."

"Naturally. Did you tell them the truth?"

She laid down her fork and looked up at him. "What do you think, Mr. Blake?"

His gaze captured hers as he leaned closer and lowered his voice. "I do like it when you call me Mr. Blake. Maybe we'll get you a naughty schoolgirl costume and I can play headmaster."

Pink flagged her cheeks, but she picked up her fork and resumed eating.

*There. That should take care of the Mr. Blake nonsense.*

Arnold brought in the soup—lobster bisque with homemade croutons. One of Trevor's favorites.

After taking a bite, Allie closed her eyes. With the smooth line of her throat exposed, those tantalizing tits peeking above the silky, black material, and it was all he could do to keep his hands to himself. But he couldn't tear his gaze away.

Her eyes fluttered open. "This is delicious."

"I'll make sure Mrs. Hubert knows how much you like it." Sounding hoarse, he took a sip of wine. Apparently this was going to be more difficult than he thought, living with Allie but not touching her. Torture, really, and he had brought it on himself.

"So, you don't have any family left?" she asked.

"No, I don't." At least none he cared to claim.

Sympathy filled her eyes. "I'm sorry. I know what that's like, losing people you love."

He gave her a cold smile. "Don't feel sorry for me, Miss Campbell. It's you who should be pitied. If you didn't care so much about your family, you'd have never agreed to fuck me."

She drew a sharp breath, shock and anger flashed in her eyes. "You're right. If it weren't for them, I wouldn't look at you twice. And I'd have slapped you into next week for the things you said to me."

Yes, this was the fiery woman from this afternoon. He was glad she'd reappeared. Much better than the sympathetic, nervous Allie.

When Arnold served roasted game hens stuffed with wild rice, she smiled sweetly and thanked him. She'd never smiled at Trevor like that. Not once. He raised a brow at Arnold as the older man left the room.

"So, what's with all the antiques and knickknacks?" She forked a piece of hen into her mouth.

"Knickknacks?"

"The tchotchkes. The miniature vases, the lockets, all the stuff in glass cases."

He blinked. "Tchotchkes? They're called *objets d'art*, Miss Campbell. There are books in the library about the various collections if you care to educate yourself."

"How very grand," she said in a fake British accent, her nose lifted in the air.

"That accent's dreadful. And yes, it is terribly grand, but then so am I."

"You really are an arrogant ass."

"But a charming one."

She rolled her eyes and finished her meal.

Once custard was served, Trevor turned to Arnold. "Thank you. We'll call you when we're done."

"Very good, sir."

Trevor refilled his wine glass. "Did you enjoy dinner, Miss Campbell? I thought for a moment you might lick the plate clean."

Little lines near her eyes betrayed her stress, but she hid it well behind a smile that seemed almost genuine. "The food was delicious."

"I'm so gratified." He leaned back in his chair and studied her.

Her body stiffened under his scrutiny, and she cast her gaze on the flickering candle. He didn't like it when she wasn't relaxed with him. Even an angry response was much better than this tense nervousness.

He rose from his seat and held out his hand. "Come, Miss Campbell."

A look of panic raced across her features, but she quickly mastered it. Taking his hand, she didn't speak.

Instead of leading her out of the dining room, he walked to the terrace doors. When she realized he wasn't taking her upstairs, the tightness around her eyes lessened—somewhat.

As they stepped outside, Trevor turned to her. "What do you think?"

In silence, she gaped at the lighted garden before her. A traditional English garden really, with stone paths and herbaceous borders and a profusion of flowers.

"This must cost a fortune to water," she whispered.

Keeping hold of her hand, he led her down the steps and onto the garden path. "Yes, I believe it does."

The comforting smell of blooming flowers enveloped him as they strolled beneath a dark sky, the half-moon partially visible through the clouds. "Do you like it?"

Her lips parted and she swiveled her head, taking in the trees, the roses, the purple and pink delphiniums. "Of course, it's beautiful. How in the world do you grow all this here?"

"Most of the area was dug up and fresh soil brought in. You're absolutely right though, it's a frivolous expense. I've been thinking about tearing it out and putting a tennis court here instead." They walked further toward the grotto swimming pool. "Do you play, Miss Campbell?"

"Not as well as you. You're just trying to get a rise out of me. You're not going to get rid of this garden. You wouldn't have gone to all this trouble if it wasn't important to you."

With a sudden movement, he stopped and faced her. He wrapped an arm around her waist, pulling her into him. Her eyes widened and she drew in a surprised breath.

"Never presume to know me, Miss Campbell." He reached out with his other hand and caught a lock of her hair, rubbing it between his finger and thumb. It was just as soft as it looked.

She stared at him warily, her hands flat on the lapels of his jacket.

He pulled her closer, his palm hot against her cool, bare back, felt her breasts press against his chest. He wondered what her nipples looked like—pink and dusky or just a shade darker than her pale skin? He let go of her hair and moved his thumb slowly across one of her golden eyebrows.

Her breath quickened. Those blue eyes darkened a bit. As he slowly leaned forward and kissed her temple, her lashes fluttered, tickling his cheek. Bloody hell, he was rock hard and he hadn't even kissed her properly.

Leaning his head back, he tenderly brushed his hand across her jaw, then ran his finger over the seam of her lips. Those full, pouty lips. They parted and her eyes drifted shut.

He dipped his finger in her mouth, then traced her upper lip with his damp fingertip. His own breath was shallow, his heart racing. He edged the tip of his finger in her mouth once again. "Suck," he whispered.

Her eyes shot open, and she jerked her head away, so that his finger was no longer touching her. "No."

He stroked the naked skin along her spine, felt her shiver. "You're having difficulty with the 'every whim' part of the program, aren't you, darling? If you want to end this arrangement now—"

"I don't." Staring daggers at him, she grabbed his free hand and lowering her head, licked his finger from base to tip like it was her favorite treat. Then she slid it between her plump lips and began to suck. Gently at first. Leisurely. With a moan, she swirled her tongue around him. Her head bobbed up and down, her eyes never leaving his as she gave a porn-star performance. Scraping her teeth against his knuckle, she increased the suction, pulling him further inside.

Good God.

His cock pulsed with the rhythm of her mouth and got even

harder, if that were possible. By forcing Allie to do this, he'd just fucked himself. And not in a satisfactory way.

Abruptly, she jerked the finger from her mouth with a pop and dropped his hand.

"Happy?" she asked.

~~~

It was getting harder to suppress her reactions to him—the anger, the anxiety. And the attraction. That tug she felt when he took her in his arms and stroked his fingers along her jaw. When he kissed her temple and looked at her with stormy gray eyes. She'd almost softened toward him, too, until he reminded her yet again about their little transaction. Every whim, her ass.

He constantly kept her off balance—cold and sarcastic one second, hot and sensual the next. He was toying with her, and she didn't like it.

He gazed at her with a mixture of amusement and something else she couldn't quite define. "Well done, Miss Campbell. Now, we need to get back. I still have some work to do this evening."

"More poor people to exploit?" She couldn't manage to keep the hint of bitterness out of her voice.

"Widows and orphans to destroy, puppies to kick." He sighed deeply. "So much evil to do and only twenty-four hours in a day."

She glanced up at him. "You're not funny."

"You, on the other hand, are terribly amusing."

As they walked back to the house, she let her hand trail over the velvet petals of a yellow rose. "If you miss England so much, why did you leave?"

He stopped, that nasty smile hovering on his lips. "Wherever did you learn your sucking skills, Miss Campbell? You're exceptionally good at it. Had a lot of practice?"

She let go of the rose petal and twirled toward him to lash out, but when she did, her finger caught the tip of a thorn. "Damn." She stuck the bleeding finger in her mouth.

"Let me see." Taking her hand, he brought it closer to his face and squeezed.

"Ow, stop that." She tried to yank out of his grasp, but he tightened his hold.

"Don't be such a baby. It's only a scratch." Drawing a folded white handkerchief from his pocket, he wrapped it around her finger and applied pressure.

This time when she tried to pull away, he let her go. She clutched the handkerchief and resumed walking. She didn't look at him, didn't ask any more personal questions.

With his hand on her bare back, he led her to the house, through the dining room, to the foot of the staircase, where he'd felt her up earlier in the evening. Her cheeks grew warm thinking of his hand on her breast, squeezing it like he owned it. Which, for the next two months, he did.

But that was nothing compared to what was coming. She was going to have to show him the whole enchilada, let him touch whatever he wanted. She was on the verge of freaking out when he gazed down at her with a mocking smile.

"Good night, Miss Campbell. Try not to dream of me." He ran his fingers down her spine before striding toward his office.

She stood alone on the bottom step, completely confused. Her heart slowed to a steady beat, and the threatening tide of panic began to subside.

So, that was it? No sex? He must be playing another game, one that only he knew the rules to. But she was too tired to figure them out tonight.

Grateful for a reprieve, she whisked off her shoes and, grabbing the hem of the dress with her uninjured hand, lightly ran up the stairs to the safety of her room. She shut the door behind her and locked it. It wouldn't keep him out, but at least she might have some advance notice if decided to barge in.

She went to the bathroom and unwrapped her scratched finger. The initials embroidered on his handkerchief read TWB. Trevor William? She scoffed, glancing at herself in the mirror.

"You're an idiot, Allison. Who gives a crap what his middle name is? The man was about to take over your house and kick your family out on the street." No matter how many flowers he planted or how gently he wrapped her bloody finger, he owned her ass. And she'd better remember that.

In the bedroom, she removed the dress, letting her hand drift over the expensive fabric before hanging it up in the closet. Then, she threw on a pair of men's boxer shorts and an old, faded T-shirt before grabbing the phone off the side table. Allie needed to call her father and explain the situation. She could only imagine what Monica told him, and he must be worried by now.

He answered on the first ring.

"Hey, Dad."

"My God, Allie, what the hell is going on? Monica said you're living with Trevor Blake."

"Sorry I couldn't talk to you in person, but when I came to see Mr. Blake about the loan, he offered me a job," she said, forcing enthusiasm into her voice. She didn't want her father to suspect anything was wrong.

"Allie, he's throwing us out of our house. You can't work for that man."

She sank down on the bed and, plucking the gray duvet with two fingers, took a deep breath. "I'm going to be his assistant, Dad, and in return, he's going to forgive the debt you owe and pay off the mortgage and the rest of the medical bills."

"Why? Why would he do that, Al?"

She hated lying to him. But it was necessary. "He liked my

initiative. I'm not getting much of a salary at this point, but I have room and board and I'll gain a lot of experience." She winced as she said the words. She didn't really want the kind of experience a man like Trevor Blake would give her. *Hot, consuming sexual experience.*

Her father laughed. "That's amazing, Allison. I'm so proud of you."

He wouldn't be proud if he knew the truth. She closed her eyes and kept her voice light. "Can I talk to Brynn?"

"Let me see." He came back a minute later. "She doesn't want to talk right now, but she'll come around. She doesn't like change and you left so suddenly…"

Allie cleared her throat. "Okay. So, what are you going to do about work?"

"When have I ever not worked?" He sounded testy, then sighed. "Sorry. I haven't been completely honest with you. I, uh, sold off all my tools a couple of months ago. The business has been in trouble for a long time."

She closed her eyes. "Why didn't you tell me?"

"I didn't want to worry you." He laughed, but there was no humor in it. "And I guess I didn't want to admit I'm a failure."

"That's not true. Don't say that."

"It is true. Anyway, I've started doing some odd jobs for a friend, fixing up some rental properties, repairing old appliances on the side. It doesn't pay much, but since Mr. Blake has forgiven the loan and offered to pay off the medical bills…Allie, you can't know what a relief this is." He let out a sob and sniffed a couple of times. "Sorry, I just can't believe he's doing this. Thank him for me."

Allie felt a lot of things toward Trevor, but gratitude wasn't one of them. "I'll come by tomorrow and check in."

"By the way, we're out of paper towels. And coffee filters."

"Paper towels are under the sink and coffee filters are in the pantry, third shelf down." She pressed her lips together. He was going to fall apart without her. This was a mistake, moving in with Trevor. But what choice did she have?

~~~

Allie was awakened by tapping, then a rattle of the door handle. Disoriented, she rubbed her eyes and tried to figure out where she was. Right, Trevor Blake's house. She stumbled out of bed and unlocked the door. Standing on the other side of it was a middle-aged, round-faced, cheerful bundle of energy with curly red hair.

"Good morning, miss," she said in an English accent. But hers wasn't fancy, like Trevor's and Arnold's. "I'm Frances. Sorry I wasn't here yesterday to greet you proper. My day off." Clad in a black dress and black tennis shoes, she hustled into the room and pulled back the curtains, flooding the place with light.

"Nice to meet you," Allie said before she walked back to bed and huddled under the blankets. She couldn't do cheerful this morning, she was too exhausted.

"Time to rise and shine. Mr. Blake is waiting on you."

Allie groaned and checked the time. Seven o'clock wasn't early, but she'd spent the night in tears. Her eyes felt swollen and grainy. "Tell Mr. Blake to stuff it." She pulled the covers over her head.

Frances laughed. "Oh, I won't be doing that. Come on now, love." She played tug-of-war with the blankets but managed to yank them out of Allie's clutched hands. "You need to get up. Mr. Blake says you have a full day ahead of you."

Allie glared at Frances but stopped herself. It wasn't Frances's fault she was in this mess. Sitting up, she pushed a stray piece of hair out of her face. "Okay, I'll be down in a few."

"I'll have a nice cup of coffee waiting for you. How do you take it, love?"

She was beginning to like Frances. "Lots of cream and sugar, please."

As Allie climbed out of bed, she had to wonder what Frances

and Arnold thought about her. Did they know she was Trevor's mistress? She was probably one in a long line of women who stayed in this room, servicing Trevor Blake. She shouldn't care. He'd be on to the next girl soon, and Allie could get back to her family.

She washed quickly and changed into a pair of faded jeans and a blue T-shirt. *Screw the makeup.* If Trevor Blake didn't like her face in its natural state, he could suck it.

Just like she had sucked his finger last night. He'd stroked his hand absently up and down her back as she took him in her mouth. His hand against her skin…

*No, focus.* She couldn't afford to get distracted. He was waiting on her, and she needed a clear head. She trotted down the stairs and ran into Frances.

"I was about to come and get you. Mr. Blake is getting a mite peevish. Follow me, dear."

"Aren't we going to the dining room?"

"No, until last night, we hadn't used it in years." She came to a stop in front of a doorway that opened to a blue and white room. It seemed cheerful and homey—and not a knickknack in sight.

Allie poked her head in the door and the rich smell of coffee called to her. Trevor was already seated at the table, BlackBerry in hand.

"Don't stand there hovering, Miss Campbell. You may have all day, but I assure you, I do not." He never looked up from his phone as he spoke.

She sat at the opposite end of the table, as far away from him as she could get. Arnold waited by a sideboard.

"What would you like for breakfast, miss?"

Trevor set aside his phone and looked up. "Give her some of everything, Arnold."

She glared at him. "Hey, English, I'm in the room, and I can answer for myself."

He quirked a brow. "You're a bright little ray of sunshine this morning, Miss Campbell. And do sit next to me. We have things to discuss and I feel as if I'm looking at you from across a football pitch."

With a sigh, she moved down the length of the table, but before she could pull out a chair, Arnold was there, pulling it out for her.

Frances placed a cup of steaming coffee on the table, and Arnold gave her a full plate of bacon, eggs, sausages, and toast. She smiled at them. "Thank you."

"That will be all for now," Trevor said. "You've got quite a fan club going, you know." He nodded toward the door that Frances and Arnold had exited.

"I'm sure they like all your mistresses." She didn't look at him as she placed her white linen napkin on her lap.

"Perhaps. And while the top of your head is as delightful as the rest of you, eyes on me."

Picking up a piece of toast, she lifted her head. "Yes?"

"You need to sign these." He set a stack of papers in front of her. "My lawyer put these helpful little pink strips to show you where."

She dropped the toast and wiped her hands. After eyeing the papers with suspicion, she peered up at him. "What are they?"

"You said you wanted everything in writing. This states that I'm paying off all your family debt and in exchange, you will grant me whatever favors I desire." Holding the pen, he smiled. "No matter how perverse."

# Chapter 4

ALLIE GASPED. "IT DOES not say that."

"Read it if you don't believe me."

She could, but what difference would it make? That's exactly what she was doing: giving him sexual favors in return for money. Basically, she was attesting to the fact that she was a whore. She snatched the pen from his hand and signed next to all the pink strips.

"Excellent." He handed her the BlackBerry he'd been fiddling with. "I've programmed in my numbers." He reached into the inner pocket of his suit jacket and pulled out a credit card. "And I have a personal shopper waiting for you. Simmons will take you anywhere else you need to go." He scanned her *Get Lucky in Vegas* T-shirt. "I took the liberty of compiling a list."

"You did what?" she asked, still reeling from the sex contract. Now he was going to dictate what she wore? "You made me a shopping list?"

He pushed back from the table. "No appreciation necessary. Seeing you in a natural fiber will be thanks enough." He scooped up the papers she'd signed and patted her head as he left the room.

"Wait," she called, but he didn't come back. Damn him.

She rubbed the top of her head where he'd patted her. Allie was getting tired of his condescension. But what could she do about it? She'd just signed papers to make her role official. She couldn't back out now.

Maybe that's why he hadn't wanted sex last night. Maybe he was waiting to get all the details down in legalese.

Fingering the embossed numbers on the credit card, she frowned. Some women would kill for this opportunity, to live here, to have all their expenses paid—to have sex with Trevor Blake. She wasn't one of them.

She tucked the card in the pocket of her jeans. Then, plucking a strip of bacon from her plate, she went to find Simmons.

Allie had the blond chauffeur drop her off at home first. While he remained in the car, she let herself inside. Since she was rarely home by herself during the day, she stood in the living room, taking in the quiet—except for the high-pitched whine of the refrigerator. Somehow, her dad never got around to fixing it.

Making her way to the kitchen, she surveyed the damage. A carton of milk had been left on the counter, coffee grounds were spilled in the sink, and a dirty pan sat on the stove. She hoped her dad had at least remembered to make Monica and Brynn lunch.

Allie put the milk away and found the pork chops from yesterday still in the fridge, so she wrote her dad a quick note on how to prepare them and propped it next to the coffeepot. And she needed to remind her father that Monday was trash day. He always forgot.

She washed a load of laundry and cleaned up the kitchen. Then, taking one last glance around, she knew she couldn't put it off any longer. It was time to go to shopping.

⁓

Six hours later, she was exhausted. Nancy, her nice but rather manic personal shopper, made Allie try on more clothes than any one person could possibly need. And as Simmons and Arnold made trip after trip from the car to Allie's room, she watched the bags pile up around her. For what she'd spent at Agent Provocateur on underwear, she could have bought a used car.

"Why don't I bring you a cup of tea, miss?" Frances asked from the doorway. "Then you can have yourself a nice hot bath, and I'll put these things away for you."

"No, that's okay. I'll put everything away myself."

With a frown, Frances looked at the dozens of bags littering the room. "But it's my job."

Some of the things on Trevor's list were pretty risqué—barely there thongs with ruffles, completely transparent teddies, and sheer waspies—corset-like bands that circled the waist with garters dangling from them. She'd never seen one before today. She was used to buying her underwear in packages of six.

"I don't mind," Allie said.

"All right, but I'm bringing your tea, and that's that."

Once Frances was gone, Allie pulled out the more questionable purchases of the day and shoved them in a dresser drawer. This really was mistress wear.

The fact that Trevor had specifically requested all this made her stomach knot in worry. The man obviously knew what he wanted, was used to women wearing this type of thing. Allie was comfortable in an old T-shirt and pajama pants. Trevor's other women must be in a completely different sexual category. Allie would never measure up. Not that she cared what Trevor thought. If he didn't like her lack of technique, too bad. Maybe he'd send her home.

Frances reappeared with a tea tray. "Make sure you eat, now. You hardly touched your breakfast. I'm going to run you a bath."

Falling onto the bed, Allie grabbed a sandwich and ate. She had finished her second cup of tea by the time Frances reentered the room.

"All ready. In you go, and I'll put away the rest of your things."

While being waited on still made her feel like a diva, Allie gave in. With a smile of thanks, she slipped into the bathroom. Humidity from the hot water made her skin damp, and the tub brimmed over with frothy bubbles that smelled of lavender. She hadn't had a bubble bath since she was a little girl.

Quickly shedding her clothes, she pinned up her hair before sliding into the water. God, it felt good—soothing and warm. She'd just started to drift off when the door opened. Thinking it was Frances, she smiled and opened her eyes to find Trevor staring at her.

Allie's heartbeat kicked up a notch. "What are you doing in here?" Granted, it was a stupid question, but he'd taken her by surprise. She sank further into the suds and slapped an arm over both breasts as if she were a virgin in a Regency novel. She knew she was behaving like an idiot, but that didn't stop her from covering the girls.

"What do you think I'm doing? Taking tea with the queen? I'm here to speak with you, of course." He'd removed the jacket and tie from this morning, undone a couple buttons at his throat, and rolled his sleeves up to his elbows. With his black hair and wicked gray eyes, Trevor looked sexy and disheveled. He strolled into the room and parked on the side of the tub. Stretching out his legs, he made himself at home. "Did you have a good day, Miss Campbell?"

"Shopping on a rich man's dime. Oh, yes—I've reached the pinnacle." Every word carried the sting of sarcasm.

"You haven't come close to the pinnacle, Miss Campbell. And you'll know when you've reached it, because you'll be screaming my name." His eyes met hers as he scooped his hand into the tub, skimming her thigh in the process. She skittishly shifted her leg and watched him, her attention fixed, as he brought a palm full of bubbles to his lips. He blew them at her, and a bubble blob landed on her nose.

He laughed when she crossed her eyes to stare at it. Swiping at it, she left an even bigger blob on her face.

"Allow me." Trevor bent toward her. He was so close she could see the lighter flecks of silver in his eyes. Softly, he brushed off the bubbles. "There." He slid one finger across her jaw. "Did you get everything on my list?"

He still didn't move back. His clean scent teased her and mixed with the lavender. It was a compelling combination. The open collar of his shirt left a V-shaped gap, exposing the hollow of his throat. Allie's gaze flickered to the pulse beating there, lifted over his stubble-covered chin, lingered for a brief second on his firm lips, and finally, she stared into his eyes. "Your list was ridiculous."

He held her gaze for a moment before brushing her lips with his own. Then, straightening, he again trailed his hand through the bubbles, but this time, he lowered his fingers into the water and found her leg. She froze when he slid his palm along her calf, rubbing down to her ankle until he held her foot. "My lists are never ridiculous. You can try everything on for me after you get out of the tub."

She tried to pull away, but he kept a firm grip on her heel and took it out of the water, placing it on his leg. He didn't seem to care that his pants were getting soaked.

"Forget it, English. I spent the whole day trying that stuff on, and I'm not going through it again."

He began kneading the bottom of her foot, and his soapy hand slid up the arch, to her toes, then back down to her heel. He increased the pressure right where she needed it. "So you don't enjoy shopping?"

"Maybe your other mistresses love it, but I don't."

"You seem very preoccupied with my mistresses, Miss Campbell. Afraid you won't measure up?"

Again, she tried to pull her foot from his hands, but he held on and continued to massage. She wasn't going to lie—at least not to herself—his thumbs pressing into her arch felt wonderful. She almost sighed in pleasure but caught herself at the last second. She barely refrained from thrusting her other foot in his lap and having him rub that one too.

"So, you do this type of thing all the time?" she asked.

"Rub women's feet?"

"Pay them to have sex with you? If that's the case, God only knows what you've caught. You could be a walking petri dish."

His face became a blank mask. "If I recall, it was your idea to barter your services."

"I didn't hear you protesting." She sank further into the water. "I want you to wear a condom. Every time."

"That's terribly unfortunate, Miss Campbell. I like to ride bareback, feel every sensation as it were. No barriers. Just my skin against yours."

Now her cheeks were on fire. But she wouldn't back down. "Tough. I'm not taking any chances."

Sighing heavily, he shook his head in mock sadness. "Though it will be a tremendous sacrifice, I suppose I could glove up. But just so you know, it won't be the same."

"You're still not funny."

He continued to rub her heel, edging toward her ankle. Switching up the pressure, he'd rub firm circles into her muscles one minute and use a soft caress the next. Then, with deliberate, leisurely strokes, his hands glided up her calf to circle the back of her knee. The look in his eyes dared her to stop him.

And she should have. She should have protested, slammed her legs together, but she didn't move. She was mesmerized by those gray eyes, the slick hands, and the skillful fingers dancing across her skin. It had been so long since anyone had touched her like this. She wanted more.

Leaning slightly forward, Trevor's fingers trailed even further north. When he reached her inner thigh, his grazing touch was so light it almost tickled. His hand moved closer—closer to her aching core.

Her mouth parted. Just another inch and he'd reached it.

Then he slowly, too damn slowly, slid one finger inside her. Closing her eyes, Allie held her breath, waited for him to move. *This shouldn't be happening.* She didn't even know him. But it felt too good to stop.

"Open your eyes."

Heart pounding, she heeded his command and watched his impassive face as he slipped another finger inside her. Scissoring them, he used his thumb to trace around her clit. Back and forth, those fingers came together and slid apart, alternately stretching and filling her. She'd never felt anything so delicious.

In only moments, an orgasm rocked through her body. Allie's eyes drifted shut as she arched her back. With one arm still hiding her breasts, her hands clenched into fists and her toes flexed.

"Look at me," he said softly.

Once again, her eyes flickered open. Trevor's jaw tightened, his was breath choppy.

As he continued to move within her, waves of pleasure rippled from her pussy outward. The cooling water lapped over her hips until the aftershocks subsided. But as her body relaxed, Trevor's fingers stayed buried deep inside her. "The next time you come, Miss Campbell, you will scream my name. Count on it." Then he gave her an arrogant grin and very gently removed his hand from her body.

Angry at herself for being such an easy mark, for being so desperate that she virtually panted for his touch, she plunged her free hand into the water and fumbled around for the loofah. She flung it at him with her left hand, but it still managed to hit him square in the chest with a wet thud. "Get out."

He rose to his feet, his now-soaked white shirt transparent and plastered to his sculpted body—his defined pecs, his lean abdomen. He was every bit as hard and ripped as she'd imagined. She wanted to touch that chest and see for herself how firm it was. Skim her hands over each and every abdominal ridge.

And then she noticed his erection. His very large erection.

"Don't stare, darling. Unless you'd like a closer look?"

She should be embarrassed, but instead, she actually wanted a closer inspection. How big was it? How thick? Her heart pounding, Allie pulled her gaze away from his cock. It was more difficult than it should have been. "Get. Out."

With a smile, he walked to the door. "See you at dinner, Miss Campbell."

After he was gone, Allie took a deep breath and submerged herself beneath the bubbles. But she couldn't wash away the memories of Trevor observing her when she was at her most vulnerable, the way he carefully watched her reaction with his heated gaze, never taking his eyes from her as his fingers moved inside her. It was more intimate than anything she'd ever experienced. And she didn't even like him. So how was she supposed to face him after that?

~~~

Standing at her bedroom door, Allie smoothed her hand down the front of her light blue dress. Okay, so Trevor finger banged her earlier. Hardly the end of the world. And he watched her have an orgasm. Big deal. It was a biological reaction. Like sneezing.

And she shouldn't be embarrassed about their condom conversation either. That was just taking care of business. True, she was on the pill. Had been for years. She started in college and kept up the habit, even though no man had been anywhere near her since... Trevor Blake. He had been near. He'd been inside her.

She ignored the heat flooding her cheeks. Stupid blushing.

Grabbing the door handle, she gathered her courage and left the room. But when she walked down the stairs, Trevor wasn't waiting for her this time. He wasn't in the dining room either.

Holding out a chair, Arnold dipped his head in greeting. "Mr.

Blake has been tied up with business. I'm afraid he will be unable to dine with you this evening."

Although Allie had been nervous about seeing him again, she was actually disappointed by his absence. God, what was wrong with her? Was she getting that Stockholm Syndrome thing, where she identified with her captor?

She needed to get a grip. She didn't have Stockholm Syndrome, and if Trevor couldn't join her, that was a good thing.

Arnold served her a bowl of green soup and retreated. She felt like an idiot, eating alone at the long, polished table. Though for once, she could relax. She didn't have to be on guard with Trevor at her elbow, watching her, teasing her with that droll, sarcastic sense of humor. She was happy to eat in peace. Very happy. Ecstatic, in fact.

After dinner, she was at a loss for what to do, so she decided to wander around the first floor and look at the antique knickknacks. And Allie didn't care what Trevor said, an auction house was just a fancy yard sale but with older shit.

She started at the far end of the house, nearest the dining room, and stepped into a salon...parlor? Sitting room? She didn't know its official title, but it was wallpapered in egg-yolk yellow. It didn't seem like Trevor's style at all. Not that she was an expert or anything, but his office contained large, comfortable leather chairs and that huge wooden desk—warm, manly furnishings. A few expensive-looking landscapes as well. But this room was the exact opposite.

Fussy and filled with hand-painted Chinese cabinets and porcelain bowls, an enormous Buddha watched her from the corner. So... the Asian room, then? Really, theme rooms? Well, this was Vegas.

She walked out into the hall and glanced down at a case that held antique gunpowder flasks. Why did Trevor buy all this? Did he wake up one morning, suddenly fascinated with carved Spanish daggers? Because there were seventeen of them mounted in individual glass boxes and hanging along one wall.

As she drifted from room to room, she saw stunning landscapes, busts of ancient Roman women, and a flock of porcelain shepherds scattered across a mantel. She hoped he had a killer security system and a hell of a lot of insurance.

Finally, she stumbled onto a round room in the back of the house with a giant flat-screen TV and a squishy, overstuffed green sofa. Kicking off her shoes, she curled her legs under her and grabbed the remote from the coffee table.

At least he had satellite. After the insurance company had denied the experimental treatment her mother needed two years ago, Allie's family had dropped their cable and every other nonessential expense—not that she had much time to watch television anyway.

Flipping through the stations, she settled on a thriller she'd already seen. Her mind wandered as she watched. She'd tried to call Brynn this evening before dinner, but no one answered at the house. And her call went to voice mail when she'd tried Brynn's cell. She'd call again once she got back up to her room. Brynn couldn't shut her out forever.

With her chin propped on her palm, Allie's eyes drifted shut.

———

Trevor found her curled up on the sofa, her face lovely and relaxed. He wished he could relax. After he'd seen her lounging in the tub all pink and glowing, after caressing her soft, wet skin, he'd spent two and a half hours in the gym, punching a bag, running on the treadmill, lifting weights. He'd wanked off in the shower, but it had barely taken the edge off his aching cock. He'd finger fucked her for God's sake. He hadn't planned on touching her at all. His lack of self-control was bothersome. And bringing her here was a mistake, one of the worst ideas he'd had in a good, long while.

He grabbed the remote and turned off the television. Allie didn't move. Her legs, bent at the knee, were long and bare. The hem of her light blue dress had risen to the curve of her perfectly shaped bottom, revealing the hint of a round globe. He hadn't seen her ass yet. Or her breasts. He'd touched her, watched her come, but hadn't gotten so much as a glimpse of the best bits.

Crossing his arms over his chest, he couldn't pull his gaze away from her. With a deep breath, he forced himself to look away from that luscious ass and back to her face, her tousled hair.

He'd made up his mind this evening. He was going to have to keep his distance. No more naked Allie. No more bathtub visits. No more touching. It was just too bloody frustrating.

He should send her home to her family. It was stupid, keeping her here without shagging her senseless. But every time he thought about letting her go, he rejected the idea. And she hadn't cleared her debt. Besides, he liked taunting her, saying outrageous things, watching those cheeks fill with color.

Bloody hell, when had he turned into such a rambling twat?

Reaching out, he poked her in the arm. Her brows furrowed, but she didn't awaken. So he grabbed a strand of white-blond hair and tickled her nose with it. Still asleep, she brushed at her face with one hand.

"Miss Campbell," he whispered. With the strand of hair still in his hand, he ran it along the seam of her lips. "Oh, Miss Campbell."

"Go away." She shifted her bottom against the back of the sofa, making the dress ride up further. He sneaked a peek and saw half of her peach-shaped ass hanging out, just waiting to be palmed.

With a scowl, he poked her again. A little harder this time. "It's midnight, Miss Campbell. You should be upstairs in bed, before you turn into a pumpkin."

She groaned.

Sighing, he bent and scooped her up. Her light fragrance surrounded him, making him want to haul her up to his room and spend the rest of the night buried inside of her. Did she smell that good all over? He'd love to find out. Instead, he shifted her a bit and carried her out of the room. As he walked toward the stairs, she snuggled herself more comfortably in his arms, resting her head against his shoulder. She felt right there.

As soon as it crossed his mind, he stopped cold. That was a bloody stupid thought. She was just new, that was all, a novelty in his life. He stared down at her beautiful face. He would grow tired of looking at it. And it wouldn't take two months either.

He leaned his head down and whispered in her ear, "I'm going to take you upstairs and fuck you senseless, Allison."

Her eyelids flickered. "Mmmkay." Suddenly, her eyes popped open and realization crept in. She began struggling then, her hands pushing at his chest.

"Oh good, you're awake." He set her on her feet.

She stood in front of him and tugged at the hem of her dress, smoothing it over her hips as she looked up at him with sleepy eyes. "What's going on?"

"I was carrying you to bed, Miss Campbell. But I'm glad you awakened before I had to drag your bum all the way up the stairs. There are a great many of them, and you were becoming quite burdensome." He spun her around by the shoulders, reached out, and gave her bottom a little pat. His hand wanted to linger, but he made himself pull back. "Off you go. Nighty night."

She looked up to the top of the stairs and back at him. "Aren't you coming?"

Curling his lip, he thrust his hands into the pockets of his trousers. "Unfortunately, no."

———

When Allie opened her eyes the next morning, the sun was barely up. She glanced at the clock next to the bed and groaned. Six-thirty and she wouldn't be able to go back to sleep. Not after thoughts of last night flooded her brain.

He'd sent her toddling off to bed as if she were a child. She was here for his sexual needs, and every time he didn't demand she meet them, anxiety filled her, ballooning larger until she felt ready to burst. If Trevor didn't want her, why didn't he just let her go? She was convinced he was playing some twisted mind game. Still, what could she do about it?

Throwing back the covers, she headed for the shower. When she walked into the breakfast room, almost an hour later, Trevor's chair was empty. She gazed around the room for a second, then Frances entered with a carafe of coffee.

"Hungry, love?"

"Just coffee, thanks." Allie refused to ask about Trevor. If he wanted to go AWOL during meal times, it wasn't her business. "Frances, can I use a car this morning? I have some errands."

"Certainly, there's a car in the garage at your disposal. Mr. Blake also requested that you meet him in the foyer at noon." Frances set a cup in front of her with a wink and left.

As Allie sipped her coffee, the house remained eerily quiet. It was like living in a museum. She missed the whine of her old refrigerator, the sound of her sisters' bickering.

After jogging up to her room and grabbing her purse, Allie made her way outside and around the corner of the house. In a garage that was larger than her own home, Simmons cleaned the interior of the limo. He shut off the vacuum when he saw her. "Good morning."

"Good morning. Hey, I need to borrow a car." She eyed the six vehicles parked inside. There was a little yellow roadster she liked the look of, but the thought of wrecking the vintage car made her nervous.

"How about I drive you?" Simmons nodded toward the limo. "I'll be finished in a second."

Allie shook her head. "That's okay."

"Then why don't you take the Mercedes? It's all gassed up and ready to go." He plucked a set of keys dangling from a hook.

Allie took them and slid behind the wheel, adjusted the seat and mirrors. The mixture of new car smell and expensive leather was intoxicating. Much better than the Festiva's odor of old burger wrappers and exhaust fumes.

She slowly and carefully drove across town. She didn't want to add to her debt by dinging Trevor's car.

She pulled up to the house and parked on the curb. In the driveway, her dad was bent in half beneath the hood of his old Ford truck. When Allie slammed the Mercedes' door, he lifted his head and did a double take. Grabbing a rag at his side, he wiped his wrench as she approached.

The lines around his eyes seemed deeper, even more pronounced than they had only two days ago. "Hey, Al. Very fancy ride."

Allie shrugged and moved to hug him. "Mr. Blake's letting me use it."

He stepped back, out of reach. "No, Al, I don't want to get you all dirty."

She glanced down at the black-and-white sundress she wore. "Oh, right. How are things going? Everybody doing okay? Did Brynn put the towels in the dryer yesterday?"

He tossed the wrench in the toolbox. "You better come inside, Al. We need to talk."

# Chapter 5

"WHAT'S WRONG?" ALLIE TRAILED her father to the kitchen and watched him wash in the sink. Her mom hated it when he cleaned up in the kitchen, but she could never break him of the habit.

He grabbed a paper towel and wiped his dripping hands. "Monica didn't get home until three this morning. Wouldn't tell me where she'd been."

"Oh my God, this is crazy. What is she thinking?" Allie started walking out the door, ready to confront her sister, but his voice halted her steps.

"Don't bother. She was gone again this morning when I got up."

Allie faced him. "And you have no idea who she's with, where she's gone?" She placed her palm on her forehead and sighed. "That kid is driving me crazy."

"Brynn thinks Monica has a new boyfriend, some guy she met at a party."

Fear mixed with the anger churning inside her. Who knew what kind of parties Monica had been going to? Drinking for sure. Drugs? Maybe. "At a party," she repeated. "Do we even know this guy's name?"

Her dad shook his head and leaned against the counter, rubbing his bloodshot eyes. "No. I know it doesn't make sense, but this is how she's dealing with your mom's death. She's grieving."

"We're all grieving. That's no excuse," Allie said. "You call her friends, and I'll check online, see if she's updated her status. Maybe she posted something that will help."

"Those friends of hers aren't going to tell us anything. You should know that by now."

"So we do nothing? Monica can't keep going on like this, Dad, and you shouldn't let her."

He dropped the grease-stained hand from his face. "What do you want me to do, Al? She's eighteen. I can't force her to come home." He pushed away from the counter and sat at the kitchen table.

Allie dropped down next to him and grabbed his arm. "Dad, she's irresponsible. She's going to get herself into real trouble. What would Mom say?"

He jerked his arm back, shaking off Allie's hand. "Mom's not here. In case you haven't figured it out, we're on our own." His deep voice boomed. "And I know I'm failing her. I don't need you to tell me that." Pushing out of his seat, he stormed off, his work boots pounding against the floor before he slammed out of the house.

Allie jumped at the sound. God, she was so tired of all this. But she couldn't sit there, worrying about Monica for the rest of the day. She needed to keep busy. So Allie forced herself to get up and clean the kitchen. After she swept the floor, she threw the neglected towels in the dryer and did another load of wash.

In the girls' room, she found Brynn sitting cross-legged on one of the twin beds, her laptop open in front of her. "What are you doing here? Aren't you supposed to be at what's-his-name's place?"

"Trevor." Allie plopped down on the bed and tapped her elbow against Brynn's arm. "And there's nowhere else I'd rather be. I've missed you."

"Huh, right."

"I tried calling you last night, but you never answered."

"I know. I was still mad at you." Brynn leaned over and rested her head on Allie's shoulder for a brief second before moving away. "Monica was out all night. When she got home, World War Three started."

Allie sat motionless. Brynn actually touched her. Voluntarily. It had been a long time since her sister had sought any kind of comfort, and Allie wasn't going to make a big deal about it, but she wanted to throw her arms around Brynnie and hug her back. Maybe this was progress. She cleared her throat. "Yeah, I heard. Any idea where she is now?"

"No, but she's dating some new guy. His name is Brad, and he's a total douche."

"Do we know the douche's last name?" Allie asked.

"No, she unfriended me, so I can't spy on her. I'm not even sure where they met. But he's older than her. Like as old as you."

"Yeah, twenty-five is ancient," Allie said. But it wasn't funny. Monica was headed down a dangerous path, and the last thing she needed was some loser leading the way.

Brynn picked at the toe of her tennis shoe. "My guidance counselor had a meeting with Dad yesterday."

Well, hell. Allie didn't know how much more bad news she could take. And Brynn was always the quiet one, she never got in trouble at school. "Why didn't he tell me? Is everything okay?"

"Yeah. Dad said you were too busy with your new job and we shouldn't worry you with this stuff."

This was exactly the type of thing she should know. She was gone for two days and look at what happened. Monica was missing and Brynn had trouble at school. "No, honey, I'm never too busy for you. Tell me about this counselor meeting."

Brynn rolled her eyes. "Ms. Castor thinks I'm depressed because of Mom. Like um, hello? She says I'm not engaged enough. I need to add some extracurriculars and start participating in class more. Like it's not enough that I get straight As? Now I have to talk too?"

"What did Dad say?"

"Dad totally agreed with her. He sat there staring and nodding like he was hypnotized. Now I have to join at least one club." She poked herself in the chest. "You know I'm not a joiner."

It might be good for Brynn to break out of her shell a bit, make a couple new friends, speak up once in a while. But, if Allie sided with the school counselor, she'd further alienate her sister. She chose her words carefully. "I know it's unfair that she's forcing this on you. But maybe you can pick something that's not too terrible? Maybe Spanish or Math Club?"

Brynn's eyes widened. "Do you *want* me to get beaten up on the bus?"

"No?"

"I'll figure something out. She gave me a book to choose from. But I am not talking in class, so she can just get over it." Brynn was so adamant, Allie simply nodded and kept her own mouth shut.

Then Brynn peered up at her. "Can you make me a grilled cheese or something?"

Allie couldn't remember the last time she didn't have to prod Brynn to eat. "Yeah, of course. Want tomato soup with it?"

"Do we have goldfish?"

"No, but we could go get some." Allie reached out and patted Brynn's leg.

"Okay." She nibbled her lip. "And maybe we could watch a movie or something?"

Allie wrinkled her brow. "I don't know. You're not going to make me watch another teen vampire movie, are you?"

Brynn actually smiled. "Maybe."

"You're cruel, Brynnie. Very cruel."

Allie was supposed to be back at the mistress mansion by twelve, but to hell with that. Her sister needed her. Trevor Blake could wait.

---

Trevor stood in the foyer and glanced at his watch for the seventh time in the last twenty minutes. He tried calling the cell phone he'd given Allie, but it kept going to voice mail. He shouldn't have let her go off on her own, should have had Simmons drive her. What if she had gotten into an accident?

No, that was ludicrous. Of course she hadn't been in an accident, she was simply defying him. And that had him fuming.

He'd paid off her family's debt, forgiven her father's loan, bought her a whole new bloody wardrobe, and kept his cock to himself. All that he asked in return was that she be here at noon. So he could take her to fucking lunch.

A smile tugged at the corners of his mouth. Well, she would regret this little act of rebellion. Yes, she would very much regret inconveniencing him today.

He stalked to his office. Loosening his tie, he shoved back his chair and fell into it as he stared blankly at one of the computer screens. Mistress, indeed. It was high time he got what he'd paid for.

Trevor worked throughout the afternoon. By the time Allie finally got home, it was five forty-seven. Arnold informed him the minute she arrived. Instead of demanding an explanation immediately, he let his anger simmer as he continued to work until dinner.

A few minutes after seven, he sauntered into the dining room and cast a glance her way as he took his seat at the head of the table. She looked lovely in the navy dress. He knew for a fact she would look even lovelier out of it.

She glanced up at him. "Sorry about this afternoon. Monica didn't come home until three this morning and now she's missing. Brynn was upset and needed me. Her school counselor is making her join a club. I know that doesn't sound like a big deal, but it is to her."

He arched a brow. "I don't care about your family troubles, Miss Campbell. Stop boring me with your domestic problems. You're here to see to my needs, and so far, you've been abysmal." He took a sip of wine and stared at her over the rim of his crystal glass.

"I apologize, Trevor. My family problems have gotten in the way of fucking you. Would you like me to suck you off while you eat your salad?" She smiled as she offered to blow him, but underneath that sweet expression was rage. And he was delighted to see it. It made things so much more interesting when Allie was losing her shit.

"No thank you, Miss Campbell, I think we can wait until after dessert." The thought of Allie on her knees, taking him between those lush lips had his cock hard in seconds. He took in her stiff back and frozen smile. Her breasts were pushed up over the edge of her dress, giving him a mouth-watering glimpse of their full-ness. He wanted to see them, touch them. He planned to make her ache just as he'd been aching. She needed to be taught a lesson for ignoring him.

When she hadn't made it home at the allotted time and hadn't called to say why she was late, he'd felt... He put down his fork and rubbed the center of his chest.

Fuck that. He wanted her. He'd paid for her. He was going to have her.

She needed to be put firmly in her place. He'd punish her for wasting his time. He would have been more productive today if he hadn't been worrying about her. And for that she would pay.

---

Allie grabbed her wine and drank half the glass. Was he really going to ask her to blow him after dessert? Could she go through with it? She'd told herself a million times that's why she was here in the first place, but the anticipation was making her crazy.

As she picked at her food, Trevor seemed deep in thought, and whatever he was thinking about didn't make him happy. He scowled, his fingers white where he gripped the fork. Then suddenly, he laid it down on the side of his plate and rubbed his chest.

Placing her hand on his arm, Allie leaned toward him. "Are you all right? Are you having chest pains?" She was worried about him. Not that he deserved it.

He blinked a few times before glancing at her. Immediately, the scowl was replaced by his taunting smile. He stared into her eyes before gazing down at her hand. "Actually, I was thinking about you crawling under the table and taking me in your throat while I ate my cheesecake."

Allie snatched her hand back and smiled sweetly. "Just let me know when you're ready." Like hell. She had no intention of doing any such thing and would probably poke him with her fork if she thought he was seriously suggesting it. However, it was her fault for stupidly bringing it up in the first place. So, maybe no fork poking. Maybe.

"I think I'm ready now, Miss Campbell. Neither one of us seems to be interested in our food tonight. Let's retire to the drawing room, shall we?"

She gazed into his hard, gray eyes. Her heart began to pound. This was it, time to put out and shut up.

He stood and moved behind her, pulling her chair back before taking her hand. Leading her out of the dining room and up the stairs, through one hallway and then another, they reached a large room at the back of the house. This room seemed more to Trevor's taste—long leather couches, book-lined shelves, and tall windows that looked out onto the lighted garden. She wandered around, nervously touching things here and there—the inlaid cigar box on a side table, the globe in a brass base, the bust of some Greek or Roman man with half a nose. The room was dimly lit by one large table lamp in the corner.

Trevor moved to the wet bar by the windows. The lighting left him in the shadows, making his cheekbones more pronounced, giving him a wicked, almost sinister look.

Allie took a deep breath and willed her heart to slow down. He wasn't going to hurt her. They'd made a deal. "So, what's the safe word?" Again, she'd blurted it out. She could usually control herself, but around Trevor, she couldn't keep her mouth shut.

He glanced up as he poured a bit of brandy into a snifter. "Would you like one? The brandy, I mean, not the safe word."

She nodded and dropped down on one of the sofas. He handed her a glass before sitting across from her.

Swirling the brandy, he studied her. "Afraid I'll bring out a whip and handcuffs?"

Allie took a sip of her drink, feeling the fire of it burn the back of her throat. "How would I know? No pain though, that was our deal."

"Right." He nodded slowly. "So what would be an appropriate safe word, do you imagine?"

Allie shrugged. He made her feel silly for even bringing it up.

"How about 'ouch'? Will that do, Miss Campbell?" He raised a brow and took a sip from his glass.

"How about 'stop what you're doing or I'll cut your balls off, you bastard'?"

Narrowing his eyes, he pretended to consider it. "Seems a bit wordy."

She fought a smile. "All right, how about"—her gaze darted around the room and landed on the globe—"Uruguay?"

Grinning, he silently toasted her with his glass. "Uruguay it is. So if I cause you any pain—"

"Or discomfort."

He nodded, his eyes never leaving hers. "Or discomfort."

"Or if I feel the slightest bit uneasy."

His lips thinned. "Now you're reaching, Miss Campbell."

"It was worth a shot."

"To Uruguay."

She toasted back and took a sip, dropping her eyes to the faded red-and-blue Oriental rug beneath her feet. She couldn't remember feeling this nervous, not even the first time she had sex. Prom night—Andy Watson. Of course, she had half a bottle of strawberry wine in her to take the edge off her nerves. She took another sip of brandy. Definitely better than strawberry wine.

"Where did you go just now, Miss Campbell?" His voice, sharp and clipped at dinner, was now soft and seductive. Was this how he would sound during sex? She imagined him using that persuasive tone to murmur in her ear, to coax her to come. It would definitely work.

Allie raised her eyes and drank him in—the straight blade of his nose, the intelligent eyes, the hollows beneath his strong cheekbones. So handsome. He was commanding and controlled and at ease with himself. Everything she wasn't. Everything she wanted to be.

"I'm right here. With you." And she meant it. She was still nervous, but she was aroused too.

"I'm glad." They stared at each other until Trevor's eyes drifted over her, slowly moving from her face all the way down to the tips of her new designer shoes. She felt that look against her skin, like a caress. "By the way, I do like the dress. What are you wearing under it?"

"I believe your people call them knickers." Allie glanced away, feeling self-conscious, then took a deep breath and looked back. She took another sip of brandy, her hands shaking slightly, her pulse racing.

"Show me." His voice sounded deeper than usual.

She licked her lips and her nipples got hard. Dazed, she realized he could do that with just his voice, make her breasts ache for his touch.

"Please." It was the way he said it that got to her. Humble and demanding at the same time.

She placed her glass on the round table and slowly rose to her feet. Her knees were wobbly and her heart pounded. But when he looked at her that way, like he wanted to devour her, she got excited. She wanted him to look at her, to touch her the way he had in the bathtub.

She was surprised at her own reaction. Allie'd never thought much of sex, but she had never met a man as sexual and blunt as Trevor either. She knew it was wrong—this whole situation was wrong—but seeing his beautiful face and imagining what he could do with those strong hands made her damp.

Shutting out all her doubts, all her problems, she focused on this moment. She wanted Trevor for herself, for how he made her feel—like she was the most desirable woman he'd ever seen.

With trembling fingers, she unzipped her dress, letting it pool at her feet. She stood before him in a navy demi bra and matching thong. Her hard nipples probably showed through the transparent lace. The panties were a wisp of silk between her legs.

Trevor's gaze lingered on her breasts. "Come here." Setting down his glass, he held out his hand.

She placed her fingers in the center of his palm and took three steps forward until she stood between his long legs. Glancing up at her, he ran his hands along her outer thighs. His gentle touch made her stomach flutter. Then he leaned forward and placed a chaste kiss on the triangle of her thong.

Allie gasped, leaned her head back, and tried to catch her breath. Why that was so erotic, she couldn't say, but that small kiss made her knees weak.

When he looked up at her again, his cheeks were ruddy. She could feel the heat coming off him in waves. He smelled crisp and woodsy and manly, and she took a deep breath, wanting more.

He played with the little bows on either side of the thong. "You're so lovely." His thumbs slipped under the thin straps and slowly, ever so slowly, he pulled them down over her hips, past the curve of her ass. Then, he stretched his hands outward, ripping the fragile material from her body, exposing her before tossing the shredded scraps on the floor.

Allie covered herself. "Do you know how much that cost?"

He pulled at her hands, held them away from her body. "Not a clue." He leaned back against the sofa. "Straddle me."

After hesitating for a moment, she did as he commanded while he continued to hold her hands, helping her as she planted her knees on either side of his legs. Lowering herself onto his lap, she felt vulnerable and exposed but so turned on she could barely think. The light woolen material covering his hard cock brushed against her core. She was almost dizzy with want.

Trevor dropped her hands and spanned her waist with his own, squeezing lightly. When his thumb circled her belly button, Allie swallowed. This was tame stuff, and yet her nerves sizzled and fired in response. She was ready to explode and he'd barely touched her.

As his hands glided around to her back, Allie grabbed his shoulders. He unhooked her bra, his hands stroking as he slipped the straps over her shoulders and let the lacy cups fall away. His gaze traveled to her bare breasts. He leaned back, still completely dressed, his hands resting on her thighs. Staring at her nipples, he licked his lips. "They're pink. Gorgeous pink."

She released his shoulders so that he could slide the straps down her arms and remove the bra completely. Then, arching her back, she thrust her breasts toward him. "Trevor," she whispered.

His eyes returned to hers. "Tell me what you want, Allie. Tell me what you want me to do."

She was breathing hard, panting. "Touch me."

"Where?" His voice was rough.

"Everywhere."

He moved his hands up her thighs to the rounded cheeks of her ass. He clutched them, kneading her flesh. "Here?"

She closed her eyes for a second. Each touch, each squeeze made her slick with moisture. She opened her eyes and, reaching out, plunged her fingers into the soft, dark waves of his hair. She leaned down, her lips barely brushing his. "Yes."

He let go of her ass and moved his hands up to her hips, his thumbs resting right above her mound, then one lightly slid downward and flicked her clit. "Here?"

She shuddered and licked the seam of his mouth, capturing his bottom lip, sucking it. When he inhaled sharply, she smiled and pulled away. "I said everywhere."

He thrust his hand into the hair at her nape. "Not good enough. I want you to tell me exactly what you want, Allison, in lurid, filthy detail." Using her hair as leverage, he pulled her down for a hard kiss that let her know he was in charge.

His tongue swept inside her mouth, stroked hers, made her throb. She tilted her hips forward and rubbed her clit against his erection. His slacks, rough against her swollen lips, provided delicious friction.

Letting go of her hair, Trevor broke the kiss and grabbed her hips, stilling her. "I'm waiting."

Allie looked at him, confused and irritated that he'd stopped her from grinding against him. "What?"

"Details. Tell me."

She reached out and jerked at the knot in Trevor's tie. She took in his face, his dark eyes, his parted lips. "I want to feel your skin against mine." She pulled the tie out of his collar. Then she hastily unbuttoned his shirt. In the process, she ripped one of the buttons off and heard it ping against the wall.

"Do you know how much that cost?" Trevor mocked, sounding winded.

"Nope." She pulled the shirttails from his waistband and tugged his jacket and shirt over his broad shoulders, pinning his arms in the process. She reached out and squeezed his biceps. "You feel so good, so hard."

In response, he leaned toward her and began trailing light kisses across her shoulder. "You're so soft." He captured the skin on her upper arm between his teeth and gently bit.

"You need to be naked," she whispered.

"Yes." He pulled back and tugged the shirt and jacket down his arms, ripping at his cuffs. More buttons flew, and soon his arms and chest were bare.

She sat back and got her fill of him—masculine and lean with hard-ridged muscles. This was sex. This was what everyone talked about, that out-of-control need. She felt it with him.

With one hand, she reached out and ran her finger over his collarbone, down the center of his smooth chest to the waistband of his pants.

"Allie." He took her hands in his and brought his head forward, kissing her chin, her cheeks, her neck. His kisses were fast and tinged with desperation.

"Touch me, Trevor. Touch my breasts."

He released her hands and tenderly, with the pads of his fingers, traced little patterns along the sides and tops. "Like this?"

She shivered and shook her head, strands of her hair spilled over the backs of his hands. "No."

"Tell me," he growled.

"My nipples." When he brushed his thumbs over the hard points, she groaned. "More. Harder."

He obliged, pinching them between his thumbs and forefingers, pulling them out and then easing them back but never relinquishing his hold.

Allie ran her hands up and down his arms as he tortured her. Once again, she began rubbing herself along the edge of his hard-on. She moaned at the sensation. Suddenly, she couldn't stand it anymore. She needed to see his cock, feel it without any obstacles.

Reaching down, she unbuckled his belt. "You're still not naked."

"We should remedy that immediately." Trevor pushed her hands aside and unfastened his pants. Lifting his ass to remove them, Allie had to hang on to his arms or get bucked off.

When he'd finally gotten rid of the last barrier between them, she glanced down at his long, thick shaft and bit her lip.

"Problem?" he asked, watching her.

"No. Just big."

"Naturally."

She smiled at his arrogance and attempted to wrap her hand around him. Her grin widened at his gasp. His dick jumped in her hand, and using her thumb, she circled the head, wiping the bead of moisture across the tip. "Now tell me what *you* want." She threaded one hand through his hair, rubbing her lips along his jawline. When she got to his ear, she teased the lobe with the tip of her tongue.

Trevor grasped her chin in one hand, forcing her to meet his gaze. "If I told you what I wanted to do to you, Miss Campbell, you'd never stop blushing."

Something about having his dick in her hand made her feel bold, in control. "Try me."

"I want to tongue fuck you. I want to slide my cock between your tits while you pleasure yourself. I want to watch as you take me in your mouth. I want you in every way imaginable and some I haven't even thought of yet. But right now, I want to fuck you so hard, you'll forget your own name."

Oh God, she wanted that too. All of it. She kept her grasp on him, sliding her hand down to the base of his dick and back to the tip. "Yeah, that sounds good."

Letting go of her chin, he nibbled his way down her neck. Once he latched on to her breast, she became so focused on her own pleasure, she let go of him and clutched his hair with both hands. He continued to lick at her breast and with one hand, reached between them. When he slipped a long finger inside her pussy, she shuddered.

"More," she whispered.

Then a knock sounded on the door. "Mr. Blake, Miss Campbell."

# Chapter 6

Allie froze, but Trevor continued to play with her. The feel of his tongue against her breast was heaven, still she clenched her hands into fists, grabbed his hair, and tried to pull him off.

"Sorry to disturb you," Arnold called through the door, "but Miss Campbell's father is on the phone."

Trevor quit sucking, but his finger remained inside her. "She'll be there in just a moment, Arnold."

"Very good, sir."

"Oh my God," she whispered. "What if he'd come in?"

Trevor withdrew his finger and reclined, resting his head against the back of the sofa. Keeping both hands clamped on her hips, his cock jutted between them. "He'd have something to put in his wank bank, I suppose."

With a snarl, Allie pushed out of his arms and scrambled off him as she searched for her bra. She found it lying halfway under the sofa and slipped into it. The thong was ripped and useless.

She glanced down at her feet and realized she was still wearing her shoes. How did she not know that? Grabbing her dress, she hastily shimmied into it, reaching around to zip it up in the back.

Trevor stood and watched her silently as he pulled on his clothes. He picked up her thong and tucked it into his pocket. "Come here," he said. Without waiting for her to comply, he pulled her to him. "Your hair is a mess." He combed his fingers through it, tugging at a few tangles. "There."

On shaky legs, Allie walked to the door and opened it. Arnold had left the phone on a silver charger in front of the door. She glanced up and down the hallway, but it was empty. Relief flooded her. Arnold probably knew what they'd been doing, but Allie didn't think she could face him right now.

Bending down, she picked up the phone and hit the talk button. "Dad?"

"Sorry to bother you, Al." She could hear the weariness in his voice.

"What's wrong?"

"Monica came home. Just thought you'd like to know."

Allie ran a hand through her hair and winced. Trevor hadn't gotten out all of the tangles. "Where the hell has she been?"

"She's got a boyfriend, Brad something. Truth is, I don't know what to do. I don't want her seeing this guy, but I want to give her a safe place to come home to."

"But you have to think about Brynn," she said. "Monica can't keep treating the house like it's a hotel. They both need stability and consequences." And Allie's leaving hadn't helped in either department. She turned around and found Trevor listening to every word, an indefinable look on his face. "Listen, Dad, I'll come over tomorrow morning and we'll talk about it. Okay?"

"Sure. Night, Al."

She clicked the off button and let her eyes drift toward Trevor's crotch, allowed herself to stare for an instant at his still-hard dick. She had to admit, it was an impressive specimen.

"Your family drama is becoming quite tedious, Miss Campbell."

She walked to the side table and placed the phone next to the cigar box. The man had fingered her twice now, and he couldn't call her by her first name? "It's been tedious for a long time, *Mr. Blake*."

He narrowed his eyes at that. "How long will you be gone tomorrow morning?"

She shrugged. "I don't know."

He strode toward her, and her heart stopped, waiting to see what he might do. But he didn't stop, didn't slow down. He walked right past her. "Good night, Miss Campbell," he said as he left the room.

She stared at the closed door, reeling from the rejection. They'd almost had sex and that was it? *Good* fucking *night, Miss Campbell?*

The desire was gone now, making Allie feel restless. And angry. Her father was dealing with all this Monica crap, and she was busy giving Trevor a handy. And he seemed completely blasé about the whole thing.

She rubbed her forehead. Well, of course he was unaffected by it. He probably did this type of thing all the time. Hooked up with people. Kept mistresses.

He was on a different sexual page, and she needed to catch up fast. She had a feeling if she didn't, she wouldn't walk away from this mess with her heart in one piece.

The next morning, Trevor was seated at the table when Allie stepped into the breakfast room. She wore a pink dress, and it looked pretty on her, but he noted the dark circles beneath her eyes. Apparently she hadn't been able to sleep either. "Good morning, Miss Campbell." The words came out as a growl.

Allie frowned. "What's wrong with you?"

He raised his brow. "I didn't get laid last night." At first, he'd been intent on punishing her for standing him up. But when he'd seen the nervousness in her eyes, when she'd asked for a safe word, all thoughts of punishment disappeared. Instead, he found himself seducing her. And she had been so sweetly enthusiastic, ripping at his shirt, asking for his touch, that all he'd wanted to do was sink inside her. He wanted to satisfy her every desire. Until Arnold's bloody intrusion. Cock blocked by his own butler.

After he'd left her, he swam laps in the pool for over an hour and still had a raging hard-on. In fact, his cock was rock hard when he woke up this morning. Getting all dressed up with no place to go made him pissy.

Allie rolled her eyes. "Yes, because your dick is always the priority." She took a sip of coffee.

"Since it's why you're here, Miss Campbell, my dick is the only thing that should concern you."

She set down her cup and picked up a fork. "Believe it or not, Mr. Blake, my family trumps you *and* your little you." She pointed her fork toward his lap. "Sorry, but that's the way it is."

He clenched his jaw at the Mr. Blake reference. "Yes, well, that is unacceptable." He passed her the small pitcher of syrup for her pancakes. "And since you and your family cannot seem to solve your own little crises, I'll be accompanying you today."

-----

During the forty-minute drive, Trevor checked his email while Allie ignored him—wouldn't look at him, wouldn't speak to him. Other than telling him to keep his "lip zipped" around her family. He pretended like her silence didn't bother him.

She was angry, of course. And she'd protested his presence in her family business until she finally realized her arguments wouldn't work. And while he hadn't known her long, he hated it when she shut him out.

When Simmons pulled the limo up to the crumbling driveway of the Campbell home, Trevor scanned the cracked front steps and the peeling, faded paint, marveling at its shabbiness. This was what all the fuss was over, this tiny, rundown house? Had it been like this when the mother was well, or had it gone downhill with her health?

Trevor followed Allie to the front door, and she gave him a warning look over her shoulder before walking inside. The interior was as decrepit as the exterior. The furniture was old and worn, a faded blue blanket nearly covered a tear on the sofa. Stuffing spilled out of the ripped, faux leather chair.

"I'm home," Allie called.

Her father, Brian, whom he had met on three previous occasions, stepped out of the kitchen with a tired smile. "Hey, Al." But as soon as he caught sight of Trevor, the smile dropped. "Oh, Mr. Blake. Didn't know you were coming too."

Trevor held out his hand. "Sorry for the imposition. Good to see you again, Mr. Campbell."

Allie's father nodded and shook hands. "Call me Brian. And thanks for giving Allie a job. I'm very grateful."

Trevor glanced at Allie, saw her assume a phony smile. He could now tell the difference from the real thing, and the smile she wore was as fake as the leather on the ripped chair.

"Please have a seat, Mr. Blake," she said.

"Thank you, Miss Campbell." Trevor sat and crossed his legs. "Just ignore me." He waved one hand.

"Dad, where's Monica?"

Brian shrugged. "Still in bed. She walked in last night like nothing was wrong and made herself a sandwich. Said she'd been with her boyfriend. I don't know who he is or what he does." He blew out a breath.

Allie stalked down the hall, her arms swinging at her sides like a cadet on parade. "Monica, get your sorry ass out of bed. Hey, Brynn." The house had thin walls and he heard everything as if he were in the same room.

Brian shifted uncomfortably and scratched his chin. "Sorry you have to be here for this, Mr. Blake."

"No apologies necessary."

Stomping down the hallway, a young girl with a mess of honey-colored hair and a long T-shirt that barely covered her ass made her way to the living room. She pulled up short when she saw him. "Who the hell are you?"

He stood and gave her his most charming smile. "I'm Trevor. You must be Monica. I've heard so much about you." He held out his hand.

The girl looked at it as if she didn't know whether to shake it or slap it away, but eventually took it in her own and did the former. "Hey."

Allie stepped into the room with a young girl hovering behind her. She was a couple years younger than the bitchy one and stared at him like he was a rare species she'd found in the wild.

He turned the charming smile on the young girl with dark hair. She would be lovely when she was a bit older. Not as lovely as Allie, but still very pretty. "And you're Brynn."

She nodded and blushed.

"I'm Trevor. Wonderful, now we're all acquainted." He sat back down and graced them all with a pleasant smile.

Allie glared at him, then turned to Brynn. "Can you make Mr. Blake some coffee?"

Brynn scampered off to the kitchen.

With a sigh, Allie pointed to the sofa. "Sit down, Mon."

"You're not the boss of me, Allison. I'm an adult, just like you."

Trevor almost laughed. She sounded like a six-year-old in the schoolyard.

"You're acting like a spoiled ten-year-old," Allie said.

Brian perched on the sofa, his elbows resting on his knees. "Who is this boy you've been dating, Monica?"

The girl shrugged and flopped on the sofa next to her father. The long T-shirt rode up, giving a flash of purple-striped knickers underneath. Trevor noticed. Monica watched him as she played with a strand of hair. "Like what you see?"

Trevor's smile turned arctic. "Not particularly, no."

That wiped the shit-eating grin off her face. Allie was spot-on, the girl was a brat.

"Answer Dad, Mon. Who is this guy? We know his name's Brad. What's his last name?"

Monica's brows pulled together and she managed to look affronted that someone dared to question her. "It's none of your business. And I'm going to kick Brynn's ass for spying on me. God, I hate this family."

Brian took a deep breath. "We're all upset about losing your mom, but you're screwing up your life, sweetheart."

Monica pressed her lips together and two angry-red patches dotted her cheeks. "I'm sick of people saying that. I know what I'm doing." She leapt to her feet. "It's my life. And it's not because of Mom. It's because I'm a woman who can make my own decisions."

Allie gestured with one hand. "Bullshit. You're a child who throws a temper tantrum every time you don't get your own way. And if you skip any more school, you're not going to graduate. Do you think Mom would be proud of you right now?"

"Fuck you, Allie. You're not Mom. I was as close to her as you were, but you act like you're the only one she loved." She ran out of the room and down the hall. She slammed the door so hard, the whole house rattled, leaving the poorly painted landscape hanging above the sofa at crooked angle.

There was a moment of silence.

"Well," Trevor said, "she is a delight."

Allie and Brian swiveled their heads and looked at him.

Allie wagged her finger. "Stay out of this."

Brian shook his head. "I'm sure Mr. Blake is trying to be helpful."

Trevor put on a grave expression. "I do apologize. Wouldn't dream of intruding."

Allie glowered and uttered "jackass" under her breath.

Brynn walked in with a clear, red plastic tray with three mugs.

She set it on the coffee table and handed Trevor a full cup. "Is black okay?" she asked. Her gaze lifted as far as the knot in his tie.

"Lovely, thank you."

Brynn nervously tucked a strand of hair behind one ear. "What's going to happen now?" He noticed she spoke to Allie, not Brian. Curious.

Allie sank down on the sofa. "It's up to Dad."

"I don't know what the hell to do. God, I wish your mom were here."

"I'm worried about Monica. She's doing some really stupid shit, and this Brad guy is trouble. Brynn thinks he's in his mid-twenties."

"What do you think, Al?" Brian asked. "Should I ban her from seeing this guy? And what about school? I can't force her to go."

For some reason, Trevor found himself becoming angry. "You are the girl's father. Why is it Allison's responsibility to make a decision?"

Allie stabbed him with a look, then turned back to Brian. "I'm not sure what to do, Dad."

Trevor took a sip of his coffee—and almost sputtered. Good God, that was dreadful. He smiled at Brynn. "Excellent."

She ducked her head, her skin a fiery red.

"Why isn't the girl in school?" he asked.

Allie smiled at him. He was beginning to hate that phony smile. "First of all, it's Sunday, so no one's in school."

He shot her a look.

"Second, she's still in high school."

"But she's been skipping a lot," Brynn said.

Allie nodded. "She had a full ride to UNLV but decided not to take it."

"What are her plans, then?"

They all shrugged their shoulders.

"I see. Well, it's been lovely, but Allie and I have to go now."

With a smile, he stood and held his hand out to her. She stared at it the way Monica had a few minutes before.

"I'm going to walk Mr. Blake to his car, and I'll be right back." She set down her cup and stood.

"No, afraid not," he said. "We really have to go."

With narrowed eyes, Allie smiled. "I have to stay."

Brian stood as well. "No, it's all right, Al. You go on."

Trevor turned to Brynn. "Thank you for the coffee, love."

"You're welcome," she whispered.

His hand on her back, Trevor walked Allie to the car and waved off Simmons, opening the door himself. Once he slid in beside her, Allie faced him. She was furious, her blue eyes darker, flashing.

"I quit."

"You can't quit, my sweet, you've barely even started. Furthermore, you couldn't possibly pay back all that you owe me." He took her hand in his and, with a mocking grin, kissed the back of it. When she tried to snatch it from his grasp, he allowed her to pull away. "I think you're suffering from too much responsibility and low blood sugar. You barely touched your breakfast. What sounds good, Asian fusion or Italian?"

<hr>

Allie didn't say much on the way to the restaurant. It was pointless to argue with him. But she was frustrated—with her family, with Trevor, with her life. Sitting across the table from him in one of the most expensive Asian restaurants in the city, she gazed out at a fountain along the Strip.

Trevor ordered without consulting her. Big surprise. After several minutes of silence, he leaned toward her. "They're not helpless, you know. They're fully capable human beings. Even the young one. She won't perish without you."

"You don't understand."

"Then explain it to me."

Allie stared into Trevor's eyes and found herself unable to look away. The spell was broken when the waiter brought a huge platter of food and set it between them.

"Do you really want to know?" she asked once he'd gone.

Trevor nodded. "Yes, I really do. Now hand me your plate. I'll play Arnold, shall I?"

She took a steadying breath. She didn't like talking about it, but she had to make him understand. "My mom got sick five years ago. Breast cancer. I left college and came home to look after the girls. I thought it would only be one semester, maybe two. She had a mastectomy and chemo, and for nine months the prognosis was good." She picked up her fork and ran the tines over the tablecloth. "But then they found a lump in the other breast." Allie stopped for a second. She glanced out the window and watched the water spray toward a bright blue sky. She cleared her throat. "Eventually, it metastasized to her bones. She had radiation, hormone therapy. They even tried this experimental medicine." She licked her lips and looked at him.

Trevor said nothing as he handed her a plate.

"Last Easter she broke her leg. She'd just been standing there and suddenly, she collapsed." Allie gazed down at the platter but didn't see the food. She saw her mom, who looked so much like Monica, wearing a bright red chenille bathrobe, asking if anyone wanted another pot of coffee, then she fell to the ground.

"One minute she was fine, the next she wasn't." Allie took a sip of her wine. With a trembling hand, she set her glass down and it clinked against her plate. "She died in November, right before Thanksgiving."

She saw nothing but compassion in his eyes. Sardonic, self-absorbed Trevor she could handle. But a Trevor with real feelings and a bit of empathy? No way.

She blinked back the tears that were threatening to spill over and once again cleared her throat. Talking with Trevor, telling him about her mother's illness, made her chest feel a little lighter somehow. She rarely spoke about it with her family. Her dad would start crying and leave the room, Brynn would do the same, and Monica barely mentioned Mom anymore.

She found Trevor staring at her, those gray eyes sharp and compassionate at the same time. "What about you?" she asked. "How old were you when your parents died?"

His eyes became shuttered and the compassion was gone. In its place was his normal, slightly taunting gaze. He stabbed a shrimp with his fork and held it up to her. "Mmm, try the lobster sauce. It's delicious."

Allie let him shovel food into her mouth. "Very good. Is it painful to talk about? Your parents, I mean?"

His face became devoid of expression, and he fed her a piece of braised Kobe spare rib. "Not at all, I assure you."

He was hiding something, she could feel it. But what else was new? "Tell me something about yourself. All I know is that you're a businessman who collects things like engraved metal biscuit tins. Which in case you didn't know, is odd."

His gaze lowered to her lips. "I enjoy long walks on the beach and living each day to the fullest. My turnoffs are rude people, and I adore Virgos."

Allie couldn't help it—she burst out laughing. He'd looked so serious and earnest when he'd rattled off that stupid list. "You're out of luck then, because you don't live near a beach, you're the rudest person I know, and I'm not a Virgo."

"But I don't love you, darling, so we can cross that off our list." He forked a piece of duck and held it to her lips.

Well, that sobered her up. He didn't love her and she didn't love him. But to hear him say it made her heart stutter.

They finished lunch without any more personal revelations and when they hopped into the limo, Trevor instructed Simmons to take Allie to her home. But he made her solemnly swear to be back at the mansion by six.

"I promise. And thank you, Trevor."

"Yes well, you were becoming tiresome." Then he pulled out his phone and ignored her for the rest of the drive.

—⁓—

Trevor spent the afternoon catching up on work. And thinking about Allie. That sad lot she called a family was dragging her down. Needy, the whole mess of them.

As he walked through the upstairs hallway before dinner, he glanced into the glass case that held the engraved biscuit tins Allie had mentioned. Everything displayed in the house had been a part of his grandfather's collection—the old man's obsession, really.

Trevor often wondered what his grandfather would think of him, here in Vegas. Dragging half of England with him. Building a garden in the middle of a desert. It smacked of a sentimentality he'd never openly admit to. If Allie's family was her weakness, this was probably his—hanging on to the past, to the grandfather who'd given him a home.

He stopped in front of Allie's room and knocked on the door.

After a moment, she poked her head out and frowned at him. "What? I was back before six." She clutched the lapels of her pink robe with one hand.

Her skin was still damp and she smelled divine. He watched as a single drop of water slipped from the hollow of her throat down her upper chest, to hide beneath the satiny folds of material. He wanted to follow its trail with his tongue. Under his gaze, Allie's nipples beaded. He needed some quality time with those breasts too. He'd had a sampling the night before. Now he wanted more. When his eyes drifted back to her face, her cheeks were as pink as the robe. "I appreciate your punctuality, Miss Campbell. I thought we might have a drink on the terrace before dinner."

"Oh." She swallowed. "Okay." She sounded a little breathless. Her voice was a little huskier. He wanted her to say his name with that voice.

Trevor perused her, from the top of her blond head to her bare toes, peeking out from beneath the hem of the robe. "Or I could come in and we could delay dinner by an hour. Or two."

She clutched the robe tighter. "I'm not on the menu, English." She slammed the door in his face.

In spite of his aching cock, he smiled. Yes, this was why Allie was here. She amused him.

He propped himself against the wall and waited. "Tick tock, Miss Campbell."

"Don't rush me, Mr. Blake." The words drifted through the door.

Trevor studied his nails. "I'll be sure to order a schoolgirl uniform tomorrow. I can't wait to see you in plaid." He knew it irritated her when he called her Miss Campbell, but he nearly gnashed his teeth when she reciprocated. "I'm coming in there to help if you don't move it along."

She opened the door then and stepped out into the hallway. She looked lovely in the ivory lace dress, the V-neck displaying a delightful view of her plump breasts. Her bright, straight hair looked soft and shiny. He found himself reaching out to touch a strand but thrust his hand into his trouser pocket at the last instant.

"What?" Brows furrowed, she blinked up at him. "Why are you scowling like that?"

Fuck it. He pulled his hand from his pocket and sank his fingers into the hair at the base of her neck. He massaged the back of her scalp, and with his other hand, he grabbed hold of her waist and jerked her toward him. She tottered on her heels and flattened her hands against his chest to steady herself.

His gaze skimmed over her face. Her eyes widened and her glossy lips parted.

"Trevor," she whispered, "what's wrong with you?"

Leaning down, he kissed her possessively, tasting the sweetness of her lips, sliding his rough tongue against hers. He let go of the tight hold on her hair and let his fingers sift through it, feeling its silky texture. He couldn't get enough of her lips. Of her fresh scent. Of her hands running over the contours of his back beneath his jacket.

He was achingly hard. Again. Still.

Trevor moved his other hand from her bare back to her bottom and squeezed, felt the lace rough against his palm before gradually pulling his mouth away from hers. He missed the contact.

Allie's full lips appeared poutier as she glanced up at him. He licked his own. "I think I'm wearing your lippy."

Stepping back, he took a handkerchief from his pocket and dabbed at his mouth. He looked at the light pink streak against on the white fabric before she took it from his hand. Her eyes met his as she reached up and rubbed at his upper lip.

"There, I think that's all of it." She still hadn't lowered her eyes, and they gazed at each other for a long moment.

Trevor tucked the cloth in his pocket, then ran a finger down her cheek.

Allie shuddered slightly. "Thank you for letting me go back home today."

He placed his hand on her back, brushed his fingertips over her bare skin. God, she was soft. "How did it go with Monica?"

They made their way to the stairs and Allie's fingers grasped the banister. "Not well. After she calmed down, I tried to talk to her, but she still wouldn't tell me Brad's last name. However, she did promise to go to school this week. Of course, that was after I threatened to follow her to class or maybe stick a tracking device up her ass."

Trevor scoffed. "How innovative of you." He led her out back and onto the wide terrace. Arnold had set up a small bar to one side.

"What's your poison, Miss Campbell?" His cock was still hard and watching her gracefully move around the patio in that short dress wasn't helping.

Allie smiled. "Can you make a cosmopolitan?"

"Of course I can. I simply choose not to."

"You take one part vodka—"

"Yes, yes, all right." He began mixing ingredients into a shaker and poured the contents into a martini glass. "Here you go." As he handed her the glass, their fingers touched, and he felt that spark again. Honestly, he was like a schoolboy with his first crush. It was embarrassing.

Allie's eyes found his. "Thanks."

Trevor let go of the glass and moved back to the bar. "I will have a very manly scotch, thank you." He poured himself a glass of single malt and walked back to her.

"Come on, there's something you need to see." He held out his hand.

Allie stared at it before linking her fingers with his, and he helped her down the flagstone steps. They strolled along the path, toward the bottom of the garden to the small pond. He led her to a bench overlooking a hill. Two mountains in the distance framed the sunset. He squeezed her hand. "See there?"

She gasped. The water reflected the orange and pink hues that streaked across the sky. "It's beautiful." She shifted on the bench and placed her hand on his thigh, letting it rest there too briefly. "You're so lucky, Trevor, to have all this."

"Am I?" He'd never felt particularly lucky. Fortunate perhaps, not lucky. But sitting next to her, in his extravagant garden, he felt something like it for the first time.

They sipped their drinks and watched in silence as the sun fell, a dark purple sky replacing the orange glow. A few stars popped out. And Trevor was…at peace.

"When I was little," Allie said, "my dad used to drive us out to the desert to look at the stars. He had this old telescope, and we'd take turns trying to find the different constellations. My mom would pack cookies, and Monica would never shut up, and Brynn used to fall asleep on the way home."

He stretched his arm along the back of the bench, brushed the hair off her shoulder. "That's a lovely memory."

She nodded. "I think so too."

He sighed. "We should go in soon. Arnold will have a coronary if the food gets cold."

As they stood, she tucked her arm in his. He glanced down at the top of her head and suppressed the urge to kiss it. Good God, he was becoming treacly sweet, and it was slightly nauseating.

She peered up at him and smiled. "Thank you for showing this to me."

"You're most welcome." He felt himself smiling back.

He led her through the fragrant garden and toward the lighted terrace where he noticed someone lounging on one of the chairs. Stopping in his tracks, the tendons in his hand strained as he clutched his tumbler of scotch.

Allie pulled to a stop beside him. "Who's that?" she whispered.

Trevor glared at the woman making herself at home with a glass of champagne in her hand.

"Hello, Mother."

# Chapter 7

"MOTHER?" ALLIE GASPED. "I thought your parents were dead?"

Gracefully, the woman uncrossed her legs and rose from the lounger. "Trevor, dearest, what have you been saying about me?"

"Nothing good, I assure you."

Allie glanced between the two and winced at the cold expression on Trevor's face. She hadn't known him long, but she'd quickly learned that look always spelled trouble.

Allie switched her attention back to his mom—his beautiful, sophisticated mom—and saw the resemblance. Her hair, the same dark shade as Trevor's, brushed the tops of her shoulders. Her tilted eyes were gray as well.

"Who's your little friend, darling?" She nodded toward Allie, her inspection thorough.

Trevor's muscles stiffened beneath her hand, but he adopted a casual tone. "This is Allison Campbell. Allison, this is my mother, Margaret Tremayne Blake del Santos Quinn Arceneau..." He narrowed his eyes. "What was the last one, Mother?"

She smiled at him. "Beauregard."

"Yes, that's it, Beauregard. Can't believe I forgot." He peered down at Allie. "Lived on a farm, that one."

Margaret took a sip of champagne. "He lived on a ranch in Texas, as you very well know." She turned to Allie. "Call me Mags, darling. Everyone does."

Trevor extracted his arm from Allie's and strode toward the bar. With his back to them, he poured himself another drink.

"I tried calling several times last week," Mags said.

When Trevor turned around, he wore his most annoying smile—the sarcastic, nasty one. "I've been busy, as you see." He pointed his glass at Allie.

Mags drained the last of her champagne. "Your father's inside, taking a call. He should be out in a moment."

Trevor's body stilled, his glass froze in midair. Then he seemed to snap out of it, and if Allie hadn't been watching closely, she might not have noticed.

"Father's here?" Was that a hint of panic in his voice?

Seconds later, a tall man in his late fifties stepped onto the terrace. He was as strikingly handsome as Trevor, and Allie imagined that Trevor would look just like him in about twenty-five years.

Trevor had parents. He flat out told her he didn't have any family. Why would he lie about that?

"Hello, Son. Any scotch left for me?"

Saying nothing, Trevor poured his father a glass and handed it to him.

As he accepted the drink, his gaze fixed on Allie. "Well, well, who have we here?"

"This is Allison." Trevor's voice was so frigid, it chilled her. "She's *my* mistress. So no poaching."

Allie clenched her fists and bit back the vehement denial that sprang to her lips. This was the role he wanted her to play? Well, fine. Every time she started to feel something for Trevor other than contempt, he got nasty and she remembered why she disliked him. She turned to his father with a polite smile. "How do you do?"

"Aren't you a stunner? Good work, Trev."

Mags gently poked him in the ribs. "Be good, Nigel. Leave the poor girl alone."

Nigel wrapped his arm around Mags's waist and gave her ass a little pat. "All right, love."

Trevor stared up into the dark sky. "What have I done to deserve this?"

Mags raised a brow. "Quite a lot of mischief, I imagine. Now stop being so melodramatic, darling, and refill my glass." She handed her flute to him. "And you, Allie—or is it Allison? Do you need a refill?"

Allie might need more than one to deal with all of these batty Brits. "Yes, champagne sounds lovely."

Trevor handed Allie a glass before refilling his mom's. "And it's Miss Campbell to you, Mother."

"Nonsense. Let's eat, darling, or I'm going to expire." Mags slowly turned toward the house.

"And I'm melodramatic?" Trevor walked over to Allie and placed his hand on her back. She took a page from Mags's book and jabbed her elbow in his rib. But she wasn't teasing.

"Umph," Trevor groaned softly. He leaned down and whispered in her ear. "Behave yourself, darling, or you won't get your pudding."

Allie jerked away from him and hurried inside. He caught up to her and pulled out her chair before taking his seat at the head of the table.

Arnold served the first course, a lemony fish soup, and retreated. She didn't blame him. Allie wished she could slip away to her room too. The tension coming off Trevor was so thick, it was hard to breathe.

"Son, you must be wondering why we're here," Nigel said. "Mmm, this soup is quite nice."

Trevor leaned his elbow against the armrest of his chair and sipped his scotch. "I'm more curious about when you'll be leaving."

Mags placed her hand on Trevor's arm. "We're getting married, darling. Isn't that wonderful?"

"Yes, delightful. Who are your victims this time? And is it a double ceremony? That would be quite novel."

"Don't be silly, dearest. We're marrying each other. Again." Mags grinned, clapping her hands together.

"Well." Trevor raised his glass. "All the best to you."

Allie couldn't understand the anger in his voice. Wasn't that every child's fantasy, to see their parents get back together?

"I'd like you to be my best man, Trev." His father wiggled his eyebrows. "Maybe even have a little stag party?"

Trevor threw his head back and laughed. "You must be joking."

Nigel frowned and Mags pouted. She even managed to make her pout look sexy. Really, the woman had a gift. Maybe that's why Trevor was immune to Allie's own eye-batting, lip-biting trick. He'd seen his mother use it too many times.

"I don't know what's more amusing, the two of you marrying each other—again—or the fact that you're doing it in Vegas. Maybe we should lay odds on how long it will last this time." He raised a brow. "I'll give it seventeen hours before you're screaming like a banshee, Mother." He nodded at his father. "And it will be six weeks at the most before you have your cock inside another woman."

Allie gasped, but no one noticed.

Still laughing, Trevor raised his glass and drained it. "Yes, cheers to the happy couple." He pushed back from the table, threw down his napkin, and blew out of the room.

Mags smiled. "Well, he took that better than I expected."

"Quite," Nigel said.

With wide eyes, Allie looked to Arnold, who had silently walked back into the room, but he was no help. He wore his professional butler face as he stared at the wall.

"So, Allie darling, how long have you been sleeping with my son?"

Once the last dish had been swept from the table, Allie smiled at Mags and Nigel, made her excuses, and all but sprinted out of the room. She didn't know what to make of them. Time for some answers.

She rapped lightly on the door of Trevor's office and slipped inside. Without waiting for an invitation, she wandered into the room.

He flicked his eyes from his computer screen. "May I help you, Miss Campbell?" He'd taken off his jacket and tie, and rolled up his shirtsleeves. Despite the casual appearance, this wasn't the man who had kissed her so passionately in the hallway before dinner or showed her the beautiful sunset from the foot of his garden. That Trevor had been replaced by the uncaring business-man she'd first met.

"No, not really."

"Then why are you here? I'm very busy at the moment."

Allie walked behind the desk. Leaning over his shoulder, she stared at some sort of spreadsheet filling one of the screens. "Just making sure you weren't playing solitaire."

Trevor glanced down her dress. "I can see all the way to your pussy, Miss Campbell. Did you come here to fuck?" His gaze lin-gered on her breasts.

She recognized his tactic. He always said something shocking when he wanted to push people away. He'd done it with his parents at dinner, and now it was her turn.

She straightened. "I came to see if you were all right. And to say I think you're an ass."

"I'm fine, and duly noted. Please shut the door on your way out."

Instead of leaving, she parked herself on top of his desk. "No." Swinging her legs back and forth, her calf brushed his upper arm. "You lied about your parents." She kicked off her shoes. "Why?"

"I never actually said they were dead. You assumed. And do get down, you're blocking my monitors." But he wasn't looking at the monitors. He was staring at her legs, where the flared skirt had ridden above her knees.

Allie flattened her hands on the hem and raised it another inch. "These monitors?"

Trevor's steely gaze flew to hers. "Are you toying with me, Miss Campbell?"

Allie's heart began to pound as she leaned forward. This felt dangerous, like she was walking a very thin line, and with one misstep, she could tumble. Whether Trevor wanted to admit it or not, his parents' sudden arrival had upset him. She wanted answers, yes, but she also wanted to coax him out of this foul mood so that he'd talk to her. "Maybe," she teased. "Do you like to be toyed with, Mr. Blake?"

His eyes narrowed at the title. "Do you?" Grabbing hold of her hips, he slid her ass across the desktop until she sat directly in front of him. "Put your feet on the armrests."

Biting her lip, Allie glanced back at the door. "What if someone comes in? Arnold could interrupt us again."

"Always a possibility. But you started this game, Miss Campbell. Are you brave enough to finish it?"

Was she? When he looked at her with those gray eyes, so full of sexual promise, she felt brave, powerful. She didn't know what this was, this insane attraction between them, but she wanted to explore it. Taking a deep breath and gathering her courage, Allie placed the toes of one foot onto Trevor's chair. It caused her skirt to hike up to her hip. Then she propped her other foot on the opposite armrest. Her breath quickened, waiting to see what he'd do next. "Well?"

Trevor let go of her waist and glided his hands down her hips, over her thighs. With the tips of his fingers, he grazed her bare legs before gripping her knees and spreading them even wider. His gaze drifted down her body, idled over her breasts until finally it rested on her covered pussy. "Your knickers are wet." He let go of one knee to brush his thumb across the lacy triangle of her panties.

Gasping at his delicate touch, Allie gripped the edge of the desk.

Trevor's eyes darkened as he watched her. "Do you like that, Miss Campbell?"

She nodded.

"Sorry, love, can't hear you."

"Yes. I like it when you touch me."

"When I touch you where?" With his thumb, he pushed aside the elastic and traced over her slick folds. "Here?"

"Yes." Allie glanced down. Trevor's tanned arm was a sharp contrast to her ivory skirt. Through the transparent material of her thong, she watched his thumb glide up and down her pussy. "That feels good."

"Do you want more?"

She was tired of being fingered. He was the one always toying with her. Time to be bold, tell him exactly what she wanted. And she wanted him. Every hard inch. Allie stretched toward him, framed his face with her hands. "Trevor. I really, really want you inside me now. Please tell me you have a condom."

"Several." He pulled his hand from her, let go of her knee, and reached around to grab his wallet. Opening the flap, he withdrew four.

Allie grinned. "You're very optimistic."

"Really? Is that how you see me? I prefer practical." Tossing the condoms and wallet on the desk by her hip, he lowered his head to kiss her inner thigh. When he hooked his fingers into the waistband of her panties, he gazed up at her. "Take them off or rip them off?"

Allie placed her hands back on the desk and angled her ass up. "Take them off. You have no respect for the lingerie."

With aching slowness, he began to remove them. One centimeter at a time. It was torture. After a minute, she gave up.

"God, fine. Rip them."

Trevor smiled at her. "Good choice." Once again, he pulled

his hands outward, tearing at the fabric. Then he gently removed her feet from his chair, pushed it back, and stood between her parted legs.

Allie touched his exposed throat. "You're always overdressed for these things."

"I could say the same about you." He reached around her and unzipped the dress, tugging down the bodice until her breasts were exposed. "That's much better."

She worked her arms free until the dress was simply a band around her waist. As Trevor leaned forward to capture her lips with his, Allie freed his buttons, desperate to get her hands on that magnificent chest again. Then parting the edges of the shirt, she ran her hands across his pecs. His skin was warm, so smooth.

Trevor palmed one of her breasts, flicking the nipple. At the same time, his tongue stroked hers.

Clutching his shoulders, Allie felt like every nerve in her body was on fire. Her pussy ached, her breasts tingled, her pulse raced. She twisted her head to the side, breaking the kiss. She let go of his shoulders to rip a packaged condom off the strip. "Why are you still wearing pants?" she asked.

"That's a good question," he said, his lips moving against the side of her neck. "God, you smell good enough to eat." He unfastened his belt and Allie heard the metallic slide of his zipper.

"Absolutely," she said. "But second round, all right?" She reached into his trousers and grabbed hold of his shaft. It was as long and thick as she remembered. Using her thumb and middle finger, she stroked his cock, felt it twitch against her hand.

Trevor grabbed her wrist, and then without warning, he plucked her from the desktop and, spinning, dropped her into the chair.

Shocked, she gazed up at him with wide eyes. "What?"

He stroked himself. "Suck."

Allie stared at the engorged head, just inches from her mouth.

This was like her first night here, when he'd demanded she suck his finger. She'd felt embarrassed and resented it. But now, staring up into Trevor's face, his pleading eyes, she knew she was in control here.

She ran one finger along the length of him. His dick jerked upward in response. "All right, but on one condition."

"What's that?" His voice had never sounded so gruff.

"You can't come."

He titled his head back, his breath merely shallow gasps. "Fine," he gritted out.

Allie grabbed the base between her finger and thumb, then darted her tongue across the tip.

Trevor threaded his fingers through her hair. "More."

Taking her time, Allie licked the entire length of him. "Do you like that, Trevor?" When he didn't answer immediately, she said, "I can't hear you, love."

Using her hair as leverage, he tugged her head backward and stared down. "Careful. You don't want to get ahead of yourself, darling. And since you asked, I do like it. In fact, I'd like to fuck your mouth. I'd like to shoot streams of come down that lovely throat of yours. But I won't. This time."

So maybe she wasn't as in control of the situation as she thought. Trevor was completely unpredictable. That excited her too.

He relaxed his hold on her hair, and she leaned her head toward him once more. With long, slow strokes, she licked his shaft, tracing the tip of her tongue over his glans. She lowered her mouth over his head, sucked gently.

"Allison." He groaned her name.

Encouraged, Allie took more of him in her mouth. She found she liked the taste of him. Grasping the base, she worked her fingers in tandem with her mouth. Glancing up, she watched Trevor. He'd closed his eyes, clenched his jaw.

Allie bobbed her head up and down, increasing the speed, before easing off. Then she started the whole process over, licking the length of him, teasing him. As she took more of him in her mouth, her own pussy ached. She wanted to take him to the brink and pull back. Make him suffer just a little bit, the way she was suffering.

Trevor's hands tightened on her scalp. "That's enough. Stop, Allison."

She lifted her head but kept her fingers wrapped around him. "Stop? And here I thought you had some self-control, English."

He grasped her chin, brushing his thumb across her lips. "Don't push me."

She was tempted to do just that. But she was too needy, her body ached for him.

Without turning away, he fumbled on the desk for the condom, removed it from the wrapper, and had it rolled on in seconds. Then, grabbing her waist, he lifted her from the chair. "Wrap your legs around me."

She did, locking her feet behind his back. He settled on the edge of his desk while she clung to his shoulders.

Allie closed her eyes as Trevor reached down between them. He guided himself inside her—just the tip at first, and it wasn't nearly enough. She craved all of him. Then, sinking his fingers into her hips, he thrust upward and pulled her further onto him at the same time.

The width of him stretched her. She'd wanted this, wanted to feel him inside her, filling her. It was incredible.

Sliding her up and down his cock, Trevor simultaneously moved his hips and found a pace. Allie just hung on and enjoyed the ride, although the sensations were almost too much. After a four-year sexual hiatus, his large cock stung, but it felt so damn good at the same time. Pleasure and a little pain.

Opening her eyes, she found him staring at her, closely watching every expression on her face. God, he was gorgeous. Those cheek-bones, those firm lips. She rubbed her own across the edge of his whiskered jaw. "Trevor." She dug her fingers into his back. She was close. "Don't stop," she begged.

"Say please, darling." He still had the haughty attitude, but the words were stilted as he tried to catch his breath.

"Don't fucking stop, English." Tilting her head up, she bit his chin.

With a groan, Trevor increased the tempo, raising her hips and then slamming her onto his shaft over and over.

When she came, every muscle in Allie's body tightened. She scraped her short nails across his back. "Trevor."

When she said his name, he came too, his hands tensing on her hips as he shuddered. Breathing hard, she continued to cling to his shoulders as he clutched her ass. His chest was slick as it rose and fell heavily against hers.

Allie pressed her cheek to his shoulder and closed her eyes. She'd never experienced anything like that. Would it always be this intense? If so, she could become addicted to him.

After a few minutes, Trevor moved off the desk. Allie lowered her legs, and falling onto the chair behind her, she continued to pant while her heart slowed to its normal rhythm.

"You may toy with me anytime, darling." Pushing her hair from her forehead, Trevor bent down and gave her a scorching kiss. Just then, her stomach growled. He smiled against her lips. "How can you be hungry? You ate less than an hour ago." He straightened and redressed himself.

"I was too busy to eat. Between fending off a very inappropriate interrogation from your mother about our sexual habits and questioning her about you, I barely ate a bite." She stood and shoved her arms back into her dress. Turning around she presented her back to Trevor.

He zipped her up, giving her ass a little swat when he was through. "My parents know nothing about me. I'm surprised they remember my middle name."

"Oh my God, you sound like Monica. 'Nobody understands me,'" she mocked in a British accent. "Listen, there's a diner off the Strip that sells amazing hamburgers." She spun around to face him.

He'd tucked his shirt into his pants. "I'll text Simmons for the limo. He can take you." He reached around her to pick up his BlackBerry from the desk.

She snatched it out of his hand and set it down. "There's absolutely no reason to drive to a diner in a limo unless you're sixteen and on your way home from the prom." She found her shoes next to his chair and slipped into them. "By the way, why did you tell your parents I'm your mistress? That was an asshole move."

"My father likes to shag any female with a pulse. I did you a favor."

"And yet…it felt like an insult. Besides, he's marrying your mother for heaven's sake."

"That wouldn't stop my father, you know. I meant what I said. The man can't keep his John Thomas in his trousers." He moved around her to plop down in his chair.

"John Thomas?"

"Yes," he said. Reaching for her, he grabbed her arm and pulled her onto his lap. "John Thomas, cock, prick, willy. His penis."

She rolled her eyes. "Got it. So why did you let me think your parents were dead?"

His fingers squeezed her leg, putting just enough pressure on her thigh that she almost shivered. "Are you ready for round two?"

Allie crossed her arms, pretending that the warm pressure of his hand wasn't making her skin tingle or her nipples tighten. Should she feel this way right after a deliciously powerful orgasm? Seriously—he was addictive.

Gazing out the window into the lighted garden, she cleared her throat. "I'd have thought you'd be glad your folks are getting back together. Instead, you're in here, pouting like a child."

He yanked his hand from beneath her skirt and shoved her off his lap. "You're not here to think, Miss Campbell. Now run along. I have work to do."

His words stung. Not only was she back to Miss Campbell, but he had also reminded her she was here for one reason. She'd fulfilled her obligation and now she was being dismissed. The satisfying afterglow she'd felt a moment before dimmed to a flicker.

"Right, I'm the whore. Sorry, I won't forget again." She made her way to the door.

"Wait." His command stopped her in her tracks. "I thought you were hungry."

Without looking back, she reached forward, her hand on the doorknob. "I changed my mind."

"So did I. I'm feeling peckish after all."

She dropped the handle and turned.

The look in his eyes was intense, but with a blink it was gone, and the old, sardonic Trevor was back in place. "So, tell me, what's so special about these hamburgers?" He unfolded himself from the chair and grabbed his jacket.

—◦◦◦—

The diner was a kitschy throwback to a 1950s soda fountain. Doo-wop music played from a jukebox in the corner. Could anything scream Vegas more than Elvis movie posters plastered to the wall and a disco ball hanging from the ceiling? Trevor hated it on sight.

Allie munched on a double cheeseburger and onion rings. "Mmm. This is the good stuff. My mom used to bring us here after back-to-school shopping when I was a little girl."

"Fascinating." He was still aggravated that she'd referred to herself as a whore. She wasn't a whore, far from it. She was sweet and funny and responsive to his touch. Being inside her had been fucking fantastic. Mind-numbing.

And why was he becoming so heated about a word, anyway? She could call herself what she liked. He had other things to worry about, like how fast he could get rid of his parents.

Allie stole one of his fries, and he lightly smacked her hand. "What was it like for you, growing up with only one set of parents and playing the role of big sister?" Allie and her family were like a foreign tribe he wanted to understand, but he didn't know the language. His stepsiblings, temporary though they were, had been dreadful.

"It was nice," she said. "Lots of laughter, lots of bickering with my sisters, but not in a hostile way, like it is now. We were happy. Until my mom got sick." Her eyes clouded with sadness. "Your parents must have hurt you very much."

He looked down his nose at her. "Fuck your sympathy, Miss Campbell. I don't need it. I'm perfectly content with my life. I doubt you can say the same. And I don't need you to analyze me either. You're a hotel clerk, not a shrink. When we get home, I'll show you what your role is. I do hope you're comfortable on your knees." He hated that she felt sorry for him, viewed him as weak. He had rubbed along very nicely without the benefit of two competent parents, thank you very much. He'd had his grandfather, after all.

Allie stared at him silently for several moments, her blue eyes assessing him and eventually shrugged. "Yeah, I got the memo, I'm your whore. I'll buy kneepads tomorrow. But I could see they upset you. Whatever went on in the past, I think it's kind of nice that they want to include you in the wedding."

There was that goddamned word again. *Whore*. Hearing it pissed him off. So did her opinion of his parents. "You don't know what the bloody hell you're talking about." He glanced down at her plate. "Are you almost through? I still have work to do."

"At ten o'clock at night?" she asked, munching on an onion ring.

"Foreign stock markets open at different times. There are countries other than yours, Miss Campbell. I know it's hard for you Americans to comprehend that."

She sipped her shake. When she released her straw, she handed him an onion ring. "Try one."

He bit it in half. "Now let's go."

"In a minute. So, what do you invest in? Besides small businesses?"

He pushed his plate away. "Stocks, bonds, money markets, commodities. Why?"

"Just curious. Did my dad seem like a good investment to you?"

On paper, yes, Brian Campbell seemed like a very good investment. He owned a small used-appliance business that had turned a profit, and he wanted to expand into commercial refrigeration. All well and good. He didn't need much capital—at least it wasn't much to Trevor. To Brian, it had been a small fortune. But Trevor's gut had told him no. And he rarely went against his gut.

But he'd been slightly—ever so slightly—moved at Brian's optimism and his story of three daughters, one in college. Brian was a happy family man who wanted to give his wife and daughters a good life.

Against his better judgment, Trevor had loaned Brian enough money for tools, equipment, and office space. It had been a mistake, not following his instincts.

But if he had, Trevor never would have met Allison. Since she breezed into his office, she'd been playing havoc with his schedule and his libido. Still, he wasn't sorry she was here with him. "I loaned him money, didn't I? I must have thought so."

"You know the business wouldn't have failed if my mom hadn't…" Her voice trailed off.

"But the reality is, she did get sick. She died, and your father defaulted, and you're paying off his debt." He knew he hurt her, could see it on her face. That lovely, delicate face. But he didn't care. She needed to toughen up, the way he'd had to. Playing the what-if game was a waste of time. His voice softened. "It's no good wishing things were different, Allison. You'll never get ahead that way. Accept what is and use it to your advantage if you can. If not, move past it."

She pushed her plate away and leaned toward him. "I don't want to get ahead, English. I just want to get my family on track. That's the difference between us. I give a shit about people." She jabbed her finger at him. "You only care about yourself. And that's what makes you an asshole. Now, I'm ready to go."

She stood and waited for him to do the same. When they stepped outside, her spine was rigid beneath his touch, and she hugged herself against the cold night air. Trevor shrugged off his jacket and dropped it over her shoulders.

"Thank you."

They didn't speak on the way home. Inside the house, he walked her to the bottom of the steps, and before she could dart off, Trevor grabbed Allie's arm. "You're not a whore. Don't ever refer to yourself that way again. It offends me."

He turned on his heel and walked away, leaving her huddled in his jacket, holding on to the banister.

# Chapter 8

ALLIE WALKED INTO THE breakfast room the next morning and found Trevor sitting in his usual spot, phone in hand. He glanced up and did a double take.

"What the devil are you wearing, Miss Campbell?"

Allie almost smiled at the look of horror on his face. She stared down at her green polyester vest and black slacks. "My uniform, Mr. Blake."

When Arnold set a full plate in front of her, she glanced down in confusion. "Are these baked beans?"

"Mr. Blake Senior asked for a fry-up. Very popular back home."

Allie stared at the toast, hash browns, a tomato, bacon, sausage, a fried egg, and baked beans.

"If you eat all that, you'll explode," Trevor said. "And by the way, Arnold, Mr. Blake Senior doesn't pay the bills around here. I do. So I'll thank you to listen to my breakfast orders, not my father's."

"Of course. When he makes his next request, shall I refer him to you, sir?"

"Just tell him to sod off."

The butler bowed and left the room, leaving Trevor to glare after him.

"Why so pissy?" Allie asked. "What's the big deal about your father ordering breakfast?"

"This isn't a hotel, Miss Campbell, and speaking of which, why are you wearing that hideous uniform?"

Allie took an experimental bite of toast and beans. A tasty combo. "Well, Mr. Blake, my boss doesn't like it when I show up for work wearing jeans and a T-shirt."

He twitched a brow. "I'm your boss."

"Well, now I have two. C'mon, Trevor, I have to give at least a week's notice, otherwise, I'll leave everyone in the lurch."

"You're here to see to my needs. How can you do that if you're not actually here?" He bit out the words, his eyes dark with irritation.

"After last night, if you're still so desperate for sex that you can't make it through an afternoon, you should look into a good recovery program. This town's full of 'em." She patted his hand. "You're not alone, and admitting you have a problem is the first step."

"Very amusing, Miss Campbell, but I made my expectations perfectly plain from the beginning. You're welshing."

Allie looked up from her plate of fried goodness. "I am not welshing. I have a responsibility to my coworkers. Besides, you're always busy in the afternoons—buying and selling and ruling over your little domain—far too busy for an afternoon shag." She ate a bite of tomato, egg, and toast. "This is good."

Trevor gazed at her plate, his lip curled in disgust. "It's coronary inducing." He stroked his smooth jaw with one hand. "Mmm, maybe I *should* let my father request it. In fact, I think I'll encourage it."

Allie laid down her fork. "That's not funny."

"What's not funny?" Mags sashayed into the breakfast room. She wore a royal blue peignoir with matching marabou feathers at the collar and wrists. She looked fabulous, her face perfectly made up, her hair tousled like she'd just rolled out of bed after a very satisfying tryst.

Trevor rose from his seat and held a chair out for his mother. "Father's demise. I would find it very amusing."

Arnold walked to the sideboard.

"Just coffee and dry toast, Arnold." She turned to Trevor. "You have a treasure in that man, darling."

Arnold set the coffee and toast before Mags as she examined Allie. "Why are you wearing that very ugly clothing, dearest?"

"This is my work uniform."

Mags's eyes shifted from Allie to Trevor. "I thought she was your mistress. Isn't that enough to keep her occupied?"

Trevor tapped on his phone. "One would think so."

"Apparently you're doing something wrong, darling, otherwise, she'd be in bed until noon."

Allie pushed away from the table and stood. "Please quit talking about me like I'm not here. It's annoying." Irritated, she strode through the maze of hallways and left the house. As she walked toward the garage, she jerked to a stop.

"Good morning, Miss Campbell," Simmons said, waiting for her. "Mr. Blake said you have to take the limo."

Allie rolled her eyes. "Of course he did."

She had Simmons drive her home first. Letting herself in with a key, she walked into the living room. "Hello," she called.

"Al?" Her dad stepped out of the kitchen. "What are you doing here? And why are you wearing your uniform?"

Damn, she'd forgotten about being Trevor's assistant. She was having a hard time keeping track of all the lies. "It's a part-time thing. I wanted to see Brynn before she went to school. What time did Monica come home last night?"

"She didn't, and no phone call either." He sighed and turned back toward the kitchen.

Allie followed. "What are you going to do, Dad? Are you going to let this go on?" She wanted him to take the lead for once. Make a stand. Be a parent.

Leaning his hands on the counter, he sighed. "I wish I knew what the right answer was. What's your take on it?"

She gazed out the window. She was used to this, making decisions that affected her sisters. But she didn't like it. She never knew if she was doing the right thing.

It started when her dad worked crazy hours and her mom lay in bed, sick from chemo. Allie would decide where the girls could go, coordinated schedules, and checked their homework. Taking care of her mom on top of it had been exhausting. Some days, the responsibilities were almost too much.

"Maybe you could invite Brad over for dinner or something? Talk to him. If he cares about her—"

"I already suggested that." Brian pushed off the counter and crossed his arms. "She won't introduce us. She comes and goes at all hours. She has no consideration."

Allie nibbled her lip. "You could always give Monica an ultimatum."

Brian laughed. "Yeah, 'cause that always works so well. If I paint her into a corner, I'm going to lose her."

Allie had a sinking feeling they'd already lost Monica. What would her mom do in this situation? Allie didn't have a clue.

Her father remained silent for a few minutes, then nodded. "You're right. If she can't follow the rules, she can't stay." He stared at the floor, shaking his head. "But I can't tell her. Will you talk to her?"

Mutely, Allie nodded. Looked like she was going to have to play bad cop. Again.

"I need to get ready for work." He patted her shoulder as he walked by. "At least you're doing okay for yourself, Al."

But Allie wasn't doing okay. She was floundering. She regretted having to make the hard choices. She had virtually abandoned Brynn. And now she was stuck with Trevor. Her life was a disaster and every time she tried to do the right thing, it got worse.

She couldn't think about that now. *No time to wallow.* Focus.

First, Monica. Then make breakfast for Brynn, pack her lunch, load of laundry, and clean up.

With a sigh, Allie set down her mug and dug her phone out of her pocket. She left a message for Monica before grabbing a skillet and a couple of eggs. She'd finished slathering butter on the toast when Brynn walked into the room.

"What are you doing here, Al?"

"You know Dad always overcooks the eggs."

Brynn sat at the table. She glanced at Allie's uniform. "I thought you quit your job?"

Allie was tired of hearing about that damn job. She set a glass of juice and the plate in front of her sister. "It's part-time."

Brynn poked at her food. "So what's it like, living with that guy?"

Allie sat across from Brynn. "I'm not really living with him." *Liar.* "I just stay in the same house. His parents came into town last night, and they're a little nuts, but interesting."

Wide-eyed, Brynn forked a bite of egg into her mouth. "What do you mean nuts?"

"They're not crazy. I don't think." She glanced at the rooster clock. "More eccentric than loony. Mags is over-the-top glamorous, and Nigel is…" She shrugged. "I'm not sure what he is, exactly. But apparently they're getting remarried. Oh, and I had baked beans for breakfast."

"Gross." Brynn pinched off a piece of toast and crumbled it on her plate. "So, they're divorced?"

"Yeah." Allie wondered how old Trevor was when his parents split and how he'd gotten along with all of those stepfathers. Had Nigel remarried too? She felt a little sorry for Trevor. That kind of background had to be rough. Poor little rich boy. She blinked at Brynn's messy plate and put the arrogant English ass from her mind. He wouldn't want her sympathy, in fact, he'd punish her for it, like he had last night. Dismissing her and lashing out when she'd shown an ounce of compassion. And anyway, Trevor wasn't her concern. Brynn was. "How's your government class? Did you finish your project?"

She asked Brynn questions about school and her few friends. It seemed normal and almost comforting.

As Brynn finished getting ready for school, Allie finished her list of chores and walked into the living room. Her dad stood by the door, keys in hand.

"Did you remember to take out the trash?" she asked.

His shoulders slumped. "Damn, I knew I'd forgotten something."

"I'll take care of it."

He leaned forward and pressed a kiss to her cheek. "Thanks, Al. Let me know when you hear from Monica."

"Sure."

---

Nigel walked into the breakfast room and gave Mags a kiss on the cheek. "I saw your bird from the window upstairs, Trev. I'd give that little totty a right seeing to if I were you, my boy."

"But did you see her clothes, darling?" Mags asked.

"Hideous," Nigel said with a little shudder as he walked to the sideboard and grabbed a plate. "Ah, a full English."

Trevor ground his back teeth and forced himself to remain seated. He'd made a bad move last night, letting his parents see how they affected him. Allie had tried to pull him out of his dark mood. She'd succeeded. In fact, he couldn't get the memories of her naked body out of his head. But at the diner, he'd acted like a beast to her. She was right, he was a bit of an asshole.

Nigel grabbed the seat Allie had vacated a few moments before.

Trevor ignored them both. He sipped his coffee and continued to read his email.

"Now, Trevor," Mags said, "we'd like to talk about the wedding."

He didn't bother looking up. "I can't stop you, Mother."

"What about being my best man, Trev?" Nigel asked.

Mags heaved a dramatic sigh. "We shouldn't have sprung the news on you like that last night. I know you were upset, my poor lamb." She reached out and stroked a finger down his cheek.

Trevor wrenched his head to the side. "Hardly."

Nigel snorted. "Threw quite a wobbler, you did. You always were a sensitive lad. But that's neither here nor there. I think we should wear kilts. What say you, Mags?"

Trevor didn't know how much more he could take. His mother's pseudo concern made his eye twitch, and his father's blithe attitude made him want to punch something. Nigel's nose might do, for starters.

Mags closed her eyes and purred. "I love a man in a kilt. Of course, I love a man out of a kilt."

"You naughty minx," Nigel said. "Perhaps we should go upstairs, and I'll show you exactly what one wears under a kilt."

Trevor savagely stabbed at his phone while his breakfast threatened to make a reappearance.

"So, Son, what about it? Kilts?"

"I don't give a damn what you do, old man. I will not be attending the wedding, so whatever your plans"—he tossed his napkin on the plate—"make them without me." He pushed back from the table and walked out of the room.

Arnold hovered in the hallway, and with a sigh, Trevor stopped in front of him. "Find out how long they'll be here. And please, do whatever is within your power to make them hasten their leave, yes?"

"Of course, sir."

Trevor started walking on but stopped and turned around. "Oh, and Arnold?"

"Sir?"

"You really are a treasure." His stoic butler's cheeks actually turned pink. Allie's little blushing problem was catching. He smiled as he walked to his office.

———

"What do you mean I'm fired?" Allie had worked at The Lucky Shamrock Hotel and Casino for four years. She'd never been late, never been rude to a customer. "I don't understand." Sure she was quitting anyway, but fired? Now she'd have that on her resume. *Trevor.*

Her manager, Rick—or as everyone called him behind his back, Rick the Dick, which was not terribly original, but perfectly accurate—shifted his eyes to the maroon-colored carpet. He took a deep breath, straining the already burdened buttons of his bright green vest. "I don't know what to tell you, Allie. You've been a great employee, but we're letting you go. Sorry."

He scuttled away from her, but she hopped in front of him, blocking his exit. "He got to you, didn't he?"

Rick hunched his shoulders. "I don't know what you mean," he muttered as he brushed by her and hightailed it to his office.

Trevor's arrogant fingerprints were all over this. She'd come in this morning, like she had almost every weekday morning for the past four years, only to find Rick waiting for her with a pink slip.

Shelly walked over and put her arm around Allie, pulling her into a hug. "I'm sorry, sweetie. I didn't know, or I'd have given you a heads up."

In her late forties, Shelly's choppy, white-blond hair and gamine features made her look a dozen years younger than she actually was. Allie was going to miss her.

"I know you would have."

Shelly pulled back, a puzzled frown on her face. "What do you mean *he* got to Rick? Who's he?"

"Hang on," Allie said. She glanced at the man standing at the front counter, waiting to be checked in. Although she was royally pissed at both Rick and Trevor, this guy didn't deserve to take the brunt of it. Besides, he was staying at The Lucky Shamrock, so his day was about to get worse. This place wasn't exactly a five-star luxury experience. She put on her best customer service smile and attended him. After she was through, she walked back to Shelly.

"Don't tell anyone, okay?" She waited for Shelly to nod. "It's a really long story, but my dad owed this guy some money. He agreed to forgive the debt if I went to work for him."

"Doing what, breaking kneecaps?"

Allie laughed. "No, but he doesn't want me working here anymore. He wants my undivided attention."

Shelly's brown eyes bulged. "Allie, does this creep want you to sleep with him?"

Allie opened her mouth to lie, but nothing came out. She was so damn tired of lying. She wanted to pour out her troubles to someone else for a change.

"Oh my God." With her hands on her hips, Shelly's lips thinned into a frown. "You are so not doing this."

"He hasn't actually forced me do anything. But I've moved into his house and—"

"Well, you can just move out."

"It's not that simple," Allie said. "I owe him."

Shelly lowered her voice and leaned her head toward Allie's. "You are not going to sleep with some creepy old man."

"He's not old. Or creepy. He's...he's kind of amazing in that department." She felt the rising tide of heat fill her cheeks. The whole experience had been a wakeup call. Allie discovered she loved sex. At least Trevor sex. Then he'd turned defensive and cold at the diner and ruined it.

Speculation dawned in Shelly's eyes. "You like him," she accused, wagging her finger under Allie's nose.

"Maybe. Except when he pulls crap like this." She hiked her thumb toward Rick the Dick's office.

"Oh, honey, I'm telling you, this will end in heartbreak. Some guy is trying to buy your affection. It's not right. You deserve a man who will love and respect you. You're a beautiful person, Allie, inside and out."

She had no doubt this whole thing with Trevor would end in disaster. And heartache? Probably. Allie shook her head. "I'd better go before security tosses me out. And you'd better get to work before he fires you too."

"He wouldn't dare. I know where the bodies are buried. Screw work. Let Rick the Dick handle the front desk for a change. We're going to have ourselves a three-martini breakfast." Shelly grabbed her purse and tugged Allie toward the door.

Allie dug her heels into the carpet. "It's not even ten o'clock."

"It's always happy hour in Vegas, honey."

# Chapter 9

ALLIE WAS A LITTLE drunk. Okay, maybe more than a little. She'd had two and half cosmos with her lunch—lunch being a bowl of communal pretzels sitting on top of the bar.

Simmons had told her to call when she needed a ride, but she was tired of being told what to do. On the sidewalk, she gave Shelly a sloppy hug good-bye before climbing into a taxi.

"Take care of yourself, kid," Shelly said.

Outside of the mansion, Allie tossed a twenty to the driver before stumbling into the house. Inside was cool and dark. She leaned against the front door for a moment, wishing she had another drink. Her mouth was so dry.

She had decided at the bar that she was going to have a little talk with the British bastard. He had some splainin' to do, Lucy. He couldn't just pick up a phone and get her fired like that.

As she looked around the foyer, Allie wondered briefly where his parents were, but the thought flew out of her head as quickly as it formed. Arnold and Frances must be busy too. That was good. She didn't want to be interrupted.

She weaved her way down the corridor, slapping her hand on a glass case to steady herself. This one held elaborate antique brass finials. Trevor collected the weirdest shit. Pretty but weird. Carefully, putting one foot in front of the other, she made her way to his office without faltering too much. She dispensed with knocking and flung open the door, slamming it behind her.

Trevor sat behind his desk, sans jacket. His shirtsleeves were rolled up and his tie…hell, she didn't know where his tie was. He held the phone to his ear and gave her a dirty look as she staggered into the room.

Allie didn't care who he was talking to. Whoever it was could wait. Right now, she wanted all of his attention, and she was just soused enough to not care if it pissed him off.

She walked over to the desk and jerked the phone from his hand. "This is Mr. Blake's assistant. He'll have to call you back." She hit the end button and tossed the phone down on the desk.

Slowly, Trevor stood. His nostrils were a little white around the edges, and his gray eyes narrowed as they pinned her like one of the butterflies on display in the upstairs hallway. "What the bloody hell do you think you're doing, Miss Campbell?"

"You"—she shook a finger at him—"are an ash."

His brows lifted. "You're drunk."

"You bet your ash I'm drunk. I'm drunk as a skunk." She unbuttoned her vest, pulled it off, and threw it at his head.

He calmly plucked it from his face and placed it on the desk. "Do you always make it a habit to drink before"—he glanced at his watch—"two in the afternoon?"

"Maybe." She started unbuttoning her long-sleeved white blouse. "Or maybe I'm just mad you had Rick the Dick fire me." She pulled the blouse off and tossed that at him too.

His gaze got stuck on her breasts. She glanced down at her sheer white bra, the one with cups shaped like sea shells. Everything was on display. She shrugged. He'd seen it all anyway.

"Pardon?" he asked.

"Rick the Dick," she said, unbuttoning her slacks.

"Why are you undressing in my office, Miss Campbell?" He licked his lips and watched her pull down the zipper.

"Because you're in here, Mr. Bloody Blake. Where the hell else would I shtrip?" She kicked off her black tennis shoes as she let the pants drop over her hips, giving him a good view of how little her panties were concealing.

"But why are you taking off your clothes at all?" He ran a hand over his mouth, his eyes fixed on her body.

Allie stepped out of the slacks and stumbled a bit as she bent to pick them up. When she straightened, she felt a little woozy, so she stopped moving for a second and placed a hand on her forehead. "The room's a little spinny." Then she hurled the slacks, hitting him in the chest.

Trevor stepped around the desk, and as she reached behind her back to unhook the bra, his hands settled over her arms, preventing her from moving. "Allie, what is going on?"

"I'm here to fuck you. That's why I was fired, right?" She tried to pull out of his hold, but his grasp was too firm. "Let go of me."

"Allison, stop." He spun her in his arms, so that his chest rested against her back. She could feel his shirt buttons press along her spine. Could feel the hardness of his cock press against her ass.

"Oh God, I'm so dizzy."

"Yes, I'm sure you are." As he spoke, his lips brushed her cheek. "Now, I'm sorry you were fired, but I told you from the beginning you would have to quit."

"And you couldn't give me one week to do it? Housework and blow jobs. That's apparently all I'm good for."

He sighed in her ear. "Let's get you dressed." He rubbed his hand along her forearm. "And that's not all you're good for. You've taken care of your family, Allison, and put your own needs last. It's admirable."

Why did he have be *nice*? That was just like him, to knock her for a loop when she least expected it. She was pathetic. He paid her one compliment, and she was ready to crumble. Trevor had tried to take her house. Had taken her car. He was sarcastic and nasty and lashed out like a whip whenever she asked him something personal. He didn't care about her, but when he touched her, all higher-level brain function stopped and her hormones took over.

"No." She pushed her back against his chest. "No, you are not doing this to me. I am pissed. And I want my job back. And my car. And my fucking life." Suddenly, tears welled in her eyes and she began to sob. Letting go of his arms, she buried her face in her hands and cried tears of grief and anger that she had kept pent up for the last six months. Tears for her family, for her mom. Tears for herself and the life she should have had.

Trevor petted her hair, soothing her. "You've been brave for so long, darling. Let it all out. Shh, it's going to be all right."

His kind words made her cry harder.

Dropping her hands, Allie turned to face him and wrapped her arms around his waist, letting her forehead rest against his chest. "Liar," she choked out. "It's not going to be all right. It sucks, and it's going to keep on sucking because that's what life is."

"You don't believe that. You've just had a bad day." He rubbed little circles along her bare back with one hand and continued to stroke her hair with the other.

."Thanks to you."

Trevor maneuvered her over to the chair in front of his desk and pulled her onto his lap. She turned toward him, resting her head on his shoulder.

"I'm a rotten man."

"The worst," she sniffed. "And I'm going out to look for another job tomorrow."

"Mmm," he said against her cheek. "We'll see."

"I mean it, Trevor. I have to work. When you get another mistress, what am I going to do? I have to have a job."

He didn't say anything but sat, holding, stroking her, comforting her. God, she was so damn tired. Not just from the crying jag, but from her life.

She didn't know how long she sat in his lap, but eventually she lifted her head. Trevor wiped a tear with his thumb and kissed her cheek before standing with her in his arms and placing her gently back in the chair. She didn't even bother to cover herself. She was too weary to care.

He moved to the desk and gathered her clothes, all except for the vest, which he dropped into the trash can. He held his out his hand. "Let's get you dressed. Although I'm fine with nudity, Arnold is such a prude."

Her eyes were swollen, and she was a little sick to her stomach as she placed her hand in his. On shaky legs, she stood. "Do you know why I took a job at such a crappy casino?"

"Yes, because they worked around your schedule when your mother was ill." He briskly helped her into the sleeves of her blouse and buttoned her back up, as if she were a child. Then he knelt before her and guided her feet into the slacks, one foot at a time.

"I hate you," she whispered. She clutched his shoulder as she lost her balance, but Trevor placed his hands on her hips and held her steady.

Gazing up at her with serious eyes, a sad smile touched his lips. "I hate myself sometimes." With his hands still wrapped around her, he bent forward and lightly kissed her belly button. He took a deep breath and fastened the button and zipper on her slacks. Before he could stand, the office door opened.

"Oh, good, darlings you're here." Mags swept into the room but came to a halt at the sight of Trevor kneeling in front of Allie. "Are you proposing, dearest? Let's see the ring."

She swished forward and grabbed Allie's hand. Mags looked at her bare finger with a frown. "Where's the ring, Trevor? All of my husbands had a ring. Although Francois put it in the soufflé, and I almost choked to death. Nevertheless, he had a ring."

Trevor climbed to his feet. "I'm not proposing, Mother. I was helping Allie get dressed. She feels a need to shed her clothes in my presence."

Allie blushed furiously. "You know what, Mr. Inappropriate?" She shoved her finger into his chest. "I've had it with you. And I've had it with your sharky remarts."

Trevor raised his brows. "Of course you have." He turned to Mags. "Now, Mother, I need to get Allie to bed because, as you can see, she's a bit wankered."

"What *does* she do for a living, darling? And where can I sign on?"

---

When Allie awakened, the room was dark. Rubbing her eyes, she moaned, stretched her legs. Her mouth was desert dry and her head throbbed.

She glanced at the clock on the bedside table. Almost time for dinner. She wasn't sure how long she'd been out, but she clearly remembered what had happened in Trevor's office.

Allie buried her head in the pillow, feeling totally conflicted. Did she want to go back home? Yes. Did she want to walk out and never see him again? No. She was starting to *like* him, for God's sake. She wanted to have sex with him again—just to make sure the first sensational time hadn't been a fluke. But she was also angry because he was ruining her already complicated life. What a mess.

When she sat up and swung her legs to the floor, the throbbing in her head grew stronger.

A knock sounded at the door, and before she could call out, Trevor walked in. The light from the hallway kept him in silhouette. "Ah good, you're up. How are we feeling?"

His loud, chipper voice pierced her skull. "Keep it down, English."

"Poor Miss Campbell." He strolled toward her and flipped on the bedside lamp.

"Ugh." Allie squinted and held up a hand to shield her eyes from the brightness.

"Have a hangover? That's what happens when we drink our lunch."

"*We* didn't drink our lunch. I did. So, stop saying the royal we."

"Still cross, I see."

"Maybe your sparkling personality is rubbing off on me."

He smiled. "You should be so lucky." Trevor held out his hand. "Here."

She looked down at the two pills in his palm.

"It's just aspirin to help with the headache you're undoubtedly feeling."

"I need water."

With a deep sigh, as if she were the most tiresome person in the world, he walked to the bathroom and came back with a full glass. "Open up."

Allie obediently opened her mouth, and he popped the pills on her tongue, then handed her the glass.

"Do you need help getting dressed? Again? Although undressing you is much more entertaining."

Ignoring him, she stood and walked into the bathroom. She very quietly shut the door behind her and locked it. Hopefully, he would take the hint and leave while she took a shower. Doubtful. He didn't take hints. Subtlety was wasted on Trevor.

Allie shed her clothes and stood under the hot water. It felt good on her gritty skin.

After she toweled off, Allie drank another glass of water and brushed her teeth. Close to feeling human again, she looked at herself in the mirror. Her damp hair was a tangled mess and her eyes were slightly bloodshot. Never again. Day drunk wasn't pretty.

As she gently ran a brush through her hair, she heard a noise in the other room. Grabbing her robe off the hook, she shrugged into it and opened the bathroom door.

Trevor had taken off his dinner jacket and lounged on the bed, leaning against the headboard. His large body seemed to take up most of the mattress. What would it be like to share a bed with him? And what did he sleep in—pajama pants? Nothing at all? Her cheeks grew warm, and she cinched her robe a little tighter.

His eyes swept over her, lingering on her chest before lazily drifting up to her face. "You keep staring at me like that, Miss Campbell, and we'll definitely be late to dinner."

She gathered the lapels of her robe together with one hand.

"Then why don't you give me some privacy?"

He shifted to his side, propping himself on his elbow. "You didn't give me any privacy this afternoon. I was in the middle of an important business meeting. Your little strip show was very distracting."

She took a deep breath and tried for calm and unaffected. "I apologize for that. I don't usually drink, but when I get fired for no reason—"

"How long are you going to be angry about that, love?"

She took a step toward him. "You took away my livelihood. Yeah, I'm angry. And I'm sure I will be for quite a while, so get used to it." The aspirin hadn't kicked in yet, and her head was pounding. Why did she even bother? She never won an argument with him. The deck was stacked against her.

"I told you to quit, Allison. And I'll provide whatever you need. You've only to ask."

She forced a smile. "Some privacy would be great."

She hated being indebted to him. She didn't want him to provide for her. It made her feel weak and helpless, a feeling she'd been acquainted with since her mom got cancer. She was tired of feeling that way.

"Are you trying to get rid of me, Miss Campbell?"

"Yes. Now scoot." She made a sweeping gesture with her hand.

He looked affronted. "I have never scooted in my life, nor do I intend to start now. I want to watch you get dressed." His eyes grew darker and his voice deepened. "There's no need to be shy. I've seen everything you have to offer, touched most of it, tasted a bit." His gaze slid over her once more.

She was tempted to drop her robe and hop on the bed with him, but her pounding head would hamper the enjoyment. And he wasn't going to leave. The more she insisted, the more entrenched he'd become. *Stubborn.* Yes, he could be a jerk, but this afternoon, he'd held her and consoled her. Trevor Blake was infuriating and impossible to figure out.

His eyes met hers and he smiled. A slow, sexually charged smile. He was remembering last night, she could tell. She hadn't been able to think about much else either.

When he stared at her with that heated gaze, she felt completely naked and exposed. Her nipples pebbled against the slinky robe.

To cover her reaction, she stalked over to the dresser and plucked out a bra and a matching pair of panties. "You love to hear yourself talk, don't you?"

"Yes, I fascinate myself."

"Well, that makes one of us." She swung back around to face him.

"I said I want to watch you dress, Miss Campbell. Every whim, remember?"

She glared at him as she walked to the closet. "Tough. I've got a headache and I'm not in the mood."

A frown marred the line of his mouth. "Would you like to skip dinner and rest? I could have Frances send up a tray."

She was a little touched by his thoughtfulness. "No, I'll be okay."

"All right, but if you don't move it along, the terrible twosome might decide to join us in here."

She grabbed a dress and walked back into the en suite, leaving the door open. "What is the deal with you and your parents, anyway? What did they do that was so terrible?"

She shimmied into her dress and put on a little makeup. When she was done, she walked into the bedroom. "Well?"

Trevor stood and grabbed his jacket, pushing his arms through the sleeves. "Are you going to dinner barefoot? How bohemian."

"Fine." She pulled a pair of black heels from the closet. "Don't tell me."

———

When she slipped on her shoes, her dress rode up over the backs of her bare thighs. It was bloody difficult to keep his hands to himself. If he hadn't been such an ass last night, he would have had another taste of her. He remembered how soft her legs were. How long and lean. He wanted to be on top of her next time, with those thighs wrapped around him, his cock deep inside her. She'd been so very ready for him last night, tight and wet.

Good God. He was turning into a right wanker. Damn near every waking thought was centered on Allison and how to get her naked.

Then she walked into his office and did it for him.

When she had hung up his phone, he'd been in the middle of discussing expansion plans with a small bakery. It wasn't a terribly important call, even though he'd told her it was. But business trumped everything else. Even Allison.

Until he realized she was drunk.

And then she started taking off her clothes, one horrible uniformed piece at a time, all the way down to the sheer bra and knickers. Her breasts were truly stunning, a goddamned work of art.

If she hadn't been drunk... But she had been drunk. Then she started crying. Tears undid him every time. Allison's tears had gutted him.

But he'd told her from the beginning he wanted all of her attention. She hadn't listened. He'd kept his end of the bargain, paying off her debts, letting her keep the house. Was it so wrong that he expected something in return?

Perhaps he really was the asshole she accused him of being. He'd gotten her fired, after all. It took a two-minute phone call to the casino owner. Two minutes, and he'd altered her life. Again. But he wanted her here, not stuck in that hellhole, miles off the Strip. When she'd looked at him with those accusing blue eyes, he actually felt a little guilty. He rubbed his chest as he held the bedroom door open for her and followed her to the top of the stairs.

He was doing her a favor, really. She needed money. He had money. Wasn't living here, taking tea with him, sunning herself by the pool much more pleasant than wearing the green waistcoat and dealing with tourists? Of course it was. She was just being stubborn.

He wrapped an arm around her waist, and they descended the stairs. He savored the feel of her body pressed against his. In her room, he'd had to restrain himself from stripping her out of that robe and touching every single inch of beautiful, pale skin.

He led her through the hallway and she preceded him into the drawing room, where his parents waited. But he kept hold of her hand, stroked his thumb across her palm. He didn't want to let go.

"There you are, children," Nigel said, leaning on the mantel. "We were about to come looking for you."

That's exactly what Trevor had been afraid of.

"Don't worry. Mags and I know what it's like, don't we darling? Can't keep your hands off each other, eh?"

His mother looked at her ex and future husband and smiled.

Grinding his teeth, Trevor fought for patience. When the hell were these two going to get tired of whatever game they were playing and get out of his bloody house? He told Arnold to find out their plans, but they had been just as cagey with his butler as they'd been with him. They insisted on blathering about a wedding that would never take place.

Mags rose from the sofa and walked to Allie, taking her other hand and pulling her from Trevor's side. Like a possessive child, he wanted to yank her back. Why he had such a stupid reaction, he didn't know. But it made him feel out of sorts.

"I'm so glad you're rested, dearest," Mags said.

Trevor ignored both of his parents and moved to the bar. "What would you like to drink, Miss Campbell?"

"Soda water, please."

"Are you sure you don't want to continue this afternoon's bender? I could line up some tequila shots for you."

"Just soda water."

"So, Allie, I've decided that you"—Mags paused for dramatic effect—"should be my chief bridesmaid."

"Um…what is that exactly?" Allie sat at one end of the sofa and accepted the glass from Trevor without looking at him. "Like a maid of honor?"

Trevor perched on the armrest next to her, his leg brushing her arm. He reached out and touched a strand of her hair, wrapping it around his finger like a spring. She smelled of citrus and flowers, and he inhaled deeply as he gazed at the shades of gold shining through it.

Mags touched Allie's knee. "Exactly. Won't it be fun? We can have a hen night."

Allie twisted and looked up at Trevor. "Bachelorette party," he translated.

"Oh, well, I don't know how long I'm going to be here."

"Nonsense, darling, Trevor is half in love with you already. I have a feeling you might be here permanently."

He unwound the strand of hair he'd been toying with and dropped it. "Don't be stupid, Mother."

"Ow." Allie glared at him over her shoulder and rubbed her head.

He donned a neutral expression as he sipped his scotch. "Apologies, Miss Campbell."

"How could he not be in love with her?" Nigel asked. "Look at the girl. She's perfectly lovely."

"And given half a chance, you'd fuck her sideways." Trevor smiled coldly at Nigel. "Yes, Father, we know. If there's a woman in the room, you need to prove that your cock still works. We get it." Trevor wanted nothing more than to pick the man up and throw him out of his house.

Nigel shot Trevor a disappointed frown. "There's no need for that, Son. It's all in the past."

Mags sat up straight. "We should go in to dinner. I'm famished."

# Chapter 10

ALLIE NODDED POLITELY AS Mags went on about dresses, shoes, cakes, and bouquets, but her mind was on Trevor and his father. Despite his bland expression, Trevor had sounded so bitter. Was he upset because his father slept with other women in general or one woman in particular? The next time she saw Frances, Allie would pump her for information. She had turned on The Blake Family soap opera, but started watching in the middle of an episode and was confused by the characters and plotlines. Of course, she could ask Trevor for details, but he'd only say something nasty and shocking, so what was the point?

"How does that sound?" Mags asked.

Allie tried to remember what they had been talking about.

Before she could respond, Trevor spoke. "She wasn't paying attention, Mother. If you were the slightest bit aware of anyone other than yourself, you would have seen Allie's eyes glaze over ten minutes ago."

Mags's smile dimmed just a little. "Sorry, darling, I forgot that wedding plans are tedious for everyone but the bride."

"You've done it enough times, you should remember. Why not get married by an Elvis impersonator and quit bothering the rest of us?" Trevor said.

Allie glanced at him. Despite his biting words, his face was perfectly pleasant.

"Sorry, Mags," Allie said. "I do want to know all the details. My mind just wandered for a second. Now, what are you wearing?"

"We'll go shopping tomorrow, dearest, and pick it out. We'll pick out your dress too."

Oh God, not more shopping. Allie managed a smile. "Sure."

"Allie doesn't like shopping, Mother."

Mags appeared confused for a second, then began to laugh. "Don't be silly. All women love to shop."

The rest of the dinner passed slowly. Mags chatted away and Allie tried to appear interested, Trevor interrupted with biting, sarcastic remarks, and Nigel remained quiet. When it was finally over, Trevor excused himself and went to his office. Allie, not the slightest bit tired after her drunken nap, knew she couldn't stand any more of Mags's cheerful prattling and Nigel's brooding silence.

She excused herself and, on her way to her room, stopped by the library on the second floor and snagged a couple of books relating to Spanish daggers. She wanted to know why all of these collectibles were so damn interesting to Trevor. Then she changed clothes and called her dad.

"Hello?" His voice sounded anxious.

"Hey, Dad, have you heard from Monica? I called her this morning and left a message, but I haven't heard back."

He sighed. "No, I thought you might be her."

Damn that kid. "Let me know if she calls?" Allie asked.

"Yeah, same here."

She asked to speak to Brynn and flipped through the dagger book until her sister picked up the phone.

"Hey, Al," Brynn whispered, "Dad's freaking out over here."

"He's worried about Monica. You still don't know Brad's last name or who his friends are?"

"Uh, no. I don't hang out with stoners."

The book dropped from Allie's lap. "Is it just pot or something else?"

Brynn sighed. "I'm not sure, but I found a bag of pot under

her mattress. Don't tell her, okay? She'll kill me if she knows I was snooping."

"I promise. But you have to let me know if you find anything else."

"Okay." There was a long pause. "So, are you stopping by home this week? I mean, I know you're busy. You don't have to come, I was just curious."

Although she might claim otherwise, Brynn needed her, needed the stability she provided. "Tomorrow morning. I'll make you breakfast." If Trevor had any objections, too bad. Allie had responsibilities.

"French toast?"

"You got it, Brynnie."

After she hung up, she tried to concentrate on the book, but antique Spanish daggers, even the kind made from Toledo steel, just couldn't hold her attention. What if Monica was doing something worse than sparking up? Allie had a bad feeling about this Brad guy.

She should have kept a better eye on Monica, should have searched her room, checked her phone.

Frustrated and restless, she grabbed her robe, threw it on, and opened her bedroom door. Glancing out to make sure no one was loitering in the hall, she padded from room to room, examining the *objets d'art* on display.

She stopped to look at carved salt cellars. Snuff boxes were grouped together on a shelf in the library. The top of each held an engraved herald or crest. What was the appeal of all these items? Trevor didn't seem obsessed with the collections, yet he must be. She couldn't swing a dead cat without hitting some encased doodad.

As she drifted through the second floor, her mind turned over the situation with Monica, but she'd come to no conclusions. If her sister chose not to answer her messages, there wasn't much Allie could do but worry.

She made her way to the round TV room and settled herself

onto the squishy sofa, curling her feet beneath her, and began changing channels. She wasn't in the mood for crime shows, news shows, or movies, but when she spotted an ugly pair of green earrings on a shopping channel, she paused.

"Good God, you're not thinking of buying those," Trevor whispered in her ear.

Allie jumped and spun her head. "Don't sneak up on me like that."

He plopped on the sofa next to her, his thigh touching her leg. "How would you like me to sneak up on you?"

"How about not sneaking at all? And I can't buy anything. I don't have a job anymore."

Trevor reached over and took the remote control out of her hand, hitting the off button and tossing it on the sofa cushion. He gazed at her out of the corner of his eye. "What's wrong, love?"

She untucked her legs, pulling the edges of her robe closed. "My sister's missing."

"Monica?"

She nodded.

He picked up the pink satin sash and rubbed it between his fingers. "Missing how?"

"Like she's gone. Trevor, I need to be at home with my family."

"When was she last seen? Is she really missing, or is she with the boyfriend?" He shifted toward her, stretching his arm along the back of the sofa.

"She's been gone for two days, no one's heard from her, and apparently, she's smoking pot."

He gasped. "Not the dreaded marijuana."

She jerked her tie out of his grasp. "It's not funny. My sister's out there"—she flung her arm wide—"doing God knows what with some punk ass guy we know nothing about. She's throwing her life away."

He gripped her chin, forcing her to look at him. "I'll find out who this Brad person is, all right?"

Surprised at his offer to help, she nodded. "What's this going to cost me? Nothing with you is free."

He swooped down and kissed her. When his tongue stroked hers, she reached up to touch the side of his face, but he pulled away too quickly. "There, paid in full." She ran a finger over her lips. That brief kiss wasn't enough. Why did she have to feel this way about him? He was everything she didn't want—high-handed, arrogant, snide.

He watched her reaction with hooded eyes. They stared at each other in silence until Allie began to feel her cheeks heat up.

*Comforting, funny, confident. Sexy as hell.* All right, so he had his good points.

She swallowed at the sensual allure in those smoky gray eyes. "I think you hurt your mom's feelings at dinner." She didn't really want to talk about his mother. She wanted to lean forward and kiss him back. She wanted to stroke the prominent cheekbones, to feel the rough stubble on his chin. But after last night's after-sex dismissal, she was a little hesitant to make the first move.

He plucked at her hair and, just like in the drawing room before dinner, twirled a strand around his finger, unwound it, and twisted it again. "My mother doesn't have feelings, she has histrionics."

Allie turned her head slightly to look up at him. "She was hurt, Trevor. I could see it in her eyes."

He shrugged. "She'll get over it."

She knew it was useless to discuss it with him anymore. He had an amazing way of blocking out anything he didn't want to hear.

Letting go of her hair, he brushed his finger lightly down her cheek.

She smiled and slapped at his hand. "That tickles."

Trevor raised both brows. "Are you ticklish then, Miss Campbell?" His eyes twinkled, and without warning, he struck. His fingers scurried over her ribs and stomach. He squeezed her knee until she was twisting away from him.

Laughing, Allie tried to push him off but couldn't. His hands seemed to be everywhere at once. When he lightly squeezed her side, Allie couldn't take anymore. The safe word they had talked about suddenly popped into her head. "Uruguay." She laughed as she said it. With a grin, he kept tickling and she pushed at his chest. "Uruguay, Uruguay."

He stopped squeezing but kept his hand pinned to her waist. He was halfway on top of her now, and her robe had parted, leaving her legs bare.

Allie froze beneath him. Her breath came in shallow gasps. Once again, his gaze snagged hers, and she was unable to look away. She reached up and smoothed a dark lock of hair off his forehead.

"Allison."

---

Her white cotton T-shirt peeked between the edges of her robe. Shouldn't be sexy, but it was. Long, blond hair fanned out over the sofa cushion, trailing toward the floor. She fluttered her lashes, her eyes locking with his, and she bit down on that pouty lower lip.

"I need to fuck you again." He was surprised at how harsh his voice sounded, but he was on the edge here and he didn't know how much longer he could watch her, ache for her, and not fucking take her.

"'Kay." It was a faint whisper.

*Okay?* She was on board then?

Clamping both his hands on either side of her head, he took possession of her mouth. He slid his tongue against hers and bit at her lip, not too hard but probably enough to sting. Then he licked at it and nibbled, more gently this time.

During their encounters, both in the salon and in his office, he'd hardly kissed her at all. He hadn't realized what he'd been missing. Allison was delicious. God, he loved the way she tasted. Sweet and hot. Loved the way her tongue met his, the way she sucked on it. And when she moaned into his mouth, he moaned too.

She murmured in the back of her throat as she moved her legs restlessly beneath him. Then Allie grabbed his wrists, stroked her hands along his arms, back and forth, scratching her short nails against his skin. Even that felt brilliant.

Abruptly, she let go of his arms and clutched his shirt in her hands, pulling him closer.

In response, Trevor fisted her soft hair, tilted her head back against the sofa pillow, and continued to devour her. Every bit of finesse deserted him, and he was like a randy schoolboy on his first time out. Their teeth bumped and he knew he was being too rough. She didn't seem to mind though. She met him kiss for searing kiss, thrust her tongue against his, stroking it with her own.

Allie continued to clutch at his shirt as her legs tangled with his. Then she rotated her hips, grinding on him, moving against his straining cock. Oh, fuck, that felt good.

He wanted to touch her body, feel those breasts. In a moment. Maybe two, because right now, he couldn't stop kissing her, couldn't stop sticking his tongue down her bloody throat.

Allie wrapped one leg around his waist. Exactly what he'd been thinking about earlier. She squeezed his waist with it, and he shifted until his cock was aligned with her pussy. Then he moved against her, angling himself, rotating as he pressed against her.

*So hot.*

He was on fire. The feel of her consumed him, burned him up. He couldn't remember wanting anything the way he wanted Allison.

Allie's moans became more frequent, more urgent as she continued to grind against him. He hadn't dry humped anyone since he was fifteen. But it felt so damned wonderful, he just kept rubbing against her, enjoyed the friction.

Keeping his mouth on hers, he let go of her head and jerked the tie of her robe loose. Then he pulled it open and off her shoulders.

Allie broke away, tore her mouth from his, and shrugged out of the robe. "Hang on, let me get rid of this." As soon as her arms were free, he found the hem of her shirt and whipped it over her head.

With his weight on his hands, he leaned away to look at her. For a long moment he simply stared at the beauty that was Allison Campbell—that lovely face, the wide, blue eyes, the lush mouth. Ah, those full, pink-tipped breasts. Then his mouth was back on hers, demanding a response.

She gave him one. She sank her fingers into his hair, tightening her grasp, pulling at it. It almost hurt. And he loved it. Loved the way his body heated at her touch. Loved the way he fit against her. Perfectly, like they were made that way.

He clasped her thigh, smoothed his palm across her soft skin, working his hand higher until he cupped her ass through the thin material of her shorts. He forced his mouth off of hers. "Why are you wearing so many damned clothes? Bloody nuisance." Then he leaned back down and pressed his lips to hers once more.

He grasped the waistband of the shorts and pulled them down. Allie helped by lifting her ass off the sofa and yanking on the other side. With reluctance, Trevor raised his head and stopped kissing. "Drop your leg, darling. Shorts need to come off." He was all but gasping, his chest brushing her bare breasts with each exhalation. Those gorgeous bare breasts. Dipping his head, he took one in his mouth and sucked.

"Trevor." She pulled on his hair until he raised his head. "Why am I always the naked one, huh?"

He smiled down at her. "Part of my master plan."

She ran her tongue across her lips—they were dark red and swollen. She slid her calf over his ass and down the back of his thigh, taking her time, caressing him with her leg.

He groaned. "You're killing me, Miss Campbell." He drew the shorts over her legs and dropped them on the floor.

"We've had sex. Can we dispense with the Miss Campbell?" She was winded too. He liked that he'd done that, made her heart pound, made her breathless with his kisses.

He grinned. "Maybe I have a naughty nanny fantasy."

She let go of her viselike hold on his hair and laughed. God, how he loved that sound. She smoothed her hands along the sides of his face, brushed his cheek. "Let's get you naked too."

"Marvelous idea." He leaned back, keeping his knee wedged between her thighs, and with one hand, unbuttoned his shirt. Allie didn't help him. Instead, she ran her own hands across her breasts and watched as his shirt disappeared.

With great reluctance, he moved away from her to stand. "Do that again. Touch yourself."

Her eyes on him, she hesitated a moment, then did as he'd asked. Pulling her bottom lip into her mouth, she lightly circled her fingertips over her nipples. They jutted out, begging for his attention.

Trevor's gaze didn't leave her as he found a condom. "More." He grabbed his cock through his pants, gave it a stroke as he watched her.

She cupped her breasts, then moved her hands lower, with agonizing slowness, down her taut stomach, over her smooth legs. Finally, her fingers danced over the small triangle of blond hair. She let her legs fall open and parted the lips with two fingers, giving him a captivating view of her damp pussy.

He ran a hand over his mouth, closed his eyes, and took a deep breath. He needed to get control or he'd embarrass himself—that also hadn't happened since he was fifteen.

After a minute, he opened his eyes and kicked off his shoes, and in seconds was as naked as she. Still touching herself, her gaze flowed over him, taking in his chest, his abs, and stopping at his cock.

He wanted to protest when she moved her hand away from that lovely cunt, but when Allie sat up and balanced on her knees, crooking her finger at him, he closed his mouth. "Come here, English."

Enthralled, Trevor stepped closer and cupped the back of her head. When she circled both hands around his cock, he groaned. But when she rubbed his tip across her nipple, he almost came on the spot.

"Fuck, Allison."

"In a minute," she said with grin.

Reaching out, Trevor squeezed her breasts together and placed his cock between them. God, he'd fantasized about this. Often. The real thing was much better. Allie dropped her hands as he pushed himself between her tits. It was almost more than he could to take.

Allie grabbed his hips. "Self-control. No coming allowed."

"Ladies first," he agreed.

As he thrust his hips forward, the tip of his prick poked the bottom of her chin. He pulled back and drove forward once more. This time, Allie lowered her mouth and licked the head. *Bloody fucking hell, that felt good.* He did it a few more times, but the combination of her mouth, her tits, and watching his cock slide between them was too much.

"I can't take any more of that, love." Relinquishing his hold on her breasts, he tore the condom wrapper open with his teeth. After he sheathed himself, he had her on her back in a flash.

Never letting his eyes stray from her face, he cupped her breast, grazing her nipple with his thumb. She arched and dug her short fingernails into the back of his hand. Ah yes, Allie Campbell had very sensitive breasts. He would have to do something about that.

Bending his head, he swirled the tip of his tongue around the areola, denying her what she wanted, licking in smaller circles, nibbling his way toward the center but never touching it.

"Trevor, please." She twisted her head and looked at him.

He stopped. "Please what, darling?" He smiled cheerfully.

"I hate you."

He leaned down and nipped the underside of her breast, causing her to gasp. He was dying, wanting to be inside her, but he so liked playing with her. "Please what?" he prompted.

"Suck me, English."

Only then did he lick the rosy-pink point. He scraped his teeth along the length of it, pulled it in his mouth, and flicked it with the tip of his tongue. Then he moved his head to the other breast and carefully bit down. She leaned her head back, exposing her white throat. He hadn't explored that part of her yet. But he would. Eventually, he would become acquainted with every bloody inch of her.

Keeping his mouth clamped on her breast, he moved one hand to her pussy, rubbed the pad of his finger against her slit. She was slick and ready. Using his thumb, he circled her clit and slid a finger inside. She was smooth and wet, and she smelled so good. All the while, he continued to sweep his tongue across the hard flesh of her breast.

Allie writhed beneath him and again grasped his hair with one hand. "I want your cock, Trevor."

"Yes." He kissed her, almost tenderly as he slipped his finger from her body, but he wanted to be in her so badly, he ached.

She wound both of her legs around him this time. He brushed his lips over one of her heated cheeks as he thrust inside her. To the hilt. Oh God, yes. "Talk to me, Allison."

She stroked his back. "Fuck me, Trevor."

There was no place he'd rather be than inside Allison Campbell. He felt the walls of her pussy clench around his cock. Then he ran his lips across hers. "Do that again. Tighten up."

She did as she kissed him back. *Tighten and release.* Over and over until he thought he'd go mad from it.

Then he began moving, slowly at first, pulled out almost completely, then stroked back inside of her. *Heaven.* In and out, faster and faster.

Allie's soft moans had him straining. He wanted to hold off for as long as he could.

She reached down and touched herself as she looked into his eyes.

"Filthy details, Allison. Tell me what you like."

"I like…" She licked her lips and continued to move her fingers in small circles over her clit.

"Tell me," he ground out.

"I like it when you take control. And when you fuck me hard."

He obliged and slammed his cock into her, retreated, then did it again. "Come," he ordered. He couldn't hold out much longer. "Come for me, Allison."

She did, bowing her back, shoving her breasts upward. He watched them sway as he continued to pound into her.

He felt his balls tighten, and came. It was intense and powerful, draining him as he continued to pump. Even after he was empty, he thrust a few more times, burying his face in her neck. Her long hair tickled his cheek and he smiled against her damp skin.

She ran her hand up and down his back, kissed his temple, smoothed the hair away from his face with her other hand. He lay on top of her, unable to move.

How long they stayed that way, he had no idea. He didn't care. He felt too good.

Finally, he roused himself and leaned back as he gazed down at her. She was asleep. He tried not to jostle her when he stood, but she opened her eyes and stared up at him. Her gaze tracked him as he removed the condom, wrapped it in a tissue, and tossed it in the trash.

He walked back to the sofa and, bending down, pushed aside a strand of her hair. "Are you all right, love?"

"Mmm hmm." With a smile, she stretched her arms over her head. His eyes strayed to her breasts once more.

"I don't remember the last time I felt this relaxed." When she sat up, he straightened, giving her some room to move. She reached down and grabbed her clothes. As she pulled on the thin, white cotton shirt, he couldn't take his eyes off her. She stood and hiked the shorts up her legs, over her hips.

She glanced over at him, taking in his face, chest, finally lowering to his cock, which had started to rise again. "Are you going to get dressed?" Her eyes remained fixed.

"Haven't decided."

"But you said Arnold frowns on nudity."

He swiveled his head left and right. "I don't see him around, do you?"

She looked like she was fighting a smile. Crossing her arms, she angled her head. "Are you telling me that you're going to prance around the house buck naked?"

He looked down his nose at her. "I've never pranced in my life, nor do I intend to start now." A slow smile crossed his lips. "But the naked bit, well, that sounded like a challenge to me."

# Chapter 11

THE NEXT MORNING, ALLIE cracked one eye and glanced at the clock. She couldn't remember the last time she'd slept until nine o'clock. "Shit." She sat up, the covers falling from her naked breasts. She'd promised to make French toast for Brynn.

She glanced down, saw a bruise along the side of one breast. "Trevor." She'd spent most of last night having lots and lots of mind-blowing sex with him. His tongue wasn't just good for smart-ass remarks. She smiled at the memory. It was really good at other things too.

She glanced over at the side of the bed where Trevor had spent the night. Picking up the pillow, she shook out the indentation where his head had been and mussed up the covers. She didn't want Frances to know he'd been here. Silly but true. She was embarrassed. A mistress who didn't want the help to know she was boinking their boss.

She hopped up and scanned the room for her clothes. The robe lay on the floor by the door. Her sash lay half under the bed. She jerked on the robe and snatched the tie around her waist, then bent over and peeked under the dust ruffle. How the hell did her T shirt and shorts wind up there?

A knock sounded at the door and Frances walked in with a tray. "Oh good, miss, you're awake."

Allie dropped the dust ruffle like it was on fire. "Good morning."

Frances set the tray on the table next to the bed and bustled over to the curtains, pulling them back, letting the bright morning light spill into the room.

"Thanks, Frances, but you didn't have to bring this to me."

"Mr. Blake thought you might like to have a lie in this morning. He said you had quite a late night."

Her cheeks flooded with heat. British bastard. Was he going to put it on a mobile billboard and parade it up and down the Strip?

"Said he kept you up late, watching a movie. Loves those old movies, he does. Just like his grandfather, God rest his soul."

Allie's shoulders sagged in relief at hearing his excuse. Wait, grandfather? "Yeah, that was sad." She cast her eyes to the ground. She felt a little bad, playing Frances like this, baiting her for information on Trevor, but he never talked about himself.

"Oh, I know. Gutted, Mr. Blake was. Like peas in a pod, they were."

"Did his parents attend the funeral?"

"Mrs. Mags attended, of course." Frances stepped into the bathroom. She emerged a minute later with an armful of dirty towels.

Allie cast her eyes around the room, trying to think of what to ask next. "So, Trevor spent a lot of time with his grandpa?"

"Almost every holiday. Not like he had much choice, mind you."

"What about his parents? Why didn't he spend holidays with them?"

The older woman stiffened her spine. "I don't gossip. You'll have to ask Mr. Blake if you want those kinds of details."

"I did. You know he's never going to tell me. At least give me a hint. Or tell me why they got divorced in the first place."

Frances pursed her lips as though she'd sucked on a lemon and walked toward the door.

"What did Nigel do to Trevor?" Allie's words were rushed.

Frances took a deep breath and turned around. "I'll tell you this. There's a reason why Mr. Blake don't like seeing his parents none, but it's his tale to tell. Mrs. Mags expects you downstairs in half an hour. Going shopping for the wedding." With her head held high, she left the room.

---

Allie sipped her coffee and reached for her phone. She texted Brynn, saying she was sorry for missing breakfast but she would be home after school.

Brynn texted back that she had a club meeting and was going to study for a test with a friend afterward. Allie hoped it was true. Her little sister needed to socialize more. Brynnie seemed far too isolated these days.

Allie still planned to stop by the house, maybe throw together a quick dinner and stick it in the fridge. Her dad wasn't known for his cooking skills, and Allie hated the thought of them eating sandwiches while she dined on Mrs. Hubert's four-course meals.

After drinking her coffee, Allie stepped into the shower. As she stood beneath the warm spray of water, lathering her sex-sore body, thoughts of last night came pouring back. Trevor between her legs, Trevor touching her, sucking her, entering her from behind while she held on to the headboard for all she was worth. The last two days made up for the last four sexless years.

She donned a pretty bra and panty set to match her red-and-white polka-dot sundress. She slipped on a pair of kitten-heeled sandals and made her way to the foyer, where Mags waited for her.

"Good morning, darling." She kissed Allie's cheek. "The beef-cake chauffeur is waiting for us. Let's go." She donned enormous sunglasses and headed outside.

Allie trailed after her. Once they'd settled into the back of the limo, Allie avoided glancing at Mags and stared out the tinted window instead. How could she look at the woman when Allie kept thinking about the nasty, amazing sex she'd had with Trevor the night before? Awkward.

"Are you and Trevor having a spat, dear?"

Allie turned her head, her eyes wide. "No."

"Because he was terribly cross this morning. More so than usual, even."

Really? Allie would have guessed he'd be in a great mood—very sated and relaxed. Maybe she was the only one who thought the sex had been amazing. Earth shattering. Hotter than Vegas in the middle of August. What if it was just another shag to him?

"What's Nigel up to this morning?" Allie was desperate to change the subject.

Mags sighed. "He took breakfast in the bedroom. I'm afraid he's pouting, as the Blake men are prone to do."

"It's none of my business, Mags, but why is Trevor so angry at the two of you?" Normally she wouldn't have asked such a nosy question, but Trevor wouldn't tell her anything and neither would Frances.

The older woman said nothing for several seconds. Then she sighed. "The truth is, Nigel and I were never very attentive parents. I'm a passionate woman"—she placed her hand on her chest—"and Nigel is, well, let's just say he has extremely powerful lusts."

Allie almost winced. "I shouldn't have asked. It really is none of my business. I don't need to know the details—"

"When Trevor was young, Nigel and I were too caught up in our stormy relationship to give him the attention he needed." Mags carried on as if Allie hadn't spoken. Like mother, like son. "We divorced when Trevor was six. I remarried"—she flicked her wrist—"several times. And Nigel remarried too. Also several times." Her eyes narrowed briefly.

"Poor little Trevor got lost in the shuffle. I moved to Spain with one of my husbands, then to Australia with the next, to France, and finally to America. I just returned to England a year ago, where I reconnected with Nigel, and well, here we are."

Allie stared at Mags with an open mouth. "What about Trevor?" Was this why Trevor never spent holidays with his parents—no, screw holidays. How about every day? "Where was he during all this? With Nigel?"

Shifting her legs, Mags twisted the diamond rings on her fingers. "Trevor went to boarding school when he was eight. Nigel and I thought it would offer him some continuity. And of course, he stayed with my father until then and spent holidays there as well."

That was the grandfather, the one who watched old movies with Trevor. *Two peas in a pod.* Allie knit her brow. "Hang on, eight years old?"

Mags shrugged. "Boarding schools take children at a very young age. We thought it was for the best."

For whom? Allie tried to imagine what it would be like to have two completely self-absorbed parents send her away at the age of eight. Her parents had always been loving and caring, not only to her and her sisters, but to each other. Yes, her dad checked out mentally when her mom got sick, but before that, he'd been a good dad. Poor Trevor.

"Why didn't he stay with you during the holidays, Mags? Or Nigel?"

Mags swallowed. When she removed her sunglasses, her eyes were shiny with tears. As she blinked them back, her long lashes fluttered rapidly. "I realize I've been a horrible mother, Allie. I do know that. I feel it every time I'm in the same room with him. I've always been too involved in my own life, so has Nigel. That's why we're here. We want to set things right with Trevor. We want him to be a part of this wedding so that we can all move forward. A new beginning."

Allie shook her head and tried to keep the judgment out of her voice, but it was difficult. "I don't think it works like that." They had damaged Trevor, abandoned him. How could he just get over that and move on?

The limo stopped in front of Crystals. Simmons opened the door for them, and Mags replaced her glasses before exiting first. As she stood at the entrance, her smile seemed forced. She smoothed her hand down her tight blue dress. "Well, we'll just have to hope for the best with Trevor, won't we? I think I'll get married in red this time. I'm so tired of dreary white." She nodded at Simmons before strolling through the door.

---

"What about this one, darling?" Mags stepped out of the dressing room wearing a very short, red bandage dress with a plunging neckline.

Allie was speechless. "I hope you're not getting married in a church. That dress is sinful."

"I was thinking about having it in Trevor's garden." Mags turned around and viewed her backside in the three-way mirror. "Of course, I haven't told Trevor yet." She twirled around and faced Allie. "How do I look?"

Allie smiled. "Beautiful." In fact, Mags looked more sexy and voluptuous than ever. Perfect for a Vegas wedding.

Mags's hands drifted over her breasts, her flat tummy, and hips, then smoothed their way across her ass. "I don't like to brag, but I do look hot." She grinned. "Oh, darling, who am I kidding? I love to brag."

Allie smiled. That was such a Trevor thing to say. He was more like his mother than he realized.

"Now, what are you going to wear, Allison? How about something white and frothy? Like *Changing Rooms*, the bridal version?"

"I'm not sure what that means, but it's your wedding, Mags." Allie shrugged. She didn't want to wear something white and frothy. She wasn't sure she wanted to be in the wedding at all.

After hearing about Trevor's childhood, Allie understood his animosity toward his parents. And while she liked Nigel and Mags, Allie disapproved of them too. She felt protective of Trevor, didn't want to see him get hurt again. She knew he was a grown man, perfectly capable of taking care of himself, and she already had too many people to take care of. Still, she worried. That was the one thing she was good at.

Allie watched Mags and the saleswoman flit around the store while she remained in the comfy chair and sipped sparkling water. Mags indulged in champagne, but after yesterday, Allie was sticking to nonalcoholic drinks. She reached out to the mirror-covered square table and nabbed a toast point covered with caviar. After one bite, she grabbed a napkin and wrapped up the rest of it, sticking the whole thing back on the table. Sipping her water to rid herself of the fishy, salty taste, she heard her phone buzz and pulled it out of her purse.

"Where are you?" Trevor's tone was clipped and impatient. The exact opposite of last night. Then, his words—whispered in a husky, sexy accent—had shocked and excited her. But now he acted like it never happened. So, last night really hadn't meant anything to him.

Her heart skipped a couple beats. She was being stupid. For him, this was the norm—sex was just sex. He didn't attach any importance to it. But she felt like an idiot for being so satisfied and content this morning.

She took a deep breath. "I'm great, English, thanks for asking."

"Fine. Allison, how are you, darling? Well, I hope. Now, where in the bloody hell are you?"

"I'm in one of the most exclusive department stores in town, learning that caviar is disgusting and they should leave the poor fish eggs alone."

"You're shopping with my mother, then?"

"You got it, Slick." She leaned back over the tray of goodies and picked up another toast point, this one with pâté. She nibbled the edge. "Oh, this is fantastic. The caviar was horrible, but the pâté is delish."

She heard a long, deep sigh. "Don't ever call me Slick again, Miss…Allison. And the way you're moaning over that pâté has me as hard as a rock. Why don't you come home and take care of that for me?" Suddenly, she felt lighter. He'd been affected by the hot sex too. So glad to know she wasn't alone.

She smiled and sipped. "I think I'll stay right here. Besides, your mother is picking out a bridesmaid's dress for me."

"There's not going to be a wedding."

"She wants to have it in your garden. And you should see the dress she plans to wear. It's barely there and fire-engine red. Sorry, English, but I think there's going to be a wedding. And if your mother has her way, you'll be wearing a kilt." She smiled and hung up the phone. It was nice to get one over on him for a change.

Mags came back with a one-shouldered, ivory, beaded mini dress. "What about this, Allie, love?"

"I thought you were going with the red dress, Mags."

"Not for me, for you, dearest." Then she got a thoughtful look on her face. "Although, it is my size." She walked back over to the mirror and held it in front of her. She sighed. "No, this is for you. I'll get one in blue."

⌇⌇⌇

At two o'clock, Mags was still going strong and showed no signs of letting up. She actually liked trying on clothes. Allie left her in the capable hands of the saleswoman and let Simmons drive her to her home.

When he held the car door open for her, he tipped his head. "Just let me know when you're ready to be picked up."

Allie let herself into the house and glanced at the cluttered living room—clothes, shoes, newspapers covered every surface along with a fine coating of dust. In the kitchen, dirty pans littered the sink, there were cracked eggshells on the counter, and two bags of trash sat next to the back door.

Seriously? Her dad couldn't even take out the trash?

Trevor was right. Her family was fully capable of managing this stuff without her. Her dad especially. Allie wasn't their damned maid, and she wasn't even living at home anymore. Instead of clearing out the living room clutter, she would make a to-do list. But she wouldn't be able to function, thinking about the germs breeding in the kitchen.

With a sigh, she kicked off her shoes and began loading the dishwasher. She had just poured the dish soap when she heard the front door bang.

Allie grabbed a hand towel and strode to the living room, a smile on her face. Brynn made it home after all. But the smile faded when she saw it wasn't Brynn but Monica. She stood with her back to Allie, facing a guy in his mid-twenties. He rubbed his hands up and down Monica's ass and squeezed it like he was checking a ripe tomato.

"What the hell, Monica?"

Her sister jumped and spun around. The guy—Brad?—smirked.

Monica's eyes widened. "What are you doing here, Allie? Are you checking up on me?" She sounded defensive. Her clothes were wrinkled and she looked pale.

Allie narrowed her eyes. "That would be a little hard to do,' considering you've been gone for days and haven't bothered to let anyone know where you were."

Monica stepped toward her. "I don't have to check in with you. You're not the boss of me."

Allie crossed her arms. "Really? That's all you can come up with, 'you're not the boss of me'? How about acting like the responsible adult you think you are and letting Dad know you're still alive?"

Monica moved past her, slammed into Allie's shoulder, and

stormed to her room. Allie glanced at Brad. What an asshole. She supposed he was good-looking in a just-got-out-of-jail kind of way, with his longish blond hair and darker stubble.

He gave her the once-over, his eyes lingering on her breasts. "You, uh, must be the big sister."

"Yeah. And you must be the dick Monica's boning."

That wiped the smirk right off his face. "She said you were a bitch."

"Get out."

He crossed his arms. "Monica invited me in. According to her, you don't live here anymore. So, I have a right to be here."

Allie walked over to the phone and punched in 911. "Yeah, I'd like to report an intruder."

He sneered at her before turning to slam out the door.

She apologized to the dispatcher and hung up before making her way to the girls' room. Standing in the doorway, Allie watched Monica throw clothes into a duffel bag.

"Don't try and stop me, Allie."

"Is that possible? Or are you so far up Brad's ass, you can't even listen to reason?"

Monica paused, a T-shirt in her hand. "You know, when you came home from school, everyone was so grateful—Allie the Savior, taking care of the family. And you love it don't you? You love that Dad lets you make all the decisions. Makes you feel important. Well, you're not making my decisions, and if you try and stop me, I'll kick your ass."

Allie drew herself up, placed her hands on her hips. "You and who else?" Their eyes locked in a contest of wills. Monica backed down first and shoved the T-shirt in the bag.

"Are you even going to let Dad know where you'll be staying?" Allie asked.

"It's nobody's business. Besides, I don't want you guys coming over and nagging me to move back home." She crammed a handful of underwear in the bag.

Allie shook her head. "You're making the biggest mistake of your life, Mon. Don't do this—at least not until you graduate. You're so close to getting that diploma."

Monica zipped the bag and slung it over her shoulder. "I love him. I know you don't get that, because you're too busy being perfect to have a life, but we love each other. I want to be with him."

Allie took a deep breath and willed away the tears stinging the backs of her eyes. Yelling at her sister wasn't a good strategy. Allie walked into the room and tentatively touched Monica's hand. "Fine, but stay here until graduation. You only have one more month."

Monica shrugged her off. "You don't understand. I don't care about school. I have to be with him. I want him all the time, like I'll die without him. He wants me to move in with him and that's what I want too." She walked out of the room and headed toward the front door.

Allie followed her. Her sister was screwing up her life and there was absolutely nothing Allie could do to stop it.

Monica gripped the door handle but didn't look back. "Tell Dad I'll call in a few days."

And then she was gone.

# Chapter 12

WHEN SIMMONS PICKED ALLIE up, she climbed into the backseat of the limo with Mags, who rattled on about wedding details. Allie nodded, pretending to listen and mulled over the situation with Monica. She'd made a mistake letting Monica provoke her. Maybe if Allie'd been less confrontational, she could have at least learned Brad's last name.

When they stepped into the house, Frances stood in the foyer, waiting for them. She organized Simmons and Arnold as they schlepped the bags up the stairs, Mags trailing behind, yakking all the way.

Allie walked down the hall to Trevor's office. She hadn't seen him all day and she missed him—the biting wit, the too-handsome face, the sexual innuendo. She couldn't blame it on the champagne, since she'd had none. It must have been the toe-curling sex.

She softly knocked on the door and stuck her head inside. Trevor, seated behind his desk, glanced over and motioned her forward. A dark-haired man in a suit sat across from him.

Trevor rose and the man stood as well, buttoning his jacket. "Get back to me on the condos, Alex. By the way, this is Miss Campbell." He gestured to her. "Miss Campbell, Alex Pade, my attorney."

Alex shook her hand. "Pleasure."

"Nice to meet you." She stepped toward the center of the room and looked out at the garden. She'd never get any work done with a view like that.

Trevor followed Alex to the door and locked it, then strolled toward her slowly, with a predatory gleam in his eye. "You hung up on me, Allison."

Her heart began to pound. He was unpredictable when he was in this kind of mood. A mixture of wariness and excitement filled her. And he'd called her Allison in that deep, sexy voice. That made her stomach flutter. "You were in denial about the wedding. I assure you, your mother plans to go through with it."

"I don't give a fuck about the wedding. You hung up on me." He circled her. She turned her head, trying to track his movements.

He stopped behind her and whispered in her ear. "I think you deserve to be punished."

She nodded. "Probably."

He stepped in front of her. "What's wrong? What's happened?"

"Just more family drama. The kind you don't like hearing about, so please, continue with the lecture."

His lips twisted as he raised one brow. "I had something more exciting than a lecture in mind. But it's no fun when you're like this." He walked back to the desk and sat. "I'm waiting."

With a sigh, she flopped herself down in the chair across from him. "Monica came home with Brad the Douche. She packed her stuff and is moving in with him. I met him."

"I assume since you so eloquently referred to him as a douche, your fears about him weren't alleviated?"

"No. He's steeped in bad boy. He's every teen girl's fantasy."

"Did you manage to find out his last name?"

"No."

With his elbows on the desk, he linked his fingers, his eyes narrowed in thought. "What about a plate number?"

Allie blinked. "Like a license plate?" She slapped her forehead. "Shit, I didn't even think of that." God, she was a fuckup. First, she'd left Brynn high and dry this morning, then she'd blown it with

Monica. She should have looked out the window and made a note of what the douche was driving.

"It's all right, Allison."

She leaped to her feet. "No, Trevor, it's not all right. I was supposed to make Brynn breakfast this morning. I know that you don't understand how important that is, but trust me, it's important. She needs me right now, and I'm not there for her. My other sister is shacking up with a loser and dropping out of high school. What is she supposed to do with her life if she doesn't even have a high school education?" At some point, she'd started pacing back and forth in front of the desk. "And I don't know what to do about any of it. So please, oh wise one, who lives in a fucking mansion and has servants and weird-ass collectibles and a garden that costs more to water than I made in a year, how is everything all right?" She stopped to glare at him.

He glared back and rose from his seat. "It's not my job to fix your life any more than it's your job to fix your family's. And I've worked very hard for everything I have. And those weird-ass collectibles, as you put it, were my grandfather's. I don't need to apologize to you or anyone else for what I've acquired. So, fuck off."

She reeled back, felt like she was gasping for air. The man had no compassion, no human decency. Of course, it was no wonder, considering the two crazies who didn't bother to raise him. Still, that didn't excuse his stupid platitudes. She pointed a finger at him. "You fuck off, English." She turned and stalked to the door, but when she tried to open it, she couldn't.

"It's locked," he said coldly.

She spun around. "I know it's locked. I can see it's locked. I don't need you and your snotty British ass to tell me it's locked. Okay?" She unlocked the door, threw it open, and marched to her room.

Trevor thought about taking dinner in his office. It's what he was used to, and it would be a hell of a lot better than eating another meal with his parents. He bloody well didn't want to see Allison either. How dare she get angry with him because her life was shambolic? It wasn't his fault.

*Well, it's partly your fault.*

Fine. So he'd insisted that she come live with him instead of at home, where she could serve Brynn breakfast. What the bloody hell was so important about making breakfast anyway? Wasn't her father at least capable of doing that much? For God's sake, even Trevor could make toast and tea.

And yes, he had her car towed. And got her fired.

But Allie's life had been falling apart before Trevor came along. He'd forgiven her father's debt, paid off the house, paid the hospital bills. In fact, now that he thought about it, he was a goddamn saint. She should be thanking him. Instead, she paced in front of his desk, ranting like a madwoman.

No, he wouldn't cower in his office. This was his house, and the rest of them could go hang. They were the interlopers.

He shrugged on his suit jacket, adjusted his tie, and left his office. He found them in the drawing room, sipping on cocktails. His cocktails. His drawing room.

"Trevor, darling, come join us." Mags patted the sofa next to her. She wore a bright blue frock that showed too much cleavage, as usual. A large sapphire and diamond necklace decorated her neck.

"What can I get you to drink, Trev?" Nigel stood next to the drinks cart, an obnoxious grin on his face. *Wanker.*

"I'll fix myself something." He flicked a glance at Allison, sitting on the other sofa, her posture rigid. She made a point of not looking at him.

Things had been so good between them. What the hell had happened in less than twenty-four hours?

Her family issues, of course.

He gave his father a vicious smile and fought the urge to shove the old man out of the way. "Do excuse me, Father."

Nigel stepped aside. "Was just telling the ladies that we should go out for dinner some night this week. Vegas has some bloody decent restaurants. Maybe take in a show afterward. What do you say?"

Trevor splashed two fingers of single malt into a tumbler and took a healthy swallow. "I don't know why you people continue to include me in your plans. If I wanted your company, I'd have invited you here. When did you say you were leaving again?"

Nigel just toasted him. "Cheers, Trev."

Trevor ignored him and walked to the sofa. He dropped down beside Allie, his hip fitting snugly next to hers.

She pressed her lips together and glanced, not at him, but in the opposite direction, toward the mantel. "Do you mind? You're in my personal space."

He leaned toward her and whispered, "My cock was very much in your personal space last night. And you, darling, loved it." That got her attention.

She swung her head toward him. "Shut up," she said through clenched teeth.

"What's going on? You two having a tiff?" Nigel propped himself on the armrest next to Mags.

"I think they are, darling. Trevor was very cross this morning." Mags sipped her champagne, her eyes fluttering between them.

"It's time to eat." Trevor stood and offered his arm to Allie.

Glaring at him, she stood and slipped her arm through his. As they made their way to the table, Trevor leaned toward her. "I keep thinking about you, naked on the sofa. Shall we meet in the media room again this evening?"

"Fuck off," she said, her voice so low he barely heard her.

"That's exactly what I'm proposing."

Once in the dining room, he pulled out her chair and took his own seat at the head of the table. Nigel seated Mags, and Arnold served the salad.

"Allie and I went shopping for the wedding today. Are you still thinking about kilts for you and Trevor, love?" Mags gazed up at Nigel.

"Haven't decided. What do you think, Trev?"

Allie smiled at him. Her fake smile. The one that danced on his last nerve.

"I think you would look great in a kilt, *Trev*." She turned to Mags. "And have you told Trevor your wedding plans for the garden? I was thinking that tree next to the grotto might need to come down. That way, you'd have an unobstructed view of the waterfall." She forked a piece of lettuce in her mouth, looking rather smug as she chewed.

Sticking his hand beneath the table, he grasped her knee and squeezed gently. She grunted, her mouth full. "I don't see that as an option, do you, Miss Campbell?" He squeezed again, a little firmer this time as she tried to pull away.

"Oh, the grotto sounds lovely. And the waterfall would look beautiful in pictures, wouldn't it, love?" Mags asked Nigel.

He reached out and tapped her nose with a finger. "Whatever you want, Mags, it's yours."

Trevor let go of Allie's knee and watched her face. She gazed at Mags and Nigel with a longing he didn't understand. What was she thinking? Clearly, she didn't find them as annoying as he did.

As dinner progressed, his repulsive parents cooed at each other and Allie ignored him to poke at her food. Nothing pissed him off more than being ignored.

Trevor was about to squeeze her knee again when Arnold stepped into the room. "Miss Campbell, your sister has just arrived."

Allie jumped from her seat. "What? My sister's here?" She threw her napkin on the table and hurried toward the dining room door.

Trevor stood as well. "Which sister?"

"A very young girl, brown hair." Arnold glanced at Allie. "She had a suitcase with her."

Allie all but ran to the foyer, Trevor close on her heels.

Brynn stood near the front door, her eyes darting around the room. When she saw Allison, relief filled the girl's face. "Allie."

Allie grasped her by the shoulders. "Oh my God, what's wrong? How did you get here? Is Dad okay? What's wrong?" The words tumbled out of her, falling one on top of the other.

"I'm okay. I took a cab."

"Does Dad know you're here?"

"No." Brynn shook her head, her hair covering her face.

Trevor moved forward. "Why don't we take her to the salon upstairs? Arnold, would you be so good as to have Frances prepare a room and perhaps bring a tray of sandwiches?"

"Very good, sir."

Allie threw her arm around the girl's shoulders and followed him up the stairs. Trevor looked back and gave what he hoped was a reassuring smile. "I hear you had to join a school club? Ghastly, being a joiner." He shuddered. "So, what did you finally settle on?"

Brynn quickly glanced at him before her eyes bounced away. "Um, photography. I kind of like taking pictures."

"I'd like to see them sometime." Timid, she would be at home behind the camera, watching everyone around her, observing but never participating. Perhaps Allison was correct, Brynn did need her. But that didn't mean he was letting Allie go. The very thought made him... He grimaced. Fuck, he didn't know how he felt. But he wasn't ready to give her up. He reached the salon and held the door for the pair of them. "Ladies."

Brynn, her eyes wide, practically gawked as she twirled in a circle.

"Wow." She reached out and touched the bust of a long-forgotten Roman nobleman. "Is this for real?"

Allie guided Brynn to the leather sofa and lowered herself next to her sister. "Now, tell me what's happened. Why are you here, Brynn?"

Trevor stood with his back against the door, his arms crossed. He'd known Allie would be difficult, knew she came with a full set of family baggage. Well, this was what he got for his trouble—little sister turning up unexpectedly. But she wasn't so bad, really, this little girl. Could hardly be more of a pain in the ass than his own parents.

And Allie was very gentle with her, very loving. Allison Campbell was a good person. A great lay but a good person.

"I'm leaving home. I just want to be with you, Al." With her eyes cast to the floor, the poor girl looked miserable.

"Brynn," Allie said, "you know you're a terrible liar? You have a tell, kid."

Brynn's eyes drifted to Allie. "I do miss you."

"But?"

"Dad's dating."

Allie let out a little laugh. "Brynn, honey, that's crazy."

"He's seeing my guidance counselor, Ms. Castor. I overheard them talking on the phone last night. He was laughing, and he called her Karen."

"I'm sure you misunderstood. Maybe they were discussing you."

Brynn looked up then. "He's been gone two nights this week. He said he had some errands to run after dinner. You know Dad doesn't do errands, he leaves all that stuff to you. Mom's only been dead for like, six months. It's disgusting."

Allie glanced up at Trevor, her face ashen.

He pushed off the door and walked forward, taking a seat across from them. "You're welcome to stay here, Brynn. For as long as you need to. But you have to tell your father where you are."

Brynn looked at him like he was a god. "Thanks. But"—she turned to Allie—"can you do it? Call Dad, I mean? I don't really want to talk to him right now."

Allie gave her a wry look. "Yeah, I bet you don't."

"Are you mad?"

"No, but promise me you'll never leave home like this again. We already have one runaway in the family. Nobody likes a copycat, Brynnie."

He suddenly felt de trop. Standing, he made his way to the door. What possessed him to offer up his home to Brynn, he wasn't sure. But the poor little thing seemed so sad and lost, he couldn't possibly turn her away. Plus, Allie wouldn't be happy with her sister miserable at home. When Allison's happiness had become a priority, he didn't know, but for some reason, making Allie Campbell happy was suddenly very important to him.

He stood in the hallway and impatiently waited for Allie and her sister. Eventually, they emerged. Brynn looked a little better, but Allison looked worse, and she had that awful plastic smile affixed to her face.

"Brynn, love, Frances is waiting for you at the end of the corridor." He pointed down the hall. "She'll take you to your room. Let her know if you need anything."

Pressing her lips together, Brynn nodded, wrapped her arms around her middle, and walked down the hallway. When she was out of sight, Trevor turned to Allie. "I think I'm running a bloody hotel." Allie gave a little laugh and he smiled at the sound.

"Why don't you go ring your father? He must be worried sick." He grabbed her hand and laced their fingers together, leading her toward her room.

"I can't believe he's dating again. It's surreal, you know. We just lost my mom and he's ready to move on."

"Men tend to get over these things faster, plus, your mother was sick for a long time." The words were out of his mouth before he could pull them back.

Allie stopped in the middle of the hall. With a sigh, Trevor turned and faced her. "I'm terribly sorry. That was a callous thing to say."

She gazed up at him in the dim hall light. "Yeah, it was."

He lifted her hand, kissing the back of it. "I'm sure he loved your mother very much."

She glanced up at the ceiling and flattened her lips. "Sorry I yelled at you today. It wasn't your fault. I was frustrated, and I took it out on you." She sighed and shifted her focus to him.

Trevor lifted one shoulder. "No harm done." He leaned forward and placed a small kiss on the corner of her lips. "Go call him. I'll be in the office if you need me."

⁓⁓⁓

Taking a deep breath, Allie willed herself to calm down. She'd already flown off the handle with one family member today—better not make the same mistake twice.

She grabbed her cell and called home. When no one picked up, she tried his phone. He answered on the third ring. Allie could hear loud voices and laughter in the background. "Hello?"

"Dad, it's Allie. Where are you?"

"Hey, Al, I'm kind of in the middle of something. Can I call you back?"

"Brynn's here. She took a cab to Trevor's and she's spending the night. I'll make sure she gets to school in the morning and then I'll come by the house. We need to talk." She hit the end button and frowned.

What the hell was going on? Her father wasn't worried sick. He didn't even know Brynn had left. One daughter missing and the other had run away. And her dad was out on a fucking date. Unbelievable.

She had done her best to take care of her family—she'd failed miserably, but at least she tried. What had her dad been doing? He'd left everything to Allie and lost the business. Didn't he give a damn about all that Allie had sacrificed for her sisters? For him?

It hurt like hell, feeling used.

Immediately, she regretted the thought. She didn't quit school and take care of her mom and sisters because she wanted her dad's gratitude. She did it because it was the right thing to do.

*But it was time to reclaim her own life.*

She squelched that little voice in the back of her head. This *was* her life. She had chosen it, no one had forced it on her.

That didn't mean she wasn't still pissed. Of course her dad deserved a life, especially after what he had gone through with her mom, but it was well past time that he picked up the slack at home.

She left her room, intending to check on Brynn. In the hallway, she met Mags and Frances, the latter carrying a tray of food.

"I'm taking a nibble to your sister. I brought an extra cup because I thought you'd want to join her. Mr. Blake said to make sure you eat a sandwich since you barely touched your dinner. He was very adamant."

Of course he was. "Thanks, Frances."

Mags held up a champagne bottle and a glass. "I thought I'd join in too, dearest. Come along." Holding the bottle aloft, she wiggled her ass down the hall, leaving Allie and Frances lagging behind.

Brynn's room was in the same wing as Allie's but around the corner. Painted a pretty shade of robin's-egg blue, it was a little bit smaller than Allie's room, with no sitting room attached.

Brynn sat on the bed with her knees drawn up, her arms tightly hugging them. She watched Mags with wide eyes.

"Hello, my dearest." Mags patted Brynn's cheek before kicking off her designer heels and lowering herself to the bed. "We've decided to keep you company. What fun."

Brynn's eyes skittered to Allie with a WTF look.

"Brynn, this is Mr. Blake's mother, Mrs..." Allie stalled, unable to remember Mags's last last name.

"Call me Mags, my little cherub."

Frances poured tea and handed out sandwiches. "You poor lamb," she said to Brynn. "Press nine on that phone if you need anything at all." She whisked the tray off the dresser and was gone a moment later.

Mags sipped from her flute. "That woman is priceless. Now, what is wrong with you, my pet?"

Brynn opened her mouth to speak, closed it, and looked helplessly at Allie.

"Brynn just needs a little time to settle in, Mags," Allie said.

Mags tsked. "Now, children, don't try to hide the truth from me. I'll just have to force Frances to tell me, and then she'll feel guilty for being a tittle-tattle."

With a sigh, Allie briefly explained her family's situation and Monica's recent departure with bad boy Brad.

"Allie, dearest, why didn't you tell me all this?" Mags asked.

"I didn't want to unload my problems onto you. Anyway, Brynn's upset because my dad has started dating—"

"My guidance counselor, Ms. Castor."

Mags put her arms around the girl's shoulders. "So many changes," she said.

In a move that surprised Allie, Brynn buried her head in the crook of Mags's shoulder and cried. Trevor's mother petted Brynn's hair and murmured soothing sounds. After several minutes, Brynn finally pulled away, her face splotchy and damp. "What did Dad say? Was he mad that I left?"

Not wanting to hurt Brynn further by telling her the truth, Allie lied—seemed like she was doing a lot of that lately. "He was fine with your staying here for the night."

Brynn looked relieved. "Thanks, Al."

Picking up her champagne glass, Mags raised an eyebrow. "Now finish your tea, girls, and eat something."

Brynn went for the cookie first. "What are these called?"

"Jammie Dodgers," Allie said. "They're Trevor's favorite."

—⁓—

The next morning after breakfast, Allie showed Brynn the garage. Simmons gave her the grand tour and Allie didn't know if her sister was more impressed with the cars or the hot blond chauffeur. When he was through showing Brynn the classic roadster, he tossed Allie the keys to the Mercedes.

"So, what do you do for Mr. Blake?" Brynn asked Allie as she climbed into the car.

"Oh." Allie stalled while she buckled her seat belt. "Answer letters, bring him tea."

"Why can't Arnold or Frances bring him tea?"

Allie swung the car around the circular drive. "They're busy running the household."

"Oh. He seems okay. I mean, it's nice of him to let me stay and everything," Brynn said. "Are you in love with him or something?"

"Of course not," Allie snapped. "What would make you say that?" She quickly scanned her memory from last night. Had she done something that would give Brynn the impression that she and Trevor were involved? She came up blank. Facing forward, she pulled out onto the street.

"I don't know. I just thought last night, when we were talking to him in that salon place, the two of you sort of seemed like a couple."

Allie didn't say anything else as she drove Brynn to school, but her heart was pounding. A couple? No, they weren't a couple. She was temporary. This whole situation was just temporary.

She pulled up to the school and turned to her sister. "Good luck on your English test."

Brynn grabbed her backpack off the floor. "It's a biology test and thanks."

"Right, sorry." Allie had English on the brain.

Brynn stepped out of the car and slipped the pack on her shoulder before leaning her head back inside. "Are you going to pick me up after school?"

"I might be out with Mags, so maybe Simmons will have to pick you up?"

Brynn's face turned almost purple. "'Kay." She slammed the door and trotted into the building.

Oh no. Brynn had it bad for Simmons. Allie closed her eyes. She couldn't worry about Brynn's crush right now either. She needed to deal with her dad before he left for work.

She pulled out of the school lot and drove home. Without bothering to knock, Allie walked into the house and found her dad whistling to himself in the kitchen. His salt-and-pepper hair had been freshly cut, and his cheeks were smooth and stubble free for a change.

"Hey," she said, placing her keys on the counter.

He stopped pouring coffee into a travel mug and set down the pot. "How's Brynn?" He grinned at her.

"Seriously? Your middle daughter drops out of high school and moves in with her boyfriend. Your youngest daughter runs away, and you're 'how's Brynn'?" She hadn't meant to start with accusations, but damn it, she was pissed. He acted like he didn't have a care in the world.

The smile slid off his face. "I didn't know she was gone because she sneaked out. And she's going to be punished for it when she gets home."

"Why? You never punished Monica. Besides, she doesn't need punishment, she needs your attention."

He picked up the carafe of coffee and continued to fill his mug. "I made mistakes with Mon, and I don't plan to repeat them with Brynn. Besides, Monica's an adult. Karen thinks we should give Brynn some space right now, but she needs boundaries and consequences."

"*Karen* thinks she needs boundaries? Brynn's guidance counselor?" She crossed her arms, felt her muscles lock in place. "Well, Karen can fuck off."

Brian moved toward her, his lips pressed into a thin line, his finger in Allie's face. "You don't talk to me like that. This is my house and I'm still your dad. My private life isn't any of your business." He dropped his hand, took a deep breath, and stepped back.

His house? It wouldn't be his house if she hadn't agreed to sleep with Trevor. And it wasn't her business? Everything that happened to this family was her concern. Pain spread through her chest—but that pain quickly turned to anger. "No, Dad, it became my business when I moved back home and started taking care of Mom, the girls, the house." She uncrossed her arms and waved them around the kitchen. "I've been holding this family together because you've been too wrecked to do it. I came over yesterday—you couldn't even take out the goddamned trash. Suddenly, you're talking about boundaries?" She shoved a finger into her chest. "I've been picking up the slack around here, not you. I've been making all the tough choices. So, yeah, I think I'm entitled to have an opinion. And dating Brynn's guidance counselor when Mom just died? Not cool."

She had given up everything for this family, and now that he had a girlfriend, Allie's sacrifice didn't matter. She'd had to make the hard decisions while he dealt with his grief. But apparently, his grieving time was over and he'd replaced Allie's mom so fast it was a slap in the face.

He scrubbed his hands over his cheeks and then stuck them in the pockets of his faded jeans. "I know I haven't been acting like much of a father lately. I've put too much on you, Al. Parentalizing you, Karen calls it, making you the parent instead of me. I'm sorry about that."

She shook her head and pressed her lips together. It was like looking at a stranger. What was wrong with him? "So, you're talking about our family to your new girlfriend?" She pivoted on her heel and began moving from the fridge to the back door. She had gone all in and lost. Her dad was moving on, Monica was a disaster, and Brynn would be subjected to a woman she couldn't stand. Allie'd made this deal with Trevor—for what? None of it mattered.

She turned to her father. "Brynn doesn't want this. Don't you care about that? Think about how she's going to feel with a new woman around here, telling her what to do, psychoanalyzing everything she does. You barely paid her any attention in the last six months, now all of your attention is going to be on this Karen." She was panting and her throat felt tight.

He sighed and shook his head. "Brynn will come around. Karen's a nice lady, and I really like her. She makes me happy."

Allie laughed bitterly. "Happy? Who's fucking happy?" Tears filled her eyes, and she couldn't seem to catch her breath. "You know what? You're selfish—"

"I'm selfish? How the hell am I selfish, Allison?" He unpocketed his hands, thrust them toward her. "I watched the woman I love die. Slowly, painfully. For five long years." Tears began rolling from his bloodshot eyes. "I can only hope and pray that Monica comes to her senses, but I can't force her to come home. I know I've been unfair to you, burdening you, and all right, that was selfish. But wanting to move on with my life? Wanting to find love again?"

Allie wiped the back of her hand across her nose. "No, you need to care about your family for once. Maybe focus on your daughters for a change. But you only care about your sex life and that makes you worse than selfish, Dad. And Brynn can stay with me as long as she likes, since I'm the only one who gives a damn." She ran out of the house, slamming the door behind her.

# Chapter 13

"WHAT DO YOU THINK of Allie's dress, dearest?" Mags sauntered into the office.

Trevor glanced up from the computer screen. "Sorry?"

Mags held a dress by the hanger. "Allie's dress? For the wedding?"

"She's wearing white? I thought that was the bride's prerogative. Look, I'm very busy. I don't have time for this right now."

She held the dress in front of her and examined it. "I'm tired of white. I'm wearing red this time. Plus, Allie looks stunning in it."

"Mmm hmm." Trevor dismissed her and the wedding from his mind and returned to the stock analysis.

"Although, I think Allie would make a lovely bride."

There was always the risk in buying a stock on its way down. Most likely it would go lower still, but Trevor always trusted his gut and his gut told him to buy.

"I want to be a grandmother."

He bought a few hundred shares, sat back, and smiled. He didn't care for gambling in the casinos that much, but he loved gambling in the market. It was a rush to prove the experts wrong.

"How many do you think you'll have?" she asked.

What was she on about? Oh yes, Allie's dress. "What does Allie think?"

Mags glided into a chair. "How would I know, darling?"

"Well, didn't you have her try it on?"

With her head tilted to one side, Mags smiled. "You haven't been listening to a word I've said, have you? Just like your father."

He pierced her with a look. "I'm nothing like him."

"Oh, darling, why can't you forgive him?"

"I don't wish to discuss this. As I've said, I'm busy." He clicked his mouse, shifted to another monitor, and looked at the cost projections for a design team that wanted to borrow money. Didn't seem like a good fit.

"He's made mistakes. But he's sorry. Do make up with him."

"He married Anna. I'm not likely to forgive that any time soon."

Mags flicked her fingers. "I'm not thrilled with his choice either, but you and Anna had broken up."

"Yes, that was kind of him to wait. Would have been damned awkward if she and I had still been fucking."

She took a deep breath, her lip pursed. "He's changed, Trevor darling. I promise."

Trevor assumed a neutral expression. "I don't really care one way or the other. When are the two of you leaving, by the way?"

He picked up his phone and texted Allie, wondering how the talk had gone with her father. Probably a disaster—much like the conversation he was having right now. Parents were nothing but a pain in the ass.

"Not until after the wedding."

"Mother please, we both know there's not going to be a wedding. Go back to England or, better yet, Italy. You've not had an Italian yet, and you do love the warm weather." He picked up his cup and took a sip of coffee.

"I think you and Allie should have a Christmas wedding. Think of how much fun that would be. She could wear a white dress trimmed in fur." Mags clapped her hands.

Trevor choked, coughing for a full minute. "How did we get from your marrying an Italian to my marrying Allie? Which is never going to happen, by the way." He set his cup down with a little more force than was necessary.

"Why not? She's a lovely girl. She's caring and kind. She'll give me beautiful grandchildren."

Trevor eyed her with irritation. "You were a dreadful mother. What makes you think you'd be a better grandmother?"

Mags winced, almost imperceptibly, but Trevor saw it. He'd hurt her. Too bad. She'd never given a damn about him. He rubbed at his sternum and pulled a roll of antacids from the desk drawer, popping a couple in his mouth. This fucking ache in the middle of his chest was growing tiresome. "I need to get back to work."

"Yes, of course, darling." She rose from the chair and grabbed the dress before she exited the office.

Trevor watched her go and pushed any guilt he was feeling to the side. What did he have to feel guilty for? After all, he hadn't abandoned *her*.

His phone vibrated. He glanced at the brief text from Allie. Things hadn't gone well with her father. He wasn't surprised. No man liked to be told whom he should date.

---

Allie's mind went over her father's words. He wanted to be happy. Of course he did. But at what price? Brynn had two and a half more years at home. She shouldn't have to spend it with her dad's girlfriend. Seeing the woman at school and home? Every kid's nightmare. Why couldn't her dad understand that? His newfound happiness came at the expense of his daughters.

Allie rubbed her forehead as she drove. She still needed to find out Brad's last name and where Monica was staying. Trevor had hired a detective. Maybe he had some information by now.

When Allie arrived at the mansion, she met Frances in the foyer. "Did Mags want to go shopping today?" Aside from the actual shopping, Allie enjoyed spending time with Trevor's mom. She was funny and charming, despite the constant wedding talk.

"Mrs. Mags is in the garden."

"Thank you." Allie wandered outside and found Mags sitting on a bench under an arbor covered with bright pink flowers. This early in the morning, the temperature was mild and the sun felt good on her skin. "These are pretty." Allie touched a whisper-soft, cone-shaped petal.

"It's a pink trumpet vine," Mags said. She seemed distracted as she stared blindly at the tinkling fountain in front of her.

Allie hovered near the arbor for a minute. When Mags didn't acknowledge her, she moved toward the house. "I'll leave you alone."

"No, I'm sorry, dearest. Do come sit." She patted the bench. "But I warn you, I'm not very good company today."

Allie settled in next to Mags. The garden was so peaceful. She could see why Trevor kept it, despite the cost. "It's beautiful here. Almost doesn't seem real."

"Yes, quite."

Allie closed her eyes, listened to the birds chirp, the splash of the fountain. Inhaling deeply, she sighed. She could almost relax—if only she could forget her problems.

"He hates me, you know."

Opening her eyes, Allie turned to Mags. "What?"

"Trevor. He hates me, well, really, both of us. I can't blame him. We've been quite useless as parents."

Allie reached out and touched Mags's hand. "He doesn't hate you."

"We probably deserve it. I am worried for him though, that he'll wind up bitter and alone. But you're good for him, Allie. You're the light to his darkness." Mags squeezed Allie's hand and looked at her with a sad smile. "Please don't hurt him. His heart is very fragile, you see."

Fragile? Trevor? He was sarcastic and uncaring. He was a hardened businessman who got what he wanted.

*Then why had he let Brynn stay? Why did he offer to find Brad?*

Because he wasn't totally hardened. That didn't make him fragile, though. Just made him…Trevor.

Withdrawing her hand, Allie shook her head. "Trevor and I aren't like that." She contemplated the fountain, some kind of sea serpent with a twisted body and water shooting out of its mouth. "I mean, we don't have that kind of a relationship."

"Don't let him fool you, dearest. He cares for you. I can tell."

"Well, I think he cares for you too, Mags."

"All right," Mags sniffed, "that's enough. Self-pity is dreary and I'm tired of it. I think we should go cake tasting. I want something spectacular, with so much fondant, my teeth will ache." She stood and looked around. "You're right, it is beautiful. My son has very good taste."

Allie stood as well and smoothed down her skirt. "Do I have time to stop in and see Trevor first?"

"Yes. I'll get ready and meet you in the foyer in an hour."

They parted once they entered the house, and Allie made her way to Trevor's office, but for once he wasn't there. She found Frances in the Asian room.

"Is Trevor home?"

The maid adjusted a sword on the wall, then shifted a porcelain bowl to the left. "He's at the indoor pool."

"I didn't know there was an indoor pool."

"In the very back of the garden, toward the bougainvillea and to the left. It's a glassed-in structure."

Allie really needed to take time and explore the garden—the rest of the house too. There were probably a dozen rooms she had never seen. Trevor's room in particular. But surely she would have seen a bloody glassed-in pool. Uh-oh. She was picking up Englishisms.

She walked outside, took a left at the red bougainvillea, which climbed up the brick wall. She picked her way through the narrow flagstone pathway and finally saw it—a glass rectangle, completely surrounded by shading palm trees, like an oasis.

When she stepped inside, the warm, moist air hit her and the smell of chlorine was strong. She watched Trevor cut through the bright blue water with powerful strokes. A pair of lounge chairs and a table stood off to the side, and Allie made herself comfortable until he was finished.

He must have seen her out of the corner of his eye because as soon as he touched the end of the pool closest to her, he dipped his hair back in the water, then leaned his forearms on the concrete. "Take your clothes off and come for a swim."

Rivulets of water slid down his broad shoulders and she was more than tempted. "I can't," she said, forcing her gaze from his chest to his face. "I have a date with Mags."

He rolled his eyes and sank beneath the surface. He reemerged a few seconds later and hoisted himself out of the pool.

Allie followed his movements as he toweled his chest. He rubbed circles around his pecs, his nipples were hard, and she remembered flicking her tongue over them the other night. He had groaned when she did it and demanded she do it again. Her eyes dipped lower. The navy swim trunks rode low over his hips, showing off the hard ridges of his abdomen. Her fingers itched to touch him again.

Trevor walked forward and, reaching out, palmed her cheek. "If you keep that up, I'll bloody well fuck you right here and now."

Shivering at his touch, she peered up at him, wanted to lick every inch of his body. But that would take longer than an hour— well, if she did it right. Letting her eyes roam over him, she noticed his hard cock was good to go. "We're in a glass pool house. Anyone could see us."

"I'm willing to take that risk. With Brynn staying here, I can't sleep with you at night. My mother's commandeering most of your day. Are you trying to kill me?"

"It's killing me too, but I have to meet your mother in an hour." That refusal should have sounded firmer. But looking at Trevor practically naked…and wet—it melted her resolve.

Although she and Trevor had been together only a few times, she missed him. Missed those hot lips on her skin. Missed his wandering fingers and his talent for finding new erogenous spots. The man had skills.

And while she should be self-conscious about the transparent walls, instead, she was completely turned on. She doubted anyone would come looking for them, but the possibility made it a little naughtier.

Trevor tossed the towel back on the table and leaned down. Cupping the back of her head, he whispered against her lips, "I can do a lot in an hour." He kissed her then. Not the demanding kisses from the other night. Tender and coaxing, this kiss seduced her. She leaned back against the lounger and he followed her, placing his knee between hers. His leg and swim trunks left her skirt wet, but she hardly noticed. Though his skin was cool, his touch heated her as his free hand caressed her neck, tracing over her collarbone and skimming the tops of her breasts. Craning her neck, she kissed him back and clutched his shoulders.

She wanted this, needed it. It was the only thing that felt right lately, being in Trevor's arms. That didn't make sense, but it was true. She felt like herself with him. Her old self, before she had so many responsibilities. Free and alive and young. She liked feeling this way. Even if it was only temporary.

He gradually pulled away, releasing her. She slid her hands down his shoulders, still slick with water, over his arms to his wrists. "Forty-five minutes. I'll have to shower and change."

"Deal," he said. Allie stood and quickly shed her clothes while Trevor peeled the wet trunks from his hips.

Feeling like a seductress, she sprawled on the lounger and raised her arms above her head, drawing his gaze to her breasts. She knew he liked watching her, so she lowered one hand and placed her index finger in her mouth. Allie almost grinned as she watched his cock lengthen in response. Trevor grasped it in his hand and gave a tug. She liked watching him as well.

Pulling her finger from her mouth, she drew it down her chest and around her areola. Then she cupped her breast and pinched the nipple. Hard.

Trevor groaned and gave his cock another slow stroke. "You know I love it when you do that."

"I know," she said. "Come here, English." His eyes darkened and his breath became labored. She loved that she had that effect on him. Made her feel like a goddess.

In a hot second, he lowered his body onto hers, thrust his hands into her hair, and kissed her. Reaching down, Allie grasped his cock, rubbed her thumb over the head. His hips were still chilly and damp. It felt good against the muggy air.

Trevor licked his way down her throat and latched on to one of her breasts. "Please suck harder." When he obliged, she moaned in pleasure.

Before she was ready, he'd left her breasts and kissed a trail to her stomach. He stopped at her hipbone, biting hard enough to make her gasp. "Trevor."

"Spread your legs wider," he said. "I want to see you."

Allie flattened her knees to each side, opening herself to him. "Lick me." She didn't ask timidly this time, she demanded.

He glanced up at her. With his hair slicked back and his face flushed, he seemed wilder than before. Maybe it was the atmosphere, maybe it was the filtered sunlight, but the lust in his eyes heightened her own desire. "Lick you where, Miss Campbell?"

"My pussy. I want your tongue on my pussy."

He grinned then. "You're learning." He lowered his head and licked the length of her.

Allie grabbed a fistful of his wet hair and closed her eyes. Yes, she'd definitely missed Trevor. Normally he took his time—long, slow swipes of his tongue as he buried his fingers deep inside her— but today he didn't linger. He lapped at her quickly, his tongue darting into her, twirling in a fast circle. It felt amazing, and when he moaned against her, the vibrations from his voice sent shivers racing across her heated skin. Then he pinched her clitoris. The sensation was overwhelming and she shattered a few moments later. Letting go of Trevor's hair, she clutched the sides of the lounger, crying out. The sound echoed through the tiled room.

While she recovered, Trevor gave her one last taste before rubbing his cheek against her inner thigh. "I don't have a condom with me," he said, gazing up at her.

Allie reached down and ran her hand over his damp hair. "Finish what you started the other night."

He frowned until she pressed her breasts together. "You want me to fuck your tits?"

She nodded. She wanted to take him like this, felt herself growing wet again just thinking about it.

"I'm going to come this time, Allison."

"Seems fair," she said, still panting. That orgasm had left her a little dizzy as it ripped through her body.

Trevor moved up the lounger and, grabbing hold of the headrest, slowly slid his dick between her full breasts. "God, yes."

With his brows drawn, Trevor peered down, watching himself glide between her tits. A look of intense pleasure crossed his features before he closed his eyes. "You feel incredible." He increased the pace, thrusting forward and back. "I'm going to come, Allison." His body tightened as he shot a long stream onto her chest, another rope of come landed on her neck. Still, he continued to piston his hips.

Once he pulled away, Allie let go of her breasts. "I need another forty-five minutes with you, love." He leaned down and kissed her forehead. As he moved to grab his discarded towel, he kept his eyes trained on her.

To tease him, Allie rubbed her middle finger along her breastbone, swirling his semen in a circle and dragging it over her nipple. "Too bad you'll have to make due with a quickie."

He closed his eyes for a second and licked his lips. "God, you drive me insane. You know I'm going to be thinking about this moment for the rest of the bloody day."

She liked that she sent him over the edge, distracted him. "I hope so."

He lowered himself to the lounger and nudged her hip aside until she scooted over. With gentle strokes, he wiped his come from her chest. "How are we doing on time?"

Allie's hand trailed over his leg. "I think we're good."

Trevor tossed the towel aside and stretched out beside her. Throwing an arm around her waist, he nuzzled her ear. "I take it things didn't go well with your father this morning?"

She shook her head and petted his forearm. "No. Not even a little bit. Is it okay if Brynn stays a few more days? I know it's not what you had in mind when we made this bargain—"

"Allison."

She stopped talking and glanced over at him. His spiky black eyelashes emphasized the light gray, almost silver, irises. The black band that edged the lighter shade provided a striking contrast. She could lose herself in those eyes.

He bent his head and ran the tip of his tongue across her lower lip and briefly sucked it into his mouth. Leaning back a fraction, he remained close, their lips almost touching, but not quite.

"I told you Brynn could stay as long as she needs to. It's fine. In fact, I'll meet the two of you for tea in the conservatory."

She smiled.

The smile he gave her in return, a genuine smile that formed little commas next to his mouth, caused her heart to skip a beat.

"I love these cookies," Brynn said. She was the most relaxed Trevor had ever seen her. The girl would always be shy by nature, but she seemed to be getting used to him. She smiled, and her gaze darted away, settling on the fountain. "And thank you for the gift card and docking station. That was nice of you."

He wanted to make sure she was comfortable. Allie had mentioned the girl liked listening to her iPod, so he simply instructed Frances to get what was needed. It was nothing, really, yet by the look on her bright red face, Brynn was pleased. "You're most welcome. And the biscuits are British, of course." Arnold only served them for Allie and Brynn.

In fact, both sisters had Arnold wrapped around their fingers. With great flair, he'd presented them with little frosted fairy cakes, their initials written in pink icing. Trevor didn't get a little cake with his initials. When Allie and Brynn moved out, his butler might very well decide to go with them.

He frowned and pushed the thought aside. The very idea of Allison not living here made him uneasy. She wouldn't always be here, but the when of it was his decision. And right now, he wanted her here. In his bed. Straddling him.

With a sigh, he shifted in discomfort. He needed to be inside Allie again. As soon as possible. The brief excursion in the pool house had only whetted his appetite, rather than easing it.

Trevor grabbed a biscuit. The fountain tinkled softly in the background. This really was a most peaceful room. The air was cool and dry and the flowers gave off a heady perfume. Maybe this should become a ritual, taking a few minutes out of the day to have tea with Allie.

She smiled at him. "Your mother finally picked a wedding cake."

He threw her a droll look. "Excellent. I've worried myself silly over it." He popped the last of the biscuit in his mouth and then wiped his hands on the napkin. "Do try the watercress sandwiches, Brynn. They're quite nice."

Brynn plucked one from the tiered tray and peered at it with suspicion. "What's watercress?" She lifted the top layer of bread and sniffed the sandwich.

"Watercress is an herb. Served on these tiny, crustless sandwiches at teatime." He picked one off the tray and took a bite. "Mmm." He closed his eyes and smiled.

Brynn laughed and took a small bite. After chewing a few times, she shrugged. "It's all right," she said.

"Well, they can't all be Jammie Dodgers."

"She's getting red velvet to match her red dress," Allie said.

Trevor sighed and glanced at her. She'd changed into a peach-colored dress and her bra pushed her breasts up and outward. The memory of this morning, working his cock between those lovely tits, made him hard. Slowly his gaze traveled to her eyes, which he found glaring at him. Whoops. Wouldn't do to be caught gaping in front of Brynn. Still, if Allie didn't want her breasts to be admired, she shouldn't put them on display—but he very much enjoyed it when she did.

"Did you hear me?"

"Yes, darling, red velvet."

Brynn, who had been looking over the tray of food, paused. "You call your assistant darling?"

Trevor noticed Allie turning a lovely shade of pink. It made him smile. "I call everyone darling. Darling."

"It's a British thing," Allie said. By the downward turn of those lush lips, he knew his little slip had upset her. She could rail at him later. In fact, he looked forward to it.

He drained his cup and stood. "Well, ladies, delightful as always, but I must get back to work."

"Mr. Blake, there are some things we should go over soon." Allie gave him a hard stare.

"Of course, Miss Campbell. I'm at your disposal."

Trevor left the conservatory with a smile. But when he walked into his office and saw his father looking over the brass armillary sphere sitting on the bookshelf, the smile turned into a scowl. "What do you want, old man?" He walked to his desk and settled into the chair behind it.

"We need to talk," Nigel said, spinning one of the rings.

"I can't imagine why." He kept his gaze trained on his computer screen.

"Trevor, we've done this bit. I know I've been a bastard. And I am sorry. For all of it, Son."

"Well and good. Close the door on your way out, would you?"

Nigel stopped fondling the sphere and walked toward the desk. "Your mother very much wants the wedding to be a family affair."

"You've always been particularly good at affairs."

Sighing, Nigel fell into a chair with careless grace. "Are you ever going to get over Anna?"

"Oh, do me a favor," Trevor said, disgusted. Over Anna? He was over that slag long before his father came sniffing around. Still, it was bad form. Man's code and all that. But what did he expect from such a tosser?

"I'm sorry I hurt you, Trev. And I'm sorry I wasn't a better father to you. But Mags and I would like to try and make it up to you."

Trevor batted his lashes. "Are you going to buy me a pony?"

Nigel scratched his jaw with one hand. "I know we haven't been the best of parents. The memories you have aren't all pleasant ones, but there were good times, you know."

"Mmm, yes. Remember my sixth birthday party? In the middle of opening presents, Mother accused you of fucking around. You went tearing off in your sports car, she proceeded to get drunk on champagne and cry hysterically. One for the memory books."

Nigel rubbed a hand over his mouth and shifted his eyes to the left. "Yes, well, you're not six anymore. This is for your mother, Son."

"I've missed most of her weddings." Trevor paused and stroked his chin. "No, I take that back. I've missed all of her weddings. Yours too, in fact. Why should this one be any different?"

Nigel stood and straightened his suit jacket, tugged at his cuffs. "You will be there. You will give your mother this, and she will be happy." With a stiff back he left the office, slamming the door behind him.

Trevor gripped the armrests on the chair and sneered. It was always about their happiness. His mother was little more than an incubator and his father, a sperm donor. Why didn't they just leave him the hell alone?

When Allie came in seconds later, he hadn't begun to rein in his anger.

"What's wrong with your dad? I just ran into him in the hall and he seemed really upset." She knitted her brow and approached the desk. "Trevor, what happened?"

He tapped a few keystrokes and brought a prospectus up on the screen. "I keep getting fucking interrupted and I'm busy. Get out." He knew it wasn't fair to unleash his anger on her, but he didn't want to be bothered just now. He was tired of his parents and their infernal wedding chatter. Tired of not being able to shag Allison whenever he bloody well wanted. Tired of having so many people invade his office.

Instead of heeding him, she sighed and walked over to the desk, hopped on top of it, and tilted her head forward, looking at his screen. "I talked to your mom today."

"I'm sure it was a riveting conversation. What do you want?"

"I wanted to remind you to take it easy around Brynn. I don't want her to think I'm anything but your assistant."

He still didn't look at her. This investment expected a twelve percent rate of return. No one could guarantee twelve percent in this economy, no matter how aggressive. He didn't trust it. And he always trusted his gut. *Except when it came to Brian Campbell and his beautiful daughter.*

"Fine, no more slipups in front of Brynn."

"Have you heard from the private detective? Does he have any news about Brad?"

"When I know something, you'll know something. Are we through?"

She opened her mouth to speak but hesitated. "About the wedding—just because you don't want to hear about it, doesn't mean it's going to go away."

His mouth kicked up on one side as his gaze took her in from head to toe. "You look good in that color, love. Use that credit card I gave you and go find something in the same shade. You can show me later." He dismissed her by picking up his BlackBerry and punching out a text.

Allie reached over and grabbed the phone from of his hand. She remained unfazed at his withering glare. "Your mother thinks you hate her, Trevor."

"She wouldn't be wrong." Standing, he reached for the phone and plucked it out of her hands. "I have business to take care of right now, Allison."

"You have to make this right. I know they hurt you, but she's your mom."

He smiled, felt his lips pull up at the edges. "I don't have to do anything. And I think you've forgotten your place in the scheme of things, darling. You're a fuck toy, not my conscience. Now, run along."

# Chapter 14

THREE DAYS. THREE DAYS and she hadn't dropped that plastic smile once, at least not in his presence. It was enough to make him mental. And why didn't anyone else notice? Even Brynn was oblivious to the fact that her sister was miserable.

And it was his fault.

Trevor knew he'd gone too far the instant he said *fuck toy*. He'd been cruel, thoughtless. He was a bloody bastard.

After he said it, she'd looked momentarily stricken, then assumed that irksome expression and jumped down from his desk. "You're right. I'm here for sex. I won't forget again." She walked out of his office, the line of her back straight.

He opened his mouth to call her back and decided against it. He could apologize, should, really, but he knew her. She'd give him that horrible grin and tell him it was fine, all was forgiven. She'd be lying, of course.

And she shouldn't forgive him. He didn't deserve it.

Three days ago, when she gazed up at him at the indoor pool, those lovely blue eyes had eaten him up. He knew she wanted him, just as he had wanted her. But now she wouldn't even look at him. Oh, she was accommodating and said all the right things, but she wouldn't look him in the eye.

That first night, when he'd met up with everyone in the drawing room before dinner, he'd tried to get her attention. But her gaze swept past him, over him, never settling on him. Brynn began thanking him profusely in what he supposed was English as she prattled on about the names of the songs she'd bought with her gift card. He'd tried to look attentive and properly interested in what she had to say, but his eyes kept straying to Allison.

Dinner was a disaster. Nigel had shot Trevor disappointed glances. Allie had just smiled. And ignored him. Mags had kept a conversation going almost single-handedly and was very good at drawing Brynn out of her shell. The girl blossomed under a little bit of female attention. She must miss her mother terribly.

His gaze rested on Allison as she played with her food. How taxing it must have been, putting her life on hold to take care of a dying mother and two sisters. He couldn't imagine it, couldn't imagine using all of his focus and energy to take care of someone else. Allie deserved a medal. And all he'd done was hurt her, call her names—foul names.

"Why so moody tonight, dearest?" Mags had asked.

"What do you mean tonight?" Nigel asked. "He's always been moody, even as a little boy. Would much rather play with his cars and trains than be with people."

Taking a deep breath, Trevor narrowed his eyes and held his tongue. Brynn was in the room after all, and he didn't want to scorch her ears. He could have told his father to sod off, could have reminded his mother that the only person he saw for days on end was his grouchy nanny who rarely spoke to him. They didn't know how he behaved as a child, as they were rarely home. Instead, he smiled at Brynn, turned to Allie, and bowed his head slightly before leaving the room.

For the next three days, he'd insisted on taking tea with Allie and Brynn, forced Allie to take strolls with him in the garden before dinner. And every night he challenged her to a game of chess in the library. He'd tried to provoke her, tease her, eventually got nasty with her. She looked right through him. And smiled.

When they were alone together, she would look anywhere but at him and ask, "Would you like to have sex now, Trevor? I'm here for your pleasure." It was as impersonal as if she'd asked about the weather. *"Is it hot out, Trevor? Would you care for some sunscreen?"* With that robotic, goddamned expression firmly in place.

He'd been gobsmacked the first time she said it. And saddened. By the fourth time, he smiled coldly. "When I want sex, you'll know. The way you'll be able to tell is when my cock is inside your pussy, Miss Campbell." She hadn't asked again.

By Saturday, he'd had enough. He planned on taking her to dinner, leaving Brynn under the watchful supervision of Arnold and Frances. His parents were still in residence, of course, but he wouldn't leave a goldfish in their care.

"Be in the foyer at seven," he'd told Allie over tea.

"Yes, of course. Is there anything special you'd like me to wear?" She held her cup aloft and glanced at his tie.

He all but gnashed his teeth. "I'm sure whatever you come up with will be satisfactory."

Clueless Brynn texted and ate a sandwich. How could she not see the difference in Allie? How could she not see through the fake congeniality? It was baffling.

"No." He shook his head. "Wear an evening dress." He let his eyes drift to her breasts and linger there. "If I don't like it, you'll change." He flung himself out of the chair and left the room.

"What's wrong with him?" he heard Brynn ask.

Good God, what wasn't wrong with him? He was a miserable fuck and desperate to break through to Allie. Couldn't take another minute of that polite, phony attitude.

At seven on the dot, she descended the stairs in a dark red, strapless dress that exposed a good deal of cleavage, with her hair piled on top of her head. She was beautiful. Or would be if she'd wipe that gormless expression off her face.

He offered his arm, and she hesitated for the briefest instant before taking it. Out front, Simmons waited next to the limo. Trevor climbed in next to her, and she sat as stiff and taut as a wire.

"Would you care for champagne, Allison?" He lifted the chilled bottle and poured some into a waiting flute.

"No thank you, Trevor. I'm fine."

Just to get a rise out of her, he handed her the glass with an evil smile of his own. "I insist."

"All right, then. Thank you."

*No more*—he wanted to shout the words at her. He'd reached the end of his tether. He missed her, the real her, the one who lectured him and shivered at his touch and was fiercely loyal to her family. He had to do something to shake her out of this. Why couldn't she just say something vicious to get even?

With narrowed eyes, he poured a glass for himself. "Take down your hair."

"What?" She looked momentarily startled before the composed look he'd grown to despise settled back over her features. Handing her drink to him, she reached up and took out a few pins, loosening her hair. She ran her fingers through the long strands and then placed her hands in her lap. "Is this better?"

With a critical eye, Trevor studied her face and hair for several seconds. "No, it's not. Put it back up."

He settled in his seat and watched her struggle to finger comb her hair and refasten it with the pins. Still, she seemed unflappable.

His gaze swept over her new coif. It was messier than before, and he liked it. Yes, he was tired of this phony pretense. He wanted her back. So, tonight he was going to do everything in his power to make Allison Campbell come unwound.

~~~

Allie tried to ignore him. He was doing everything he could to get a rise out of her, but she wouldn't be goaded into an argument. He wanted a mistress, not a girlfriend—sure as hell not a friend. He didn't want advice about his family. He didn't want to be called out on his ridiculous behavior toward his parents. Fine. That was just fine with her.

She was a fuck toy, so be it. He wanted sex, she'd give it to him. Without emotion this time. Without aching for him, without feeling anything at all. Because fuck toys didn't have feelings. And that's why she was there. To pleasure him whenever he wanted. British bastard.

In the meantime she would be cheerful and pleasant. He thought he could rattle her cage, but he'd underestimated her. He thought he was dealing with an amateur. He must not know she was employee of the month fifteen times in the past four years. When she spoke to him, she pretended he was just another hotel guest and assumed her customer service face—the peaceful, unruffled expression that calmed even the most belligerent tourist.

She ran a hand over her hair. "Is this all right, Trevor?" She let her gaze bounce on him before looking away. That was one thing she couldn't bring herself to do—look at him. She couldn't gaze into those light gray eyes and not want to burst into tears.

*You're a fuck toy.* Those words had ripped her to shreds. No, she hadn't just been hurt by what Trevor had said, that was too mild a description. She felt as if she had a gaping chest wound.

The thing was, she had actually started to like him, thought they had a connection, a bond. But Trevor didn't have bonds with people. He had employees, not friends.

That's what she was, his employee. So she held on to that customer service smile like it was a lifeline and she was drowning. Because if she didn't, he'd see how much he'd hurt her.

She felt his cold gaze flash over her. Out of the corner of her eye she saw him shrug and raise a brow. "It looks fine, I suppose."

Allie just smiled at the comment and turned her face toward the partition. She didn't know where they were going for dinner, didn't care. In the past three days, she'd interacted as little as possible with Trevor. Except when he'd made her take tea with him, go on ridiculously long, rambling walks in the garden—which under normal circumstances she'd have enjoyed—and forced her to play chess with him until late in the evening.

The last activity had her nerves frayed. She kept expecting him to try and seduce her. And she would give in to him too, because, as she'd reminded herself enough times, that's why he kept her around. But to actually let him kiss her, touch her, slip inside her body would be almost more than her faux cheerful attitude would be able to take. So, she'd tried to prod him into sex, at least that way she would be in control. *"Would you like to have sex now, Trevor?"* He'd been shocked the first time she said it. His eyes widened, his cheeks paled. But she kept asking, in a cool, polite voice. But after a while, he'd snapped back and she didn't dare push him any further. Knowing Trevor, he'd take her up on it out of irritation.

And to be honest, for all her pep talks to herself about having sex with no emotion, she was almost positive she couldn't do it. The times they'd had together haunted her. She dreamed about them, played them over and over in her mind. She'd never felt so satisfied, so emotionally connected. She knew Trevor didn't feel the same. He'd told her that in a dozen different ways.

No, she needed to keep up the pleasant façade, needed to keep her emotional distance. It was the only way she'd survive this. Survive him.

Simmons dropped them off at one of the largest casinos on the Strip. Trevor didn't speak at all but placed a hand on her lower back and guided her through the door and into the elevator. As they slowly climbed to the twenty-first floor, he stood with his back against one wall, his hands thrust in his pockets, and stared at her.

She looked straight ahead and did her best to ignore him but could see his reflection in the brass doors. It was going to be a long night without Brynn, Mags, and Nigel as a buffer.

The doors slid open, and still not speaking, Trevor escorted her to a restaurant she'd only heard about. It was even more beautiful than she'd imagined. The white and ivory décor should have felt impersonal but, instead, was inviting. As they were shown to their table, Allie's eyes traveled upward to the enormous glass bubble chandelier that encompassed the middle of the restaurant. The maître d' took them to a corner table by the window, which allowed them a view over the lighted city, making the Strip's neon signs look exotic in the night sky.

Trevor held Allie's chair before taking the seat across from her. "What do you think, Allison?" he asked, nodding toward the view.

"It's very nice." She watched his jaw tighten. She was getting under his skin and she was glad. He deserved it.

She picked up a menu. She'd never heard of most of the dishes listed, but when the waiter appeared, Trevor ordered for the both of them. She hated when he did that.

"I think we'll start with the caviar and a bottle of '96 Cristal. Then we'd each like a tasting menu with the wine pairings. Thank you." He handed the waiter his menu.

She didn't like caviar. He probably remembered that and ordered it on purpose. Allie thought back to some of her worst customers. The ones who were angry about having a room too close to the ice machine. The drunk ones she'd caught peeing in the hallway. The ones who called her a fucking bitch for not having two queen-sized beds in one room. She smiled as she handed the waiter her own menu.

Trevor leaned back in his chair. "You look lovely tonight." He didn't sound happy about it.

"Thank you." Her eyes skidded over him and got caught in his gaze. Those gray eyes were so penetrating, so intense... She blinked and looked away, directed her attention to the street below. She ignored him, refusing to look his way again until the waiter brought their champagne and caviar.

Trevor fixed her a plate of blinis and topped the thin pancakes with a scoop of caviar and a dollop of crème fraîche. "Here you are, darling. Eat up."

Allie took the plate and nibbled the blini. This stuff was disgusting. She swallowed it with a gulp of champagne.

Wearing a concerned frown, Trevor reached out and patted her hand. "I forgot, you don't like caviar, do you, darling?"

"It's fine."

"It's an acquired taste. You'll get used to it. I'm sure that if I ate…" He waved a hand at her. "What did you eat? Something made of hamburger no doubt." He gave an affected shudder. "I'm sure it would take me a while to get used to that." He gave her his most charming, sexy smile.

"I'm sure it would."

She poked at her food and even managed to choke down a couple bites by the time their dinner arrived. The waiter poured a red wine, and when she glanced down, she wasn't sure what was on her plate. A small steak with something on top.

"Filet Mignon Rossini," the waiter said. He turned and left.

"Steak with foie gras, black truffle, and cabernet sauce." Trevor cut into this steak.

Allie did the same. After taking a bite, she decided it was the best thing she'd ever tasted in her life. She glanced up to find Trevor staring, a strange look on his face. When he saw her notice, his blank mask slid in place. She shifted her gaze and stared at his nose.

"How is it, darling?"

"Very nice, thank you." Her cheeks were becoming sore from smiling so much. But she wasn't backing down. Not when it bugged the hell out of him.

"By the way, since we're here, I got a room. We haven't fucked in a few days, what with the relatives in the house. Try your wine, love. It's absolutely delicious."

Allie continued to smile, but it was an effort. He was pushing her as far as he could. He wanted her to break. And a part of her wanted it too. She wanted to tear into him, tell him what an ass he was, how much she hated the sight of him. Still, she refused to give him the satisfaction. And she knew that her pleasant persona was driving him apeshit and this was his retaliation. Well, she wasn't backing down. He wanted a fuck-toy mistress, he was going to get it. With both barrels.

She tilted her head, her heart pounding in her chest. No fear of tears now. She was pissed. "Whatever you want, Trevor." She took another bite of steak, but it had lost its flavor.

"Excellent," he said in an equally pleasant tone.

Allie cut her food but ate little of it. Eventually, the waiter took away her almost-full plate. She wanted to eat, just to show him she wasn't bothered, but her stomach wasn't that strong. She felt unsettled and suddenly nervous. Could she go through with it? Or would she back down and let him win?

The waiter was back immediately with a green sorbet. Her stomach twisted into knots.

Laying down his spoon, Trevor regarded at her coolly. "Not hungry? Anxious for the rest of the evening?" He didn't seem to expect an answer. "I know how you feel. Let's get out of here, yes?"

He pulled out his wallet and left a few folded bills on the table, then walked around and pulled back Allie's chair. He leaned down and whispered in her ear, "So nice to have an eager partner."

When she stood, he placed a hand on her elbow, guiding her out of the restaurant and back into the elevator.

What was it going to take to wipe that insipid expression off her face? He couldn't take it anymore. This wasn't Allison. The Allison he knew was loving and gave him hell and pulled him out of his cross moods. This woman was a bloody automaton, and it was pissing him off.

They got off on the seventeenth floor. He pulled the key card out, and with an electronic whoosh, the door opened. "I knew we wouldn't be here that long—unless you're up for multiple rounds, darling—so I didn't book a suite. Hope you don't mind."

"Not at all." A king-sized taupe-covered bed dominated the space.

He spun her around and, with his hands on her shoulders, pulled her to him, her chest pressed against his. "Have you missed fucking me, Allison?" If he'd been hoping for a blush, a gasp, or any reaction at all, he was sorely disappointed.

"Yes, of course," she said. "Would you like my hair up or down?" She stared past him with wide blue eyes and waited, that stupid smile etched permanently on her lips.

Trevor was in a vicious mood. He knew exactly what she was doing. At first, she'd been acting aloof and pleasant because he'd hurt her, but now she was doing it just to get his wick. Well, if she thought she could push him over the edge, she didn't know who the hell she was dealing with.

He released her and took a step back to slide out of his jacket. Tugging at his tie, his gaze never left her face. "Hair down."

He watched as she once again removed the pins, placing them on top of the dresser to her right, her hands shaking slightly.

Good. She wasn't as indifferent as she pretended.

She ran her fingers through the long tresses and rubbed her scalp a few times before letting her hands fall to her sides. Her hair was in disarray now.

He unbuttoned his shirt but left it on and unfastened the cuffs. With detachment, Trevor looked her up and down. "Take off the dress."

He watched her throat move as she swallowed. She hesitated briefly, then reached behind her and began to unzip the back.

"No, slowly. I want to savor it." His voice was icy, but he was hot, wanting her so badly, he ached. But if he showed her one ounce of empathy, then she'd continue this idiotic behavior, and he was going to end it, once and for all.

She still refused to look at him, pinning her gaze to his collarbone. Taking her time, Allie unzipped the dress and slowly peeled the dark red satin over her breasts. Her strapless bra was red as well. Trevor gritted his teeth as his cock grew even harder. Rubbing a hand along his chin, his heart slammed into his chest. He'd missed this—seeing her skin, her breasts, her long, smooth legs. Missed touching her.

Allison leaned forward, giving him an eyeful of her plump, confined breasts as she slid the dress over her hips and thighs, finally stepping out of it and tossing it on the bed. She turned toward him, and it took a moment, but her eyes slowly made their way to his before dancing away, that polite, annoying smile glued to her lips.

He took one step toward her. The smile dimmed a bit. He took another step, and her eyes widened and filled with panic. Damn, he didn't want that reaction either. He wanted her as she had been, receptive and laughing and touching her body. He wanted what they'd had before, not this…lack of emotion, this detachment.

Reaching out, he pulled a strand of her hair between his fingers, rubbed the silky texture. Then he bent toward her. He'd wanted her mouth, the taste of it, the feel of those full lips beneath his. But she turned her head at the last second, and his lips grazed her jaw.

He snapped his head back, eyes narrowed. "I'm in charge here, Miss Campbell." He wanted to kiss her, had been fantasizing about it. He liked kissing her, goddamn it. "Every whim, remember?"

"But fuck toys don't kiss." She smiled serenely. "Would you like me to touch you now?"

Livid. No, he was past livid. Couldn't remember being this

pissed off. Ever. She wanted to play with him? Fuck her. Literally. He would slam inside her and she could wear that smile while he did it. He didn't give a damn.

"Take your knickers off." He was breathing hard and fast. Pulling the shirt off his shoulders, he let it drift to the floor.

She hooked her thumbs in the waistband of her thong and wiggled her hips as she slid the red material off her legs. She straightened and placidly stared at his throat.

With his jaw clenched, he unbuckled his belt, jerking it out of its loops and tossing it on the dresser. She wanted to push him, aggravate him—to what end? Was this the reaction she wanted? His anger?

"Now the bra," he bit out.

She stretched her arms behind her and unhooked it, holding the cups over her breasts with her hands. Her disheveled hair slid over those full tits, making his cock throb. The dark blond hair covering her pussy had him licking his lips.

"Drop it."

Her smile tightened a bit before ratcheting up a notch, and she dropped the bra at her feet. Dear sweet Lord, she was the most beautiful woman he'd ever known. And she wouldn't look him in the fucking eye.

Trevor rubbed his chest. "Allison." His voice was so hoarse he almost didn't recognize it. "Look at me."

Swallowing, she lifted her chin and stared at his forehead.

"Look at me, Allie. Please."

"I am, Trevor." The smile slipped, but she tried to hold on to it. And failed. She pressed her lips together in a grimace.

He should be glad. Glad that fake expression was gone. But in its place was a look of such sadness, such despondency. "Look me in the eye," he pleaded.

She stood there, naked and beautiful, and hesitantly, finally, met his gaze. "What would you like me to do now?"

She could do anything she wanted, demand whatever she liked. He would be clay in her hands.

Damn her. He couldn't go through with it. Couldn't touch her like this. He'd tried to push her, get her to surrender, but he was the one who broke. He glanced away, ashamed. "Get dressed." He grabbed his shirt and jacket, hastily shrugging into them. "I'll meet you downstairs in the lobby." He turned on his heel, closed his eyes for a moment, then left the room.

# Chapter 15

ALLIE LET OUT A shaky breath and staggered three steps to the bed, falling onto it. *No time for crying*. She wouldn't give him the satisfaction. Still, tears flooded her eyes. Looking up to the ceiling, she blinked them away.

Why had he left? Wasn't this what he wanted? Yes, he wanted to push her, she got that much, but this was Trevor. He never stopped until he got his way. But he'd stopped with her.

So what? That made him a hero?

She brushed a stray tear from under her eye. With trembling legs, she went into the bathroom and splashed cold water on her face. Her cheeks were pale for a change, and she felt sick to her stomach. She walked back into the room and numbly put her clothes back on, shoved the hairpins into her purse. She stared at his belt, lying there on top of the dresser, and left.

Trevor stood near the entrance, waiting for her to join him. He didn't say a word as he led her out of the casino and into the limousine. Simmons held the door for them, and when Allie climbed in, she stared straight ahead. If she looked at Trevor and his cold, blank face, she'd wind up in tears again.

The car moved forward. As it pulled into traffic, Trevor reached out and grasped her hand, pulling it onto his thigh. Surprised, Allie did glance at him then, but all she saw was his profile.

"I was angry and I hurt you. I'm a complete and utter ass. Please forgive me." He still didn't look at her, but he gave her hand a little squeeze.

Now he apologized? Now, after that craziness upstairs? After forcing her to the brink, almost pushing her into fucking him? She pulled her hand out of his and placed it back in her lap but kept her eyes trained on his face. "No."

He turned then. "What can I do?" His voice sounded raw and jagged.

She shrugged. She tried to plaster the smile back on, but it was gone for good. Her heart had shattered like a piece of glass and she was hollow. "I don't know."

He took her hand again and placed it on his cheek. "Tell me what a horrible prick I am. Hit me. Throw something at me. Just forgive me."

Her tears came now. They flowed freely, and she was powerless to stop them. "I'm not sure I can."

He pressed his lips into her palm. "I won't give up until you do."

Allie didn't speak again. She was confused, and although still angry, Mags's words came back to her. *His heart's very fragile, you see.* Allie heard the vulnerability in his voice when he asked for forgiveness.

Part of her—the small, stupid part—wanted to comfort him. God, how pathetic. The only thing that was fragile around here was her brain.

*But he apologized.* Trevor never apologized.

Did he get an award for acting human? He should have apologized days ago. Should never have said such a hateful thing in the first place.

When they pulled in front of the house, Simmons opened the door. Allie tried to muster a smile for him but couldn't manage it, so she nodded instead. As she walked across the drive, she felt Trevor's presence behind her, but he didn't touch her, didn't place his hand on her back or elbow. She shouldn't miss it.

When she walked through the door, Brynn sat waiting on the bottom step with her arms clutching her knees. She hopped up when she saw Allie.

"Where have you been? I've been trying to reach you for over an hour."

Allie rushed to her sister, placed her hands on her Brynn's shoulders. "What's happened? Are you all right?"

Trevor moved behind her. She could feel his body heat at her back.

"What's wrong, Brynn?" he asked.

"Monica's in jail. She needs bail money."

"Oh my God." Allie's hands fell. Trevor gently gripped her arms, offering support. She fought the desire to lean back against him, to take comfort from him. No, she could handle this on her own. She tried to pull away, but his hands tightened. "Why was she arrested?" she asked.

"Possession of pot and underage drinking."

"Crap, I need to call Dad."

"I already tried," Brynn said. "I got his voice mail. I couldn't get ahold of you either."

"I'm so sorry." Allie ran her hand down Brynn's long hair. "I had it on vibrate and forgot to turn the ringer back on."

"Where are Arnold and Frances?" Trevor asked.

Brynn shrugged. "They were busy, and I didn't want to bother them with this."

"No reason to worry your father right now, Allison. I'll call my attorney and take care of it." He reached out and patted Brynn's head before walking past them toward his office. "It'll be fine, I promise," he said, glancing over his shoulder.

Allie guided her sister up the stairs and into her room. Brynn pulled away and flopped down on the bed while Allie walked into the closet. "How did Monica sound?"

"She's in a cell with a bunch of drunk people. She sounded scared."

Allie shimmied out of the dress and threw on a pair of old jeans and a sweatshirt. Walking back into the bedroom, she stuck her hands in the shirt's front pouch and settled herself next to Brynn.

"Is Monica going to be okay, Al?"

"Yeah, she will. But first we need to see if we can get her out of jail."

"You're not going to make me go back home, are you?"

She rubbed Brynn's back. "No, but Dad has the final say." Not that he seemed to care one way or another. And that's what pissed Allie off the most. She was worried sick about her sisters while her dad was probably out having a great time with his new girlfriend. Resentment and frustration warred with the anger. She was tired of being the responsible one. She closed her eyes. But that's why Brynn was here in Trevor's home, and it was why she was going to bail Monica's sorry ass out of jail. Her sisters needed her. Allie wasn't going to abandon them.

"I don't know why Dad gets to make the decision," Brynn said. "You're the one who does everything. And I like it here. Mags and Nigel are funny. Besides, I'm going to be in the wedding. Mags asked me to be...what did she call it? Not flower girl. Junior bridesmaid, that's it." She smiled. "I like them. Why doesn't Trevor?"

Allie smoothed a strand of Brynn's dark hair, flipping it behind her shoulder. "They weren't always the best parents."

A knock sounded at the door.

"Come in," Allie said.

Trevor stepped into the room. He'd removed his tie and unbuttoned the top two buttons of his white shirt. Her eyes drifted to his and this time, she didn't look away.

"I found your sister. She's in the North Las Vegas Detention Center. We can bail her out now."

Allie stood. "Let's go."

"I want to go too," Brynn said.

"No, you stay here." She slipped her feet into a pair of tennis shoes. "We'll be back soon."

Trevor held open the sedan's passenger door for Allie before walking around and climbing behind the wheel.

"You don't have to do this, you know. I can handle it myself," she said.

He started the engine and pulled through the gate. "You've been dealing with this by yourself for too long." He twisted his head and glanced at her.

"I don't need saving, Trevor."

"Really? So you have the fifteen hundred dollars for bail money, do you?"

Gritting her teeth, she stared out the window. She owed him big time, and it was always there between them, like an invisible wall. She was tired of being indebted to him, wished they were on equal footing. *Then you never would have met him.*

"We could, of course, allow her to rot for a few weeks until her trial. How does that sound? She is eighteen, after all," he said.

"Fine. So what do you want in exchange for this loan?"

When he didn't answer her, she unhooked her seat belt and moved closer to him, placing her hand on his leg, creeping it closer to the juncture of his legs. When she stroked his semi-hard dick through his fly, she whispered in his ear, "What's fifteen hundred dollars worth, Trevor? How many handies will it take?"

He sharply pulled over to the side of the road and threw the car in park before turning on her. He grabbed the back of her head, drawing her face close to his. "Stop this at once. I want your forgiveness, you ungrateful brat."

She did laugh then. How very Trevor-like. Demand forgiveness and insult her in the same breath. "Tough. I don't want to forgive you. You don't deserve it."

He leaned down and kissed her hard—and all too briefly. "I

know I don't deserve it." He let her go and gripped the steering wheel, rotating his shoulders. "Now, put your seat belt back on."

She sighed and snapped her belt in place. Just when she thought she had a handle on him, he did something surprising and thoughtful. It was irritating.

"Besides, I've never bailed anyone out of jail before. I can cross it off my bucket list."

She slanted him a look. "Glad you think this is funny."

He reached out and picked up her hand, bringing it to his mouth. "My lawyer assures me he can get the charges dropped if she enters a drug rehab program." He lightly kissed her fingers. "And I heard from the detective today."

"What?" She jerked her hand from his grasp. "Why the hell didn't you tell me? What's Brad's last name? Who is he?" She twisted in her seat and glared at him. The passing headlights cast shadows onto his profile.

"I didn't tell you because I was angry. The longer you kept that hideous smile in place, the more I wanted to throttle you."

He was unbelievable. Yeah, this was the Trevor she was used to dealing with, the selfish jerk who did whatever he wanted and couldn't care less about anyone but himself. "What's. His. Name."

"Bradley. Thomas," he said, mocking her cadence. "There, does that tell you everything you want to know?"

She took a deep, steady breath. "Here's a wacky thought. Why don't you just tell me what the detective said, so I won't have to beat it out of you?"

"Well, we do have a safe word—Uruguay."

"Trevor—"

He sighed. "Fine. He's twenty-four, has three prior arrests, two for drugs, one for a DUI. He's lives in a house in North Las Vegas, and he's three months behind on rent."

Sounded like even more of a loser than she thought. "What does he do for a living?"

"No job on the books. The detective thinks he sells drugs. Pot mostly. He's living with four other people, two men, two women, not including your sister."

"Perfect. How much are the detective and your lawyer going to cost me?"

There was a long pause. "You know, darling, you're beginning to piss me off." His pleasant voice belied his words.

She knew from experience, the more polite and cheerful he got, the angrier he was. Well too bad, she was angry as well—angry at him, Monica, her father, her dead mother. Oh God, no, that wasn't true. She wasn't mad at her mom. How the hell could she be mad at her mom for dying? Allie missed her every day.

She sighed and rubbed her forehead. She was a bitch for even thinking such a thing. Her mother had been warm and big-hearted and cared about people. She'd depended on Allie, had asked her to do one thing—take care of her family.

It shouldn't be so goddamned hard. Why couldn't her dad and sisters just do what they were supposed to do? She had. She'd quit school and come home. Allie hadn't complained, run off the rails, or started dating someone inappropriate.

She needed to fix this. And she'd start by accepting Trevor's help. She couldn't get Monica out of jail by herself, even though she'd argued otherwise. She'd get Monica home and talk some sense into her. True, that hadn't worked the thousands of other times she'd done it, but she had to keep trying. It's what her mom would want.

———

Trevor looked around the detention center with distaste. There was an odious mixture of alcohol and unwashed bodies—never a pleasant combination. The uniformed man behind the glass took their money, Allie signed a couple of forms, and then they waited for over an hour in uncomfortable molded-plastic chairs.

Allie remained silent, but glared at him every once in a while. Usually after he said something he thought was rather witty. But at least she was looking at him again.

He'd been serious before. He would stop at nothing until she forgave him. Bailing her sister out of jail was a start. And the irony wasn't wasted on him. Allie had asked him to forgive his parents three days ago, and he'd been angry at her interference. Now she wouldn't forgive him, and it was tearing him apart. She was right—he didn't deserve it, but he wanted it just the same.

Clutching her release papers, Monica stepped through the door, clothed in jeans and a dirty pink T-shirt. Her hair was a snarl of tangles and her cheeks were blotchy from crying. Dark makeup circled her eyes.

Monica ran toward them, flinging herself into Allie's arms. "Thank you. Thank you for getting me out."

Allie hugged her back. "Are you okay?"

The younger girl nodded. "Yeah. I'm good." She glanced at Trevor with puffy eyes. "What's he doing here?"

Trevor stepped forward. "Let's get out of here."

Allie kept her arm around Monica's shoulders. "He's the one who bailed you out."

Trevor held the door, and Allie threw him a look as she passed through it. "Thank you," she mouthed.

He didn't want her gratitude. Not really. He wanted things to be the way they were before his mouth got in the way—comfortable in each other's presence, the sexual awareness bubbling beneath the surface of every touch, every glance. He wanted her to want him.

Once they reached the parking lot, Allie rubbed Monica's back. "So, why didn't Brad bail you out?"

Monica stiffened, stepped away from Allie. "Don't start, okay? He's on probation."

"So? What does that have to do with it?"

Monica said nothing but looked away.

"Was he with you when you got arrested?" Allie came to a stop in the middle of the lot.

"It wasn't his fault," Monica said.

"So he just left you there, by yourself?"

"He didn't want to leave me, but if he gets into trouble again, he'll go back to jail."

"Maybe that's where he belongs."

"Shut up, Allie." Monica clenched her hands at her sides. "You don't know him, so why are you even talking about it?"

"I met him. He's an asshole."

"And he's not?" Monica pointed at Trevor.

Allie took a step toward her sister. "He's the asshole who bailed you out. You should be on your knees, thanking him."

Monica sneered. "Isn't that your job?"

"You little—"

Trevor smoothly stepped in between them. "I think we should go back to my house and get a good night's sleep." He took Allie's arm in one hand and Monica's in the other and all but hauled them toward the car.

"I want to go home," Monica said.

"Finally, you're talking sense." Allie peeked around Trevor's chest to look at her sister. "Have you called Dad yet?"

Monica tried to pull out of Trevor's hold, but he tightened his grip. "No, why should I? And I'm not talking about that home. I mean where I'm staying with Brad."

"Are you kidding me? You're going back to the loser who left you to get arrested?"

"Shut up—"

Trevor gave both of them a shake. "Both of you shut up. Now, who's hungry?"

"I'm calling Dad," Allie said when they walked through the front door of the mansion.

"Yeah, you do that," Monica said in a snotty tone.

When Trevor led Monica to the drawing room, Allie remained in the foyer and tried calling her dad. It went to voice mail and she left a message, feeling angrier by the minute. Where the hell was he, and why couldn't he just pick up the damn phone?

She turned to find Trevor leaning against a display case of bird eggs. Suddenly, a wave of exhaustion overwhelmed her, leaving her drained. "Why are you doing this anyway?"

"Standing here? In my own foyer? Because I can."

She took a step toward him. "Why are you doing this for Monica?"

"Bailing out teenage delinquents is a new passion of mine. Although she's quite a little bitch."

"You don't get to talk about my sister that way, and you can't buy forgiveness, Trevor."

He pushed off the glass case and slowly moved toward her. "Doesn't hurt to try." He cupped her cheek, his thumb stroking along her bottom lip.

It felt good, his touch. And it shouldn't, because he wasn't right for her. He was callous and uncaring and selfish. Most of the time. And they made a deal, one that didn't leave room for the emotions churning inside of her.

He leaned closer, his mouth a whisper from hers. She wanted his kiss, his touch, even though her feelings were still bruised from his hurtful words.

He kept his eyes open, locked on hers, as his lips softly brushed her own.

"Oh look, Nigel, they've made up."

Trevor closed his eyes. "Fuck," he said.

She snapped her head back. This interruption was a good thing. She had been weakening toward him, and she needed to stay strong.

It was just a bargain. She needed to remember that and not let her feelings get tangled up.

"I'll go see if Brynn's still awake," she said. "I'm sure she'll want to see Monica." Allie nodded at Mags and Nigel as she ran up the stairs.

Trevor straightened. "When are the two of you leaving?"

"I don't know what you and Allie fought about, Son, but you've been like a bloody thundercloud for the last few days," Nigel said.

"Where did everyone go?" Monica asked, stepping into the foyer.

"Oh, this one's new. Are you starting a harem, dearest?" Mags asked.

Trevor stared at the ceiling and sighed. Then he roused himself. "This one's off-limits too," he said to Nigel.

"Son, how many times do I have to tell you? I'm with your mother."

Mags swished forward in a bright green caftan, her arm extended. "I'm Mags, Trevor's mother. I tried to teach him some manners, I really did."

Trevor scoffed. "Was that in between your second and third marriage, or your third and fourth? Because I can't remember."

Nigel walked forward and smacked Trevor on the back of the head. "Behave." Then he turned to Monica. "I'm Nigel."

"Monica, these are my parents, such as they are." He nodded toward the two nightmares who'd created him. "This is Monica, Allie's middle sister. We just bailed her out of jail."

"Ooooo, what were you in jail for, darling?" Mags threw her arm around Monica's shoulder and walked her out of the foyer.

Trevor turned to Nigel. "I'm quite serious you know, about leaving these girls alone. If you so much as look at one of them sideways, I'll kill you."

"I keep telling you, Trev, I love your mother."

"Right." He glanced toward the stairs where Allie and Brynn

stood. "Brynn, we busted your sister out of jail, and we brought you a burger to celebrate."

Brynn gave him a tired smile. She'd obviously been asleep. Her dark hair was flat on one side and she wore a pillow wrinkle on her cheek.

"Thanks. For the burger and for breaking Monica out."

"Go to the drawing room and get something to eat before Mags beats you to it." He nodded his head toward the hallway. Brynn walked by and tucked a strand of hair behind one ear.

Trevor draped his arm around Allie's shoulder and led her away. She shrugged it off, but he yanked on the hood of her sweatshirt, forcing her to keep pace with him.

"Guess she hasn't forgiven you after all, Son," Nigel said, before jogging back up the stairs.

No, she hadn't. But she would. It would help things along considerably if he could get Mags and Nigel to leave. They popped up at the most inopportune times.

In the drawing room, Monica perched on the love seat next to Mags. Brynn sat cross-legged on the floor, throwing tater tots in the air and catching them in her mouth.

"Oh, darlings, Monica has been telling us about her new friend, the prostitute. Tell them." Mags rubbed her hands together. "This is dreadful."

Monica gave Mags a confused, sideways glance. "There was a hooker in the cell with me who got cheated out of her money. So she hit the guy in the head with her shoe and the heel got stuck in his skull. She was covered in blood."

Trevor sank onto the sofa and pulled Allie down next to him. "What a charming story. One I'm sure you hope to tell your children." He said to Brynn, "Pass me a bag of fries, would you? And give Allie a burger."

Brynn dug into the grease-coated white sack and pulled out a burger and a bag of fries, handing it to him. "Here, Trevor, catch." She threw a tot. It hit him on the forehead and landed on his trousers. He simply picked it up and tossed it in his mouth.

Then he peeled back half the wrapper and handed it to Allie. "Eat this." He held out a fry. She gave him a look but let him feed it to her. "You hardly ate a bite at dinner, love."

"I wonder why."

When he gazed up, Monica, Brynn, and his mother stared at him with wide eyes. "What?" he asked with a frown.

"So are you two, like, dating? I thought she was your assistant," Monica said. "What is she assisting you with?"

Trevor glanced over at Allie and found her cheeks had turned bright red. Almost as red as the bra and knickers she wore earlier. "I suggest you tone down the snotty attitude and show your sister a little respect."

Monica tried to hold his gaze but eventually dropped her eyes. He didn't imagine this subdued change in behavior would last long. Didn't seem her style to back down from a fight. Being in jail must have really shaken her.

"And she is my assistant," Trevor said before eating another fry. "Anyone who says otherwise can go back to their own home." He gave each one of them a hard look.

"Dude, you just posted bail for me. It's none of my business."

He nodded. "Good. And on that note, I'm going to bed."

He stood, dropped his fries on top of the coffee table, and walked out the door.

# Chapter 16

As soon as he was out of earshot, Monica threw Allie a smug look. "The two of you are totally doing it."

"Shut up, Mon," Brynn said. "At least she doesn't have a criminal record."

"Now, now, girls. Let's not fuss." Mags clapped her hands. "Monica, Frances prepared you a room across from Brynn's. She can show you the way." When Monica and Brynn just stared at her, Mags gestured in a shooing motion. "Well, go on. Get to bed."

Allie had never seen Mags in such a commanding mood before. She seemed almost maternal.

Once they were gone, Mags began gathering wrappers, packages of ketchup, and the rest of Brynn's tots, tossing them into a sack. "Your sisters are charming, Allison."

"Thank you. I'm not sure how charming Monica is these days. We did just bring her home from jail, after all."

Mags placed a hand on Allie's arm. "You know why Trevor is doing all this—bailing out your sister, allowing Brynn to stay here?"

Allie didn't want to discuss Trevor. Besides, talking about him to Mags felt like a betrayal somehow. "You know Trevor, he's unpredictable. He can be nice when it suits him." She wadded up the napkins and tossed those in the sack along with her uneaten burger.

"Nice?" Mags actually threw her head back and laughed. When she sobered, she tilted her head, her eyes sparkling. "Trevor's never been nice. Not even as a child. No, my darling Allie, he's in love with you."

~~~

The next morning at the breakfast table, Trevor glanced up from his phone. "Why are you staring at me?"

"No reason." Allie lowered her gaze to her plate, but her eyes had other ideas and, against her will, kept returning to his face.

"Do stop, Allison. It's annoying. Unless this is your subtle way of telling me you've forgiven me and want to fuck?"

"It's all about fucking with you, isn't it?"

"Yes, it's been four frustrating days, and I'm so goddamned hard all the time, I could cut rocks with my cock." He glared at her, as if it were her fault.

In a way, she supposed it was, but her mistress duties had been derailed by the arrival of his parents and her sisters—and of course his own ass-clown behavior.

Mags had been so far off base last night it was laughable. Trevor didn't love her. He wanted her. He even wanted her forgiveness—at least he seemed sincere about that—but it wasn't love.

"So, what do you want to do, English, throw down on the breakfast table?" she asked.

He leaned toward her. "God, yes." Trevor gave her a look of such longing, such heat, she felt seared by it. He picked up her hand and brushed his lips across her palm.

Maybe she could lock the door. A quickie would take what, ten minutes tops? No, what was she thinking? His parents were in the house, and her sisters. And she was still mad at him. But when Trevor touched her like this, every rational thought fell out of her head.

Then Mags and Nigel walked into the room. Trevor dropped her hand like it was poison. "Oh, you two again."

Mags, swathed in the green caftan she'd worn the night before, lowered herself into a chair. "I've been rethinking the wedding."

Nigel, dressed in a paisley robe, poured himself a cup of coffee and sat down next to Mags. "Do you know what sounds good this morning? A round of golf. Eh, Trev? Let's hit a few."

"The whole thing is all wrong." Mags pressed her hand over her heart and her large diamond engagement ring winked in the light. "I simply can't do it."

"I knew it wouldn't last. When are you leaving then?" Trevor asked.

Mags raised her brows. "What are you talking about, darling?"

"The wedding." A little smile played on his lips. "I knew you wouldn't go through with it."

She laughed. "Who said we're not going through with it?"

"You did, just now. Not two seconds ago."

"I bought new clubs. Let's give them a go," Nigel said. "Haven't got much play in lately."

Mags touched Nigel's sleeve. "Darling, I'm parched."

"I'm terribly sorry, my love. Would you like juice or coffee?"

"Both, of course."

"Goddamn it, Mother," Trevor exploded. "What the bloody hell are you talking about?"

"Don't yell at your mother, Trev. It's bad form." Nigel rose, and as he did, his robe parted, giving Allie a full view of little Nigel. Which wasn't so little. And it appeared as though he manscaped. Everything.

She tried to hold it in but couldn't. Erupting with laughter, she slapped a hand over her lips. Shaking, tears ran down her face.

Trevor turned his angry gaze on her. "What the hell has got into you?"

"Your father just flashed me," Allie said, trying to catch her breath.

Nigel smiled. "Whoops." He returned from the sideboard and placed a glass of juice and a cup of coffee in front of Mags. "Sorry that you saw my dangly bits, Allie. Sometimes the boys need fresh air."

She tried to stop but wound up laughing harder. His parents were bananas.

Trevor clenched his jaw. "You"—he pointed at his father—"there are children in the house, you perv. Wear some fucking clothes to the table." He pointed at Mags. "And you. You said you were rethinking the wedding."

"What? Oh." Her brow cleared. "Red's not the right color. And now we'll have to change the flowers. And of course the cake I picked will never do." She sighed and sipped her juice.

With jerky movements, Trevor stood. "You two are leaving today. Do you hear me? I've had enough." He marched to the door and threw it open.

"We're not golfing then?" Nigel called after him.

⸺

Trevor strode to his office. They were a pair of nutters, his parents. After all these years, he still didn't know why he let them burrow under his skin. But when his father flashed Allie, Trevor couldn't keep his anger in check. For God's sake, the man had not an ounce of shame.

A knock on the door brought him out of his thoughts. Allie poked her head inside. "I'm going to run home and talk to my dad."

"Fine."

"Are you all right?" she asked.

"I assume you're referring to the two barking mad people who made me?"

She smiled and nodded. "Yes, them."

"What the hell is the point of getting married? They've had ten weddings between them. Why go through it again?"

Allie walked to his side of the desk and perched on the corner. "Marriage obviously means something to them."

He rubbed his chin and made a disgusted snorting sound—one that was very unbecoming. He vowed never to make that sound again. "It's just another excuse for my mother to plan a party."

"I'll bet every time they take those vows, they have the best of intentions."

Trevor laughed. "Did you hear yourself just now? Vows, as in promises." He waved his hand. "Their intentions are bloody pointless."

She toyed with the hem of her pink dress. "Would vows mean something to you? I mean, if you made a promise to someone, would it be important for you to keep it?"

He looked up at her and noticed for the first time that she was sitting on his desk, her bare legs within reach. He wrapped a hand around her knee. "I don't want to talk about parents. Or marriage. Or promises." He slid his hand down her soft calf.

"Of course you don't." She gently pulled her leg from his grasp and stood, smoothing her skirt over her hips. "Trevor?"

He wanted her, here on the desk, and to hell with whoever came barging through the door. "Hmm?"

"It's none of my business, but how long are you going to let Monica stay?"

More complications—his parents, her sisters. He had a feeling there would be no desk sex in his immediate future. "Of course it's your business. She's your sister. And I really hadn't given it any thought. By the way, I bought the house Brad's been living in."

Allie stilled. "When?"

"I had my attorney, Alex, make an offer late last night. The landlord was thrilled to wash his hands of it. There are five people living in a two-bedroom house, and they've made quite a mess of it. But, I figured at least this way, I could ensure that Monica has a place to live."

She looked at him, her brow furrowed. "Why did you do that?"

"Because I can." She seemed surprised, and he didn't understand why. She already had too many worries, and if this eased her mind, why wouldn't he?

―∽∾∽―

Allie left the office and walked out the front door and around to the garage. Of course he could afford to buy a house. It meant nothing. *He did it for you.* That little voice that kept giving Trevor a pass when he acted like a jerk, or gave him more credit than he deserved when he did something nice, was getting louder. More annoying and difficult to ignore too.

But this gesture wasn't personal. Like he said, he did these things because he could, not because he wanted to make her life easier or better. Or to please her. It was his nature to take charge. He was bossy like that.

She walked into the garage and found Simmons polishing a car.

Her feet practically skidded to a halt. "Is that…" She pointed to the shiny Festiva. It looked just like her car but without all the dings and dents. And it was bright, cherry red, not the faded orangey-red she remembered.

Simmons smiled. "Yes, Miss Allison, it's yours. Mr. Blake had it fixed, painted, and detailed." He walked around to the front and patted on the hood. "There's a brand-new engine, new transmission, new brakes and tires. It's practically a whole new car."

"This is *my* car?"

Simmons chuckled. "One and the same." He snatched the keys off the wall and handed them to her. "Here you go. Take her for a spin."

Allie cleared her throat and blinked back tears. Trevor wasn't a sweet man. He wasn't a kind man. And yet…he had taken in her sisters, he was gentle with Brynn, made sure Monica had a place to stay. He could have totally taken advantage of her the day she was sloppy drunk. Instead, he took care of her. And he'd begged for forgiveness. Now he brought her car back.

She didn't know what to think about any of this, how to process it. But right now, she needed to talk to her dad, have it out with him once and for all. He needed to start acting like a father again. Then she could think about Trevor.

"Thanks," she said to Simmons, hopped into the Festiva, and took a minute to appreciate it. It smelled clean and fresh. She started the engine and smiled when it purred instead of clunked.

Trevor. That look he'd given her at the breakfast table—it made her ache. She wanted him too. Four days seemed like a long time without sex—even though she'd lived without for over four years. Now she craved him, like a gambler craved one last bet. But she couldn't do anything with her sisters in the house, so moot point.

She waved at Simmons and drove home, enjoying the familiarity of her old car. When she pulled up to her house, she saw a strange Honda sitting in the driveway. She snapped off the radio. Who would drop in at seven-thirty?

Allie used her key to let herself in. At the sight of a strange woman walking from the hallway to the living room, wearing one of her dad's T-shirts and nothing else, Allie yelped. "What the hell?"

The other woman screamed and yanked at the hem of the shirt, trying to pull it down over her hips. "Who are you?" She wore glasses and had chin-length dark hair. She was on the short side and a little heavy.

"I live here. Who are you?"

Her dad walked out of the kitchen, a spatula in his hand. His brows lifted, causing the horizontal lines along his forehead to deepen. "Allie, I wasn't expecting you."

"Yeah, no shit." She looked back at the woman. This had to be Karen, the guidance counselor. "What if Brynn was with me? And why wouldn't I be here, considering Brynn and I left you messages all night?"

His mouth opened and closed. "I forgot to charge my phone."

"Really? Well, while you were dicking around and not checking your phone, Monica was sitting in jail."

The color drained out of his face. "Is she all right? What happened? What did she do?"

"I'd like to speak to you in private." She glared at Karen, her lip curling as she glanced at the woman's bare legs. Her father had sex last night, in the house he'd shared with her mother. Allie trembled with anger.

"I'll just go get dressed." Karen scurried out of the room.

Once she was out of sight, Allie turned on him. "Nice, Dad. Brynn ran away from home, Monica's in jail, and you're shagging the guidance counselor."

He pointed the spatula at her. "I told you not to use that tone with me. Now, come in the kitchen and tell me what happened. I need to flip a pancake."

She couldn't remember the last time he'd made himself a meal and he was cooking pancakes for Karen? She tossed her purse down on the sofa and stalked to the kitchen. She glanced around. The place was a mess—spilled pancake batter congealed on the counter, newspapers and mail littered the table, and three trash bags stood next to the back door. Well, forget it. She wasn't picking up after him this time. Let Karen do it.

He flipped a pancake, then faced her. "What happened with Monica?"

"She was arrested for pot possession and underage drinking. Trevor bailed her out and she spent the night at his place."

He rubbed his forehead with the back of his hand. "Shit. This boy she's dating is trouble."

Allie gasped. "No, you don't say."

"I get it, Al, you're upset."

"Let's get one thing straight. I'm not upset, I'm pissed." She tried to control herself, but her breaths were spastic and her chest felt tight. "You've spent the last six months so depressed you could hardly get out of bed in the morning. I've been doing everything around here, the cooking, cleaning, shopping, taking care of the girls." Not to mention keeping them from losing their house and trading out medical bills on her back. Okay, so sex with Trevor wasn't exactly a chore, but she had traded herself for her family. And it was humiliating. "And now that you've replaced Mom, you still don't give a shit about Monica or Brynn."

"That's not true, Allie. I do care, and I could never replace your mother. Never."

"May I say something?" Karen stood in the doorway, dressed in a skirt and blouse, her glasses gone, her hair combed.

"No," Allie all but snarled at her.

"Yes," her dad said.

Karen stepped into the room. "It's very normal to feel anger when a parent moves on."

Seriously, a lecture about feelings? This strange woman stood her ass in Mom's kitchen, then had the nerve to talk about moving on?

Allie stared at the rooster clock and fought for calm. She pressed her shoulders down and took a deep breath, held it for a couple of seconds, then turned back to the woman. "Karen, if you don't mind, I'd like a private conversation with my father?"

"She can say what she likes. This concerns her too." Her dad suddenly looked down at the burning pancake. "Shit." He grabbed the pan, tossed it into the sink, then reached over and flipped the stove switch.

"It doesn't concern her, it concerns the family."

"Allie's right, Brian." She walked toward him and kissed his cheek. "Call me later." She smiled at Allie. "It was nice meeting you."

Allie remained silent until she heard the front door close. "You are unbelievable. You've known this woman a week and suddenly she gets to pop off about our family? What are you going to do about Monica? And Brynn? Or are you too busy sexing up your girlfriend to worry about them?"

Ignoring the dig, he leaned against the counter and folded his arms. "What do you want me to do about Monica? What can I do? And I was going to call you about Brynn today. It's time she came home."

Allie shook her head. "Forget it. She's not coming back if you're letting that woman sleep here."

His expression closed down. "I'll do what I like in my house, Allison. And Brynn is my daughter. First, you want me to act like a father, then you veto my decisions. And you're right, it's past time I started pulling my head out of my ass. Brynn comes home today."

"That's before I knew you were having sex with *Karen*. Can't you see how messed up that is?"

"This won't happen when Brynn's here. I want her home by tonight. She has school tomorrow."

"But—"

"It's not open for discussion." He gave her his back and hit the taps, filling the sink with water.

Allie felt like she'd been sucker punched. She had done everything she could for him, for their family. And now he was dismissing her.

She watched his tense movements for a moment as he scrubbed at the pan. When he refused to look at her again, she left.

⁂

Trevor stood at the window, staring out at the garden. He had more than enough work to keep him occupied, but he couldn't maintain his concentration this morning. What did she think of the car? Was she pleased? He didn't know why she would be, it was a piece of rubbish, and no matter much paint they applied, it was still an eyesore.

Allie knocked on the door and leaned into the room. "Sorry to bother you again."

He turned to her and smiled. "No bother." She looked worried. She always did after a go-round with her family. They put too much on her, expected more than they should. Her father seemed something of a cockup since Allie's mother died, and it all fell on her slender shoulders. "Want to take a walk?"

He held out his hand. As she moved forward, he watched the slight sway of her hips, her pretty, long legs. Even her sandal-clad feet were lovely, the tips painted pale pink to match her dress. He obviously needed to get laid. Badly.

She placed her hand in his, and they walked through the French doors and around the side of the house toward the roses. "I take it things didn't go well with your father?" He wove his fingers with hers as they made their way to the stone path.

"How can you tell?"

He glanced down at her. "What happened?"

"He spent the night with Karen. She was still there this morning, barely dressed, and he was making after-sex pancakes. He wants Brynn home today."

He led her to a shaded bench. She sat next to him and blew out a breath. "Brynn doesn't want to go back. She doesn't like Karen, and after seeing her wearing my father's T-shirt, I don't like her either."

"It's where Brynn belongs, love. At home with your father."

"What if she runs away again?"

Trevor slid his arm across the back of the bench and pressed her head to his shoulder. She felt rather nice there. And her hair smelled fresh and citrusy. He rested his cheek on top of it. "Well, I wish I had some words of wisdom for you. But you've talked to your father, you've played mother to your sister, even though that's not your job. And you've attempted numerous times to save Monica from being an idiot."

Allie lifted her head and glowered at him. "Thanks for the wrap-up. I know what I've done, but none of that has worked. What am I supposed to do now?"

"How about nothing?" He stroked his thumb along her bare shoulder.

She placed her hand on his thigh and twisted her body toward him. "I'm not following. What does that mean? I can't just sit around and twiddle my thumbs." When he opened his mouth to speak, she pointed a finger at him. "And I don't want to hear about twiddling your dork."

He scoffed. She knew him too well.

"Second of all, I can't just do nothing. I'm not a do-nothing type of girl. I'm a fix-it type of girl."

Trevor nodded and gathered a handful of her hair. He ran his fingers down the length of it, released it, and started the process all over again. "All right then. Fix it."

"Yes, that's what I'm talking about." She patted his leg. "How?"

"First—and this is the important part, darling, so pay attention—you must have a proper magic wand. Then, you wave it over your disgruntled family…"

She slapped his thigh. "You've got nothing? No ideas, no magic bullet, nada?"

"You see what a roaring success I've had with my own family."

She pressed her lips together. "Point taken."

"Maybe things will work themselves out."

"Uh-huh. When was the last time that happened?"

"There's always a first time for everything, love."

With her mouth pulled to one side, she peered up at him. "By the way, thanks for my car." She leaned toward him and kissed his cheek.

"You're welcome. And it's still ugly."

"This doesn't mean I've forgiven you," she said. "Not completely."

"Understood."

⁓

Allie strolled back to the house. She needed to tell Brynn it was time to go home. She left Trevor on the bench and a smile crept over her lips when she thought about him sitting next to her, stroking her. He was always touching her, rubbing his hand across her shoulder, twisting a strand of hair around his finger—very tactile, and she liked that.

As she stepped into the hallway outside of Trevor's office, she ran into Mags. "Is he in a better mood or still shirty?"

"If shirty means cranky, then I think he's better. He's out in the garden."

Mags's brows lifted. "Really? Doesn't he have important work to do?"

"I don't know, but we spent the past thirty minutes outside."

"Well done. Now, let's reconvene in the foyer in twenty minutes. We have so much to buy."

She sashayed toward the main part of the house. Allie shook her head and watched those hips glide from side to side as Trevor's mother walked away. Maybe Mags could teach her how to do that. It was an art form.

Allie found Brynn in the kitchen, rolling pie crust with Mrs. Hubert. Hands on her hips, the older woman watched Brynn's movements with a critical eye.

"You need to build some muscles, girl. Put some elbow grease into it."

Brynn stuck her tongue out of the corner of her mouth and pressed down, rolling the dough, making it thinner.

"Brynn, can I talk to you for a second?" Allie asked.

Mrs. Hubert glanced up and nodded. "Go on now. We'll make an omelet tomorrow."

Brynn grinned and wiped her hands on a white dish towel. "'Kay, thanks."

Allie followed Brynn out of the kitchen and into the foyer. "What's up, Al?"

"Dad wants you home tonight." Allie winced as Brynn stomped her foot.

"What? That's not fair. I want to stay here."

Well, Brynnie was certainly breaking out of her shell. She would have run to her room and sulked a week ago. Today, she behaved like a toddler. Allie reached out to pat her shoulder, but Brynn slapped her hand away.

"So Monica gets to stay here, but I have to go? Why? Why does she do the bad stuff and I get punished? I'm making straight As, you know. Maybe I didn't mention that?"

"You did mention it, and you're not being punished, Brynn. You have to live at home and go to school. Just like everyone else."

"At least I go to school. What does Monica do all day? She'll get to lounge around by the pool and take tea with you and Trevor. I want to take tea."

"There'll be no tea taking, okay? I have a feeling Mon's not going to be here for long."

Brynn shook her head. "This is so unfair."

"I know, honey. If I could keep you here with me, I would."

She frowned at Allie. "Really?"

Allie pulled her into a hug. "Really." When she kissed the top of her sister's head, Brynn didn't pull away this time. "Still want to go find a dress for the wedding?"

"Uh, yeah," she mumbled against Allie's shoulder.

"Mags wants to leave in twenty minutes."

Brynn pulled out of Allie's arms. "I need to go wash the flour off my hands." She spun on her heel and ran up the steps.

# Chapter 17

"What about this one?" Brynn ran her hand over a silver metallic cocktail dress with a plunging neckline.

"I think it's amazing. If you were thirty." Allie took the dress and hung it back on the rack.

"Darlings, how about this?" Mags held up a red satin dress by the hanger. It was ruched on one side and would barely cover Brynn's underage butt.

"Absolutely not. That's totally inappropriate. Brynn's only fifteen, Mags."

"No, sweetest, it's for me."

It was totally inappropriate for someone Mags's age as well. Allie took the dress and handed it to the hovering saleswoman. "We are shopping for Brynn today, not you. You have bought approximately sixty-two dresses in the last few days." Trying to keep these two on track was next to impossible.

"You're a spoilsport, Allison." Mags jutted her lower lip.

"Yeah, I'm a real buzzkill. Now, let's try to remember why we're here, ladies. Brynn needs a dress." She turned and looked at her sister. "An age-appropriate dress, one that hopefully will not break my bank account or get you arrested for indecent exposure."

"Allison, my pet, don't be ridiculous. You're not paying." Mags whisked up a glass of sparkling cider from the tray. "Nigel is."

Brynn grinned as she sipped from the champagne flute. "This is so cool. I want to shop here all the time."

Brynn was headed for a rough landing once she collided with reality. This wasn't the real world. This was like Disneyland for really rich British people or high rollers. Eventually, she and Brynn would return to their normal lives. Their normal, Trevor-less lives. Allie's landing was going to be bumpy too.

Mags grabbed dresses left and right while Allie made herself comfortable in what was becoming a very familiar chair. Then Mags thrust an armful of garments at the saleslady. "Fashion show time. Try them all on, Brynn, my pet, and then come out so Allie and I can see."

A few minutes later when Brynn stepped out in a red halter dress, the realization that her baby sister was almost grown hit Allie over the head. In a couple of years, she'd be off to college, their dad would probably be remarried, and Monica would be a jaded twentysomething. Where did Allie fit in?

"No, I don't like the red. Allison?"

Allie reined in her thoughts. She stared at Brynn then scrunched her nose. "No, not that one."

"Next," Mags said and sipped her sparkling cider. She winced slightly. "Not the same as Dom, is it darling?"

"Thanks for doing all this, Mags. Brynn's loving every minute of it. Sometimes she gets lost in all of Monica's drama."

"Well, I never had any daughters of my own. Unless you count my three stepdaughters, and I don't. This is quite fun."

A few hours later, Brynn had narrowed it down to four dresses—one deep blue, two black, and one white. She lined them all up on a rack and with her hands on her hips, stared at them. "What do you two think? I just can't decide."

Mags raised her brows. "No, it's quite impossible. We should just get them all."

"Mags, no," Allie protested.

But she couldn't be heard over Brynn's whoop of excitement.

The girl ran and threw her arms around Mags's shoulders. "Thank you so much."

"No, Mags, it's too much," Allie said.

"Nonsense. I've decided to wear seven dresses on the big day. Four seems almost paltry." She smiled at the saleswoman. "Ring them up, dearest." Then she walked to the front of the store, leaving Allie and Brynn alone.

"I can't believe I get four dresses." Brynn grinned and took another sip of cider. "I'm so excited."

"And ready for your next dance. Or three."

"She's so nice, Allie. When you and Trevor get married—"

Allie held up her hand. "Whoa, what? Trevor and I aren't getting married, Brynn. I have no idea where you came up with that."

"Sorry, Al. I didn't mean anything." Brynn looked a little wounded.

"No, I'm sorry. I didn't mean to snap. But Trevor and I aren't a couple."

"You guys live together. I know you don't really work for him, Al."

Allie scrambled to come up with something. "But I do. I'm his assistant." It sounded false to her ears, but she was sticking with it.

Brynn looked at the floor. "I'm not a little kid. You don't need to keep lying to me. It's kind of insulting." Pressing her hand to her stomach, she trailed after Mags.

Allie glanced up and saw her reflection in the three-way mirror. She was such a liar. But how could she admit the truth when she could hardly look herself in the eye?

"Darling, come along," Mags called from the front of the shop.

In the limo, Allie rode to the mansion in silence as Brynn and Mags chatted about the wedding. Staring out the window, she watched the throngs of people walk along the strip, mostly tourists with cameras and phones in hand, but some had the weary air of crash-and-burn gamblers. She could relate. Being in debt to Trevor made her feel like one of those desperate souls who risked their last chip on the roll of the dice. And came up snake eyes.

"You're very quiet, dearest."

Allie pasted on her best customer service smile. "No, I'm fine. Now, we have to think about shoes for Brynn."

Mags slapped a hand over her chest. "How silly of me to have forgotten." And she was off, discussing the merits of various designer shoes.

Allie stared out the window once more.

As soon as they reached the house and stepped inside, Monica, who'd been gripping the rail on the second floor, pounced on Allie. "Where have you been?" Her hair flew back as she jogged down the stairs. "I've been waiting for you for like, hours."

Mags patted Allie's arm as she left the foyer.

"Hello to you too." Allie glanced at Brynn. "Get your stuff together and I'll run you home."

"Seriously, Al," Monica said. "I need to talk to you."

"So talk." She watched Brynn meander toward the staircase.

Monica threw her hands up in the air. "My life is shit, Al."

Yeah, this was familiar. Crisis time. She turned her attention to Mon. "Tell me what happened."

"Never mind. You don't care. You're too busy hanging out with Mags." She reached out and tapped on the suit of armor, causing the hollow ring to fill the room. "This is your life now."

Allie's well of patience had run dry. She'd spent the afternoon with two adolescents, Brynn and Mags, and she'd had her fill. "I'm not going to beg you, Monica. Tell me if you want, but if you don't, I need to drive Brynn home."

Monica's brow rose. Usually, Allie would coax and cajole her sister into spilling her guts. Then she'd try to fix it, give advice. Look how well that turned out. No, this time, she was going to treat Monica like an adult. She was going to follow Trevor's advice and do nothing.

"Don't you even care that I had a huge fight with Brad? You're probably glad about that. You never liked him and you don't even know him."

Allie's eyes grew wide. "Why are you mad at me?"

Monica stepped toward her. "You live with Trevor now, so you don't care about the rest of us. You have designer clothes and go shopping all day with his mom. I heard Frances say he fixed your car. You're just fucking him so he'll buy you shit. You're a gold digger." She spun and ran up the stairs. A few seconds later, Allie heard a door slam.

God, she wished her mom were here to deal with this. She sighed. No, that wasn't true; Allie wished her mom were still alive because she missed her so damn much.

—◆◆◆—

Later that evening, when she stepped unnoticed into the drawing room, she was ten minutes late. She caught Trevor checking his watch, a look of irritation on his face. He probably just didn't want to be alone with his parents one minute longer than he had to.

Nigel, drink in hand, held court next to the fireplace. "Shot an eighty-two today, Trev. I dare you to beat that score, Son. We should get a round in sometime this week."

"I have a little habit I perform during the day. It's called work."

"Nonsense, dearest, you work too hard." Mags sipped on something pink and, when she lifted her head, noticed Allie. "Oh, tell him." She waved Allie into the room. "Tell my son he works too hard."

Allie rubbed her hands along her silk-covered hips and walked toward them. She felt like a fraud. She needed to remember she wasn't here as a guest or as a part of the family. She was the hired sex help. "Sorry, Mags, but it's not my place to tell Trevor anything."

He narrowed his eyes. "What is that supposed to mean?"

"Let me get you a drink, Allison." Nigel mixed up a cosmo and handed it to her.

Allie felt the weight of Trevor's gaze as she sat on the sofa. "I don't know if Monica will be down. She was pretty upset this afternoon."

"She'll come around," Mags said. "I'll check on her later. By the way, rose is a very lovely color on you, Allison. We'll keep it in mind when we go shopping tomorrow."

Allie felt her cheeks heat and took a deep, uncomfortable breath. "Okay." *Such a fraud.* She shouldn't be shopping with Mags, making friends with his mother. When would she get it through her head that this was all temporary? And as soon as Allie got used to it, Trevor would get bored, and she'd be back in her North Las Vegas house with its peeling paint and whiny refrigerator, wondering what happened.

Trevor stalked over to the sofa and sat down next to her, almost on top of her, completely invading her space. She knew he didn't like being ignored and would force her to acknowledge him. He was so damn pushy. That's one of the things she loved about him.

What? *Loved?* Who said anything about love? No, not loved—liked. One of the things she *liked* about him.

"I thought you bought a dress already?" He stretched his arm along the back of the sofa, his fingers skimming her shoulder.

She fought against pulling away from him—fought against resting her head on his shoulder, the way she had earlier in the garden. "Mags decided against that one."

"How was Brynn?" he asked, angling toward her, his face almost touching hers.

"She didn't want to go home and was freely sharing that opinion about every two minutes. But she and Dad had a long talk."

His eyes swept over her face. "She'll be all right, darling. What about you? Did you and your father work things out?" The concern in his voice melted her heart.

"No." The sting of betrayal was still strong where her father was concerned. But he had promised Brynn that he'd move more slowly with Karen. Allie wondered what slowly meant in his world, but she'd bit her tongue for Brynn's sake.

Arnold stood in the doorway, as if he'd suddenly appeared. The man was one stealthy butler. "Dinner is ready."

Trevor took Allie's arm and hauled her up next to him. Walking behind his parents, he slowed his pace and, leaning down, whispered, "You've taken such good care of them, darling." He kissed the side of her head.

She glanced up at him, at his gorgeous eyes, his sometimes cruel mouth, which was now tilted in a smile. Struck dumb, she faltered.

*Love.* She was in love with Trevor Blake. The realization ran through her, filling her with panic.

Shit. When had this happened? And how did she make it stop?

Immediately, Trevor halted beside her. "What's wrong, love? Are you ill?"

She blinked and tried to wipe what must be a horrified expression off her face. "No, sorry. I'm fine."

"Are you sure? You're quite pale."

"I'm fine." She tugged at his arm, and they resumed walking to the dining room.

Allie didn't say much as dinner progressed. She tried to act normally, but she wasn't hungry and ended up pushing food around on the plate.

What if he figured out her feelings? Would he ridicule her, pity her? Or would he simply shrug, tell her it was her problem to deal with, and pretend like it didn't matter?

Allie felt empty as she sat next to him. Her stomach was a little queasy and an overwhelming tide of hopelessness enveloped her. They would never work. They were too different, and he was too cynical.

And even if Trevor wasn't completely disillusioned by his parents and their failed marriages, he and Allie would never be able to build a relationship on the foundation they had now. She was a paid mistress and he'd never see her as something more.

It took forever before the dessert course was served. When Allie declined, Trevor did too.

He pushed away from the table and glared at her. "Let's go." He pulled back her chair, took her hand, and dragged her out of the dining room.

She glanced back at his parents, but Mags just smiled and waved with her spoon.

Allie had to jog to keep up with him. "Slow down, Trevor."

He didn't. When he reached the library, he yanked her inside, shut the door behind them, and locked it. Then, leaning against it, he folded his arms across his chest. "What the bloody hell is wrong with you? You've looked shocky all evening."

Allie debated with herself: tell him what was bothering her— not all of it, not about how she loved him, God no—or lie. But Trevor could sniff out lies like a dog on a hunt. She decided to go with the truth.

"Brynn and Monica said something today, and it made me feel…" She raised her shoulders. "Weird, I guess. That's all. I'm fine."

"What did they say?"

Allie wandered around the room. She ran her finger over a row of books—Shakespeare. "Did you inherit these from your grandfather as well?"

"Allison," he said pleasantly.

Oh no, she was in serious trouble if he was being pleasant.

"Are they old? They look old."

"We're not leaving this room, darling, until you tell me all of it."

Allie sighed and walked to the wooden chess table. Carved pieces of ivory and onyx stood in formation. She picked one up and studied it. The knight was heavy in her hand. "Trevor, it's nothing. I'm just being sensitive."

"What did they say, Allison?"

She glanced up at him. "Brynn mentioned that we're living together."

"And so we are."

"I'm fucking you for money, Trevor." She should have eased into it, but talking to him was like taking a dose of truth serum. Everything came tumbling out whether she wanted it to or not.

With his blank expression in place, he stared at her.

She set the piece on the chessboard and waited for him to say something biting and sarcastic. His eyes were dark and a tick jerked the left side of his impassive face.

"You may leave any time you wish. The debt is cleared." He turned and unlocked the door then left the room.

Allie stared after him. "Well, hell."

—◆—

He strode to his office, paced in front of the window a few times, poured himself a scotch, and drank it in one swallow. It burned down his throat.

Bloody hell.

Trevor turned and very calmly, very precisely, threw his glass at the James Ward landscape hanging across from his desk. A few drops of whiskey trailed over the painting, and the glass shattered and rained to the floor. He should clean that up. No reason why Frances should take care of his mess.

He'd been worried about Allie since she came down for pre-dinner drinks. She'd been quiet and wan, but as they walked to the dining room, she appeared to be on the verge of a panic attack. She hadn't eaten dinner, wouldn't look at him.

He merely thought she was worried about her father and Brynn.

To know she still thought of herself as a whore—it gutted him. God, he thought they were past that. But her sad eyes ripped right through him.

He couldn't have anticipated anything like her. She invaded his life, his home. His every bloody thought. He rubbed his breastbone. Now she was leaving him. He should be used to it by now. Everyone left.

Without knocking, Allie burst into the office, her gaze darting around the room. She took in the whiskeyed landscape and the broken glass before looking at him. When she did, her eyes pinned him to the floor. "Do you want me to go? Is that what you're saying? Because if that's what you're saying, you should say it to my face." She swung the door shut and advanced toward him. Allie's chest rapidly rose and fell and she rubbed her palms against her skirt in jerky, nervous movements.

He shoved his hands into the pockets of his trousers to keep from reaching out and grabbing hold of her. "I said you may leave any time you wish. What is so bloody difficult to understand about that?"

She stepped closer, her face a mask of anger. "Quit being a coward. If you want me to go, say the words."

He leaned down, got in her face. "If I wanted you to go, I would have said, 'Allison get the fuck out of my house.' Is that what I said? Is that what you wanted to hear?"

"No, you idiot." Her voice broke, and she swallowed before carrying on. "I wanted to hear that you want me without the stupid debt being in the way. That you don't just want me because you bought me."

"I want to fuck you because I like fucking you," he yelled. "I like having you in my home, is that too difficult for your tiny brain to comprehend?"

"Good, because I like being in your home. But I don't like having this mistress thing between us," she yelled back. She gave his chest a shove with her finger for emphasis.

"That's why I said the debt was cleared. Maybe you need your hearing checked." He poked her back gently.

"I can hear just fine. You're shouting loud enough to bring the house down."

"I can shout however loudly I please"—his voice raised a decibel—"as it is my goddamned house."

"Oh, I know it's your house. And this is your dress." She slapped her hands at her skirt. "And you got my car fixed and forgave my dad's loan. It's all yours, Trevor. What do I bring to the table?"

He did reach out then and grabbed her shoulders, pulling her to him. "You make me feel human." He kissed her, hard. "And you make me laugh." The next kiss was tender. "And you keep me from killing my parents." He showered her face with tiny pecks, her cheeks, her forehead, her eyelids. Then abruptly, he let her go. "But I won't stop you from leaving if that's what you want."

"That's not what I want." She put her hand over his heart.

It skipped a beat. He wondered if she felt that through her palm. "What do you want, Miss Campbell?"

She looked up at him with those impossibly blue eyes. "I want—"

There was a quiet knock at the door. "Mister Blake, Miss Campbell, is this a convenient time, or shall I come back?"

Allie leaned her head against Trevor's chest and gave a little laugh

Trevor groaned. "Come in, Arnold."

Allie spun to face the door, and Trevor wrapped his arms around her waist. "Yes?"

"Miss Monica is leaving. I thought you should know."

"Where's she going?" Allie asked.

"I'm not sure, but she's packing as we speak."

"Thank you, Arnold," Trevor said. After the butler left the room, Trevor rested his chin on Allie's shoulder. "Damn, I was hoping for makeup sex."

—◦◦◦—

Trevor wanted her to stay. Did that mean he cared about her? She shouldn't get sidetracked, thinking about Trevor and his feelings. Monica was leaving—probably going back to Brad the Douche the minute he snapped his fingers.

As she left the office and made her way upstairs, Trevor shortened his stride to match hers. Allie stood outside Monica's room, Trevor at her side. Peering down at her, he reached out and caressed her cheek.

Wanting wasn't the same as loving, she reminded herself, and knocked on the door.

"Come in."

Allie entered the room, but Trevor remained in the doorway. Clothes were strewn over every surface. How it could get like this in one day?

"You're leaving?"

Monica wadded up a shirt and shoved in her duffel bag. "What was your first clue?"

"So, I take it you've heard from Brad?" Trevor asked, lounging against the doorjamb.

"Yeah. He said he's sorry. He only cheated because I came here after being in jail. He was scared he was going to lose me, and he made a mistake."

That's what all the drama was about, Brad cheating? That was the dumbest excuse Allie'd ever heard. And her sister was moron enough to believe it. Did Monica get dropped on her head as a baby—what else could explain this level of stupidity? Allie literally had to bite the inside of her cheek to keep from trying to talk Monica out of it. Minding her own business was hard.

"Call me this week if you want to get together and have lunch," Allie said.

Monica froze and glanced up. "What? No, 'Monica you're ruining your life' speech?"

Allie shrugged. "As you've pointed out many times, you're an adult. You can make your own decisions." *Mistakes* was the word she was looking for.

"Oh." Monica looked a little deflated before she resumed tossing her things in the bag. "By the way, I need to borrow some money for a lawyer. The court said they would appoint one, but Brad said to get a real one." She paused and looked from Allie to Trevor.

"Sorry, Mon, I don't have it, and if I did, I wouldn't give it to you."

"What? Since when?" Her brow furrowed as she glared at Allie.

Allie walked further into the room and fisted her hands to keep from taking everything out of that duffel bag and refolding it. "Since you want to make your own choices. Choices have consequences." Just saying the words about killed her. She wanted to go with Monica to pick out the best lawyer they could afford—which wouldn't be much, but she still wanted to help. And she wanted to lecture Monica on the stupidity of dropping out of school and dating losers. But what was the point?

"You're just mad because I said you're fucking Trevor for the clothes and shit, aren't you?"

Out of the corner of her eye, Allie saw Trevor push off the doorjamb. He strode forward, but she placed a hand on his forearm. She felt his muscles tense beneath her fingers. But when she squeezed his arm, he relaxed a bit.

"Aren't you always talking about being a family? What good is family if you won't help me out?"

"I'm always here to listen, Mon. Call me any time."

"Is Brad coming to pick you up?" Trevor asked.

"Yeah." Monica looked under the bed and snagged a bra, shoving it into the outer pocket of the bag. She rose and slung it over her shoulder. "Thanks for letting me stay. Let me know if you change your mind about the lawyer." She moved past them and walked out of the room.

Allie watched her go and sat on the bed. Monica had zero self-awareness. How did you save someone from themselves?

"If she ever says anything to hurt you again, she will never be welcome in my house." Trevor sat down next to her. "But you did well with her. I was about to rip her to shreds, but you kept your cool."

Allie opened her mouth to speak when Arnold suddenly popped up in the doorway. The poor man looked frazzled. Well, frazzled for him—his tie was slightly askew.

"Miss Monica is having a rather loud discussion with a young man at the gate and Carl wants to know if he should call the authorities."

Trevor sighed. "Thank you, Arnold. We'll deal with it." Trevor rested his forehead against hers. "Am I ever going to get you alone?"

Allie patted his knee. "It's not looking good, English."

Mags and Nigel strolled into the room.

"Trev, who is this yob at the gate?" Nigel asked.

"I'm going to go straighten it out." Trevor stood and walked past his parents.

"Not without me," Nigel said.

Allie followed the two men out of the room. "I guess I should make sure Trevor doesn't kill Brad."

Placing a hand on Allie's arm, Mags stopped her. "What happened? Did the two of you argue?"

"We're fine," Allie said.

"Is this Brad Monica's young man?"

"Yep." Allie sped down the stairs and out the front door. Raised voices floated on the night air. Without hesitating, she ran to the gate.

When she reached them, Nigel stood with his finger in Brad's face. Carl stood to one side, ready to intervene. The embedded lights in the yard as well as the security lights by the guard house illuminated them.

"Watch your mouth, boy," Nigel said. Allie had never heard him use such a forceful tone.

"I'm just here to pick up Monica, and I wanted to meet Trev. What's your deal, old man?"

Trevor stepped forward, his chest almost touching Brad's. "That old man is my father. And you will speak to him with respect. Understood?" Ice dripped from Trevor's words.

Brad stepped back and held up his hands. "No prob. Don't get all bent."

"Monica, you may stay, but this wanker needs to go."

"You'd do well to be rid of him, love," Nigel said.

"Shut the fuck up." Brad puffed out his chest and held his hands out to his sides. "You want to go, old timer?"

"Anytime, you bloody git." Nigel leaped forward, but Carl stepped between them.

Allie placed her hand on Nigel's back. "Calm down. Mags would kill us if you mess up that pretty face." She turned to Monica. "Take your boyfriend and go, before I call the police."

Monica placed her hand on Brad's arm. "Let's just go. Please?"

Brad pulled out of her grasp. "Shut up, Monica, and get your ass in the car. I'm trying to have a conversation with Trev."

"Call me Trev one more time and I'll kick your sorry ass all the way back to North Las Vegas. Now, get the fuck out of here." He turned to Monica. "Are you sure you want to go with him?"

"Let's just go, Brad." Monica refused to look at anyone as she slunk off toward the truck.

Brad walked backward, the security lights gleaming off the chain around his neck. "See you later, old man."

Nigel, who had calmed down, moved forward. But Trevor held him back this time. "Let him go. The little twat isn't worth it."

"Did he give you the money?" Brad's voice drifted back as he climbed into his truck.

She didn't hear Monica's answer over the roar of the engine.

"What a very unpleasant asshole," Nigel said. "Imagine, calling me an old man. I'm in my prime. Just ask your mother."

"I'd rather not," Trevor said.

"Should I report this, sir?" Carl asked.

Trevor waved him off. "Only if he comes back."

Nigel walked back to the house and Carl resumed his post by the gate.

Allie looked up at Trevor. "Sorry about that."

He reached out and stroked her hair. "Not your fault, darling."

"Sure about wanting me to stay? My family is a pain, but they're mine. You shouldn't have to put up with them too."

Trevor sighed. "Yes, they are a bit much. But somehow I'll suffer through."

"At least you and your dad were on the same side for a change."

"Oh yes, he's in his prime, you know." He slid his arm around her waist and walked toward the house.

This night had been a roller coaster. When Trevor had said she was free to leave, Allie should have felt relief. The debt was cleared, she could return to her family. But she hadn't wanted to go. She knew this man would break her heart. He didn't love her, he said he liked fucking her. That wasn't the same thing at all.

# Chapter 18

TREVOR GRABBED ALLIE'S WRIST. Their earlier argument had been unpleasant, but they'd cleared the air and he was relieved she'd decided to stay. He wasn't ready to let her go. He liked smelling her perfume when he entered a room, liked having her poke her head into his office at odd times during the day. And he enjoyed sleeping next to her at night. She frowned on that with the sisters in residence. He couldn't blame her, really. So while he didn't mind them being here, for his cock's sake, he was glad they were gone.

When he reached the second-floor landing, he glanced back at Allie. She bore the same worried expression as she had the first time they met. It bothered him now. He wanted to ease her burdens.

"Come on, darling." He took her hand and pulled her down the hall and around the corner to his room. He let go of her wrist, opened the door, and allowed her to precede him.

Allie hadn't been in this room before. What a colossal mistake on his part. Suddenly, he had a burning desire to see her in his bed, her pale hair spread across his pillow.

"I can't believe Monica's going back to him. And she'll probably wind up pregnant or worse, with no education, no money." She walked over to the bed, her hand drifting across the carved bed post. She paused a moment and looked at it. "This bed is something else." She jumped up on the mattress and leaned back. "She's smart, she's pretty, and she's throwing her future away on this loser. Why?"

"Because he gives her the attention she craves." He lay down next to her, and she moved over a bit to give him room. "It's much easier to get this Brad fellow's attention than have to work at something, like school."

They lay in silence for a few moments. "You don't like the bed?" he finally asked.

"No, I do. It's just so over-the-top. I mean, you have four practically life-sized naked angels for posts." She reached out and traced the vines carved into the headboard. "How old is this bed?"

Trevor reached out and traced Allie's breast. "A few hundred years, I imagine." Her nipples budded under his fingers.

"Was this bed your grandfather's too, along with the collectibles?"

By now, Trevor had abandoned her breast, lifted the hem of her dress, and was moving his hand upward, over her hip. He slid his thumb under the strap of her knickers, rubbed her hip bone. "Yes, it was his life's work, collecting bits and pieces. He'd become obsessed with a subject." He moved his hand up to her stomach, brushed across her belly button. Her dress was hiked up, and he admired the rose-colored knickers. "Then he'd start collecting." He moved over her, pressed his hips into hers while he grasped her wrists and held them above her head. "This was my bed as a boy. My grandfather's old Georgian house was the only home I ever had." He leaned forward and took her earlobe between his teeth. Allie arched toward him and moaned.

She wrapped both of those long, smooth legs around his hips. "What about this house? Isn't it home?"

*Not until now.* He almost said it out loud but clamped his mouth shut in the nick of time. The idea was absurd. What he and Allie had wasn't about that. It was about sexual attraction, nothing else.

"I haven't fucked you in my own bed yet." He let go of her wrists, reached underneath her, and unzipped her dress, pulling it away from her shoulders and down her arms. Her nipples were visibly hard beneath the rosy satin bra. He bent his head and ran his tongue over one. He raised his eyes to watch her reaction.

Allie gave him a tender look that made him uncomfortable. In one quick move, he raised himself and stripped her of her dress. Then he settled over her again and roughly kissed her. He didn't want to talk about his grandfather or her sister and the worthless boyfriend. He wanted to pound into Allison. Over and over and over again.

She kissed him back as she pulled his shirt out of his trousers and hastily undid the buttons down the front. She pushed it off him and ran her short nails down his back. God how he loved that.

With his knees on either side of her hips, he sat up and divested himself of his shirt, then watched as she reached beneath her back and unhooked her bra. He helped pull it off and cupped her breasts, flicking his thumbs against her nipples. Allie moaned.

This was what they had, this was all that mattered—how it felt when they were together. Everything else fell away.

Moving down, Trevor whipped off her knickers. He then hooked his hands under her knees and lifted them over his shoulders. Before he pounded into her, he was going to taste her. Thoroughly.

He ran his hands up and down her legs, ran his chin alongside her knee. Biting her lip, she shivered.

"Touch yourself, Allison. You know what that does to me." He watched as she pressed her breasts together. Those lovely, full, pink-tipped breasts. His shallow breath quickened as he watched her lick a finger and twirl it around a nipple.

Groaning, he lowered himself until his mouth almost touched her pussy, and using both hands, parted her outer lips. With long, steady strokes he licked her before dipping his tongue inside her, then slowly lapped up to her clit. He circled it with the tip of his tongue, watching her with hooded eyes. "Talk to me."

Allie couldn't think, let alone talk. "Less talking, more licking," she managed to say. Palming her breasts, she ran a thumb over her nipples. It was like there was an invisible string from them to her clit. She glanced down, her eyes meeting Trevor's.

He continued to lick, his tongue darting inside her. Every muscle in her body clenched in response.

Then he stopped, planted a kiss on her thigh. "You taste sweet." He slid a finger inside of her, brought it to his mouth, and sucked it. But those stormy gray eyes never left hers. "So sweet."

She pinched her nipples into sharp points and ground her hips into the bed. "Lick me again."

"Where, darling?" He raised his brows and looked like he could wait all night for her response as he ran his chin along her lower abdomen. His coarse stubble tickled her skin.

She rubbed her lips together. "I want you to tongue fuck me. Now. Happy?"

"Ecstatic." He lowered his head and resumed. Slowly, he slid his tongue over her wet folds. Over and over. Occasionally, he'd flick the tip across her clit, making her shiver.

She closed her eyes and tilted her chin toward the ceiling. "That feels so good." She let go of one breast to reach down and run her fingers through his hair. "I'm close."

Trevor twisted his tongue inside her, then pulled it out, and replaced it with his finger. His mouth clamped over her while he added another finger. She was so wet, so ready.

But Trevor backed off. He lifted his head and slipped his fingers free.

Allie's eyes snapped open. "What? Why did you stop? Don't stop."

He rubbed his cheek against her inner thigh. "I don't want you to come yet."

"I hate you," she said, pulling at his hair. She wasn't gentle either.

Trevor chuckled against her wet pussy and started teasing her all over again. He used light strokes this time, barely touching her at all. It drove Allie crazy, and she tried to move her hips toward him, tried to press his head closer, but every time she did, he'd stop altogether. "Trevor," she screamed.

"Yes, darling, may I help you?"

She rose to her elbows. "You can, but you won't."

"Was there something special you wanted, love?"

She was practically gasping for air. "Please let me come. Or I may have to take matters into my own hands."

"Will one orgasm do or would you like two?"

She glared down at him. "Why don't we start with one and see how that goes?"

He laughed and lowered his head. This time his tongue swept over her slit, slid up to her swollen clit. It darted swiftly, lightly over her sensitive nub. When he slid two fingers inside her, she finally came. Practically bucking off the bed, she twisted her head and moaned into the pillow. It seemed to go on forever, and he didn't let up, didn't slow his pace. He curled his fingers, finding her G-spot. At least that's what she assumed it was, because she'd never felt anything quite like it. Pressure, but in a good way. The orgasm rocked through her. And once it finally subsided, she lay panting and still throbbing a bit.

Gently removing his fingers, Trevor looked up at her with satisfaction. "Happy?" he repeated back to her.

"No. I decided on two orgasms."

He moved her legs off his shoulders. Then taking his sweet time, he kissed his way toward her breasts. "I'm up to the challenge, Miss Campbell." He covered one with his mouth while his hand cupped the other and pinched her nipple.

With her legs splayed, Allie moved her hips, rubbing herself against him. "I want to feel you inside me."

He released her breast. "Yes." Maneuvering to the side of the bed, he stood, shucking his shoes, socks, and finally, thank God, his trousers. He pulled open the drawer on the bedside table, quickly ripped open a packet, and fitted the condom over his cock.

Allie closed her legs, rubbed her ankle down one shin, and watched him. "You're evil, you know, teasing me like that."

------

Trevor smiled as he watched her. She was comfortable with herself and with him. Seeing her stretched out, staring at his aching prick with a look of anticipation was driving him round the bend. And Allie knew it. "I just let you come. I don't see that as evil."

He grabbed her ankles and spun her toward him, pulling her to the edge of the bed. Once again, he wrapped her legs around his waist before gliding inside her. Wanting nothing more than to slam into her, he teased her instead, sliding in a couple of inches, then pulling back.

"Really evil," she groaned.

With a shudder, he pulled out almost all the way.

"Trevor." She cupped her breast and licked her lips.

"Yes…darling?" It was getting harder and harder to go slow, to taunt her with a few shallow strokes before withdrawing. He wasn't just torturing her, he was torturing himself. But it hurt so good.

"Fuck me hard," she demanded. "Now."

He laughed and rammed his cock home. "I've created a monster."

"Harder."

"Gladly." He drove his hips forward. Grabbing her ass, he stroked inside, long and hard. "You feel so damn good, Allison."

Then he pulled out of her completely and stepped back, unwrapping her legs from his waist.

"Seriously?" she growled.

"On your knees." Taking her calves in his hands, he flipped her onto her stomach.

Tossing her hair over her shoulder, she looked back at him with glazed eyes. "You'd better follow through this time, English." She shifted her position, propping herself on her hands and knees.

"Spread your legs."

Allie complied, and he grabbed her hip with one hand and her shoulder with the other as he slid into her. He gritted his teeth and forced himself to keep an even pace. He wanted her to come again before he did.

Allie collapsed onto her forearms and clutched the duvet. She was close again, he could tell. "Don't...stop...or I'll...kill...you." When she came this time, she leaned her forehead against the bed and moaned.

He didn't stop. Her pussy clenched around his cock, milking it. His fingers bit into her hip as he came.

---

Allie lay beside Trevor, stretched out on her stomach, and tried to catch her breath. Dear Lord, that man knew what he was doing. He'd pushed her to the brink and brought her back too many times to count.

She'd never felt this satisfied, this fulfilled after sex. Of course, she'd never been in love before either.

He reached out and stroked her ass in lazy circles, occasionally kneading it. "I came through, gave you two orgasms."

"Sorry, English, they only count when they're together. These were separate, so..."

He raised his head to glower. "You said two orgasms. You didn't specify they had to be together."

She yawned and patted her mouth. "Didn't think I needed to spell it out for you."

He grunted. "I'm tossing out a yellow card on that."

She laughed. "I don't even know what that means."

They didn't speak but lay in companionable silence for a while. Eventually, Allie rolled on her side and faced him.

"What am I supposed to do?"

He gave her a sleepy smile. "Begin by stroking, then use your mouth. It may take me a few minutes, but I'll be up to the task again in no time."

She slapped his chest. Laughing, he caught her hand and held it against him.

"I mean about Monica."

"Back to that, are we? What can you do, love? You know if you try to talk her out of it, she'll just run back to him that much quicker."

"Would you talk to her? She might listen to you."

He slid her a look. "No, absolutely not."

"You're right." She sighed dramatically and peered up at him through her lashes. "It was wrong to ask."

Trevor laughed again. "Sorry, darling, that doesn't work on me."

She leaned toward him and bit his shoulder. "Okay, so tell me what to do. I have to do something. I have to fix this."

"Why?"

"Because," she said, sitting up, "she's my sister. She's my responsibility."

Blowing out a breath, he took a strand of her hair and wound it around his finger. "Actually, she's not." When she opened her mouth to argue, he shushed her. "Listen to me. You're not her mother, you're not her father. What choices and decisions she makes are hers alone."

"So what's the alternative? Just let her come and go whenever they have a fight? Just let her continue to make stupid mistakes?"

"Again, love, what choice do you have?"

She frowned. "None, I guess."

But it was frustrating. She wanted to rescue her sister, give her guidance.

Trevor reached around and swatted her butt.

She blinked up at him. "What was that for?"

"You're thinking about your sister again. When we're in bed, I'd appreciate your undivided attention." He rolled her beneath him and claimed her mouth with his own.

~~~

The next three weeks flew by in a flurry of shopping, cake tasting, and picking out exotic and overpriced flowers. Oh, and having insane amounts of sex with Trevor.

Allie couldn't quite keep the smile off her face. Even Brynn noticed. "You seem happy," she said one afternoon after Allie picked her up from school.

"Things are going well. With the job, I mean."

Brynn rolled her eyes. "The job, right. It has nothing to do with Trevor?"

"Nope."

"I'd believe you if I didn't see the same expression on Dad's face."

Allie's smile disappeared. "Everything okay with you and Dad?" She hadn't spoken to him since the night she drove Brynn home from Trevor's house. It still felt strange and wrong, not living at home, not talking to her dad. But she couldn't bring herself to call him.

"Ms. Castor's okay, if that's what you're asking. She made dinner last night."

"How was that?"

Brynn shrugged. "Weird. Not the dinner, that was meatloaf, but her being in the house was kind of awkward. She's trying really hard."

"Do you like her?" Allie asked.

"She's okay." Brynn stared out the passenger window for a minute. "Are you ever going to talk to Dad again?"

"Of course, don't be silly." But not right now, the pain was still too sharp. She felt betrayed, used even. It wasn't right to feel that way, but she couldn't help it. She'd given up five years of her life for her family, and he didn't give a damn. She braked at a stop sign and closed her eyes, unable to shake the hurt feelings.

She wasn't ready to talk to him. Not that he seemed eager to speak to Allie either. No, this was a two-way freeze out, and right now, she didn't want to be the first one to thaw.

She didn't speak again until she pulled through the mansion's gate, waving at Carl as she passed the guard house. "Mrs. Hubert said you could help her make the tea today."

"I love decorating those cakes." Brynn opened the door and hopped out.

Every afternoon, Trevor took tea with Allie and Brynn in the conservatory. Sometimes Mags would join them. Brynn liked helping in the kitchen and had started making a little cake decorated with Trevor's initials. After a couple hours at the mansion, Allie would drive Brynn home before dinner but never went inside the house.

Besides the fight with her father, Allie's other worry was Monica. She hadn't talked to her sister since she and Brad left the mansion that night. Allie called twice and left messages, but didn't hound Monica like she had in the past. She worried about the lawyer and whether Mon was going to school. But Trevor was right, there was nothing she could do.

For his part, Trevor seemed more at ease than he had before. Even around his parents. Not that he wasn't above making snarky comments. But there was a relaxed atmosphere around the house and Trevor seemed almost content.

After dinner each night, Allie didn't know what Nigel and Mags got up to, but she and Trevor would politely excuse themselves, take a walk in the fairy-lit garden, and, when they couldn't stand it anymore, run up to Allie's room. They'd tear at each other's clothes and screw like crazy for the rest of the night.

Trevor had her talking like a sailor, trying new positions, and she had even picked up a couple sex toys from the shop Mags had dragged her into. She'd never planned on using the furry, leopard-print handcuffs or the bright purple vibrator. But Trevor found them and put them to good use.

He spent each night in her bed, curled around her. His deep, even breaths lulled her to sleep. At least once in the middle of the night, Trevor would reach for her. He'd wake her with his talented fingers drifting across her breasts, her belly, her legs, before slipping them inside her. Then, he'd turn her on her side and, while nuzzling her neck, slide into her while he toyed with her nipples. It was addictive.

She didn't know how long it would last, but she didn't dwell on that. She'd pushed aside all thoughts of her temporary situation with Trevor and decided to enjoy the time she had with him, to live in the moment. It was hard for her to do, but she was trying.

——

Three weeks. He'd been sleeping next to Allison for three weeks and he felt… What? Content? Yes, that was it. He'd even picked up an annoying habit of humming. His attorney even commented on it.

"What's up with you?" Alex asked. "Did you make another million or something?"

"Probably."

"And why are we meeting on the terrace?" Alex glanced around the garden. "We've met out here four times in the past few weeks." He reached for the sweating glass of iced tea. "Is this because of the girl you introduced me to? Allie, was it?"

Trevor raised a brow. "What makes you say that?"

Alex smirked. "That shit-eating grin you're wearing? That's what love looks like, my friend."

"Don't be stupid." Love didn't come into the equation with

Allie. He just enjoyed her company. And her body. And holding her in his arms as he fell asleep each night.

That was lust, not love.

True, it was more powerful than anything he'd felt before, but it would pass. And while he was in the grips of it, he would enjoy it, enjoy her. Every lovely curve.

He forced his mind off Allie and focused on the business at hand. He loved his work. Breathed it. Lived it. But he had a surprise for Allie tonight, and like a schoolboy, he couldn't wait to see her reaction.

"Trevor?"

He blinked at Alex. "Right, let's run the numbers."

After Alex left, Trevor decided to play hooky and take a swim with Allison in the grotto. He'd given Arnold strict instructions. Trevor didn't care if the bloody house was on fire, they were not to be disturbed. And that especially applied to his parents.

He and Allie swam and splashed each other, playing like a couple of kids. Then she sucked him off beneath the waterfall. The cool water washing over him, her hot mouth on his cock. It'd made him crazy. And it was the most relaxing afternoon he could remember.

After dinner, he told her to throw on some warm clothes and a jacket. He'd given no other details, and she had been quizzing him ever since.

"What are we doing? Where are we going?" she asked for the fourth time.

"You're like an annoying child, really." He drove the sedan out of town, past the lights and the crowds, and into the desert.

"If you're taking me to the brothels, you're in big trouble."

He laughed and snatched her hand, bringing it to rest on his leg. "Why would I take you to a brothel?"

"I couldn't begin to imagine."

He didn't let go of her hand. "You'll just have to be patient, love."

After a few minutes, he pulled the car off the road. "We're here."

She turned to look at him. "Are you planning on burying me out here? Do I have to dig my own grave too?"

"You're an idiot." He leaned forward and kissed the tip of her nose. Then he hopped out of the car and walked to the trunk where he removed a large duffel bag.

"What's that?" Allie asked.

"That is a telescope. You said your dad used to bring you and your sisters to look at the stars." He closed the trunk and began walking away from the car. "I thought you might enjoy this. We're meant to have a good view of Orion this time of year."

Allie stopped in her tracks. It took Trevor a moment to realize she wasn't walking next to him. He spun around. "What's wrong, love?" He walked back and rubbed her arm through her down-filled coat. "Are you warm enough?"

"Um, yeah." She cleared her throat. "I'm just surprised, that's all. Come on," she said, tugging on his hand, "let's have a look."

She didn't seem like herself, yet she wasn't angry or upset. He shrugged it off and allowed himself to be led further away from the road. He glanced toward the sky as he walked. It was a fine, clear night for stargazing. "You know, my grandfather used to have a telescope set up in his study. He always said if you think the stars look small, imagine how insignificant you appear to them." Trevor pulled a flashlight out of his pocket. "Here"—he handed it to her—"hold this."

She trained the light on the bag while Trevor unpacked the telescope and tripod. He set it up and punched a few numbers into the remote. He'd already preprogrammed it for their location.

"He was a good man, your grandfather?" Allie asked.

"Yes." Trevor looked into the eyepiece. "I spent my holidays at his pile outside Kent."

"What about your mom and dad?"

He raised his head from the finderscope and pulled her to him. "Look at this, Allie. It's magnificent."

She stepped toward him and lowered her head. "It's beautiful." She stayed that way for some minutes.

"Let me move it a little for you." He hit another button on the remote. "Should be able to see Sirius."

She leaned her head down to the scope. "Your grandfather was right. I do feel insignificant." She stepped back and let him have a turn. "So you never spent any time with your parents?"

"My mother used to take me for a week, sometimes two. I rarely had her undivided attention. You know how she loves drama. So if by chance she was getting along with her husband du jour, she would make a big show playing happy families. But it was always a cockup. Either my stepsiblings and I didn't get along, or she and her husband would fight. Eventually, I told her if she wanted to see me, she could come visit Grandfather. She rarely did, unless she was between husbands. I think I just saw a shooting star. Come look, maybe you'll see one too."

"You're supposed to make a wish, I think," she said, scooting in front of him.

"Wishes are for children." He placed his hands on her hips as she gazed at the sky.

"What about your dad?" she asked.

"He's very much a child."

Allie scoffed but didn't raise her head. "No, did you see him at all?"

"He would come up to school every once in a while and take me to dinner. He would say a hell of a lot of nothing, give me some pocket money, and before I knew it, he was married again. Then I wouldn't see him for months on end."

"I think they're here for you, Trevor."

"The stars?"

"Your parents."

"I thought they just wanted to annoy the shit out of me. And they're doing a smashing job." He stepped back and looked up into the sky. "It's amazing that all those lights are made of gas and dust."

"They love you."

"Stars don't love. Look." He pointed. "The Little Dipper."

Allie tipped her head back. "See it." She wrapped her arm around his waist. "They are self-absorbed. But they're trying to make amends."

Trevor grabbed her ass. Such a nice, firm little thing. He gave it a squeeze. "Ever fucked out in the desert, beneath the stars?"

"Ever given me a straight answer?"

"I'll take that as a no," he said. "I brought a blanket."

Allie shivered. "Too cold."

They spent the next hour looking through the lens at the stars. When Allie's teeth started chattering, Trevor wrapped his arms around her.

"Thank you for this." She leaned her head against his chest.

He kissed her crown. "You're welcome."

"Take me home to bed."

Home. He liked the way she said that, as if she belonged there.

He dismantled the telescope while she held the flashlight. "I'll just say this and then I'll drop it," she said.

He stopped to look at her. "Allison, you're a terrible liar."

"You're right. I'll keep bringing it up until you listen to me. You don't have to be best friends with them, but I think you should forgive them."

He finished packing up the equipment and zipped the bag closed. "I'm sure it would be good for my soul." He stood and took the flashlight from her hand and began walking toward the car.

Allie jogged to keep up with him. "I miss my mom so much,

and if I thought she'd died without my forgiveness, that she'd tried to make something right and I'd shunned her…"

He stopped and stared down at her. "I'm letting them stay in my bloody fucking house. What more do you want from me?" He blew out a sigh and ran a hand through his hair.

Allie stood on her toes and kissed his chin. "I want you to be happy."

# Chapter 19

WHEN ALLIE AWOKE THE next morning, he was gone. The filtered light shone through the curtain, and the dent he'd left in the pillow was cold. Since Trevor had started sleeping in her room, Frances hadn't been coming in to wake Allie in the mornings, probably at Trevor's request. When she looked at the clock, she realized that if Frances didn't wake her up, she would have to start setting an alarm.

He'd kept her up half the night, accepting her challenge to his sexual prowess, as he put it. She had been a big fool to tease him about having only two orgasms. And last night he'd been out for vengeance.

"Just to put your mind at ease, darling, I'm going to make you come again," he said, grinning, his head between her legs.

"No," she said. "You've proven your point. I can't come any more. Let me have some rest, for God's sake, man." She had only been half joking. He'd already made her come three times in a row and she didn't think she could take any more. She was on sensory overload by that point. But once again, Trevor proved her wrong.

His tongue and fingers drew a response from her, making her cry out as she held his head in place, her hands pulling at his hair. By the time he was finished, he climbed up to lay next to her, sounding very smug. "So, what's better than exceptional?"

"I promise, I'll never question your sexual stamina again." She lay like a limp rag, beyond sated.

Trevor pulled her against him and wrapped his arm around her.

"See that you don't, Miss Campbell. I told you, I take my fucking very seriously." He kissed her temple and fell asleep.

Now, Allie crawled out of bed, a little stiff from last night's sexual gymnastics. By the lateness of the hour, she knew Trevor had already finished breakfast, so she took her time getting ready. A long, hot bath soothed her delicious aches. When she finally made her way downstairs, she found Mags in the drawing room, nursing a cup of coffee and flipping through a bridal magazine.

"Good morning, dearest," she said.

"So, where's Nigel?" Allie asked.

"Sunning himself by the pool. He wants to have tan legs for the wedding."

"Do you think Trevor will ever forgive you?" Allie asked, plopping down next to Mags.

She gazed up from the magazine, a vulnerable look in her eyes which she quickly blinked away. Taking a deep breath, she thrust her shoulders back. "I think so. And if not, well, Nigel and I enjoy Las Vegas. We can stay indefinitely."

"I'm sorry, it's really none of my business."

"Of course it's your business, darling. Everything about Trevor is your business."

"Please don't say things like that. Trevor is…fond of me. But that's it. I don't want you to think there's anything permanent between us."

Mags's eyes traveled over Allie's heat-filled face. "You know, dearest, I've been thinking about the hen party."

Allie sighed. Trevor didn't fall far from the avoidance tree. "What about the hen party?"

"I think we should invite Karen."

Allie straightened. "Guidance counselor Karen? My dad's new girlfriend Karen?"

Mags smiled. "Yes, exactly. It would be a nice way to get to know her."

"No. Absolutely not. It's a terrible idea."

"Oh." Mags pouted prettily. "Of course, it's your decision."

Allie relaxed. "Good."

"I just thought since it was my hen party, I could invite whom I wanted."

"Mags, you don't even know her."

"Neither do you, but you're right, darling, of course." She tapped a finger against her cup. "It's just that she's been so involved in your father's life and has been spending time with Brynn."

She was right, Karen was a fixture now. Allie stood. "Fine. I'll go call her."

"And you'll be sweet and ask very, very nicely?"

Allie raised one brow. "I'll be polite, but let's not get crazy."

---

Three days later, Mags's sister flew in from London. Allie wasn't sure what to expect, but Pixie managed to make Mags seem tame. She was a few years younger, and where Mags was curvy and voluptuous, Pix was petite and slim. Somewhere in her late forties or early fifties, she looked at least fifteen years younger with a pretty, delicate heart-shaped face.

When Pix arrived from the airport, Trevor had greeted her with real affection, placing a kiss on each cheek. Her twentysomething Italian husband got a cool handshake and a cold stare.

That night, for the hen party, Pix wore a feather dress and black stacked platforms with red corset lacing along the back of the heel. Mags looked like a diva in a silver beaded dress.

Allie wasn't thrilled about going. She didn't want to spend an evening with Karen. It was bound to be tense and uncomfortable. When Trevor tried to talk her into staying home with him instead, she was almost persuaded.

"We could spend the evening in bed. I'll make it worth your

while, Miss Campbell. I'll break out the handcuffs again." He wiggled his eyebrows.

"Sorry, English. You're going to have to spend time with your father and your new Uncle Paolo."

"Uncle? The man's younger than I am."

Allie stroked his cheek. "It's just one night. You'll live. So will I." She moved toward the staircase, but Trevor snagged her hand and pulled her back.

"Don't touch the strippers darling, you don't know where they've been." He kissed her lightly before letting her go.

"Back atcha."

She walked out the front door and scooted into the limo with Mags and Pixie. They picked Karen up a few minutes later, and as soon she climbed inside, Mags poured the champagne.

"Thank you for inviting me," Karen said, looking at Allie.

Allie stuck a smile on her face. "Sure. Glad to have you."

Pix produced four tiaras and handed them out. "Ladies, it's time to get our freak on."

Karen looked a little nonplussed but gamely placed the tiara on her head. "Where exactly are we going?"

Mags's laugh tinkled like a fountain while Pix's laugh was huskier, more seductive. "You'll find out. Allie, tiara," Pixie said.

With a sigh of resignation, Allie shoved the tiara on her head. She may as well get into the spirit of things or it would be a long night. "There, how do I look?"

Mags grinned. "Like the princess you are, dearest."

"Here, girls." Pix scooped up three hot-pink gift bags.

Peeking inside the bag, Allie laughed and pulled out the contents, one at a time. "Good Lord, Pix." It was a penis paradise—rocket pockets, penis candies, mints and suckers along with a flashing pecker pin.

Karen's eyes grew huge. "Oh my."

"Let's put on our pins, darlings," Mags said. She attached hers to her one-shouldered dress. The penis-shaped pin lit from the inside with a flashing yellow light. "Now, girls, how do I look?"

With her marabou and fake rhinestone tiara and cock jewelry, she looked like a loon. But she seemed to be having such a good time, Allie said, "You look great, Mags."

Simmons pulled to a stop in front of a club that advertised an all-male review in neon. "If you ladies need me, I'll be right out here." He glanced at Allie and nodded. "You have my cell number?"

"Yeah, thanks."

As they approached the club, a shirtless hunk stood at the door taking tickets. He flashed a grin. "Welcome."

They maneuvered through the dark interior as another muscled, shirtless man led them to their table. "Enjoy yourselves."

"Oh, we will, pet, I promise," Pix said.

Allie rolled her eyes. Whether she got into the spirit of the evening or not, it was definitely going to be a long night. They ordered drinks and Allie nursed hers.

Karen leaned over. "Have you ever been here?"

"No," Allie said. "Do you feel uncomfortable?"

Karen pointed to a waiter across the room. "That was one of my students a couple of years ago. It's strange."

Yeah, Allie imagined it would be. The lights dimmed and she turned toward the stage.

A guy in a tux introduced the strippers. The music overhead blared out a patriotic theme, and one by one, hot men, their muscles bulging, stepped out onto the stage, each in a different military uniform.

"Oh, I love a man in a uniform," Mags said.

Pix smiled. "I love a man out of one."

It was like being with two middle-aged, horny teenagers.

The guys danced across the stage, ripping off their uniforms. Those tan, virtually naked men—save for the banana hammock G-strings—strutted around and froze in a series of bodybuilder poses. There were hip thrusts, gyrations, and one could work his ass like a paint shaker.

But things got really disturbing when Mr. Marine pulled Mags up onto the stage, sat her in a chair, and humped her face. Allie grabbed her phone and, laughing, sent a picture to Trevor.

Her phone immediately vibrated. Waving to Pix, she slid out of her seat and wound her way through the club to the front door. The bouncer gave her a once-over and a seductive smile. She walked further from the entrance and answered. "Yes?"

"If you ever send me a picture like that again, I will be in a fetal position for the rest of my life. Is that what you want?"

Allie laughed. "You should see you mother. She's eating it up. No pun intended."

"Oh. Good. God."

"Pix gave us a bag of penis paraphernalia. If I'm not mistaken, there's a candy cock ring with you name on it, mister."

"I'm hanging up now."

"Wait, I'm bored."

"You're at a naked male buffet and you're bored?"

Allie shrugged, even though he couldn't see it over the phone. "Yep. You've seen one waxed, naked ass, you've seen them all."

"You realize that no man thinks that way?"

"That's why you guys can be led around by your junk."

"Point taken. And I do love it when you call my cock 'junk.' So sexy."

"How about a winkie?"

He laughed. "Yes, that's much better, thank you."

"So, what are you guys doing?" She walked up and down the sidewalk, looked at the marquis pictures of the male strippers.

"Smoking a cigar, trying not to punch Paolo in his classic Italian nose. Ignoring my father."

"You want to come meet me? It's a dork smorgasbord here. A dorkgasbord, if you will."

"That is beyond tempting, love. But I'll stay here and probably drink too much."

Allie stood in silence. She wanted to tell him she missed him. She wanted to tell him she loved him and never wanted to spend another night apart. But that's not what Trevor wanted.

"Allie, are you still there?"

She cleared her throat. "Yeah, I'd better get back inside. They'll wonder where I am." She hung up without waiting for his answer.

When she walked back into the club, a muscle-packed blond was straddling Pix while she shoved bills into his man panties. Allie winced and made her way back to the table.

Mags, released from her onstage exhibition, shimmied to the music and sat across from Allie. "You must get a lap dance darling, they're so much fun."

Allie glanced over at Pix, who spanked her bare-assed friend. He wore a flag G-string, a bomber jacket, and a pair of aviator sunglasses. "No, I'm good," she yelled at Mags over the music.

Somewhere along the line, Mags had gotten ahold of a penis straw and now sipped her wine out of it. Allie's eyes found Karen's, and suddenly, she burst into a fit of laughter. Karen joined her.

After about another hour of rump-shaking good times, they clambered into the limo and drove to an upscale sushi restaurant. Mags strolled in, still proudly wearing her penis pin.

Before she sat down, Allie excused herself and went to the restroom. Karen followed. As Allie stood at the sink washing her hands, Karen stepped out of the stall, her eyes meeting Allie's in the mirror. Karen waved her hand in front of the soap dispenser and took a deep breath.

"Allie, I want you to know, I would never do anything to hurt Brynn. I feel responsible that she took off like that. Your father and I are slowing things down, trying to make sure Brynn's comfortable."

Allie could hear Trevor's voice in her head, telling her to stay out of it. She ran her hands under the dryer. "It's really none of my business."

The older woman flung the excess water off her hands. "Of course Brynn is your business. And so is your father. He told me how you took care of your mother and helped him with the girls when she was so sick."

Uncomfortable discussing this subject with this particular woman, Allie shrugged. "The two of you are adults. If you want to hook up—"

"We're not hooking up." Small lines fanned out at the corners of her eyes. "I'm in love with him. And he loves me too."

How could her dad forget her mom so quickly and fall in love with another woman he barely knew? "Look, Karen, I want my dad to be happy, but like I've told him, Brynn needs his attention right now. I'm sorry, but sometimes you need to put your life on hold for the sake of others." Allie had done it. Now it was her dad's turn.

Karen nodded, her eyes red with unshed tears. "Yes, you're right."

Allie shifted uncomfortably. "Um, I'm going to go back to the horndog sisters. I'll give you a couple minutes, okay?"

Again, Karen nodded.

Allie felt horrible as she walked out of the ladies room. She should have stayed out of it. She should have kept her mouth closed. Karen seemed like a nice lady. But Brynn was her sister, and Allie wanted to protect her.

She dropped into the chair. "Karen will be back in a second."

"I've ordered sake for us all," Pix said. She held up a small hand-painted cup.

"So, Pix, where did you meet Paolo?" Allie draped the napkin over her lap and took a sip of warm sake. The strong, clear taste burned a pathway to her stomach. She blinked back a few tears. "Whoa."

"It's potent, dearest. I don't want Simmons to have to carry you home tonight. Trevor would never let me hear the end of it," Mags said.

Pix ran her scarlet nail around the rim of the cup. "I met Paolo while I was vacationing in Cianciana. I was visiting friends, he was waiting tables in the hotel. Very Shirley Valentine of me I know, but darling, you only live once."

Karen appeared, pulled out her chair, and murmured an apology. Her face was a little splotchy, like she had been crying. Now Allie felt worse than terrible. She tried to give Karen a reassuring smile, but the older woman refused to meet her eyes.

Allie refocused on Pix. "Who's Shirley Valentine?"

The sisters' laughter filled the air.

"Oh my, you're so young," Pix said.

Mags sobered. "You're right though—you do only go around once. I've made so many mistakes in my life. Failing Trevor being the biggest, of course. But leaving Nigel was a terrible mistake."

Pix laid her hand on Mags's arm. "Don't you remember the horrible rows? You and Nigel would have killed each other had you stayed together. And Trevor is fine."

Allie wouldn't go that far. He definitely carried the scars of his parents' messed-up marriage—make that marriages.

"No, Trevor's not fine." Now Mags began tearing up. "He's been very unhappy, very angry. I wish I had been a better mother, more nurturing. And Nigel was always the one. I've always loved him."

Karen remained silent and winced when she took a drink. Allie wanted to reach out to her, but what would she say? *Yes, forget my fifteen-year-old sister? Go be with my dad, never mind that Brynn is suffering?* What an endless night. Allie wanted the comfort of Trevor's touch and his dry humor and naughty jokes so badly, she almost ached with it.

"So, when is it your turn, Allie dear?"

Allie blinked at Pix. "What?"

"I've noticed the way Trevor looks at you, like he's ready to pounce on you the moment you enter the room."

Allie's cheeks infused with heat. "You have it wrong. Trevor and I...we're just..." She shrugged.

"Don't put Allie on the spot, Pix. She and Trevor will figure things out in their own time," Mags said.

"Really though, I thought Trevor would never fall in love. He's always been so commitment phobic." She turned to Mags. "Is that the phrase?"

Mags sighed. "Yes, just more evidence that Nigel and I ruined him."

"He's not ruined," Allie said a little too loudly. Feeling embarrassed by her outburst, her gaze flashed around the room, and she lowered her voice. "He's just...in pain. And I really don't feel comfortable talking about him like this." She grabbed the sake and took a long swallow and, thanks to the coughing fit that followed, regretted it.

---

"That chap is becoming tiresome. Doesn't speak a word of English. Don't know what Pix sees in him." Nigel puffed around a fat cigar, a drink in one hand and his eyes roaming over the semiclad ass of the cocktail waitress who walked by.

Trevor raised a brow. "Really?"

"Can you believe your mother and I are getting married again?" Nigel nudged Trevor's ribs. "She was always the love of my life, you know."

"Did your four other wives know that?" Trevor let the waitress take his drink and refused a refill. He had to drive home since Simmons was escorting the women tonight.

"I fooled myself into thinking I was content. But it was all an illusion."

Trevor glanced at the roulette wheel. Paolo lost another bet. He watched as the younger man mopped his brow, then Trevor glanced at his father. "Your cock didn't seem to notice the difference."

"My heart did, Trev." Nigel patted his chest.

"Unless you want Pix and the Italian Stallion to become your physical dependents, I'd stop him from placing another bet if I were you. This asshole is running through Pixie's money like he inherited it himself."

Nigel sighed. "Oh, bugger." He walked to the table and grabbed Paolo by the shoulder.

Trevor rolled his eyes. How much longer until he could go home? He liked his home. It was comfortable there, cozy. And the thought of Allie in bed had him smiling. He loved sleeping with her. With her back to his chest, she'd curl up like a sleepy cat, press that tight ass against his cock. He sighed and looked at his watch.

Paolo and Nigel threaded their way over to him. Nigel tipped his head at the younger man. "Lost a barrelful, this one."

Paolo plunked down on a stool, propped his elbows on the bar, and buried his head in his hands. Then his head popped up. "Pix, will, how you say, kill my body." He slid his thumb across his throat.

"We've all lost our shirt a time or two, mate. And better she chop off your big head than your little one." Nigel slapped him on the back.

"I say we call it a night," Trevor said.

Nigel frowned. "It's not even midnight, Trev. What's say we go to see some tatas? Yeah?" Nigel cupped his hands in front of his chest for Paolo. "Tatas. Tits. Breasts."

Paolo's face lit up. "*Sì, tette.*"

"Yeah, see, Trev?" He pointed his cigar at Paolo.

"Take a cab." He started to walk off, only to have Nigel pull his sleeve. Trevor looked down at his father's hand and scowled. "Let go of me, old man."

Nigel clenched his jaw. "I told you not to call me old man."

"If the two of you tossers want to ogle topless women, fine, but I'm going home."

"Ah, I see what this is about." Nigel grinned and nodded. "You miss Allison. Granted, she is a lovely girl. Cheers, Trev. Very pleased for you."

Paolo's forehead wrinkled in confusion. "*Tette?*"

"Hold your horses," Nigel said.

Trevor jerked his arm from his father's grasp. "I don't know what you're on about."

"You and Allison, Son. You've finally got hit by Cupid's arrow, eh? Love is a beautiful thing."

Trevor's face became void of emotion. "I'm leaving." He strode out of the bar, through the casino. The laughter, chatter, and sounds of slot machines faded into the background. Nigel was clearly a mental case. Trevor wasn't in love with Allie. He didn't believe in it—silly, sloppy emotion. Just another word for wanting to shag someone. And that's what he wanted to do with her, shag. That was all. She was just a girl, really. A beautiful girl with an amazing smile and a spectacular pair of *tette*, but just a girl.

He rubbed his chest as he stalked out of the casino. He didn't love Allie. Period.

# Chapter 20

ALLIE KICKED OFF HER shoes and made her way up the stairs. Tonight had been exhausting. Mags was a handful, but add Pixie into the mix, and they became unhinged. Karen was a quiet, dark cloud who would have cast a pall over the evening if Mags and Pix hadn't been so enamored of their waiter—a young student named Matt. They fawned over him, quizzed him about his girlfriends, and Pix groped his ass. The sake had gone straight to her libido. Paolo had better be up for the challenge.

Allie went to her own room first, a little disappointed that Trevor wasn't already naked and in bed, waiting for her. She tugged off her dress and slipped into a sexy nightgown and robe before she headed to Trevor's room.

When she heard the shower running, she stepped into the bathroom. A wet room with no doors, her view was unhampered. He stood facing her, his head tossed back, his eyes closed as streams of water ran over his broad shoulders, down his muscled chest to his lean hips. His legs stood slightly apart, his cock jutted out, long and hard. Allie grew damp and aroused just watching him.

His gray eyes popped open. Her heart thundered at the sight of naked, beautiful Trevor.

"Come here." He held out his hand to her.

Entranced, she untied the knot on her robe and slipped it off. Her nipples hardened as his eyes raked her body. Slowly, she brushed the straps from her lacy nightgown down her shoulders and let it flutter to the floor.

Trevor's chest heaved as he took her in, his gaze lingering on her breasts. His stormy gray eyes traveled to her face. "Allison." His voice, deeper and huskier than usual, shot a bolt of desire right through her.

Without hesitating one more second, she walked toward him. He scooped her up, pressing her back against the wall, and kissed her. The warm cascade of water hit her from all sides, and soon she was slick with it.

Wrapping her legs around his waist, Allie kissed him back, bit his lip, sucked his tongue, thrust her own in his mouth as she grabbed a handful of his sopping hair. She pulled back and looked into his eyes. His eyelashes, even darker when wet, spiked together and framed his fierce eyes.

"I don't love you," he said through clenched teeth. "Do you understand? I don't love anyone." He thrust inside her, hot and hard. His fingers dug into her hips as he ground himself into her. "Allison, oh God, Allison." With each thrust, he chanted in her ear.

Allie buried her face in his neck, her tears mingling with the water.

---

She awoke in his bed the next morning. She knew without having to look that he was gone. After his declaration of unlove, he'd finished inside her. It was the first time they hadn't used a condom. Then, carefully, as if she might break with the slightest pressure, he dried her off and carried her to bed. Not a word was spoken between them as he curled his body around hers, one hand holding her breast, his leg thrown possessively over her own.

He didn't speak in the middle of the night when he stroked her body to orgasm before sliding into her. Nor earlier in the morning, when he woke her by flipping her over and burying himself inside her as he leisurely fucked her senseless.

Now she lay in sheets that smelled like him, a clean, crisp scent that made her grab his pillow and inhale deeply. When she realized how pathetic she was, she tossed the pillow aside and sat up.

Plunging her hands through her long, still-damp tangles of hair, she sighed. He didn't love her. Why did he say it? Did he suspect her feelings? Had she revealed herself somehow? Oh God, how humiliating.

With a hurting heart, she climbed out of bed. Her night-gown and robe had been folded on the small bench at the end of Trevor's carved bed. She quickly dressed and went to her room to take a shower.

Allie stepped into the en suite, and as she shrugged out of the robe and nightgown, the outer door clicked. With a towel clutched to her chest, she poked her head out of the bathroom. Trevor stood, dressed in a dark, expensive suit, a bright blue tie perfectly knotted at his throat. Hands thrust in his pockets, he leaned his back against the door.

"I went to my room, but you were gone. How are you this morning?"

Her fingers tightened on the towel. What was he really asking? If she understood that he didn't love her, didn't care about her, that it was still just about sex? Or did he really want to know how she felt this morning? All the progress they'd made over the last few weeks, all the closeness had fallen away, and she was back to square one. A fuck toy.

She shrugged. "Fine." Her eyes rose to meet his.

"Good."

They stood in silence for some moments. "I'm going to get a shower," she said, biting her lip to keep herself from bursting into tears.

"Yes, of course. I'll get out of your way." He was acting weird and formal.

When he left, she sank to the cold, tiled floor and sobbed. She cried until she didn't have any tears left, then attempted to pull herself together.

After she'd showered and dressed, Allie crept downstairs, hoping like hell she didn't run into Trevor again. She couldn't handle the awkward tension between them. And she was determined not to fall apart in front of him.

Once she was in the foyer, she heard voices raised in the drawing room. Allie ran toward the commotion and met Frances running through the hall from the opposite direction. Together, they stood in the doorway and watched Mags storm around the room.

"I can't believe you, Nigel. You are *un*believable." There were no *darlings*, *dearests*, or *sweets* to punctuate her sentence. She must really be angry. And she was repeating herself.

"Darling, I don't see what the problem is." Nigel stood next to the drinks cart, a quizzical look on his face. He watched her roam about the room.

Mags, her agitation growing by the minute, began walking faster and waved her hands over her head, like Mussolini. "Of course you don't, you stupid git."

"Watch yourself, love." He wagged a finger.

Mags threw her head back and laughed. "Watch myself. You should watch yourself, you bastard."

"I'll not put up with your name calling, my dear." Nigel crossed his arms, and his face took on the same cold, expressionless mask that Trevor assumed when he became angry.

"I'm not your dear. How dare you invite that woman to my wedding?"

"We're mates now, love, that's all." Nigel held up his hands in a pleading gesture. "Please be reasonable about this."

All of the fire seeped out of her and her body, rigid with anger a moment before, became relaxed. "Reasonable?" She raised a brow.

"How's this for reasonable?" She picked up a small bronze statue of a goddess and hurled it at Nigel's head.

He shifted to the side, narrowly escaping the projectile. "Now, Mags, that was Aphrodite. Not the thing, ducks."

She gave him a scary smile. "You're right, darling, I'm sorry."

"I should say so." Nigel dusted his shoulder. "Don't know what all the fuss is about."

"All the old jealousies are in the past," she practically cooed.

Nigel smiled. "Quite right."

"So if you invite Rebecca, I should invite Miguel. He and I are still on the best of terms. How very modern of you, darling."

"What did you say?" The smile turned to a scowl in the blink of an eye. "You will do absolutely no such thing. I forbid it."

"Oh no, we're in for it now," Frances whispered in Allie's ear.

Allie turned back and looked at the maid. "What do you mean?"

"Mrs. Mags just brought up Miguel. That's like waving a red flag at a bull, it is."

"You *forbid* me?"

Allie turned back in time to see Mags lift her chin to the ceiling. "You don't own me, Nigel Blake. I'll do whatever I please."

He strode across the room and grabbed her by the shoulders. "You will not mention that man's name in my presence, Margaret, do you understand?"

She broke free of his hold. "Miguel, Miguel, Miguel."

"You are living very dangerously, woman." Nigel's face turned purple. Allie was afraid he might stroke out.

"And while I'm at it, I may invite Francois. He asked me to move back to France just last month, you know."

"Fine," Nigel ground out, "then I'll ask Tanya. She got her boobs redone. She'd love to show them off at a wedding."

One of Mags's eyes narrowed, making her look slightly cock-eyed. She strolled across the room, picked up a bottle of gin, and threw it at him. "You are disgusting." The bottle hit the wall. The strong-smelling liquor made a stain on the pale blue paint, and glass tinkled to the floor.

"That was a new bottle."

"Well, this one's not." She chucked whiskey at his head. She wasn't even in the ballpark.

"You're aim isn't what it used to be, dear," he said in a bored voice.

"I guess I'm out of practice." She picked up a white vase with hand-painted flowers and held it over her head with both hands.

Allie felt hands on her hips and was lifted to one side. Trevor took two steps into the room and grabbed the vase from Mags's hands before she could hurl it at Nigel. "If you're going to give him a concussion, I must insist you destroy your own property to do so."

Mags's lips thinned in a straight line. "Your father wants to invite his second wife to my wedding. What do you think about that, Trevor?" Her eyes never left Nigel and his red face.

"I don't care whom you invite. I don't care if you get married at all. But if you break one more thing in this house, I'll toss you both out on your asses." He turned and left the room.

Allie gave Nigel and Mags one last look before trailing after him. "Trevor."

He stopped and glared at her. "What do you want?"

She flinched. "Sorry, I didn't mean…"

He rubbed his forehead. "Apologies, Allison, I didn't mean to snap at you. Those two drive me barmy." He thrust his hands in his pockets. "What can I do for you?"

For some reason, his formal question hurt more than his harsh words. She shook her head. "I just wanted to make sure you were okay."

Bitterness tinged his laughter. "I'm brilliant." He pivoted and went back toward his office.

Allie stood in the hallway, feeling bereft. She loved him so much, she ached with it. She knew he was going to cut her loose. And she wasn't sure how she was going to survive.

As she lingered in the hallway, Mags pushed by her with a sob.

---

That night, dinner was painful and the arctic atmosphere made Allie shiver. No one said much of anything. Trevor was withdrawn and quiet. Mags and Nigel were frigidly polite to one another.

After dinner, Trevor retreated to his office. Allie knew he didn't want to be disturbed, so she hit the media room, curling up on the couch beneath the cashmere blanket, and watched TV for a few hours. As she sat, her mind drifted. What would it have been like to hear her parents fight like that? Trevor must have been a confused little boy, new people entering his life and leaving it just as quickly.

Finally, exhausted at nine-thirty, she hit the power button on the controller. But instead of going to her own room, she went to Trevor's. The angels stood guard as she shimmied out of all her clothes and curled up under the sheets. She pulled Trevor's pillow close, inhaling his scent. Despite the pain of his callous treatment earlier, she wanted to comfort him, soothe him. She knew he was hurting. The little boy in him never got over his parents' abandonment or their manic relationship.

She woke when the bed dipped and felt Trevor try to gently pry the pillow out of her hands. She rubbed at her eyes and looked at the clock on the bedside table. "It's after midnight. Have you been working all this time?"

He plumped the pillow and crawled into bed, curling himself around her. "Yes. And I'm sorry I was abrupt earlier."

"It's okay." She stroked the arm wrapped around her waist. "They still love each other, you know, even when they fight."

"Shhh," he said against her hair. "Go back to sleep."

"Trevor?" She wasn't even sure what she wanted to say, maybe she just wanted reassurance for herself.

"Go to sleep, Allie."

She stroked his arm until she felt him breathe deep and rhythmically next to her. She was wide awake now. Her mother always fed her hot milk with vanilla and cinnamon when she couldn't sleep.

Allie crawled out from under Trevor's embrace and scooted to the edge of the bed. She looked back to make sure she hadn't awakened him, but when she saw he still slept, she quickly redressed and slipped quietly from the room.

She made her way to the kitchen and discovered Mags sitting at the granite counter, toying with a mugful of something. Her eyes were sad. She looked older and a little haggard.

"Hello, dearest. You couldn't sleep either?"

Allie rubbed her arms and shook her head. "No, I thought I'd make myself some warm milk. You?" She grabbed a sauce pan from the rack above the island and crossed the room to the fridge.

"Hot tea with whiskey." Mags took a whiff of her cup then sipped at it.

"Do you know where the cinnamon is?" Allie opened the small cabinet next to the range. "Found it."

"Allison, I'm sorry you witnessed Nigel and me arguing this morning."

Allie shrugged and poured milk into the copper-bottom pan. She added a cinnamon stick and decided to forget about hunting down the vanilla. "Frankly, Mags, it upsets me that Trevor saw that growing up."

Mags winced. "Yes. We've been dreadful parents. And now that the wedding's off, I suppose I'll leave. Probably head back to England with Pix and Paolo." She peered into her tea cup.

"What do you mean the wedding's off? Because of one fight? What about Nigel being the one that got away?"

"Yes, I thought so too." She gave Allie a wistful smile.

"So, that's it?" Allie felt an irrational anger rise to the surface. "You're not even going to fight to stay together?"

"There's been entirely too much fighting, Allie." She sighed. "You don't understand, darling. Pix was right. Nigel and I would never work."

Allie breathed out a laugh. "Trevor had you pegged from the start. The two of you are complete fuckups. Do you know how hard my mom fought for her life so that she could stay with us? Do you have any idea how painful it was to watch her die a little bit every day? You have a second chance at happiness, a second chance to show Trevor that you're not a flake."

Mags looked stricken. "Allison."

"He'd have been better off if you hadn't come back. But you guys had to turn the knife one more time. You couldn't just leave him alone." She grabbed the pan and poured the milk down the sink and tossed the pan in too.

"It's not that simple, darling."

Allie whirled around. "Nothing worth having is ever easy. God, don't you get that?" She swept out of the room and ran back to Trevor's room, craving his arms around her. He may not love her, but she loved him. And she wasn't going to give up on him. She knew he cared about her. Maybe that could be enough.

She entered his room and shucked her clothes, leaving them on the floor. As she pulled back the covers, Trevor stirred. "You all right?" he asked, his voice faint and sleepy.

Allie lay on her side facing him, one hand resting on his hip. She rained light kisses down his chest, her tongue swirling around his nipple. Trevor groaned and dragged her on top of him.

Allie straddled him and braced her hands on his wide shoulders as she leaned down to kiss him. She groaned when her lips met his. Trevor reached between them and held back the curtain of her hair.

Her nipples hardened as they brushed his smooth chest and her lips clung to his.

Pulling back, she fitted herself over his shaft and slowly lowered her body, taking him in as deeply as she could. He helped her by pistoning her hips up and down his cock. "Trevor," she gasped. She reached down and rubbed her clit, and as she came she threw her head back and lost herself in the sensations.

Trevor increased the pace. Allie's breasts jiggled as he slammed up into her. "Yes, Allison. Oh God." He clenched his eyes shut as he came, then his grasp on her hips slacked off.

Allie collapsed on his chest, breathing hard. Her hair fell over him, and he smoothed it with one hand.

"Why did you get out of bed?" He petted her hair, slowly brushing the strands back from her face.

"Couldn't sleep and I went to the kitchen for milk." She turned her face and planted a kiss on his chest. "Trevor." She raised her head. He looked so peaceful, so content in the afterglow, she didn't want to tell him about his parents.

"Yes, love?"

She smiled. "Nothing." He'd find out soon enough tomorrow. Allie rolled off his chest and laid her head in the crook of his arm.

He kissed her temple. "Think you'll be able to sleep now?"

"Um hmm." She closed her eyes and drifted off.

---

The next morning she found Trevor in his office. She bypassed breakfast when she saw he wasn't at the table. She stuck her head in the door, watched him for a moment tapping away on his computer.

"Hey, sorry to interrupt."

He glanced up but continued fiddling with his keyboard. "What is it, Allison? I'm busy this morning."

If he thought that would put her off, he was fooling himself.

She'd dealt with two teenage girls who had the leave-me-the-hell-alone-or-I'll-cut-you vibe down pat. She walked into the room. "I take it you've heard about Mags and Nigel?"

His fingers stilled. "I knew all about Mags and Nigel before they ever got here. I told you it wouldn't last. Hope you're not too disappointed."

She approached his side of the desk, leaning against it, and placed a hand on his arm. "I'm so sorry, Trevor."

"Huh." He shook her off. "Don't be ridiculous. I'm not a child, and I haven't had any illusions about those two since I was a very young boy. I don't need your sympathy."

Allie clasped her hands and took a deep breath. "I understand your skepticism and pain."

He threw his head back and laughed then—not a laugh filled with humor, but a hard laugh tinged with bitterness and anger. "Do you? Well, that's such a relief. Am I meant to share all my angst over those two bloody morons?" He pushed back from the chair and stood. He moved over and wedged himself between her legs. "I never thought for an instant those two would remarry, and I believe I told you so on numerous occasions." His voice was calm and pleasant, and he wore that blank mask she'd grown to hate.

She placed her hands on his chest. "Trevor, marriage, love, it doesn't have to be like that. My parents—"

"Your parents were an anomaly and probably only stayed together because of you and your sisters. That and your dire economic straits. Don't kid yourself that they had some kind of fairy tale, Allie. Fairy tales don't exist, and you women think if you shag someone, it means you love him. You can't bear the thought that you simply like fucking, so you make it romantic and put a name on it. It's all bollocks." He leaned down, placed a hand on the back of her head, and gave her a savage kiss. "That's real. What we have when I'm inside you, that's real. Don't wrap it in a bow and think it's anything more."

She pushed his chest to try and force him away. He didn't budge, but he let go of her head. "Don't talk about my parents that way, Trevor. My mother lay there, dying, and my father was so broken up about it—"

"That he got himself a girlfriend six months later. Oh yes, darling, he was very committed."

Allie wanted to lash out at him, hit him, hurt him like he'd just hurt her. "Believe what you want. But love does exist, Trevor, because I love you. Yeah, I know you don't want to hear it and I know you won't believe it, but there it is. I'm in love with you. And it's not just fucking wrapped in a bow, it's consuming and scary and wonderful."

He dismissed her with a look, his lips pressed together in a straight line. "I told you, I don't need your sympathy, so take your declarations of love and get out. I've got work to do." He stepped away from her and sat down in his chair, shutting her out.

She should have expected his reaction, especially given his mood. Nevertheless, she felt bruised, wounded. Dazed, she moved from the desk and, with heavy feet, walked out of the room.

She stood at the end of the hallway, her fingers rubbing her still-tender lips, unsure what to do next. Should she pack up and leave? Everything in her wanted to stay, despite Trevor's harsh treatment of her just now. She knew he was hurting—probably even more than she was—knew it in her gut. Everyone in his life had left him. Was she going to do the same? That's why he pushed people away, so they would leave on his terms and not blindside him, like his parents had done time and time again.

She left the office and went to Mags's room, where she found her fluttering like a moth around a light, darting between the closet and the bed with armfuls of clothes. "Oh, Allie dear, I've shopped so much, I think I need a new suitcase."

Allie turned to Frances. The normally cheerful, talkative maid was quiet and her forehead wrinkled into a V shape. "Good morning."

"Frances, do you think I could have a word with Mags?"

"Yes, of course." She laid a dress on the bed and squeezed Allie's shoulder as she walked by.

Allie waited until the other woman left then she watched Mags, who was still in perpetual motion. "Mags, where's Nigel?"

Mags held up two dresses, one blue, one green. "Gone, dear. Which do you think I should wear on the plane?"

"Neither."

"Well, I can't very well go naked, now can I? Although, with those perverts at security, I might as well be."

"Where did he go?"

She dropped both dresses on the bed and flitted to the dresser. "I need to send my jewels back by courier. I don't like to travel with them. Go call Frances, dear."

"No."

Mags did glance up at her then. "Sorry?"

Allie shoved all the dresses to one side and sat down on the blue silk bedcover, curling one leg under her. "So that's it? You're just going to leave him again?"

"Well…" Mags swallowed, her eyes shifting to the floor. "Nigel and I are over, Allie. I'm sure Trevor wants me out of his hair."

"So all that talk about staying in Vegas to make amends, all that was just bullshit?"

Mags tilted her head and gave Allie a disapproving glance.

"You're leaving him again."

With a sigh, Mags gathered up the dresses and moved them to a chair. Half of them slid to the floor, but she didn't bend to pick them up. She sank down on the bed next to Allie. "He doesn't want me here, darling. He told me so this morning."

"He's been telling you to leave for weeks, Mags. And you've decided to listen to him now?"

"Well…" She waved her hands helplessly.

"You're afraid he's going to give you a hard time for breaking the engagement?"

"My son hates me, Allison. It's time I faced that. Why keep butting my head against a wall, darling? It's painful, and it dulls the senses."

Allie took one of Mags's hands in both of hers. "He doesn't hate you. But if you keep abandoning him, he will. And yes, he's going to give you hell, I mean, have you met Trevor?"

Sniffing, Mags gave a little laugh.

"He needs you in his life. He's always needed you. Maybe this time, you can be there for him."

"I don't know." Mags's gaze drifted toward the door.

"Where's Nigel?"

She glanced back at Allie. "He's staying at the Bellagio."

Allie left the room. She made her way out of the house and toward the garage, where Simmons polished the side mirror on the limo.

"Can I help you with something?" he asked.

"No, I'm good. Just going for a ride."

# Chapter 21

TREVOR RAN A HAND over his face. Allie said she loved him. Poor girl didn't understand that he never expected a happily ever after—for his parents or himself. Mags and Nigel were like two children playacting. As soon as things got boring, they moved on to other playmates.

He'd said some very hateful things to Allie, caused her pain again, and he hated that, hated seeing that wounded look in her eyes. But he stood by it all. Love was a fantasy, a dressed-up word for passion.

Maybe it was simply time to end it. He rejected the idea immediately. No, he wasn't through with Allison Campbell. And as long as she understood that whatever they had was temporary, they would be fine.

Of course he was fond of her. And yes, he loved being inside her, tasting her, touching her. Her response to him was like a drug, left him craving more. He liked the way she bit her lip to study the chessboard while she contemplated her next move. The way she smelled and the way she laughed and the way she cared about her family. But that wasn't love. Far from it. That was appreciation for another person. To muck it up with talk of love was beyond ridiculous. And she needed to understand that.

He stood from behind the desk and stretched his arms over his head. He needed more coffee. Actually, he needed a swim. It would clear his head and maybe he could think of a way to clear the sadness from Allie's eyes.

He checked his computer one last time and made his way up the stairs. Once he hit the landing, Mags walked toward him. "I thought you'd left with the other one." He brushed by her and walked in the opposite direction toward his room.

Mags trotted along behind him. "I want to talk to you."

"No time," he said, looking back over his shoulder. "I'm busy today. If you need a ride to the airport, have Simmons take you." Walking into his room, he shut the door in Mags's face.

He shed his jacket, tie, and shirt, and had just started working the button on his trousers when the door opened and Mags strolled in. "Excuse me, *Mother*, I'm in the middle of something."

She waved a hand in his direction. "Nothing I haven't seen before, darling." She walked to a chair next to the fireplace and sat, crossing one leg over the other.

With a sigh of resignation, Trevor rebuttoned his trousers and grabbed his shirt from the floor, slipping his arms into it. "What is it you want?"

"Shall we eat in the garden tonight?"

"I thought you were moving out?"

"No, dearest, I've decided to stay."

Gritting his teeth, he clenched his fists. "For how long?"

"Well, that rather depends on you." She rose from the chair and stepped toward him, patting his cheek. "Until you forgive me."

His face became immobile. "No worries then. I forgave you years ago. Feel free to leave anytime."

Mags smiled. "I'm not going anywhere, darling. You may as well get used to it." She left the room in a cloud of sweet perfume. Goddamn Allison. This little ploy had do-gooder stamped all over it.

—◊◊◊—

Allie knocked on the door of the suite. Nigel answered wearing a thick terry robe with the hotel initials embroidered on the chest. His eyes were bloodshot, and he hadn't combed his wavy hair. "Allison, my dear, now is not a good time."

She edged past him. "Yeah, yeah." She glanced around the living room. "You don't have a woman in here, do you?"

"Only you. Did Mags send you?" He waved her inside.

"Um, Nige, why don't you get dressed?"

He looked down at his bathrobe and grinned. "Don't want a repeat performance, eh?"

No, she really didn't. One glance at little Nigel and she was still scarred. "Go pants up."

With a sigh, he stepped around a large entertainment unit that stood in the center of the room. He came back a moment later in old jeans and a golf shirt. "So, if Mags didn't send you…"

"I want to talk about Trevor."

"Ah. We should head down to one of the restaurants. I need a drink for this discussion." He snagged his room card off the side table, slipped it in his pocket, and opened the door. "After you, love."

They rode the elevator to the seafood restaurant, and because it was early, they were quickly shown to a table. Nigel held out her chair and made sure she was comfortable before they ordered.

When his martini arrived, he nodded. "All right, love, what's this about Trevor?"

Allie plunged once again into waters that were none of her business. "I think you should stay in Vegas."

"What makes you think I was leaving?" Nigel stirred his drink with two speared olives.

"You mean you're going to stick around? But Mags was headed back to England."

"Was?" His eyes sharpened. "Have her plans changed then?"

"I don't know, but I told her she should stay too. For Trevor's sake."

"Oh." His gaze shifted to the table and he took a sip from his glass. "I thought she meant to stay for me. That she'd had a change of heart."

"Look, Nigel, I shouldn't butt in—"

"No, it's all right, Allison." He sighed deeply. "I talked to Rebecca a few weeks ago—she was wife number two—anyway, we've remained friendly all these years. I married her on the rebound from Mags, and it was a terrible mistake. Didn't last more than a year, but I think Mags and I might have worked things out if I hadn't jumped into it with Rebecca. In retaliation, Mags married her number two, that damn Spaniard."

"So, why did you invite Rebecca to the wedding, knowing how Mags felt?"

"Rebecca's married to an old chum of mine. Went to school with Clifford. Damn fine shot on the golf course. He once shot a birdie—"

"Nige, back to the guest list."

"Oh, quite. Well, I thought we could put the past behind us, and once they were here, Clifford and I could play a few rounds. But you saw how Mags went barmy."

"So, why not just uninvite them?"

He looked a little sheepish. "Don't like to back down. It's my wedding too, you know."

Allie closed her eyes for a second. "Trevor nailed it, the two of you are morons."

"I say, Allison."

"No, I mean it. You and Mags have found each other again, after all this time. You say you love each other, you want to make amends with Trevor, but the minute you don't get your own way, you cut and run. What is that about?"

Suddenly, Nigel sat up straight in his chair and became very starchy. "Not that it's any of your concern—"

"I know it's not. But sometimes you have to make compromises to be happy. And if Mags doesn't want your ex-wife at her wedding, I think that's a pretty reasonable request. Now, what about Trevor?"

Nigel drained his glass and motioned to the waiter. "What about Trevor? I'm staying in Vegas for the time being."

"Have you told him you're sorry? Have you asked him how he felt when the two of you left him and got married a zillion times?"

Nigel shifted uncomfortably. "We're British, dear. We don't sit around and talk endlessly about our feelings. Besides, he's still upset about Anna."

"Who's Anna?"

Nigel glanced at the waiter. "Keep them coming, please. I have a feeling it's going to be a long afternoon." He gave Allie a look as dry as his martini. "Trev didn't tell you about Anna?"

Her stomach fell fourteen stories and kept dropping. "No."

"Trevor dated her a few years back. Nothing serious, but she was my fifth. Wife that is."

Allie blinked. "You married Trevor's ex?" No wonder he hated his father.

Nigel popped an olive in his mouth. "It's not like he was serious about her. They casually dated for a couple months. I apologized."

"You apologized? *For marrying Trevor's girlfriend?*"

Nigel straightened. "She wasn't his girlfriend at the time. They'd broken up, you see."

"That doesn't make it okay," she hissed.

"What do you want me to do? I've tried to get him to play a round of golf, but he's always working."

"You think bonding over a round of golf is going to fix this?" Did Trevor still care about this Anna? No wonder he didn't believe in love. There was no hope for them. She'd known it all along, but she'd let herself believe.

Her phone rang, breaking her train of thought. She groped in her bag and pulled it out. "Sorry, it's Brynn."

"Take it, dear." He sipped at his drink and glanced around the room.

"What's wrong?" Allie said in lieu of greeting.

"I'm in trouble, Al." Brynn sniffed a few times. "I got in a fight."

Allie's body froze. "Are you all right? Are you still at school?"

"Yeah, can you come and get me? Dad's out on a job, and I'm in the principal's office."

"I'll be right there." She hung up and looked at Nigel. "I have to go. Brynn's been in a fight."

Nigel hopped up from his seat and pulled out his wallet, throwing a few bills on the table. "I'll go with you, my dear."

She didn't waste time arguing but fled the restaurant, Nigel at her heels.

—◦◦◦—

She and Nigel checked in at the front office and sat on stiff chairs, waiting to see the principal. Allie nervously clutched her bag in her lap.

Nigel reached over and gave her hand a squeeze. "Brynn's a good girl, Allison. Everything is going to be all right."

It seemed like everything had gone haywire today. Brynn didn't get in fights. She didn't like conflict of any kind.

Allie glanced up at Nigel. For some reason, his casual, nonchalant air was calming.

A middle-aged woman with a short, wispy hairstyle moved toward them. "Mr. Campbell? I'm Mrs. Stanford, Assistant Principal."

Allie stood up and held her bag in front of her. "I'm Allie Campbell, Brynn's sister and emergency contact. This is—"

"Nigel Blake." He rose and shook the woman's hand.

"I can't believe Brynn got into a fight," Allie said. "She's a straight-A student. Maybe she mentioned that?"

"Step into my office, please."

Nigel stayed behind as Allie followed the vice principal. Her little sister sat in one chair, facing the desk.

Allie dropped to the other seat, her eyes scanning Brynn "Are you all right? Are you hurt?"

Brynn kept her gaze on her lap and shook her head. "I'm okay, Al."

"Miss Campbell, your sister and another girl had a heated exchange and Brynn threw a punch. The other girl managed to duck and tackled Brynn to the floor. A teacher broke it up before things could escalate."

"Is that what happened?" Allie asked.

Brynn studied her fingernails and shrugged.

Allie glanced at Mrs. Stanford. "Do you know what this was about?"

"I believe one of our staff, Ms. Castor, is dating your father?"

"Oh, great." Allie slouched in the chair and covered her eyes with one hand.

"We have a zero-tolerance policy for violence in this school. Brynn will spend the next two weeks on in-house suspension and this will go on her permanent record."

"Starting when?" Allie asked.

"Tomorrow. You can take her home now." She stood, crossed the room, and opened the door.

"Come on, Nigel's waiting."

Brynn got to her feet and shuffled out of the office. "Sorry, Al," she whispered.

"Hello, my darling." Nigel enfolded Brynn in his arms, and she hugged him back. He held her hand as they headed outside into the bright sunshine.

"What were you thinking?" Allie asked after they all climbed into the car.

Brynn shrugged again.

"Enough with the shrugging. That Stanford woman said you threw the first punch."

"Layla Anderson said some crap, and I just lost it."

She refrained from asking anymore questions on the ride home. When Allie parked in front of her old house, she turned to Nigel. "Do you want to take the car back to the hotel?"

"Oh no, I can take a taxi."

Inside the house, Nigel made himself at home on the saggy, ripped couch. He picked up the remote and flipped through the channels. "Where's the golf channel, Als?"

"We don't have cable, Nige."

"Oh." He looked a little forlorn.

"I'll be right back. Do you want something to drink or eat? We never did get lunch."

Nigel waved her off. "No, darling, I'm fine."

"Brynn, go get started on your homework and I'll make you a snack."

Once in the kitchen, Allie called Trevor. He answered on the first ring.

"Where in the bloody hell have you been?"

"Can Simmons come and pick up your dad?"

"What the … Where are you?"

"Home."

"At your father's house, then?"

"Yeah. Brynn got into a fight and is suspended."

"Where does my father fit into this picture?"

"I was having lunch with him when I got the call from Brynn."

She heard him take a deep breath. "Allison, listen to me. Those two nut jobs are not worth the effort."

"What? You…break…up…send…Sim…" And she hung up. She didn't want a lecture right now, she just wanted to make sure Brynn was okay until her father got home.

She threw together sandwiches for Brynn and Nigel, along with cookies and glasses of iced tea. She put everything on a tray and carried it to the living room. Nigel sat back, his legs crossed, engrossed in a talk show that had turned into a free-for-all with the audience members.

He hopped up when he saw her, took the tray, and set it down on the coffee table. He pointed to the screen. "Turns out, he's not the father of her child after all. They just released the DNA results and all hell broke loose. You Americans."

She reached over and flicked off the set. "What are you going to do about Mags? About Trevor?"

He took a long sip of iced tea and winced. "I don't know, Als."

"Do you love Mags, Nigel? Really love her?"

"I do. I desperately love her. But it's too late. She's already taken me back once. There's not going to be a third act, love."

She sat next to him and patted his knee. "Tell her you were wrong to want your ex at the wedding. Let Mags know she matters to you."

He gazed at the carpet and back up at Allie. "Do you really think she'd take me back? You don't know how long it took to win her affections for the second time. I could be well into the grave before she gives me another go."

"It might help if you didn't marry the first woman who flashes her boobs."

"Well, quite."

"Okay," she said, slapping her knees and popping to her feet. "I'm going to see about Brynn."

Nigel grabbed the sandwich with one hand and turned the TV back on with the other.

Allie took the tray to the girls' room. With her hands full, she kicked the door gently with her foot. "Brynn, open up."

Brynn opened the door and preceded Allie to the bed, tumbled onto it, and pulled a pillow over her face. "I hate my life."

Allie set the tray on the bedside table and pulled the pillow off Brynn. "We all hate our lives at one point or another. But you'll get through this, Brynnie."

"What's to hate about your life? It seems pretty perfect from where I'm sitting."

The man Allie loved not only didn't love her back, but he didn't believe in the emotion, had been permanently scarred by his parents and ex-girlfriend. She hadn't heard from Monica in weeks, and she wasn't talking to her dad. Yeah, things were great.

"Nobody's life is perfect. And you will get through this. What I want to know is"—she hopped on the bed next to Brynn, making the mattress bounce—"why you got in a fight in the first place."

"Stupid Layla. She said that the only reason I got an A on my paper was because my dad was fuc…er, boinking Ms. Castor. I said my command of the English language probably helped, and that if she would come up for air, instead of blowing half the football team, maybe she would pass the class."

Allie sat in shock, her eyes wide. "Brynn, you don't talk like that."

"Well, I won't anymore. One time I mouth off, I get in trouble. Dad is going to kill me."

"No, he's not. He might ground you, but kill you? No, it's too hard to hide a body."

Brynn fell back on the bed and gave an almost laugh.

"So, you threw the first punch?" Allie asked.

"No, someone pushed me into Layla, and she thought I hit her, and well, you know the rest. The algebra teacher, Mrs. McCrady, saw me get physical first, so it was my fault. I tried to tell them what happened, but it didn't do any good."

Brynn picked up the pillow and held it over her face again. Allie closed her eyes and lay quietly next to her sister for a while. Finally, she rallied.

"Try and eat something, hon." She climbed off the bed and made her way to the living room.

Trevor sat in the big easy chair, glaring at his father. Nigel untwisted an Oreo and licked the creamy center.

"These biscuits are delicious, Allison. We should get some of these at home, Son."

Trevor's face became a frozen mask. "I assume you mean your own home? Because you are not coming back to mine."

"Trevor, can I talk to you in the kitchen, please?" Allie asked.

His cold, gray eyes shifted to her. "Oh, yes. You and I are going to talk, make no mistake about that." He stood and swept past her to the kitchen.

Nigel winked at her. "Good luck, love. It's best to nod and look earnest when he's like this."

Heart beating double time, Allie followed Trevor to the kitchen. He strode toward the sink, his back to her.

"I don't like people fucking with my life, Allison." His voice was completely calm and polite, but his back was tense.

She said nothing.

"I won't tolerate it." Slowly, he turned and gave her a cold smile. "Do we understand one another?"

Allie felt herself nodding.

"Good." He started walking away, but Allie held up a hand.

"Wait, no I don't understand. How am I fucking with your life?"

He stopped. "I finally got rid of the old man, and Mags was on her way out too, but you interfered. You stopped her from leaving. Don't bother to deny it." His voice was dripping with icy displeasure.

"I wasn't going to. Yes, I talked Mags into staying. She thinks you hate her, Trevor. Is that how you want to leave things with your mom? I know she wasn't perfect, but she loves you and she wants to make it up to you."

He glared at her, like she was something disgusting. "I know you don't understand, because you had a different set of circumstances with your parents, but stay out of it. I don't care how she feels, and there is no making up for the past."

"Nigel told me about Anna. I'm so sorry."

"Why should you be sorry? It's that wanker out there who should be sorry."

She craned her head to gaze up at him. "He is, Trevor. He's been trying to apologize, but he doesn't know how."

He stepped closer. "Mind your business, Miss Campbell. You have enough trouble with your own fucking family. Some things are better left in the past."

She planted her palm on her forehead. "But can't you see the past still affects you? You're angry and you have a right to be, but maybe, if you give them a chance—"

"I'm done with this conversation." He stalked to the back door but spun around to glare at her. "I suppose you think I'm damaged. You tell me you love me, and voilà, I'm a changed man." He said something low and vicious under his breath and stepped toward her, clasped the back of her neck and pulled her close, until her breasts were pressed against his chest. "Well, I'm fine. I don't need to change. And I don't want your love. Keep it. Look at what it's got you. You loved your family so goddamned much, you sold your body to me."

"I think you'd better get the hell out of my house," Brian Campbell said.

Allie wrenched out of Trevor's grasp and glanced at her father, watched his face harden. Horror and shame filled her.

"Gladly." Trevor exited the kitchen, brushing his arm against Brian's shoulder.

Allie flinched when the front door slammed.

# Chapter 22

ALLIE STAGGERED TO THE kitchen table and collapsed into a chair. Burying her head in her hands, she fought back tears. She didn't want to see the disappointment in her father's eyes.

She heard him approach, heard the bottom of the chair scrape against the outdated linoleum. "Al, look at me, honey."

She shook her head and kept her hands over her eyes. He firmly, but gently, pried them away.

"Is what he said true? Did you sacrifice yourself for us?"

Allie didn't know what to say. Her heart felt like it had been smashed into a million pieces.

"I'm so sorry, Allison. I should have seen it. I should have known his offer was too good to be true." He let go of her hands. "I'm going to kill that son of a bitch."

"Unless I'm very much mistaken, your daughter loves my son-of-a-bitch son. So I don't think killing him is a good option right now." Nigel stood in the doorway, his gaze scanning the kitchen and landing on Allie.

"How much did you hear?" Allie asked, her stomach a tangle of knots.

"All of it." He stepped into the room. "Do you love him?"

She took a deep, ragged breath and nodded. "So much."

"He loves you too. He's just too bullheaded to know it. I'm going to call Mags. She'll know what to do." He walked back to the living room.

"I'm sorry, Dad." She felt drained and empty.

He kissed the top of her head. "You have nothing to be sorry for, darlin'."

"Brynn was suspended from school today."

He nodded. "Yeah, I better go talk to her. I really let you kids down. Your mom would be so ashamed." His chin trembled slightly.

"No she wouldn't. She would never be ashamed of you. But she'd be so disappointed in me."

He leaned away, a pained look on his face. "That's not true. She's proud of you, Al, and so am I. Everything you've done was for this family. You took over when I was too weak to do what was right." Turning, he sniffed and cleared his throat as he hustled out of the room.

Allie didn't know how long she sat in the kitchen, but she blinked when the overhead light turned on and Mags walked into the room in a swath of yellow silk.

She pulled Allie up and swept her into a hug. "My son is a beast, darling. Go on now, let it all out. There's a good girl." Mags patted Allie's back as the tears that had threatened since Trevor left finally fell.

When Allie was all cried out, she rubbed her nose on the back of her wrist. "He doesn't love me."

"Oh, my precious girl, of course he does. And how could he not? When you're not caterwauling, you're very attractive."

"But he doesn't. He told me so the night of the hen party."

Mags smiled and rubbed Allie's shoulder. "He told you specifically he didn't love you?"

"Those exact words."

She cupped Allie's cheek. "It will all be well. I promise."

Allie swallowed back a denial. Mags would only argue with her. "If you don't mind, I'm going to lie down for a while."

—⁓—

Five days later, Allie was still in bed. Brynn tried to tempt her into getting up but had no success. Brian came in every morning to check on her, but by the third day, he sounded worried.

"Al, you can't stay in bed all day. You didn't even do this when your mom died. Come on, sweetheart. I'll make you some breakfast."

Allie's response was to roll over and face the wall until he left. She didn't want to get out of bed ever again. What was the point? Life sucked, no two ways about it. She had kept her spirits up, chugged along, took care of everyone. And look what happened—one sister gone, one suspended for fighting. For five long years Allie had struggled to hold her family together and take care of her mother. Well, her mom was gone and Allie had failed miserably. Losing Trevor, having her declaration of love thrown back in her face—that was the final straw. What was the point of it all?

Time had no meaning. The days bled one into another. Brynn made sure she had a glass of water next to the bed and brought in sandwiches, which Allie didn't eat.

On day five she was awakened by someone shaking her arm so hard she dreamed she was in an earthquake. When she pried open her eyes, she found Frances and Mags peering at her with furrowed brows and thinned lips. "What are you doing here?" she asked.

"You smell, Miss Allie."

"The whole room reeks, darling. Brynn called and said you hadn't been out of bed since I left."

Mags's black-and-white-striped retro dress had Allie crossing her eyes, so she closed them. "Please go away."

"You need to get up." Frances jerked the covers back.

Allie felt like a vampire exposed to sunlight. With a scowl, she pulled the covers out of Frances's hand and covered herself back up. "Go away. I don't want to see you and I don't want to get out of bed."

"Oh, darling, he's just as bad, you know." The mattress dipped as Mags sank down next to Allie and rubbed her arm. "I've never seen him so depressed. Come back with me. And you really are quite ripe, dearest."

Allie opened one eye and glared at them both. "I'm not going back. And if you don't like how I smell, get the hell out."

"Please, Al." Brynn hovered by the door. "You're scaring me." She twisted her hands together and stood on her toes.

Groaning, Allie covered her face with both hands. She might be a complete loser, but her sister still needed her—although she wasn't much use to anyone.

Allie sat up and tried to smile. "I didn't mean to scare you, sweetheart. I'm just sad."

Brynn nodded. "I know."

"All right then, let's get you cleaned up. I'll run a shower." Frances bustled out of the room.

Mags stood. "I think we'll need to burn these sheets and your bedclothes, Allison. I'm not sure the smell will ever come out."

Allie sighed. Time to get back to her life. Her very sucky life.

She stood and was a bit lightheaded, so she grabbed hold of Mags's arm until the dizziness passed. She patted Brynn's face as she walked by. "Make me some coffee, would you, sweetie? Really strong coffee."

Frances stood next to the bathroom door, where steam flowed out in gusts. "Thanks, Frances."

Allie peeled off her smelly clothes and opened the door to the old fiberglass shower. The hot spray pelting her sensitive skin was almost painful. With heavy arms, she scrubbed herself and washed her hair. It was too much effort to condition it, and really, her split ends could just bite it.

It took every bit of energy she had to dry herself and step into the jeans, bra, and T-shirt that Frances had laid on the countertop. She reached up and swiped the foggy mirror, glancing at herself for the first time in days. She winced at her reflection. No wonder

Brynn had been scared. Her cheeks were hollow and she sported huge purple circles under her eyes.

She twisted her hair up, secured it with a clip, and brushed her teeth. That was all she was going to do, but still she lingered in the damp, steamy room. She didn't want to face Mags and Frances and especially Brynn. All she really wanted to do was curl up in bed and shut out the rest of the world.

Finally, she took a deep breath and opened the bathroom door. All three ladies stood in the hallway, Brynn with a mug in her hands. The prison guards eyed her as if she might make a run for it.

Allie looked at them in turn. "I'm not going back to bed." She took the coffee and gave Brynn a little smile. "Thanks." She blew at the surface and took a sip.

Allie walked to the living room and sat down. She leaned her head back and was almost swept away by a tide of sadness so overwhelming she put a hand over her eyes to block out everything else.

"Al?"

She cleared her throat. "Just give me a minute, Brynn."

"Let's go make her something to eat, shall we?" Frances asked. "What do you think will tempt her?"

Allie removed her hand and watched Frances lead Brynn to the kitchen. She glanced at Mags and almost lost her composure at the sympathy in the older woman's eyes.

"My darling Allison—"

"How's Nigel? Have the two of you kissed and made up?"

"We're working on it. I do love that man to distraction, even though sometimes I want to take a croquet mallet to his skull."

Allie nodded and sipped her coffee.

"He's been miserable since you left." Mags tilted her head to the side.

"Nigel? Well, tell him to go golfing. That seems to cheer him up."

"Allie, please."

"I'm not going to talk about him. I can't." Tears clogged her throat. God, she was so stupid, falling in love with Trevor Blake, the man who never cared about anyone.

They sat in silence for some minutes. Allie took comfort in it. She sipped on her coffee and felt more alert than she had in days.

Soon, Frances walked into the room, bearing a tray and a big smile. Brynn trailed after her, a look of worry still etched on her face.

"French toast. Brynn said it's your favorite." She set the tray of the coffee table.

Allie lowered herself to the floor, and for the first time in days, her stomach grumbled. "Thank you, Frances." Then she glanced around the room. "Does anyone want some?"

"You go ahead, darling."

Allie tucked into her meal, but after a few bites, she dropped her fork. "I can't taste it," she said with a frown.

"What do you mean, Al? Are you getting a cold or something?" Brynn sat next to Mags on the saggy sofa.

"It's the grief, Miss Allie."

"Grief?"

"For Mr. Blake."

She couldn't bear to hear his name. Allie pushed the plate away. "Brynn, are you getting your homework done? Did you get all your assignments from you teachers?" She didn't want to talk about Trevor. It was too painful.

Brynn rolled her eyes. "Yes, Al. But I'm missing two tests and can't make them up, so I have to take a zero."

"How's that going to affect your GPA?"

"I think I'll be all right." Brynn stared at her nails and Allie could tell she had something else to say.

"What is it? What don't you want to tell me?"

"Ms. Castor...Karen...broke up with Dad. He's been really bummed about it." She nibbled at her thumbnail.

"Brynn..."

She flung her hand down. "I just feel like it's my fault, okay? If I hadn't gotten in a fight, she wouldn't have done it. And now he's all sad, and you're all sad, and Monica's left Brad..." She covered her mouth with one hand.

Allie narrowed her eyes. "Monica's left Brad? Where is she?"

"I'm not supposed to tell." She bit her lip and rubbed her hands over her knees.

"It's all right, love," Mags said. "You need to tell us."

"She's going to be so pissed," Brynn whispered.

"Brynn," Allie said through gritted teeth.

"Fine. The douche kicked her out. I think he was mad because Trevor wouldn't give her any money. She's staying at this motel off Fremont Street."

"Oh my God," Allie muttered. "How long has she been there?"

Brynn shrugged. "A couple weeks."

Allie hopped up from the floor and stalked toward her room. She came back wearing her rattiest tennis shoes and slung her purse over her shoulder.

"What are you doing, dearest?"

"Monica can't stay there, it's dangerous. I'm going to get her. Brynn, write down the name and room number." She waited while Brynn scribbled it down.

Allie snatched the piece of notebook paper from Brynn's hand and quickly scanned it.

Mags and Frances stood up. "You can't go alone, darling. We're coming with you."

If anyone would be a target for mugging in that neighborhood, it was Mags, with her designer dress, expensive shoes, and Prada handbag. She'd attract more attention than Allie needed.

"I appreciate it, ladies. But I'll be fine. You guys stay here. Brynn, do your homework. I'll be back soon." She rushed out the door before they could follow her. Mags would never be able to catch up in those stilettos.

Allie got in the car and started the ignition. She wanted to throttle her middle sister. She held tightly to the anger and annoyance. It was much better than the sad, hopeless feeling she'd been carrying around for the past five days.

She flipped on the radio as she sat in traffic and slowly made her way downtown. When she reached The Royal Flush motel, she climbed out of the car and looked over the two-story, rundown motor lodge with disgust. The Royal Flush was one of the few motels not attached to a casino. Allie glanced at the algae-coated pool and gave a little shudder. She couldn't imagine what the rooms looked like.

She trotted to the second floor and tapped on the door. Monica answered, wearing a pair of white shorts and a pink tank top. "Not you too?"

Allie frowned. "What do you mean?"

Monica opened the door wider and Allie peeked inside. Trevor stared back at her.

———

"Allison." God, how he had missed her. She looked as if she had lost some weight. She was thinner now than when she first came to live with him, and she had been too skinny then.

She looked at him with wide eyes and didn't say a word.

"Well, are you coming in or what?" Monica asked.

Allie jerked her gaze from his. "Um, yeah." She stepped inside the room. "Trevor, what are you doing here?"

He glanced at the white-knuckled death grip she had on her purse strap. She was as nervous as he was.

He thrust his hands into the pockets of his trousers. "I received a call from Brynn. I have a feeling my mother put her up to it." And of course, he had jumped at the chance to see Allie. He missed her like he'd miss a severed limb. God, he hated her for that.

Allie's eyes swept the room as she nibbled that full bottom lip. "I'd like to speak to my sister alone, please."

He bristled at her cold tone. "I'm sorry, darling, were you talking to me or the floating nightstand?"

She glanced up at him then, anger flashing from her blue eyes. Good, anger he could deal with, but he hated it when she ignored him. "You, Trevor. I'm talking to you. I'd like you to leave so that I can speak to my sister. Is that clear enough for you?"

"Quite." He didn't take his eyes from her. "Monica, do you wish to speak to your sister alone?"

"Not particularly," she mumbled.

Trevor shrugged. "There, you see?"

"Get out."

He kicked the cold smile up a notch. "Make me."

Taking a step toward him, she kept a tight hold on her purse strap, if not her composure. "Don't tempt me. You know it's really funny that you're here—"

"Yes, I'm laughing uproariously." He flicked an eyebrow.

"Because you were the one who accused me of interfering in your life. Now, here you are." She pointed a finger at him. "Interfering."

He stepped closer to her, his shins hitting the god-awful bed that stretched between them. "Your sister asked me to be here. It's not the same thing."

Tugging her purse off her shoulder, she dropped it on the bed. "It is the same thing. It is exactly the same thing."

He glanced at the purse lying on the brown and orange swirls. If there was one natural fiber on the stained fabric, he'd eat it. "Do you know what's on that bedspread?"

Allie turned to Monica. "Will you give us a few minutes?"

Monica leaned against the dresser and watched them with wary eyes. "Um, yeah. I'll just go get a Coke or something."

"We are going to talk, Mon. And if you decide to run off again, you don't know what pissed looks like."

"Okay, Al. Jeez." She grabbed her purse, which was sitting on top of the dresser, and started for the door.

"Leave the purse, Monica," Trevor said. He didn't want to have to go on another wild-goose chase either.

"Oh my God, you two are so lame." Despite her protests, she dropped her bag and held out her hand. "Got a couple of bucks?"

Trevor reached into his wallet and pulled out a twenty. "I saw a burger place across the street. Get yourself something to eat and be back here in thirty minutes. Understand?"

"And be careful," Allie said. "This is a dangerous part of town."

"Yeah, yeah." Monica snatched the money and left the room.

Trevor turned his attention to Allie as he thrust his wallet back into his trouser pocket. "What's your big plan?"

"None of your business."

"You've made it my business, darling, by asking me to bail her out of jail. When you had your whole family move into my house, when you came to me to plead your father's case. It was fine then."

She crossed her arms and glared at him, her jaw tight. "We have new rules. I want you out of my life."

"That's a pity." He brushed his sleeve and adjusted the cuff of his shirt.

She grabbed her purse by the strap and in short, angry movements, slung it over her shoulder. Without another word, she turned on her heel and rushed toward the door.

But Trevor was quicker. Even from his position across the room, he made it to the door before she did and stood with his back against it, blocking her escape. He couldn't let her leave. Just looking at her wasn't enough. He needed to touch her, smell her. "We're not done here."

"Yeah, Trevor, we are. I expected too much from you. You're incapable of loving me, you're incapable of change. And I need more. I need a man—" She stopped and pulled a shaky breath. "I need a man who loves me beyond reason, who wants to have kids with me, grow old with me. I love you so much it hurts." Tears filled her eyes as she tapped her chest with a fist. "But I want what my parents had. And you're not the man to give it to me. So please, let me go."

He froze as still as a statue, his chest aching so badly he thought he might die from the pain. "Allison—"

"Please, Trevor." Her gaze left his eyes and drifted toward the knot in his tie. "If I stay with you, it will destroy me."

He rubbed his sternum. How could he let her go? But what reason had he given her to stay? He couldn't give her what she needed. He didn't do commitment, marriage, little league games.

Slowly, he shifted, then opened the door, and left. As he walked away from her, he'd never felt so hollow, so bereft. Not even when his grandfather passed away.

---

Allie stared at the faux wood door and blinked back tears. She was damn tired of crying. She was going to have to get used to life without Trevor. Might as well start now.

But how was she supposed to get through life without ever seeing him again? Touching him, hearing his voice?

She sat down on the bed, stared at the floor. The carpet was old, brown, and crusty with things she didn't want to think about.

She wasn't sure how long she sat, silent, hurting, but when the door opened, Allie finally remembered where she was. Monica. Right.

"Shit, Al, you look awful." Monica parked herself on the bed.

"Thanks."

"I tried to give you some time, but it's been like, forty-five minutes. Sorry about Trevor." When Monica reached out and took her hand, Allie choked back a sob. "You're still breathing and everything, but inside, you feel like a zombie? I get it. When Brad broke up with me…well, I know you think he's an asshole, but I really love him, you know?"

Allie squeezed her sister's hand. "I do."

They sat quietly for some minutes. Then Allie straightened her spine and glanced around the room. "This place is—"

"Disgusting. I know. But it's all I could afford. I finally got a job, and it sucks ass."

"Yeah, they usually do. Where are you working?" Allie asked.

"Taco Shack. And just a head's up, don't eat the Bomba Burrito. I'm not sure what they put in the sauce, but it looks like puke."

"Thanks for the tip." Allie squeezed Monica's hand once more before letting go. "I'm sorry, Mon. I'm sorry for everything. I've been so busy trying to hold it all together that I became kind of mean."

"I would have gone with 'controlling bitch,' but that's just me."

Allie shot her a glance. "I'll admit to controlling. I just wanted what was best for you. Right before she died, I made Mom a promise to look after all of you. I was really terrible at it."

"No, you weren't." Monica bumped Allie's shoulder with her own. "I've been kind of a bitch too. And Brad never cared about me. Not like I cared about him. And that's crazy painful."

Allie could relate. After all this time, she and Monica finally had something in common. Trevor didn't love her at all. And the reality of that was excruciating. If Monica was feeling the same way, Allie had nothing but compassion for her sister. No "I told you so." Just empathy.

"So what's next?" Allie asked. "Are you going to stay here?

This neighborhood is pretty scary." She didn't want to be the first one to mention home. She was trying to respect Monica's right to live her own life. Damn, letting go was hard. But Allie'd made such a crappy job of her own life, she didn't have much room to criticize.

"Think Dad will let me come home?"

Allie donned her poker face and tried to play it cool, but relief coursed through her. She'd have been worried sick if Monica stayed in this dump. "Probably. If you go back to school and follow the rules. I know that's not what you want to hear."

"It won't be so bad. And it's not forever, right?"

"Just until you figure out what you want to do next," Allie said.

"Are you moving back in too?"

Allie nodded. "Yeah. For a while. I need to figure things out myself." As she rose from the bed, she wrinkled her nose. "I think this place smells worse the longer I'm here."

Monica stood too. "Totally. And one more thing." She winced, shoving her hands in the pockets of her shorts. "I'm going to have to take summer school. I've fucked up too much this semester." She rubbed at her tear-filled eyes. "Mom would be so pissed."

Allie threw her arm around Monica's shoulders. "I think she'd be proud that you're going back and getting your diploma. I'm proud of you."

Allie helped Monica toss her clothes in a duffel bag and then drove her home. As soon as they walked in the door, Brian was waiting, ready to pounce.

"Where the hell have you been, Mon?" In three strides he stood in front of them, his eyes narrowed. "Do you know how worried we've been? Do you have any idea how terrified I was, not knowing where you were?" He reached out and pulled Monica into his arms. "Don't you ever do that to me again, you hear?"

Monica buried her face in the crook of his shoulder and sobbed.

Allie left them and checked on Brynn. Her little sister sat on her bed with her laptop open and her earbuds in. She popped one out when Allie walked into the room.

"Did you find her?" Brynn asked. "Was she mad that I told on her?"

"No, she's fine. She's moving back home and going to summer school. Brad the Douche broke her heart. I'd really like to kick him in the balls for that."

"What about you, Al? Are you staying home?" Brynn's mouth twisted to the side.

Allie pushed at a lock of Brynn's hair. "I'm staying for now. And I'm going to be all right. I promise." Allie wasn't sure how she'd get through this in one piece. But she had to try. *Survive.* That's what the Campbell family did best.

"I was worried when you wouldn't get out of bed," Brynn said. "That's not like you. And I'm going to miss them all. Even Trevor."

"I know you will, honey. He's a good man."

Brynn frowned and pulled the other bud out of her ear. "How can you say that? He broke up with you. What Brad the Douche did to Monica, Trevor did to you. You should hate him."

Allie patted Brynn's leg and left the room. She wished she could hate Trevor. It would make things a lot easier.

# Chapter 23

ALLIE HANDED THE ROOM card to the couple from Minnesota. "Here you go. Have a great stay, and if you need anything, just call the front desk." She smiled and watched them walk to the elevator. Newlyweds. Sweet.

She'd only been here for a few weeks, but she liked it. The casino was one of the larger ones on the Strip, and it was much better than her last job. Better pay, better hours. Couldn't ask for more than that.

Well, she could. She had. But she lost that hand, and it was best to put Trevor behind her and move on. Every time she thought about him, she'd flick the rubber band on her wrist. She'd done it so often, she had a bruise.

He hadn't called her, hadn't come to see her. She absently pulled at the band and let it snap back, felt the sharp sting, and took a deep breath. No more morose thoughts. She was moving on.

After work today, she even had an appointment to look at an apartment. It was time. Time to start living her own life. Serious boundary lines had been crossed with her family, and she needed to step back and put herself first for once. She'd always wanted to go back to school and finish her degree. Now was the perfect opportunity.

And she wanted Trevor. *Snap.* Damn, that was starting to hurt.

---

Trevor sat in the garden and stared at the pond. That was all he'd done lately. He didn't have an appetite, didn't have the concentration to work. He didn't even give a damn if he lost every dime. He'd ignored his lawyer's calls so often, the man had started showing up in person. Trevor just sent him away.

Nigel and Mags had moved out, but they insisted on coming over. Each and every goddamned day.

Trevor heard footsteps behind him but didn't bother turning around. Nigel. Like clockwork, his father would seek him out at the same time every afternoon.

"How's tricks, Son?"

"Same as yesterday. And the day before that," Trevor said, his gaze remaining fixed on the water.

"Swallow your pride. Go to her. She's miserable. You're miserable. Well, to be honest, you've always been a little stroppy."

"Allison called it pissy. And I can't just go to her. The ball's in her court, and it's obvious she wants nothing to do with me." But God, how he missed her. No, he didn't just miss her. He fucking loved her. He hadn't believed in the emotion. But somehow, Allison Campbell had fallen into his life and altered it completely. He wasn't sure when he finally realized how he felt. Probably when he walked out of that disgusting motel room where Monica had been staying. He'd never felt so much pain in his life, walking away from the one person who brought him joy. Yes. Fucking joy. Trevor had experienced it with Allie, but he'd been too much of a git to realize it at the time.

"So call her anyway. Send her something. Women like jewelry."

Not Allie. She wouldn't give a damn about a diamond necklace. He'd deposited millions in her bank account. He thought that would get a rise out of her, but she hadn't contacted him. Not once. He thought for sure she would reach out to him. But it was well and truly over. How was he supposed to carry on with this kind of ache in his gut? God, he even sounded like a mopey wanker. And for once, he didn't even care.

Nigel tapped Trevor's leg. "You know I'm sorry about marrying Anna."

"She never mattered, not really. Your betrayal, that's what stung."

"I know. I was a ghastly father. A worse husband, if you can believe that. To all of them. You'd think after five marriages, I'd have got it right at least once. But you, Trev, somehow you turned out better than Mags and I combined. Allison's a treasure. And if she loves you, that's saying something."

If Allie loved him so goddamned much, why didn't she call? He knew he was being irrational. He'd told her he didn't love her, taunted her when she declared her love for him. He all but packed her bags. Still, he'd made the last overture. And she simply didn't care.

He closed his eyes and laughed bitterly. What a joke. Allie realized he was a fuckwad just as Trevor finally realized he loved her.

He didn't deserve Allison Campbell. He never had.

<center>~~~</center>

"Here's your laundry room." The apartment manager, Doreen, opened the tiny closet door. The small space was big enough for a stackable washer and dryer. If she could afford one.

"One bedroom, galley kitchen, one bath."

"How much?" Allie looked around at the white walls, white ceiling, and off-white carpet with a sigh. Still, it would be her own place. It was a start.

"Nine-fifty."

Allie shrugged. "I'll take it." Why didn't she feel excited? This was a step in the right direction—new job, new apartment, new life. Without Trevor.

She worked up a smile for Doreen and followed her out of the apartment to the front office where she signed off on the credit check and sat back in the chair to wait.

After several minutes, Doreen smiled broadly. "Are you sure you don't want to look at condos?"

"I told you, I can't afford it."

"Well, according to your bank statement you can." She placed a paper in front of Allie.

Allie hadn't had any real expenses in the last few months, so she knew she had a small balance in her account. She pulled the paper closer and peered at the number. Blinking, she looked up from the paper to Doreen. "I'm going to kill him."

She barely remembered the drive from the apartment complex to Trevor's house. She was fueled by rage. How dare he? He still thought she was a whore. He still thought he could control her. She was going to have the final word on this once and for all. British ass.

When she pulled up to the gate, Carl smiled and waved.

"Glad to see you again, Miss C—"

She didn't let him finish but accelerated up the drive before screeching to a halt in front of the house. She threw herself out of the car and charged to the door. Tapping her foot, she waited for Arnold to answer, and when he did, an unfamiliar smile stretched across his mouth.

"Thank God you're here."

Frances stood behind him. "He's in the garden. Hurry now."

"The garden?" Allie echoed.

"Oh yes. Spends most of his time there," Frances said.

Allie walked through the house and flung open the French doors. Dusk fell over the fragrant garden, streaking the sky with pink and lavender. The fairy lights came on, illuminating the blooming flowers as she followed the flagstone pathway.

She found him on the bench beneath the arbor, elbows resting on his knees, staring into the water. Once she saw him, most of the anger fizzled and deep sadness took its place. She stood back and watched him, her eyes roaming over him, drinking him in. He seemed leaner, but just as beautiful. He wore cargo shorts and a wrinkled T-shirt. She didn't know he owned anything other than suits.

Allie slowly walked to the bench and sat down. "Hey."

He didn't move. Didn't look at her, respond to her.

"You put five million dollars in my bank account."

"Yes."

"Why?"

His body was tense, yet he didn't move a muscle. "Because I wanted to. I always do what I want, you know that."

She clenched her hands into fists. Why wouldn't he look at her? She couldn't argue with him when he just sat there. "I don't want your fuck money."

He turned his head then, and by the dim glow of the fading sun, she saw the despair in his eyes. "You're not fucking me."

"Well, that's what it was for, right? Services rendered? Paying off your whore? Is that what you do when you get tired of a mistress? Give her an obscene amount of money to make her go away?"

"You're the only mistress I've had, and I didn't want you to go away."

If he didn't want her to go away, why hadn't he asked her to stay? Why hadn't he called? "Keep your money."

He shrugged. "No. Give it away if you like. Start a home for wayward mistresses."

"I'm giving it back to you."

"I'll just give it back to you."

"God, you are so infuriating." She jumped up from the bench. "You think I gave you that money as some kind of payoff?"

"I have no idea," she said. "I have no idea why you do anything, Trevor. You never tell me anything, you just dictate. And then you deposit money into my account, like I'm still your little fuck toy."

He stood too, his face cold and blank. "That's not why I gave it to you. I want you to have a life. I want you to be free to follow your dreams. You've sacrificed everything for your family, you deserve to have whatever you want."

She only wanted him. "I don't want your money, Trevor."

"What the fuck do you want, Allison? Because I can't figure it out. What else do I have to offer you? You say you love me and then leave—"

"I didn't leave. You told me to stop interfering and then took pleasure in reminding me that I sold myself to you. You practically kicked me out the door."

He quirked a brow and looked down his aristocratic nose at her. "Is that right? Things become difficult and you run?"

"You're crazy, you know that? You told me you didn't love me. You told me that you wouldn't change." She rubbed her forehead and watched small waves drift across the pond. "You don't want a family. Marriage terrifies you. What the hell was I supposed to stay for? So you could continue to punish me? Push me until I snapped?" She dropped her hand and met his gaze. "What, Trevor? What was I supposed to stay for?"

His breath was choppy and his chest rose and fell as the muscles in his jaw jumped.

She waited. Waited for him to say something, anything to make her stay. *Ask me to stay.* But he remained silent and his expression told her nothing.

"I'm giving the money back, Trevor. Please just keep it." She turned and walked to the stone path that led to the house.

"Uruguay."

Her heart faltered, and she froze, her back to him.

"Uruguay," he repeated.

Biting her lip, she spun around. "I'm not trying to hurt you."

"Don't leave me, Allison." He almost whispered the words.

She knew this was huge for him. But still, she wanted more, needed it. "Why should I stay?"

"My world is empty without you. I want you home. With me."

"I want the whole package, Trevor. Love, kids, a dog."

He swallowed and nodded. "I want that with you too. But you'll have to show me how it's supposed to work, because I'm fucking clueless. And I draw the line at cats." He strode toward her and, when he reached her, swooped down and claimed her mouth with his own. His hands moved over her cheeks, caressing them. When he broke off the kiss, his thumbs teased her jaw. "I have trouble with the words, Allison, but the feelings are there. So listen carefully. I am less than nothing without you. I'm a better man when you're here. I love you. Do you understand me? I adore everything that you are."

She caressed his forearms. "I love you so much."

"Never leave me again. I forbid it." He paused. "Please."

She grinned. "Okay. But I'm going to call you out on your bossy bullshit."

"Naturally." He dropped his hands from her face and wrapped an arm around her waist. "You know, I thought you'd be here three weeks ago, when I first put the money into your account. What took you so long?"

"I haven't looked at my bank statement."

He shook his head as they walked toward the house. "I have so much to teach you about business. Rule number one, always read your bank statement." He stopped and peered down at her. "And if it's all right with you, I'd like to start a cancer foundation in your mother's name."

With tears in her eyes, she nodded. "You'd do that for me?"

He smiled. One of his rare, genuine smiles. "There isn't anything I wouldn't do for you, Allison Campbell."

# Epilogue

THE BRIDE WORE WHITE and carried pale pink roses. The blooming flowers gave the conservatory a mixed floral scent. The fountain tinkled gently as the couple recited their vows.

It was a tiny ceremony, just family and friends.

Allie squeezed Trevor's hand and watched her dad and Karen kiss as man and wife for the first time. Brynn was the maid of honor.

After she and Trevor eloped two years ago, and the weeklong lovefest that followed, Allie invited her family, Karen, Mags, and Nigel for a celebratory dinner. Sparks flew between her dad and Karen, and with Brynn's blessing, they began dating again.

Monica stood to one side with her friend, Evan, an English major she'd met on campus. He was preppy and funny. Allie liked him very much and hoped they'd become more than friends someday. But Monica's eyes kept straying to Cal Hughes. Pixie's son was in town for the weekend. With long hair and wild eyes, he was full-on bad boy—and he had the motorcycle and tats to prove it.

Mags and Nigel stood to one side, clapping for the new couple. They were living "without the benefit of clergy," as Mags put it. They seemed happier unmarried. And they'd bought a home not far from the mansion. It had taken some time, but Trevor's attitude had mellowed a bit. He wasn't as resentful, and he even played a round of golf with Nigel every once in a while.

"Our wedding was better," Trevor whispered in her ear.

"Ever regret it?" Allie asked, glancing up at him.

He looked at her with serious eyes. "Not for a second. You're the best thing that ever happened to me."

"I love you too, English."

# Acknowledgments

I'd like to take this opportunity to thank the people who helped make this book happen.

My crit pals and beta readers: Thank you for your time and support. It means so much. I heart you all.

My friends, who love me even on my crazy days: Sara, Shannon, Kathy, Alta, and Sherry. Without you guys, I'd have a lot more of them than I already do.

Leah Hultenschmidt: Thanks for loving Trevor as much as I do.

Cat Clyne: Your cheerfulness was delightful and your patience appreciated.

The team at Sourcebooks: You've helped make my dream a reality and I can't tell you how much I appreciate all your hard work.

Courtney Miller-Callihan: Thanks for taking a chance on me.

# About the Author

As a girl, Terri L. Austin thought she'd outgrow dreaming up stories and creating imaginary friends. Instead, she's made a career of it. She met her own Prince Charming and together they live in Missouri. She loves to hear from readers. Visit her at www.terrilaustin.com.

# *Against the Ropes*

## Sarah Castille

### He scared me. He thrilled me. And after one touch, all I could think about was getting more…

Makayla never thought she'd set foot in an elite mixed martial arts club. But if anyone needs a medic on hand, it's these guys. Then again, at her first sight of the club's owner, she's the one feeling breathless.

The man they call Torment is all sleek muscle and restrained power. Whether it's in the ring or in the bedroom, he knows exactly when a soft touch is required and when to launch a full-on assault. He always knows just how far he can push. And he's about to tempt Makayla in ways she never imagined…

### Praise for *Against the Ropes*:

"Smart, sharp, sizzling, and deliciously sexy."
—Alison Kent, bestselling author of *Unbreakable*

### For more Sarah Castille books, visit:

www.sourcebooks.com

# In Your Corner

## Sarah Castille

A high-powered lawyer, Amanda never had any problem getting what she wanted. Until Jake. She was a no-strings-attached kind of girl. He wanted more. Two years after their breakup, she still hasn't found anyone nearly as thrilling in bed. And then he shows up in her boardroom…

Jake is used to fighting his battles in a mixed martial arts ring, not in court. He needs Amanda's expertise. And whether she knows it or not, she needs him to help her find true happiness.

### For more Sarah Castille books, visit:

www.sourcebooks.com

# Wicked Beat

## Sinners on Tour

### Olivia Cunning

*New York Times* and *USA Today* bestselling author

## How far out are your fantasies?

When Rebeka Blake becomes the Sinners' new soundboard operator, she has no idea that red-hot drummer Eric Sticks is the only man who can give her everything her dirty mind desires...

### Praise for *Double Time*:

"Olivia Cunning delivers the perfect blend of steamy sex, heartwarming romance, and a wicked sense of humor." —*Nocturne Romance Reads*

"Snappy dialogue, dizzying romance, scorching hot sex, and realistic observations about life on tour make this a winner." —*Publishers Weekly*

"It just doesn't get any hotter or any better. On- and offstage." —*Open Book Society*

"Smoking hot sex and romance that pulls at your heartstrings." —*Romance Reviews*

### For more Olivia Cunning books, visit:

www.sourcebooks.com

# Double Time

## Sinners on Tour

### Olivia Cunning

*New York Times* and *USA Today* bestselling author

### He craves her music and passion

On the rebound from the tumult of his bisexual lifestyle, notoriously sexy rock guitarist Trey Mills falls for sizzling new female guitar sensation Regan Elliott and is swept into the hot, heady romance he never dreamed possible.

### She can't get enough of his body

Ecstatic to be on tour learning the ropes with Trey's band, The Sinners, Regan finds she craves Trey as much as she craves being in the spotlight.

### They both need more…

When Regan's ex, Ethan Conner, enters the scene, Trey's secret desires come back to haunt him, and pleasure and passion are taken to a whole new level of dangerous desire.

### Praise for *Rock Hard*:

"Sizzling sex, drugs, and rock 'n' roll…
Absolutely perfect!" —*Fresh Fiction*

"Scorching love scenes…readers will love the characters." —*RT Book Reviews*, 4 stars

### For more Olivia Cunning books, visit:

www.sourcebooks.com

# Out of Bounds

## Dawn Ryder

### He's used to dominating...

Tarak Nektosha is a self-made man, against all odds. He accomplished that by making sure he's the one in charge, both in the boardroom and in the bedroom.

### She's taking her power back...

Sabra Donovan has ambition to spare and energy to burn. So what if her last lover was a disappointment? She's never going to be anyone's plaything ever again.

Sabra's outstanding performance at a corporate photo op immediately attracts Tarak's attention, and the lines begin to blur. What happens when the one on top surrenders and the one used to obeying begins to call the shots?

### Praise for Dawn Ryder:

"Deeply romantic, scintillating, and absolutely delicious."
—Sylvia Day, *New York Times* #1 bestselling author

"Not to be missed." —Lora Leigh, *New York Times* #1 bestselling author

### For more Dawn Ryder books, visit:

www.sourcebooks.com

# *Awakening*

## Elene Sallinger

### He will open her eyes to the ultimate pleasure…

The minute Claire walked into his shop, she aroused every protective instinct Evan ever had. She looked so fragile, so lost. He ached to be the one to show her a world she'd never dreamed of, to awaken within her the passion she was so ripe to share. It only takes one touch for him to see how open and responsive she is to his dominant side. But the true test will be whether he can let go at last and finally open his heart…

### *Festival of Romance Award Winner*

### What readers are saying:

"If *Fifty Shades of Grey* intrigued you, *Awakening* will take you to a whole new level of desire, submission, and unforgettable romance."
—Judge, Festival of Romance contest

"One of the absolute best BDSM novels I have read. (And I've read quite a few.) This one is absolutely amazing!" —Autumn Jean

"Finally! A well-told story that shows the characters' vulnerabilities and how they learned to trust and love again." —A. Hirsch

### For more Xcite Books, visit:

www.sourcebooks.com

# Restless Spirit

## Sommer Marsden

### Three men want her. Only one can truly claim her.

When Tuesday Cane inherits a cozy lake house, she's not expecting to find love as part of her legacy. But how can she choose between Aiden, the loyal and über-sexy handyman she's known for years; the charming and wealthy Reed Green, a former TV star; and the mysterious Shepherd Moore, an ex cage fighter.

The only way to know for sure is to try them all... Surrounded by so many interesting men and erotic temptations, Tuesday has no intention of committing. But deep down she longs for that special, soul-deep connection. Only, which man can entice this restless spirit into finally settling down?

### What readers are saying:

"An intense emotional and sexual journey that is quite compelling." —Kathy

"One of the best adult/erotica books I have ever read.
The characters are real and believable, and the sex scenes
are absolutely scorching hot." —Rebecca

"Themes of domination and submission are fantastically well
varied throughout the story... Realistic and relatable characters
with steamy encounters at every turn." —Michelle

### For more Xcite Books, visit:

www.sourcebooks.com

# The Initiation of Ms. Holly

## K. D. Grace

### The stranger on the train

He came to her in the dark. She couldn't see him, but she could feel every inch of his body against hers in the most erotic encounter Rita Holly ever had. And now he's promising more…if she'll just follow him to an exclusive club where opulence and sex rule. She can have anything she's ever dreamed of—and more—but first she'll have to pass the club's initiation…

### What readers are saying:

"After reading *Fifty Shades of Grey*, I didn't think I would find another book as well written, but then I read *The Initiation of Ms. Holly*, and I was immediately taken in. This book is sexy, erotic, and explosive. I didn't want to put it down." —Dani

"Very, very erotic and sizzling!!! Wow, I could not put it down." —Theresa

"Everything you want in a romantic, erotic, sexual novel." —Jean

"For a fast-paced read with enough twists and turns to keep the story fresh and entertaining, you couldn't ask for a better book." —Christine

### For more Xcite Books, visit:

www.sourcebooks.com